A HALLOWEEN MURDER

MARY GRAND

B
Boldwood

First published in Great Britain in 2025 by Boldwood Books Ltd.

Copyright © Mary Grand, 2025

Cover Design by Head Design Ltd

Cover Images: Alamy and iStock

The moral right of Mary Grand to be identified as the author of this work has been asserted in accordance with the Copyright, Designs and Patents Act 1988.

All rights reserved. No part of this book may be reproduced in any form or by any electronic or mechanical means, including information storage and retrieval systems, without written permission from the author, except for the use of brief quotations in a book review. This book is a work of fiction and, except in the case of historical fact, any resemblance to actual persons, living or dead, is purely coincidental.

Every effort has been made to obtain the necessary permissions with reference to copyright material, both illustrative and quoted. We apologise for any omissions in this respect and will be pleased to make the appropriate acknowledgements in any future edition.

A CIP catalogue record for this book is available from the British Library.

Paperback ISBN 978-1-83678-464-7

Large Print ISBN 978-1-83678-465-4

Hardback ISBN 978-1-83678-463-0

Ebook ISBN 978-1-83678-466-1

Kindle ISBN 978-1-83678-467-8

Audio CD ISBN 978-1-83678-458-6

MP3 CD ISBN 978-1-83678-459-3

Digital audio download ISBN 978-1-83678-462-3

This book is printed on certified sustainable paper. Boldwood Books is dedicated to putting sustainability at the heart of our business. For more information please visit https://www.boldwoodbooks.com/about-us/sustainability/

Boldwood Books Ltd, 23 Bowerdean Street, London, SW6 3TN

www.boldwoodbooks.com

To Felicity Fair Thompson
A wonderful author, film maker and teacher. Thank you for your inspirational classes at the college, and for opening up the world of writing to me. Mary x

PROLOGUE
HALLOWEEN, 31 OCTOBER 2017

I creep along the battlements of the castle; the moon is too bright tonight. It's nearly midnight. There's an icy chill, but adrenaline rushing through my veins keeps me warm.

Ghosts whistle on the wind through the crenellations in the stone walls. Dark spirits party, it's Halloween. The veil between this world and the next is cobweb-thin this evening.

This ancient building has played many roles. It's been a place of defence, a prison, a summer residence for the rich. Tonight, it's a place of execution.

And I am judge, jury and executioner. Tonight, they must die.

I smile at the thought of them gone, already excited at the prospect of a world without them. Finally, I'll be able to breathe, to live my life. I will be free.

1

TUESDAY, 31 OCTOBER – EARLIER THAT DAY

The counter of the village shop was festooned with Halloween goods: plastic skeletons, spiders, children's masks, and bags of sweets to hand out to trick-or-treaters.

'Morning, Susan,' said Tracy, the owner of the shop.

Susan leant down and stroked Lottie, Tracy's little black spaniel. 'Sorry, it's just me. Libs and Rocco are at home. They've had their walk up the downs and I can't manage them with two bags of shopping.'

'You have a lot more in your basket than usual,' said Tracy, noting the larger loaf of bread, the vegetables and fruit, the large pizza and the packet of oven chips.

'I've got my daughter Zoe staying for a few nights with her friend LeAnne, not that I expect them to be in much. I don't know if they'll need this or not.'

'Is Zoe bringing Jamari?'

'Sadly no granddaughter this time. Zoe's wife Fay is taking Jamari to her other grandparents in Scotland. Zoe is coming on her own for a kind of reunion with four friends she was in a rock band with back in high school.'

'Gosh, they've kept in touch all these years?' Tracy remarked. 'Do they still play together?'

'Oh, no. In fact, they hardly ever meet in person now. It's all online, usually their WhatsApp group. The idea was to come over for a retirement concert for their old music teacher on Saturday but they decided to extend the stay and have a few days together first.'

'That sounds fun. They can go round some of their old haunts.'

'It's more exciting than that,' said Susan. 'As the concert is to be in Carisbrooke Castle, Maxine, one of the group, suggested they book the apartment there for a few nights beforehand.'

'But you said Zoe and a friend are staying with you?'

Susan smiled. Tracy always liked to have all the details.

'Unfortunately, the apartment only accommodates four. And so, Zoe and LeAnne agreed to sleep at my house, while the rest of the band, Nick, Annika, Maxine will stay at the castle. I think Maxine's husband is joining them. Of course, Zoe and LeAnne won't be with me much. They will want to spend most of their time up at the castle, particularly in the evenings, when it's locked up and all the staff and visitors have gone home.'

Tracy grimaced. 'Rather them than me. I wouldn't go up there after dark. Everyone knows it's haunted and, of course, it's Halloween. I'd not want to be up there.'

Susan smiled. 'I don't think they seriously believe in that sort of thing. It's just a bit of fun, in fact, I'm joining them for one of the ghost walks this evening.'

Tracy shook her head. 'I'd not be messing about with all that. There's plenty of people around here who've experienced the supernatural. We're the most haunted island in the world, you know. You take care and tell your Zoe to watch herself.'

Susan nodded in a conciliatory way. 'I'll pass on your warnings to Zoe. Thank you.'

She pushed her basket towards Tracy, a hint that she was ready to pay. Tracy ignored it. Susan guessed there was something else on her mind.

'Of course, it's not just Zoe you'll be feeding,' Tracy said, looking down at the basket. 'You have Robert staying over for the odd night now, don't you?'

Susan groaned inwardly. She should have guessed that one of Tracy's web of informants (that is, her customers) would have noticed Robert's stays. Tracy was clearly keen for an update. Susan, though, was not prepared to give this. It wasn't going to be easy to deflect Tracy, but there was one subject she knew might just do it.

'Have you heard any more about my new neighbours? First, I thought people were coming in January, then the 'For Sale' board went back up. Anyway, I noticed it came down again last week – so I guess someone may be on their way?'

Susan was relieved to see Tracy's eyes light up as she eagerly replied, 'My niece's boyfriend at the estate agents gave me the latest. It's the same man with his daughter who were going to buy in January. I don't know what the holdups were. Anyway, the exciting news is that they'll be coming one day this week, so at least we'll get to meet them.' Her face clouded over. 'I'm sorry. I was unable to find out any more details about them: confidentiality or some such nonsense.'

Tracy clearly thought she'd failed in keeping up with this particular aspect of village news, but Susan endeavoured to reassure her. 'That's fine. It's good to know I'll have new neighbours this week. Thank you. I'm sure we'll get to know all about them soon enough.'

'You're right.' Tracy leaned forward, lowered her voice. 'I did wonder if they'd pulled out because of what happened. I mean, it's less than a year since your neighbour was, well, there's no easy way to put it, murdered.'

Susan frowned. 'I know it was horrific, but he didn't actually die in the house. I doubt the buyers even know what happened. No, it's a lovely home and it will be great to have people living in there again.'

'I think you're right. It'll be good for you to have someone down that end of the close. Now, I meant to tell you, I took Lottie down to our new vets' to have her teeth checked. They were lovely with her, and they've done the place up really well. I like that they keep the dogs' and cats' waiting areas separate.'

'I've heard good things about it as well. I've signed up my two as I heard the list was filling up.'

Susan noticed a queue was starting to build up behind her and, as intriguing as all this news was, she knew she needed to get home and sort out the house.

She took out her purse and pulled out her credit card purposefully.

'There are certainly a lot of changes going on. Now, I really must be off.'

Reluctantly, Tracy began to ring up the items, but continued to chat as she did.

'It's a shame you never went for the receptionist role at the vets'; you'd have fitted in well there.'

'I was tempted, but in the end I chickened out. It's not just making appointments, is it? I'd have to do some training. I was worried I wouldn't be up to it.'

'That's nonsense. I'll let you know if anything comes up again.'

Susan filled up the bags for life she'd brought with her and finally left the shop.

***

Bishopstone, Susan's village, was a quintessential English village with a pub, a church, a few shops, a hairdresser's, a new vets' practice, and thatched cottages sitting alongside their more recently built red-brick neighbours.

It all appeared tranquil and quite idyllic on a morning like this. But, as Susan had discovered, a lot more goes on beneath the surface in a small community. The murder Tracy referred to had happened at the village church. Susan had only been living in the village for a few months at the time, when she'd found herself embroiled in the investigation.

Still, that was a year ago, and the village had moved on.

The emptier streets this morning were due to it being the October half term, the absence of pupils and their parents dropping them off at school.

Susan was grateful for the lighter mornings as the clocks had gone back over the weekend, and it was a beautiful crisp autumn day. The sky was a light ice blue, with white meandering clouds. Leaves, the colours of tiny flames, fell from the branches of the horse chestnut trees, blackbirds pecked at the few remaining berries on the bushes.

Susan made her way to her home, a cottage in a small close across the road from the shop.

As she opened the front door, her own cocker spaniels, Rocco and Libs, ran to greet her, and she wove her way around them as she took her bags to the kitchen.

For Susan, home was her refuge. For forty years she'd lived over the other side of the island in the seaside town of Ventnor with her husband, Steve, where she raised their daughter Zoe and a number of foster children. However, her marriage had screeched to a halt a few years ago when her husband had unexpectedly announced that he was leaving and she'd found herself, in her early sixties, living alone for the first time in her life.

And so she had moved to Bishopstone, and this was her new home: her own space, her own mess, where she now lived on ready meals, wearing the same old clothes, and feeling more content than she had for years.

Still, with guests arriving, in particular her well-organised and straight-talking daughter, she knew she needed to tidy the place up.

Glancing around, Susan cringed as she took in the books and papers piled up. Even her sun hat and a bag with beach towels were still stuffed in a corner. It had been a wonderful summer with lots of visits from Zoe and granddaughter Jamari. Each time they came over, she would drive to Ryde and pick them up from an early catamaran, they would head to the beach to beat the midday sun, then home to cool off. Exhausted, still smelling of suncream and clothes sticky from ice cream, she would drive them back to the pier, and wave them off. It had been a shame to see so little of Zoe's wife, Fay, but she'd needed to spend time with her own parents in Scotland as her dad had been unwell.

Susan sighed: standing around wasn't getting the house sorted. Right, kettle on.

After she poured her coffee, she remembered she hadn't had breakfast and opened a packet of biscuits.

She spent the morning basically moving piles of stuff around, most to her bedroom, and then made up the beds for Zoe and LeAnne.

* * *

Meanwhile on the mainland, Maxine, a barrister and the band member who'd arranged the stay at the castle, had left Portsmouth Crown Court and was climbing the stone steps to her chambers.

She pushed open the freshly painted door and entered the familiar musty-smelling building.

'Good morning?' asked the clerk.

'Yes, thanks,' she said, and quickly disappeared into her room. She loved returning to her familiar space, her spiritual home, its walls lined with heavy tomes and files.

As she hung up her gown and removed the tabs from round her neck, Maxine began to slip out of her court persona. She stored the horsehair wig carefully and, undoing her clipped-back hair, she shook her hair free.

She was still wearing the rest of her work uniform: the neat suit, black shoes, white blouse – they could be worn by any professional woman. But the other items were special. When she put them on, she was no longer Maxine: she was respected, listened to. She represented the law, justice.

On her desk stood a small miniature of the Roman goddess, Lady Justice, with scales and sword, a gift from her father on her graduation. He talked of his pride and then, with quiet sadness, how much this day would have meant to her mother. Maxine discovered that talking about her mother, who had died only a few years before, hadn't ruined the day, but rather completed it. It was an important lesson for future milestone events she would have to face without her mother. Maxine learned it was better to acknowledge the loss and shake hands with grief than spend these special occasions trying to push it away and treat it like the enemy.

In her heart, Maxine knew that she was a survivor, a fighter. She was now deeply committed to her work as a criminal defence lawyer. She loved it. No two cases were the same. There were always new prosecution cases to unpick, to dismantle brick by brick. Her friends didn't understand how she could take on some of her clients. 'How can you do it?' they'd say. 'How can you defend someone who is accused of something terrible?' Each time she gave the same reply: 'Everyone deserves the best defence, the best version of their story to be told. One day it could be you.' She could see from the sceptical, smug looks that they were sure it would never be them.

But then, earlier that year, in February, one of her close friends from the band, steady reliable Nick, had been arrested. LeAnne had invited the old band members to a party to celebrate the fifth anniversary of her restaurant in Ventnor. To everyone's horror, Nick, after leaving the party early, had crashed his car, been arrested and charged with drink driving.

There had been no question of innocence: Nick was guilty. It would be an open-and-shut case heard by magistrates. Despite it being the kind of work, she'd left behind years ago, Maxine had seen how frightened and desperate Nick was, and so agreed to represent him, really to be a friend to hold his hand.

However, although it had felt the right thing to do at the time, in retrospect she was sure it would have been wiser to have kept out of it all. Normally, she said goodbye to a client after the judgement but with a friend, well, there was no walking away. Since the hearing she'd had concerns about Nick as well as there being unforeseen repercussions throughout the group of friends.

She scrolled through her phone and found the message she'd received that morning from Nick.

> You are a saint, so looking forward to our week in the castle. See you later, Nick.

Honestly, he needed to stop this. She was deeply uncomfortable with being seen as some kind of heroine.

Maxine slumped into the ancient leather chair. When she'd booked this holiday for them all a year ago, she'd imagined sitting under the stars in the courtyard of Carisbrooke Castle, surrounded by the ancient stone walls, reminiscing about school and days in the band. Added to that, it would also be Halloween, perfect for ghost walks, followed by the concert in the Great Hall: what a week it would be!

Maxine sighed; who'd have imagined then what the year would hold for the group? Not only had there been Nick's arrest and court appearance, but she'd had problems with LeAnne, and then the fallout from that visit to Annika's flat last week. Given the choice, she would call the whole holiday off. But that was impossible. No one had taken up her tentative suggestion they try to cancel, and she had a horrible feeling they were all in denial about what had changed between them, all desperate to pretend they were still as close as they had been back in their school days.

Of course, there was one person on this holiday who had never been in the band, an outsider: her husband Gino.

Maxine had been married to him for two years before the other members of the band had met him eight months ago at LeAnne's party in February. At least there had been some warmth and attraction left in their marriage then. Maxine had been proud introducing Gino to them all. She knew exactly the kind of man they'd expected her to marry – someone studious, dull. Nothing had prepared them for Gino: a charming, handsome Italian builder, who'd swept Maxine off her feet on a holiday in Rome.

Maxine picked up her phone, sent Gino a text:

> I'm about to leave chambers. Meet you at the flat?

The reply came quickly.

> Sorry, can't make the 2 o'clock car ferry. I've made a separate booking to take the van over later. See you at the castle. G

The stab of pain took her breath away. She clutched her chest. Of course he was letting her down, again. She'd been in denial about Gino for months, ignoring the signs. It wasn't until last week she'd faced the truth of what was happening and finally acknowledged their marriage was over. He really had crossed the line; broken that one solemn promise he'd made when they got married.

And yet... somehow, she kept allowing herself to dream, pictured them travelling over to the island together, leaving the mainland and their problems behind. She'd even let herself imagine sharing all her memories of the castle, the setting for her childhood fantasies of dragons and princesses. And then once again she would feel his hand warmly squeeze hers, see his lips in that intimate smile that had captured her when they first met.

Maxine shook her head, pushing the images away. That way was madness and pain. This week, if Gino actually turned up, she would tell him this was the end.

Reluctantly, Maxine pushed herself out of the comfy armchair. She reached down to close the bottom desk drawer and, as she did so, she caught a glimpse of a postcard. For a moment she allowed it to warm her. She touched it gently then closed the drawer tight.

Wrapping herself in her enormous white wool coat, she picked up her bags and left the room.

As she headed to the door, the clerk called, 'You're taking leave now?'

Hearing a slice of disbelief in his voice, she turned. 'Yes, I'm finally having a holiday.'

The clerk gave her a congratulatory smile. Both knew the fear a barrister felt about taking time off. What if that big lawsuit came in while they were away? What if they came back and their caseload had collapsed? Of course, Maxine was well established now, held in high regard, but all the same, walking away was hard.

'My work phone will be on—'

'We'll do our best to leave you be. Off somewhere warm?'

She knew he was imagining her jetting off to some exotic Caribbean island and smiled. 'The weather will be similar to here. I'm going over to the island, the Isle of Wight.'

'Oh, not far then! Don't you come from there?'

'I do. I grew up in Ventnor. Do you know it?'

He shook his head. 'Only been to the island once, even though I've lived all my life in Portsmouth. Then we just got off the catamaran in Ryde, spent the day on the beach and came back. It was so odd. We felt we'd been to another country and there it is only across that stretch of water. We usually go to Spain. It feels familiar, like.'

Maxine smiled. The idea that Spain was more like home than the island a few miles away might sound odd, but she'd heard plenty of other mainlanders say it. One even asked her if people on the island lived in normal houses, whether they used English money.

'You should go again, maybe in the summer. Take a car and

drive to some of the secluded beaches. Some are empty even in August.'

'Maybe.'

Maxine grinned. They both knew he would stick with Spain.

Once out of chambers, Maxine drove to her flat in a beautiful Victorian terraced house in Southsea looking over the Solent. She could even see the Isle of Wight from here, and she liked that.

As she gathered her things together, Maxine found a copy of a CD of their band at a gig in the school hall. The quality was appalling, but it would be fun to listen to it together. She looked at the cover image: The Detention Seekers.

She and Zoe, both guitar players, had started the band, their antidote to the Spice Girls, with earnest songs about women's rights and saving the environment. LeAnne had joined purely to practise her drumming. The name of the band and the music may have been pretty ropey, but Maxine was still proud of the passion and motivation that had inspired them.

The main thing that had saved the band, ensured them any stage time, had been persuading Nick and Annika to join them. Both were so musically gifted, Nick on keyboard, Annika their amazing vocalist.

Maxine tucked the CD into the side of her bag. Maybe it would transport them back to a more innocent time. At the moment, the past seemed an infinitely safer, more appealing place to be.

2

Susan's daughter Zoe sat on the catamaran. It felt very strange to be travelling to the island without Fay and Jamari. Seeing them catching the plane to Edinburgh had been emotional. It had been a hard few months with Fay's dad being so unwell, the early-morning calls, Fay rushing up to Scotland at the weekends and for most of the summer. The stress had taken its toll on them both.

Although she was looking forward to spending her half term on the island with old friends, away from her work as deputy head in a large primary school, she had offered to miss the reunion and stay home with Jamari. But Fay had insisted it was important for her father and Jamari to spend time together, and so they'd gone off together.

Zoe sipped her coffee through the plastic lid and winced.

'Shit,' she swore under her breath, feeling the searing hot liquid burn her tongue. Although Zoe had bought it before boarding it was still boiling hot. Yet she daren't take the lid off and chance being covered in the contents. Instead, she pulled out the tiny tray in front of her, hoping the coffee would cool down before they reached the island.

Zoe was determined to have a proper chat with her mother this week. Not wanting to worry her, she had avoided telling her how ill Fay's dad was or the stress it was putting on their marriage, but there were other issues now and it was time her mother knew.

A text came through from Maxine, letting them know that she was just arriving at the castle, about to pick up the keys and attaching a sketch map of the castle. If they arrived after five, she said to phone her and she would let down the drawbridge and allow them in!

Zoe smiled: Maxine still organising them all.

Zoe looked out of the window, the sea splashing against the side of the catamaran, and then a member of the crew announced they were approaching Ryde. She felt a shiver of excitement. She was coming home.

Despite being urged to stay seated, people were standing up, jostling for position to get off the catamaran. Zoe joined the scrum.

As she stepped out onto the island she could see her mother, Susan, standing next to the car, waving.

Susan was quite short, her hair a short brown curly mass, her blue-framed glasses no longer new. Zoe mentally rolled her eyes as she noticed her mum was still wearing the old parka coat that Zoe had worn to university.

Then Zoe looked down at herself, also in jeans and an old waterproof. Granted, her own hair was blonde, cut in a very short, trendier style, and she had a few ear piercings, but she knew that she wasn't a million miles off being a younger version of her mother.

Zoe waved to Susan. Even now, in her thirties, it was lovely to come home to the familiar, and she knew how lucky she was to have her mum, a wonderfully constant support in an unpredictable world.

It had been amazing bringing Jamari over in the summer. However, Zoe was very aware that the seasons had moved on since she last came to the island. Today waves noisily crashed on the shingle, and despite the earlier sun, the day was closing in quickly, the sea and sky an icy grey. There were no sundresses and t-shirts today, no wandering with a drink in hand. Everyone was wrapped up, walking purposefully. Summer had ended.

As she approached, Zoe heard frantic barking from the car and her mother opened the car for her to greet Rocco and Libs. As she was giving them lots of fuss, she looked up at Susan. 'Can we call in at the bus station on the way to the castle? LeAnne's car has broken down. She got the bus into Newport. I said we'd pick her up there.'

'Of course,' replied Susan, 'I'm looking forward to seeing her again. I've heard good things about her restaurant.'

The dogs had calmed down now, and after Zoe had given Susan a hug, they both got into the car. Zoe buckled her seatbelt. She automatically glanced down and checked her watch.

'You're not late,' said Susan.

Zoe laughed. 'I'm not looking at the time. I'm checking my steps.'

'You're still wearing that smart watch? I thought you'd have given up on that by now.'

'Can't stop. I'm obsessed. I have to reach my target. I also track how well I've slept, keep an eye on my blood pressure, heart rate, the lot.'

'Wow, I'd hate to be constantly reminded of all that. So, how many steps do you do each day?'

'I aim for ten thousand, which is harder than you'd think.

See, for all my rushing around I've only done four thousand two hundred. The struggle is real mum!' said Zoe grinning. 'Good job we have the ghost walk this evening. Hopefully that will knock off a few more.'

Susan tutted. 'You're like your dad. I bet he's got one now.' Zoe had definitely inherited her love of running and fitness from her father.

'But you've got to keep fit, Mum,' Zoe said in her most teachery voice. 'I might get you a smart watch for Christmas.'

'Please don't,' groaned Susan. 'Anyway, I'm always out walking the dogs.'

'But it's not necessarily that many steps. You do a lot of watching them run around.'

Zoe saw her mother's grip tighten on the steering wheel, and grinned. They were both stubborn and held strong opinions but, unlike in her teenage years, they seldom had serious disagreements now. As Zoe expected, Susan changed the subject.

'Tell me, how is Jamari? Has that cold cleared up?'

'Yes, she's having to go to nursery more at the moment and she had a rotten tummy thing a few days ago. Never mind, she seemed much better yesterday. Hopefully she won't throw up on the flight.'

As they drove slowly back down the pier in a queue of cars, they chatted about childhood illnesses and then moved on to Zoe's work.

'It's OK. Thank God I'm job sharing and only doing three days a week with Fay being away so much and, um—' Zoe hesitated.

'I could come over and help out more,' offered Susan.

Zoe looked out at the familiar streets, noticed they were

passing the entrance to Quarr Abbey, made a mental note to take Jamari to see the red squirrels in the grounds soon.

Aware Susan was waiting for an answer, she hesitated. She knew her mother would come to their aid in a heartbeat but had been putting off asking her. More frequent visits would just add guilt to Fay's spiralling stress levels. There were also the possible changes she'd not told her mum about yet: if they happened it was important her mother had a good support network of friends in her new home on the island.

Forcing a smile, she turned to Susan. 'That's kind, but no, we'll be fine.' Zoe decided to move the conversation on and started to chat about the coming week.

'It will be interesting to see how this week goes. It's quite intense to be spending so much time together. I realised when we were all at LeAnne's celebration in February that, apart from Maxine, I hadn't physically met up with any of them for years.'

'I was very surprised when you told me about Nick's arrest.'

'I know. He's the last person I'd have expected to be drink driving. He ended up being given a twelve-month driving ban, a fine, and of course a criminal record. He was allowed back teaching though.'

'He was lucky.'

'He was. By the way, did I tell you LeAnne's brother, Wesley, was also arrested that night?'

'No! What happened to him?'

'He was charged with possession of drugs. He wasn't sent away but he also now has a criminal record.'

'I'm sorry to hear that,' said Susan. 'I'm afraid LeAnne's family had a bad reputation over in Ventnor. I think her uncle is in prison over here for selling stolen goods. Still, well done LeAnne for stepping out of their shadow and setting up her own business. I admire her. She's the only one in your group who didn't go to university. She's done really well for herself.'

'I agree, it's great.'

'Any news about Annika? You told me that she's with Nick now. Did that survive all the business of his arrest?'

'It did. They're living together now. Annika has a new job over here as well. Not to do with music, though, which is a shame. I'm sure she was the only reason our band was ever booked.'

'She had a remarkable voice, but I did feel her father was far too pushy. She was my pupil to start with but even though she was only six, he found her a really expensive teacher on the mainland. After that it never stopped: exams, competitions. It was never ending.'

'I'm so glad you never pushed me. As a piano teacher, you could have.'

Susan laughed. 'I'd never have tried that. You were happy going through the first few grades with me, but you hated exams. I knew there was no point in making you take them. It would have taken all the joy out of music for you.'

'I'm grateful. You taught me to read music, and that was great. I think our band was a bit of light relief for Annika, but she didn't tell her parents much about it.'

'I don't think her father realised just how hard it is to make it in the world of classical music. Still, it sounds as if Annika has managed to take charge of her life. Did you say she's a nanny?'

'She was but like I said, she has a new job now. She's working for the health service on the island, taking blood.'

'That's interesting. She never went into teaching then?'

'No way. She always swore she'd never teach and to be honest I can't see her coping with it.'

They had arrived at the bus station. LeAnne was easy to

spot short dyed white and pink hair, heavily made-up eyes which sparkled behind black catlike glasses and a black leather jacket. Zoe jumped out of the car and LeAnne ran towards her.

'Zoe,' she shouted, and they hugged.

Zoe stepped back, looked down at LeAnne's feet. 'I thought you'd shot up but it's those trainers. The soles are so thick. How do you walk in them?'

'It's called fashion, Zoe,' said LeAnne, laughing.

She picked up two large carrier bags that sat beside her wheeled suitcase.

'You've brought a lot of stuff.'

'Someone had to bring Halloween.'

At the car, LeAnne jumped in the passenger seat next to Susan.

'Thanks so much for this. My fecking car has packed up again.'

She looked back at Zoe, demoted to the back seat, and grinned. 'Notice the toning down of the language? I've had to do that. Can't go effing and blinding in the restaurant. The customers don't like it.'

She turned back to Susan. 'Good to see you after all these years. I'd swear that's Zoe's old coat you're wearing.'

'You're right.'

'You never did give a damn.' She laughed. 'Thanks for putting me up. I told Zoe I could go home to Ventnor each evening, but with the way things are with the car, this has saved me.'

'Anyway, I have a feeling if you went back to the restaurant each night, we'd never see you,' said Zoe.

'You're probably right. I've left people in charge, only a phone call away, so fingers crossed.' She turned to Susan again.

'I hear Zoe's dad's buggered off. Sorry about that. He never seemed the sort. Solid, if you know what I mean.'

'Mm.' Susan changed the subject quickly. 'I hear wonderful reports of your restaurant.'

'Thanks, yes. Doing really well. Family have been great. Mum was working with me but hasn't been so well lately.'

'I'm sorry.'

'It's this business with my brother Wesley. You know, the drug conviction?'

'Zoe mentioned it to me.'

'He wasn't sent to prison, thank God. I go in to visit my uncle over here in Parkhurst, the problems in there are a nightmare. This new drug spice is creating havoc in all the prisons.'

'What's spice?' asked Susan.

'Is that the zombie drug they were talking about on TV? I thought they said it was like cannabis?' asked Zoe.

'It's much more potent and dangerous than that.'

'Sorry, maybe I'm being naïve, but I can't see how the prisoners are getting hold of it. They must be checking visitors?' asked Susan.

'They do, but spice is scentless, dissolved in liquid. They can spray it onto, letters, even legal documents. The inmates usually smoke it then, but some have died using it. It's nasty. So, as I say, at least Wesley isn't being exposed to that. But the charges and court appearance have had a devastating effect on him.'

'I'm so sorry,' said Susan.

'It's awful. Wesley's lost his motivation to make anything of his life. Mum is so stressed by it all. It's the injustice of it that has got to everyone.'

'Injustice?' Susan queried.

LeAnne turned around to Zoe. 'Haven't you told your mum the whole story?' she demanded.

Zoe had forgotten how just how direct LeAnne could be and stammered in response, 'Um, I've not told her everything.'

LeAnne rolled her eyes and turned back to Susan.

'Well, what Zoe should have told you is that Nick is to blame for Wesley's arrest. Wesley had been out in the garden smoking with friends. Just before leaving the party, Nick, the scumbag, called the police, reporting people smoking weed. Wesley heard about it, panicked, checked his pockets, I'm guessing to get rid of any evidence, but then found a packet of cocaine. He was sure Nick had planted the coke on him. Nick had always had it in for him.'

LeAnne turned, her red fingernails digging into the side of her seat and glared at Zoe. 'That's the truth of it and there's more. When Wesely then ran out to challenge Nick, he drove his car at him, and that is why he crashed. Nick fecking tried to kill my brother.'

'Oh no—' said Zoe, shocked. She'd not heard anything about this part of the story.

'He did. Wesley told the police but of course they never believed him. They were always going to take Nick's side, even though he was off his face.'

Zoe caught her breath. She'd heard Wesley had accused Nick of the set up but never taken it seriously. As to this business of Nick driving at Wesley, that seemed even more unbelievable. And yet LeAnne seemed to be totally convinced and so no wonder she was furious with Nick. Zoe couldn't help wondering why LeAnne had come on a holiday when she would be spending the week with a man, she clearly loathed.

Zoe was relieved to hear her mother tactfully try to deflect LeAnne.

'Wesley is lucky to have a sister who stands up for him. You're a good role model for him, LeAnne. You've done so well with your restaurant. I keep hearing about it. You specialise in sustainable fish, is that right?'

'We do,' replied LeAnne, her voice moderating. 'We're very proud of what we're doing over there.'

Zoe was amazed that within a beat LeAnne's anger had dissipated and been replaced with warmth and enthusiasm. But she reminded herself LeAnne had always been like this, living life on a rollercoaster of emotion.

Whatever the reason, it was good to be able to sit back and let her mother and LeAnne chat on.

They drove out of Newport and up Cedar Hill. As they approached the unique set of traffic lights, simply red or green with no amber, the castle came into view. Looking out of the window, Zoe could sense the thick stone walls peering down on them.

Zoe had not been here since she was brought by her mother as a young child. The castle had been a fun visit: ice creams, climbing the battlements, watching the donkeys in the Well House But this evening the castle seemed far more imposing. She remembered that although partly in ruins, the walls and many of the interior buildings were intact. The past still breathed in its walls.

Susan parked in front of the castle in a small area usually largely reserved for coaches. Zoe and LeAnne just took what they needed for the evening at the castle, while Susan took Rocco and Libs out with the aim of taking them for a walk.

Zoe noticed the main car park, heaving at peak times, was practically empty. The few remaining cars, she guessed, belonged to the staff waiting for the light to fade and to welcome guests for the last of their Halloween ghost walks.

The staff were here at times when the visitors had left; some must know the castle intimately. Did they commune with the ghosts, the spirits of the castle during those hours?

Zoe shook her head. She was being fanciful: she'd never believed any of that stuff. However, she couldn't ignore the cold shiver of apprehension. Up until now the idea of being here after dark, having the run of the castle, had seemed innocent and fun. That feeling was now coloured by, what was it? Yes, that was it, she felt a knot in her stomach: one of dread, fear; one of foreboding.

3

Susan was about to leave the others to go on her walk when Zoe grabbed her arm and directed her to the entrance. 'You have to come and have a nose inside before you go, Mum. I've let Maxine know we're on our way. We can go in through the shop.'

There was an outer set of enormous metal gates. They remained propped open at this time of day. Susan knew that later they would be firmly locked, impassable, and there was no other way anyone could get in or out of the castle.

They entered the shop and ticket office, which was full of tempting preserves and chocolates as well as medieval costumes, play swords and books. A friendly member of staff welcomed them and pointed them to the shop exit which opened on to the path leading to the magnificent stone gatehouse, the original entrance to the castle on the west side. Susan looked up in awe at the impressive drum towers either side of an archway that had been defending the castle for over nine hundred years.

They walked through the archway and out into the stunning courtyard with the castle buildings. All of this protected by imposing high curtain walls. Susan noticed someone striding purposefully across the gravel towards them.

'Maxine,' shouted Zoe. She ran towards her and they hugged. 'I've brought Mum in to have a look around.'

Maxine looked over Zoe's shoulder and smiled at Susan. 'Hiya, Susan, great to see you again. It's been so long, but you haven't changed.'

Susan was pleased to see Maxine again. They'd always got on well, and she'd enjoyed the long chats they'd had in the kitchen when Maxine had been an earnest teenager putting the world to rights. Susan remembered her as a rebel with dyed pink hair and how she had been the first friend to stand proud with Zoe when she first came out in the sixth form. Today, despite the conservative jeans and blonde hair falling neatly to her shoulders, Susan could see the same burning passion for fairness and justice in Maxine's eyes.

Susan looked around at the buildings inside the castle, all so familiar from her visits over the years. To her right was the chapel, then the entrance to the Privy Garden, followed by the green lawn of the inner bailey, and then, face on, the entrance to the stable courtyard.

To her left was the start of a steep flight of steps leading to the battlements. Alongside these were the ruins of Carey's Mansion, followed by the Great Hall, now a museum, the Well House, and then the magnificent keep. A path ran through the centre of the castle grounds to a doorway in the opposite east wall, which led to the vast bowling green.

'The apartment is in the stable courtyard,' said Maxine, 'over there to the right.'

'Oh, do the donkeys sleep there overnight?' asked Susan.

'No, they go to different stables, but they're still there at the moment.'

'They were always the highlight of our castle visits,' said Zoe, glancing around. 'We dashed in, went up the battlements, then went and listened to the donkey talk in the Well House, and then raced around the bowling green.'

Maxine laughed. 'I was the same. I actually read up about the castle before coming, and I'm seeing it through different eyes now.'

'The problem with castles is that their history is so confusing,' said Zoe. She grinned at Susan. 'You were always trying to teach us about this place. Let's see – first the castle was a place for defence, then a prison for Charles I, and finally a summer residence for Queen Victoria's daughter.'

Susan grinned, 'That is a very potted history but yes, that's about right.' She looked around. 'These walls saw all that and so much more, I think that's quite magical.'

Maxine saw Susan's gaze move to the battlements. 'Do you fancy going up before the light goes? Take in the views?'

'Um, I'd quite like to, but I can't take the dogs up there,' said Susan.

'You go, Mum,' said Zoe. 'I'll look after Rocco and Libs.'

'Great. Do you want to come, LeAnne?' Maxine asked. It was the first time the women had looked directly at each other.

'I'll go with Zoe, take my bags to the accommodation,' said LeAnne.

'OK,' said Maxine briskly. 'Once you enter the stable courtyard, cross it and you'll find a short flight of steps that lead to the entrance to the apartment, behind the office and café buildings.'

'Brilliant, we'll see you there.'

'Right, Susan. Let's start the climb.'

They walked to the base of the steps, where Susan glanced at the large notice warning them of danger ahead. She grabbed hold of the metal handrail.

There were actually three uneven flights of stone steps leading to the battlements, worn away by ghostly footprints over hundreds of years. The first flight branched off to a walkway along the north side, which led behind the ruins of Carey's Mansion, all that remained of what had once been a small but impressive Elizabethan manor house.

Susan caught her breath here and prepared to ascend the second flight. At the top of these, another walkway branched again along the north side, leading to the keep.

'The keep is closer than I remembered,' said Maxine. 'I love it in there but let's continue going up today.'

There was one last short flight and then they came out on to the battlements.

The view may have been breathtaking, looking right over the island, the air incredibly fresh on her face, but Susan suddenly remembered just how scared she always felt up here. The nature of the top of a castle with its castellations meant that the dips which may have at one time allowed soldiers to attack oncoming enemies were alarming today.

A memory of tightly holding a young Zoe's hand came back. In truth, Susan's main memory of being up here was one of anxiety and that huge relief when they descended the battlements all in one piece.

Today she tried to make herself relax and enjoy the experience. This was the north side of the castle, and so the view looked over to the town of Newport and beyond.

Maxine held her face up to the sky, breathed in the fresh air. 'Gosh, that feels good. It's better air over here than in the city. Let's go this way and look down on the Privy Garden.'

Susan gingerly followed Maxine along this north side and turned onto the west side, over the gatehouse. As they approached the part looking down on the garden, Susan looked down on a ruined building tucked behind the chapel that she hadn't been aware of.

'What's down there?' she asked Maxine.

'That's the old armoury. It looks a bit bleak from up here but you can find the remains of an old fireplace so it must have been quite cosy at one time. You get there up a short flight of steps on the way to the rooms of the gatehouse. I don't know if many people go in there. Anyway, come and see the garden.'

The walled garden was carefully structured, laid out like a Lego garden with a small equestrian statue, a small fountain and neat pyramid trees.

'I like its old name of Privy Garden, rather than Princess Beatrice Garden. It reflects what a special place it has been over time, a private place for people to escape to. My sister and I would play hide and seek down here. In my mind I was a medieval princess, hiding from dragons and witches.'

'You were a very imaginative child.'

'I believed all the fairytales then, all the happy endings.'

Susan heard the stroke of bitterness which spoiled the innocent verbal painting Maxine had created.

Suddenly Maxine turned to her. 'I hope you don't mind me asking, but, well, how did you cope with your marriage falling apart?'

Susan blinked. 'I guess I went into survival mode. You start slowly to build a new life, but life's never quite the same.'

'Can you imagine ever falling in love again?'

Susan thought of Robert. She bit her lip. 'The problem for me is that word "falling". It involves trust, doesn't it?' She turned to Maxine. 'Sorry, that's a bit heavy.'

Maxine held onto the wall. She bent her head, her whole body speaking of sadness and loss. 'Don't apologise. I understand just what you mean. I allowed myself to abandon all my usual caution when I met Gino. It was so romantic: meeting in Rome, being swept off my feet. We were married within months, a fairytale day of Italian sunshine, and olive groves.' Maxine curled her hair around her finger, then turned back to Susan. 'It sounds foolish, but I really did believe I'd married my soulmate. I gave him the gift of my trust.' Her voice cracked. 'But it's not working, Susan. It's gone horribly wrong.' Maxine held her fist to her chest. 'I'd not realised heartbreak was a real thing. In my work I've seen so many messy relationships, but I'd never appreciated the hurt. The pain is frightening, it's deep in here like a shard of glass digging in.'

Susan's heart went out to Maxine as she saw the pain and fear in her eyes.

Maxine gave a weak apologetic smile. 'I'm sorry. I shouldn't be burdening you with all this. It's coming home to the island, seeing you, takes me back to our long chats in your house over in Ventnor.'

Susan smiled. 'I always enjoyed them.' And then she added more seriously, 'I'm sorry things are so difficult in your marriage. Have you thought maybe of counselling?'

Maxine gave a sad smile. 'I've given that advice to friends, and sometimes it works. But it wouldn't for us. You see, that trust I gave has been smashed to smithereens. There's no glueing that back together.'

'That's awful, Maxine. I'm so sorry.'

'Thank you, but don't worry about me. I'll get through this. I know I will.' She looked around at the castle. 'Being here puts things in perspective. Me and my problems are a drop in the history of this place, will never even get a line in the history books.'

'It's certainly a unique holiday home.'

'Yes. I do hope we can all get something out of the week. The trouble is, it's not just Gino I have to worry about. I guess Zoe told you about Nick's court case?'

'She said you acted for him. He was charged with drunk driving?'

'That's right, but I wish I hadn't got involved.'

'I'm sure Nick appreciated your support.'

'He did, but it would have been better to stay out of it. It's not like a case I can walk away from. Anyway, you forget old friends change, I hadn't realised the implications of LeAnne's brother Wesley being arrested that night: it makes it very complicated.'

'LeAnne told us in the car that she believed Nick had set Wesley up and driven the car at him.'

Maxine frowned. 'I'm afraid you only got her side of the story, and I'm guessing she's bound to stick up for her brother. She hasn't said much to me, but we've had other issues to resolve. I tell you, Susan, I'll be glad to just get through this week. Let's go round to the south wall, catch the views over the valley.'

Susan followed Maxine. Dark clouds were starting to appear, the light blue sky behind them now more white-grey.

They stopped halfway along the south wall. From here Susan looked south-west at the Bowcombe Valley. She could see for miles. Strategically, it was a brilliant position.

'Zoe said you'd moved. How are you finding it all the way over here in the wilds of West Wight?'

Susan grinned. 'It's not that uncivilised. I had family living over here. Of course, I miss Ventnor, so many lovely memories of Zoe growing up there, and the foster children who were part of our family. But with Zoe's dad gone, I needed a new start. Also, the hills were killing me!'

Maxine laughed. 'Gosh, yes. I'm not sure I could manage the one I climbed to school each day now, but we did it without thinking back then. We used to love coming to your house after school. Chaos, but always cake in the tin.'

She looked again over the valley. It was lovely to think that Maxine looked back on those times with such fondness, and for her part, Susan had loved having them all round the house. For all the stress that went along with teenage years, they felt a more innocent time.

She sighed and dragged herself back to the present. 'So, how are you finding life as a barrister? I can't imagine it's quite as glamorous as they make out on TV.'

'Certainly not, particularly if you're a criminal defence barrister. Crazy hours, pay not what people expect. And the clientele is very mixed.'

'Stressful?'

'It is, but I love it.'

'It's brilliant that there are talented people willing to take this work on.'

'I believe everyone has the right to good representation and I love fighting my corner.' Maxine looked around, her voice softening. 'You'd understand. I remember you were always fighting for some cause. You had that photo of you at some peace camp when you were younger.'

'Greenham Common. Yes, I went there. We'd only just got married. Steve's parents didn't approve. My mum, of course, thought it was a fantastic idea. I'm glad I went. I'm still in touch with some of the women I met.'

'You're an inspiration.'

Susan laughed. 'A very disorganised one.'

Turning inward to the castle grounds, they looked down on the courtyard and inner bailey and the old building that was now the toilet block. 'Apparently a little owl used to nest down there in the toilet block,' said Maxine, 'and over at the Great

Hall at dusk we should see the bats coming out. Apparently, they have recorded nine different kinds of bats here. That's why they keep lighting at night to a minimum, not to confuse them. Online I saw a photo of this baby grey long-eared bat. They're quite rare and so cute. The ears really looked enormous on this tiny thing.'

'I shall look out this evening. I got interested in bats a year or two ago, and even came over here to the pub down in the village. There's a huge pond there where you can see, I think they're called Daubenton's bats, zooming low over the water, catching insects with their feet. It's incredible.'

'You're a bat expert!'

'Hardly, but I learned not to be scared of them. All that nonsense about them getting caught in your hair and being associated with witches and bad luck. It's been very harmful for their reputation. They're so important for the ecosystem. We should be protecting them.'

'I agree. People generally now speak fondly of owls, but they were once seen as harbingers of death, which is crazy,' said Maxine. 'Mind you, one myth says they carry your soul away when you die, which I think is rather lovely.'

As they approached the final eastern wall, they found themselves enclosed in the branches of overhanging trees.

'Talking of birds,' said Maxine, 'look up there.'

'Are they crows?'

'No, they're jackdaws. See, quite a lot smaller. They nest in the holes in the walls, and use the hair from the donkeys to line their nests. Apparently, if they leave the castle, it spells doom, like the ravens at the Tower of London or something. Let's hope they stay at least for our holiday. We could do without curses on top of everything else.'

'You really have done your homework on this place. I can't

believe how much I didn't know – particularly about the jackdaws!'

'Charles I wrote about seeing them out of his window when he was a prisoner here.'

'At least I know about him being here!' said Susan, laughing.

They had reached the top of another flight of steps.

'We go down here, be careful,' warned Maxine as they clambered down.

Susan held firmly onto the rails and made her way down.

Once they'd reached the bottom, Maxine pointed to the entrance to the apartment.

'It's well tucked away,' said Susan. 'I'd heard about the apartment but never had any idea where it was.'

Maxine paused, glanced around. 'It's strange, isn't it? Hidden away. I thought I'd feel safe here, but there are so many dark corners, so many secrets.' She shook herself. 'Sorry. Come on, let's go and see the others.'

4

On the doorstep of the apartment sat a large Halloween pumpkin, its toothy grin lit by a flickering candle.

'LeAnne wasn't joking when she said she'd be decorating,' said Maxine.

The front door opened into a small hallway with a row of coat hooks and a shoe stand.

Maxine pointed to her left. 'Down there are the two bedrooms and bathroom, and this way to the right takes us to the living and dining room. Come and see, everyone.'

Susan followed her into a bright, surprisingly modern room. Most of the walls were painted grey with one statement wall of floral wallpaper. There was a small dining table, sofa, comfy chairs and TV. To one side she saw a neat kitchen area.

LeAnne and Zoe were busy hanging a banner while the people Susan recognised as Nick and Annika sat on the sofa and greeted her with a smile. They hadn't changed a lot. Both conservatively dressed, in jeans and Fair Isle jumpers, Nick with short red hair, Annika with shoulder-length mousy brown hair and old-fashioned brown-rimmed glasses.

'How was your walk, Mum?' asked Zoe.

'Great. I've learned new things about the castle already.'

'I showed Susan where the owl nests and the bats roost,' said Maxine.

'Mum knows a thing or two about bats,' said Zoe. 'I told you about her solving a murder in her village. The victim was an expert on bats.'

Maxine turned to Susan. 'I forgot you'd been involved in solving a crime. Very impressive and surprising, really. I've always seen you as someone fighting the establishment.'

'But I fight for truth,' said Susan.

'Zoe is very proud of your achievements,' said Maxine. 'I noticed there was no mention of you in the papers.'

'The police weren't too impressed with my involvement,' said Susan, 'but I was proved right.'

'You should have become a lawyer—'

Susan laughed and at that point Nick heaved himself off the sofa. 'Hi, Susan. It's been years. How are you?' He didn't wait for her to answer but turned to Zoe. 'How's the teaching? How you cope with a family and being deputy head I don't know. You must be knackered. I'll pour you a few extra drinks this week.'

'Thanks. How's the term going?'

'Cut the budget again. Music has been slashed to the bone and yet, come any event at the school, I'm meant to summon up a choir and an orchestra, and put on a Christmas production with a drama department that is down to one and a half teachers. Crazy.'

'Sounds like chaos.' Zoe looked over at Annika who was still sitting on the sofa. 'Good to see you, Annika. How are you?'

Annika stood up slowly, and stood slightly behind Nick. 'Fine, thanks. It's awesome to be staying here. I've hardly been in the castle during the day, let alone night-time.' She sounded young, like a child on a school outing.

'How's it going taking blood, then?'

'Annika's official title is phlebotomist,' said Nick with mock severity, and then, putting his arm around her shoulder, said, 'I'm very proud of her, she's done so well.'

Annika blushed and smiled. 'I'm a diurnal vampire, very Halloween. Seriously, though, I've only been doing it since the summer, and I love it. I'm based in the hospital, but I go to care homes as well. It's great having a nine-to-five job that's not too stressful. It gives me time to paint. For the first time I'm able to concentrate on it.'

'I always thought you'd be off singing in some fancy opera house by now,' said LeAnne.

'It's all a lot harder to get into than you imagine. Still, I'm singing sometimes now. Nick and I have actually started doing some gigs together, only local pubs.'

'And how are you finding Cowes? Living among all those yachty types.'

'It's dead cool, really friendly.' Annika glanced over at Maxine. 'I love the flat. Gino has done an amazing job doing the place up.'

'I hadn't realised you were in one of his properties,' said Zoe.

'Yes, I'm very lucky and, of course, Nick has moved in now.'

Nick let out a noisy sneeze. Annika turned quickly. 'Do you need your inhaler?' Turning to Zoe she said, 'We think it's the stables. He has loads of allergies. He needs to get tested properly, identify exactly what he's allergic to and then sort out the medication. He's done nothing but sneeze and blow his nose since we arrived.'

Nick gave a slightly embarrassed smile, took out a packet of sweets, and popped a few in his mouth. 'Annika worries too much over a few sneezes. I'm fine.'

Maxine interrupted. 'Now I have, as promised, bought new torches and have had them inscribed to mark our holiday.'

She rushed off back through the hallway in the direction of the bedrooms and soon returned with a box.

'They're all set up with batteries and working. It can be a memento of our holiday.' She handed round the box, for them each to pick a torch. Each had 'Band holiday – Carisbrooke Castle 2017' inscribed on the side. 'I brought eight to be on the safe side, so, of course, Susan must have one, and I'll leave the box with one for Gino and a spare on the table here.'

Susan thanked her and copied the others, putting it in her pocket.

'Good,' said Maxine. 'Right, Susan, let me show you around. It's nearly dark. Good to see it before it's completely black out there.'

'I'll join you,' said Zoe.

'I'll show you Gino's and my room first.'

They followed Maxine to a large bedroom off the main room. 'We got the pick of the rooms. We have great views over the main courtyard and well house and, if you strain your eyes, you can see the window Charles I tried to escape from.'

They left the room. Maxine quickly opened a door to show the bathroom and then took them into the other bedroom which had bunk beds. 'I'm afraid Nick and Annika have to come in here. Mind you, with their stuff unpacked it looks cosier.' Susan noticed teddy bears on Annika's bed. She found it interesting that adults clung onto their cuddly toys, even brought them away on holiday.

In this room there was also a table with a computer and

small keyboard alongside other clutter, keys, a penknife and pens.

Maxine explained. 'Nick brought some of his gear with him. He played me a composition he's working on; it's beautiful. It's a shame he doesn't have more time to commit to it, but teaching is all-consuming.'

'You're right,' said Zoe. 'I wouldn't want to be full time now. I get paid for three days but a lot of the time I'm doing admin on the other two.'

'I'm glad Nick's doing gigs with Annika now,' said Maxine. 'They're going to perform on Saturday at the concert. Her voice will be amazing in that Great Hall.' She paused, looked at Zoe. 'You definitely don't want to perform?'

'God, no. I am way out of practice.'

'I'm the same,' said Maxine. 'LeAnne would rather sit it out as well. Those two will represent us well.'

When they all went back to the main room, Susan decided it was time to leave. She needed to take the dogs for a walk and get home to see Robert before returning for the ghost walk later.

She found the leads and put them on Rocco and Libs who, sensing a walk, started sniffing and wagging their tails enthusiastically.

'Don't go walking them around here, Mum,' said Zoe. 'You get some dodgy types up here at night.'

Susan smiled: she could hear herself speaking to Zoe in the same manner years ago. It was interesting how their roles were reversing at times now.

'It's only half past four,' she replied.

'I know, but it's getting dark.'

'I'll be careful. Now, what time is the ghost walk this evening?'

'Half seven, but we need to gather in the shop about quarter past.'

'I'll come here for you all then about seven. By the way, I'll be going straight home after. Robert is looking after the dogs, but I don't want to be out too long.'

'That's fine, we'll get a taxi. I'll need to look them up though, there's no Uber on the island.'

'I've got details of Erse, the firm Annika uses,' said Nick. 'It's just one chap but his rates are very good.'

'You must mean Liam,' said Maxine, her voice sharp. 'I think Zoe could find a better taxi firm than his.'

Nick frowned. 'You don't even know him, he's great.'

'I used him because you'd given me his card when I came over recently.' Maxine glanced at Annika. 'Annika and I talked about it and agreed it would be better to use someone else.'

Nick shrugged. 'I didn't know anything about this – you've not said anything to me, Annika. We agreed it's good to support him trying to make a fresh start.'

Annika simply looked away.

Nick sighed, took out his wallet and handed a card to Zoe. 'I don't know what they're on about, but Liam's very good. Here, take the card.'

Zoe slipped the car into her purse, looked over to Susan.

'We'll see you later then, Mum.'

'Of course, I'll be off now.'

'I'll walk you out,' said Maxine.

Outside the apartment, Susan realised the deep blue-black streaks were gathering and slowly covering the sky.

'We'll not go back via the battlements,' said Maxine. 'But maybe use your torch for going down the steps here as it's pretty dark.'

Susan followed Maxine down and into the stable courtyard.

She could smell the sweet hay from the stables. Rocco and Libs were nose down, sniffing the ground intently.

'Oh, look, there's someone with the donkeys,' said Maxine. 'We can switch our torches off now and go and say hi.'

A young woman in a uniform of sage-green fleece was leading one of the donkeys out of the stable.

'I'm taking Jack off to his night quarters,' she said.

Susan was relieved the dogs remained quite calm, and she was able to stroke Jack's soft grey snout. He nuzzled her affectionately.

'He's so loving, but a bit of an escape artist.'

'He should be called Charles after the king,' said Maxine, laughing.

'Their names all have to start with the letter J. That is because, when he was a prisoner, Charles I wrote coded letters when planning escapes from the castle and signed them with the letter J.'

'I didn't know that,' said Susan. 'I'm learning a lot tonight.'

The donkey was led away, and Susan and Maxine left the courtyard through a small stone gateway that opened on to the main castle grounds.

As the light was fading, the features of the building started to disappear. Soon they would be faceless silhouettes.

'Dusk is quite unsettling, isn't it?' said Maxine. 'Neither one thing nor the other. Especially in here. It's as if the castle is coming to life.'

Susan nodded. 'I know exactly what you mean. It's very different, isn't it? I'm excited to see how it feels later when night has fallen.'

'All the ghosts and spirits will be out then. After all, it's Halloween.'

Susan pointed over to the wheelhouse. 'I wonder if we'll go

in there this evening, not for the donkey demonstration on the well, of course, but there is meant to be a ghost down the well. Someone called Elizabeth Ruffin was murdered. They found her skeleton down there.'

'Wow, that's creepy,' said Maxine. 'I'm starting to feel a bit nervous about this walk now.'

'I wasn't being serious. You're not superstitious, are you?'

'Someone said once that in the daytime they knew there was no such thing as ghosts; at night they were not so sure.'

Susan smiled. 'I've never been on a ghost walk before. I must admit I'm a little apprehensive. Not because I believe in ghosts but I'm not sure what happens. I don't like really gory stories. Still, we can all look after each other.'

'I wish I could believe that. There's an odd atmosphere in the group, don't you think?'

As they entered the archway of the gatehouse, Susan could hear their voices starting to echo against the stone walls.

'I expect everyone is a bit nervous as to how they're all going to get on. You'll be fine once people settle down.' She looked over at the shop, all lit up. 'Right. I'll see you later.'

'Yes, of course. It'll be fun,' said Maxine, but there was no smile. 'Don't forget your torch.'

Susan walked through the shop, out through the doors, and made her way out of the castle. She took the dogs along to a small wooden latch gate that led to a public walkway, around the outside of the castle walls, starting here along the south side, which faced the Bowcombe Valley.

As she opened the gate, Susan hesitated. The night was coming in quickly now; there was no one about. Should she really be doing this?

5

Susan stared at the gate leading to the path around the outside of the castle. If she fell, Zoe would never let her hear the end of it. However, the dogs were pulling, excited for the walk. Susan took a breath. Come on, it would be fine: she would use her torch and be careful.

Between the path and the castle walls was a deep grassy moat. Susan had memories of Zoe and her friends running up and down the sides as children. As she let the dogs off, she saw them make a dash down the bank.

It was as she reached the end of the first side of the castle and turned that she felt stronger twinges of unease. She was aware of being alone, the castle to her left, empty fields cut off by hedges and trees to her right. She called Libs who, she noticed, nose down, was about to make her way through to the fields. 'Not this evening, Libs, stay here.'

Fortunately, the dog spied a rabbit down in the moat and changed direction.

Susan increased her pace as she heard the frantic calls of

rooks above returning to the safety of their rookeries in the ash and oak trees nearby.

They walked to the end of that wall and turned to the north side facing the town. Susan shone her torch around, where was Libs?

She shone the beam down the moat and up on the banks. Susan saw the gap underneath an old wooden gate in the castle walls, panicked, had Libs squeezed under there? But then she heard a barking further along. Shining her torch along the bank she was relieved to see Libs barking at a rabbit that was sat on top of a lower section of wall. The rabbit bolted and Susan followed it with her torch light up a small path that led to a section of the castle where there was a gap in the main curtain wall. Her torch illuminated one of the cannons at the end of the bowling green.

Susan called Libs and fortunately she came back, joining Rocco who was standing close by. While giving them treats, she put them back on their leads.

Turning the final corner, they walked along the stretch of path that looked down over the village of Castleford. Susan felt far more comfortable walking here. There were a few lights now in the houses and it was reassuring and homely. For all that, she was relieved to get back to the car, and drive home.

Back home, Susan gave the dogs their tea and for herself heated up a tin of tomato soup which she ate with hunks of bread.

It wasn't long before she heard a car drawing up outside. Libs and Rocco pricked up their ears. They seemed to know who was coming.

She opened the door to greet Robert and his two dogs: Gem Gem, a beautiful liver and white pointer-springer cross, and

Dougie, a velvet black cocker spaniel with a flash of white on his chest.

The dogs all greeted each other while Robert wrapped Susan in his arms. She loved the way he hugged her. She felt safe, cared for, cherished.

Robert, a widowed ex-policeman, had come into her life two years after her husband had left. It had taken a while to appreciate the depth and wisdom of this man who hated the classical music and books she loved, a man who still loved rugby, tennis, and steak, while she hated sport and was a vegetarian.

He had been by her side in other investigations and picked up the pieces when Susan had scared even herself by the chances she'd taken.

But there were problems. Robert was ready to settle down. Susan was still raw and hurting from the collapse of her marriage and had no idea when or if she would ever be able to fully trust and let herself fall in love again. She was also finding she enjoyed living alone a lot of the time and was not sure if she wanted to give up her independence.

Tracy would be most disappointed to know Robert's overnight stays had been purely platonic in nature. The spare room was used. They said he was staying for convenience. It meant he could have a drink and didn't have to face the drive home after watching a late-night film. However, they both knew there was more to it than that. It was a small step forward in their relationship, as they became closer and enjoyed the companionship of spending more time together.

'How's it all going?'

Noticing the dogs were chasing each other madly around the room, Susan stepped away to open the patio doors. The cold air came rushing in, but it gave the dogs a chance to run off some of the excitement outside.

'OK so far. I've left Zoe and her friend LeAnne up at the castle. It's amazing there. They're in for quite some holiday. I've never been up there at night.'

'Nor have I, it sounds exciting.'

'Oh, I'm sorry. Did you want to come on the ghost walk?'

He laughed. 'Not really, and someone has to keep an eye on these four. The early callers for Halloween are innocent enough but some of the older kids' visits are more difficult. Their masks are getting quite gross now. They frighten me, let alone the dogs.'

As if on cue, the doorbell rang.

Susan answered to find three small children dressed as a princess, a pirate and a ghost with a mother standing a few steps behind them. After complimenting them on their costumes, she handed them the bowl of sweets. She then realised all four dogs were sitting patiently behind her and laughed. 'These are not for you. I'll have to find your treats, won't I? You're not going to need any supper at this rate.'

There were several more callers before it was time for her to leave.

'Thank you so much for dog sitting,' she said to Robert.

'We'll settle in well together. Have a good time. Don't go getting spooked by too many ghosts.'

Susan laughed and left.

* * *

She arrived at the castle to find a number of cars parked at the top. People were gathering in excited huddles for the ghost walk. It was only planned for adults, but some had dressed up in masks and capes.

The metal gates were open, and Susan walked through the shop, out through the gatehouse arch and into the courtyard.

The castle had been transformed in her absence. Tealights twinkled on the steps leading to the battlements, coloured lights danced through the stained-glass windows of the chapel. The castle had taken on a gentler persona, and Susan felt a warmth that had been missing at dusk.

And then she saw something very special. The colony of bats which roosted around the Great Hall were soaring across the sky. She stood in awe, watching them swooping and diving, hearing their tiny chirps.

Reluctantly she realised she needed to move on and began crunching over the gravel towards the stable courtyard, when she saw someone wave though the darkness. Annika was coming towards her.

'Zoe said you'd be arriving about now. I came out to make sure you were OK.'

'Thank you. I've been watching the bats.' Susan looked around. 'It's pretty, isn't it? I hadn't expected there to be lights.'

'It's dead cool. I expected the castle to feel bigger at night, but it actually feels smaller, like the walls are coming closer to you.'

Susan glanced around. 'You're right, that's exactly how it feels. So, are you looking forward to the walk? Do you believe in ghosts?'

Annika paused, looked thoughtfully at Susan. 'It depends on what you mean by ghosts. I guess everyone is haunted by something. A presence that never leaves you, is always watching you. It creeps up on you, whispers in a cold voice, taunting you, invading your dreams.'

Susan blinked. 'That's a pretty disturbing way to look at them.'

Annika laughed. 'Nick thinks I'm daft, but then I like that he's so grounded. It's why he's so good for me. I always feel safe with him.'

They walked on.

'I'm glad you're enjoying your new job,' Susan said. 'By the way, you mentioned earlier you go into care homes. I don't suppose you go into the one at Bishopstone, do you?'

'Yes. That's one of my regular places.'

'I have a friend, Alice, in there. Have you met her?'

'Of course. Such a sweet little old lady. She just sort of sits there pretending to do her crossword.'

Susan hid a smile. Alice would loathe everything about that description of her. She was kind, bright, but not sweet and she did the crossword as quickly as most people half her age.

'Zoe told me you were a nanny before working in the health service?'

'I was. The nannying was only meant to be for a few months while I went for a few singing auditions that my agent set up, but nothing worked out. I stayed for two years in the end. I finished in June as the child is off to pre-prep school. Dad suggested I rent a flat and bought me the car hoping I'd get vocal work through my agent. Dad was thinking of maybe a musical up in London. I didn't think I stood a chance and anyway I was with Nick by then. We'd reconnected when we found ourselves in the same choir. I didn't want to be away all the time. I saw this work with the blood service, and it's great.'

As they approached the stable courtyard, Susan was aware of the familiar smell of hay and donkeys, although they of course were tucked up in their night accommodation.

'Did you need a lot of qualifications for your new job?'

'They trained me on the job. I've never had a problem with needles or blood which was lucky,' said Annika, laughing. 'My only worry was how much driving would be involved. I know it sounds stupid, but I've never enjoyed it. Anyway, most days I'm based at the hospital, so those days I get a bus or taxi into work. It's all worked out well.'

'I'm glad.'

'Yes, a job with no pressure and time to myself. I've even been able to take up painting again. I'd have loved to have done a degree in art but of course Dad was all about the singing.'

'That's wonderful. It's great you're rediscovering that. Which choir are you and Nick in, by the way? Would I know it?'

'It's based in Newport. I can give you the details if you're interested. It's quite demanding. We do choral pieces. Dad has come to some of the concerts and even he admits it's very good for an amateur choir.'

'I shall look out for it.'

Annika grinned. 'I'm involved with another singing group, but I'm afraid you won't be able to watch us perform.'

Susan frowned. 'Sorry, what do you mean?'

'It's in the prison,' said Annika, laughing. 'Nick and I volunteer there, he teaches keyboards. I take a small group for singing.'

'That's brilliant,' said Susan. 'Music can be such a release for people.'

Annika nodded enthusiastically. 'I agree. It reminds me that music is about fun and enjoyment, not just passing exams and concerts.'

They climbed the flight of steps that led to the apartment.

As they arrived, the pumpkin was shining brighter than before. It looked more menacing against the darkness.

'Honestly, LeAnne has gone mad. Wait until you see inside.'

Annika opened the door, and Susan was greeted by a plastic skeleton hanging from one of the coat racks. The main room was festooned with more skeletons, with additional bats and spiders.

Maxine was busy getting everyone together, and asked Susan to take a selfie of them all. They just about managed one with them all together, but then Susan took a better one just of the group of friends.

After they had toasted each other and the holiday, LeAnne picked up a carrier bag resting in a corner.

'And now I have something special for Halloween,' she declared.

6

LeAnne began emptying the bag.

'Masks?' asked Maxine.

'Of course. It's Halloween. We have to wear them to frighten away the demons.' LeAnne laughed. 'You all look so freaked out. Don't worry, they're very tasteful; only eye masks or, to give them the right name, Columbina masks. I've also brought a pile of make-up. You can make your eyes really dark and smoky. And I've also got red nail varnish if you want your nails to drip with blood.' She laughed. 'Come on!'

Reluctantly, everyone chose a mask although they were all very similar: gold and black, decorated with black feathers and jewels that caught the light.

Susan simply tied hers on using some of the red ribbons Maxine had brought. It wasn't easy placing it over her glasses, and she found it quite frustrating. Even as a child she was never that keen on masks. She hated the way they restricted her peripheral vision. It was as if she couldn't think or talk as straight when wearing one.

No one else seemed to share her misgivings and they were all soon applying make-up and doing up their masks.

Once they had finished, Maxine took a selfie of the whole group, and then Susan suggested she take one just of the friends.

As they all huddled together, Susan noticed Nick slip his arm around Maxine's shoulder, but she gently moved his hand. At the same time, Annika stepped closer to him and laid her hand on his arm.

As soon as Susan had taken the photo, Maxine walked away from the group and looked out of the window. Annika, Zoe, and Susan sat down, but LeAnne stepped towards Nick, blocking him from his seat. 'I saw you smooching up to Maxine like that. For God's sake, get a grip.' Her voice was loud, confrontational and an uneasy silence fell on the room.

'Don't be ridiculous,' he replied crossly.

'I've hit a nerve.'

'Don't be prat LeAnne. Maxine and I are friends, and she stood by me through one of the worst times of my life.' His words were slightly slurred, his hand trembling as he picked up a bottle and refilled his glass.

Maxine stood at the side of them, touched Nick's arm. 'Leave it, Nick.'

LeAnne's eyes narrowed, and she faced Maxine. 'Doesn't it sicken you the way he idolises you like you're some kind of feckin' saint? You were just doing your job.'

Maxine stepped closer. 'Actually, LeAnne, my job would not usually involve appearing in the magistrates' court representing someone charged with drunk driving. To be frank, I'm far too good for that.' The coldness of her voice, the thin, tight lips and narrowed eyes, all spoke of Maxine's fury as she continued. 'I took Nick's case because he's my friend, admittedly one who made a very bad decision, but my friend nonetheless. I wanted to sit next to him, reassure him, support him.'

'You chose to support a coward and a fecking liar then.'

Annika, Zoe and Susan grimaced at each other and slunk back into their seats.

'Wesley's case was settled in a court of law. There was no indication of any involvement by Nick. That's the end of it.'

'The case is settled, you move on. That's how you see it? And what about if justice isn't done? What if the accused is innocent?' She pointed at Nick. 'He kept vital information from the court. He should have owned up to planting the cocaine. He's admitted he was drunk. He knows he was out of control. Not only that, but he also tried to kill my Wesley. Nick crashed because he was driving his car directly at him.'

Nick stepped forward. 'I admit I was drunk and stupid. I shouldn't have phoned the police. It was a joke. That's why I made no secret of it. I shouted it out when Wesley and his mates came in, thinking it would give them a scare as they had weed on them. Seriously, I doubted the police would come. And the idea I would drive my car at Wesley is ridiculous. Of course I never wanted to hurt him.'

'I don't believe you,' LeAnne shouted, thrusting her finger at him. 'You were out to get him.'

'Look, I know this is difficult, but Nick had no reason to launch this so-called vendetta against Wesley,' said Maxine. 'I know he was part of the team at the school that had Wesley excluded, but that was after Wesley had seriously attacked another pupil. There was nothing personal in it.'

'No motive? What about the stuff Wesley posted online?'

Nick looked away at this.

Maxine blinked, her voice lowered, more controlled. 'What posts?'

LeAnne threw her hands up. 'Nick didn't tell you?'

'I don't know what you're talking about.'

'The online abuse.' She paused, registering the confused look on Maxine's face. 'God, you really didn't know, did you? Wesley tried to keep it hidden even from me and when I tracked it down, I could see why. It was vile. Still, I tried to persuade Wesley to tell his barrister about it. It gave Nick motive to hate him. Wesley refused, said he could get into even more trouble if the courts saw it. He had actually threatened Nick and his family. So, the barrister never knew. Look, I'm not proud of what my brother did, but he was at a low point when he was excluded from school. The point is, Nick had every reason to hate Wesley.'

'I didn't know any of this,' said Maxine.

Nick glanced over his shoulder at Maxine, his face burning red and he cringed, clearly deeply embarrassed. Nonetheless, he did not speak or try to defend himself.

Maxine gave Nick a long, hard, look but then took a breath before speaking more calmly to LeAnne. 'I'm sorry Nick kept this from me, but it has nothing to do with his case, and there are certainly not enough grounds to reopen Wesley's. You're going to have to let this go.'

'But doesn't it make you wonder about Nick? He could have set Wesley up. He had the motive. You have to see that. His own case may have been straightforward, but he's not the person you thought he was. He's a vindictive liar, a violent person who tried to take the life of a young boy.'

Maxine frowned, 'LeAnne, you can't go throwing around damaging allegations against Nick. You need to rein this in. Now, you have also chosen to come away on holiday with Nick and the rest of us. You're going to have to park this at least until the holiday is over or we will all have a miserable time.'

'I can't promise that. But I have a right to be here. The rest of you are my friends, and I want to be here for the concert for Mrs Strong. But I'm not going to act as if nothing has happened and, Maxine, you're not going to shut me up,' said LeAnne. 'This isn't band practice. We're not kids. You're not in control any more.'

Before Maxine could reply, they heard the front door to the apartment open and a tall man entered the room.

Everyone turned. Maxine glanced over and with no semblance of a smile or warmth in her voice said, 'Oh Gino, you made it.'

Susan was intrigued finally to meet this man. Even with his black hair ruffled, his beard slightly unkempt and wearing a waterproof, he was remarkably handsome.

Gino put his hands up in mock surrender. 'Forgive me, amore mio. I had work to do.' He looked around. 'You all got dressed up without me.'

Gino started to shake off his large waterproof coat, and Maxine took it from him. A large torch was sticking out of one pocket. Maxine took it out, flicked the switch on and off. 'Why are you carrying this old thing around? This is the one from your toolbox. I told you it didn't work.'

Maxine tutted and Susan wasn't surprised to see the child-like scowl on Gino's face. He grabbed the torch from her and thrust it back in his pocket. 'It just needs a new battery.'

'Rubbish. It's never going to work. Good job I brought you a decent one.' She took one of the two remaining inscribed torches from the box and pushed it into his pocket.

Gino swallowed hard and turned, gave Zoe a cursory nod and then gifted Susan a warm smile, which transformed his face from the sulky child into the young man Susan guessed Maxine had fallen in love with. 'I'm sorry, I've not had the pleasure of meeting you.' The slight tinge of an Italian accent added warmth to his words, and his eyes were such a deep, dark brown that Susan was momentarily captivated.

Maxine coughed, seemingly to compose herself. 'This is Zoe's mum, Susan.'

Susan smiled. 'Lovely to meet you, Gino.'

He didn't do anything embarrassing like kiss her hand, but she felt the full effect of his smile. Divested of his coat, she had to admire the way he wore the handmade shoes, cashmere jumper, all accentuated by a gold signet ring and Gucci watch.

He looked around again, ran his fingers through his beard, and seemed to pick up on the strained atmosphere. 'Have I missed something?'

'We've just been sorting a few things out,' said Maxine, glancing at LeAnne.

'Maxine has, of course, been defending me magnificently,' said Nick. 'You have one smart wife there. She saved my life, you know. Funny how you can know someone most of your life and never realise just how special they are.'

Maxine scowled. The others shifted awkwardly.

'Why shouldn't I say it?' said Nick. 'Maxine is one in a million. Smart, beautiful. I never appreciated how amazingly talented she is before all this.'

'How much have you been drinking?' Maxine demanded.

Without speaking, Annika got up from the sofa, shot a dagger-like glance at Maxine and gently took Nick's arm, guiding him back to their seat.

'That's right, take control of your man,' said Gino, his lips tight, hands clenched.

Susan glanced at Zoe. They rolled their eyes at each other. She hoped Gino was speaking ironically.

He didn't smile, though, and the warmth she had felt radiating from him seemed to have disappeared as he continued.

'Remember that flat was let to Annika. It's only because of my goodwill you are allowed to stay there. You're fortunate to have such a good landlord.'

Nick glared at Gino. 'Good landlord? Always dropping into the flat unannounced. You're meant to give notice, you know, and I'm sure you're not meant to be using Annika's safe.'

'It's my place. I can do what I want,' said Gino. There was threat in his words.

'But Nick is right,' said Maxine sharply. 'You have to give notice to tenants before visiting a property.'

Gino turned away from Maxine, neither spoke, leaving an icy silence.

Zoe intervened, using her most teacher-like voice. 'Right. I think it's time we got ready for the ghost walk. It's nearly half past seven. We're late.'

'You're right,' said LeAnne. 'Who's ready to meet the Grim Reaper?'

'Why do you say that?' asked Maxine, frowning.

LeAnne laughed. 'It's Halloween and everyone knows he is seen here on the walkway at the first level of the castle wall: a man in all black with a dark shroud, hiding his face, carrying a great scythe, warning everyone to leave this place.' She laughed. 'God, Maxine. I was only joking. Now, Gino. You need a mask.'

The gold and black mask suited Gino. His dark eyes sparkled through the slits. He seemed to recover his good humour and was laughing as he got them all together again for a selfie on his own phone. Susan again offered to take one of the group.

After this they started to get their coats on, ready to leave. Looking over at LeAnne in her short leather jacket, Annika in her pink faux fur with the enormous pockets, and Maxine in her white wool coat, Susan was more than glad she had her old parka. It seemed much more suitable wear for an icy walk around an old castle.

'Don't forget your torches,' called Maxine. 'Apparently, we go up the steps. We'll need them.'

Susan felt in her pocket to check she had her torch from earlier. It was a good size, fitted in easily.

As Maxine turned off the lights, and people switched on their torches, Susan glanced around the group. She felt a shiver of apprehension. The beams from the torches caught the glitter and feathers on the masks, from which their eyes stared. With their faces partially hidden, it was harder to judge what everyone was thinking or feeling, yet their eyes seemed to stare out at you as if they could see into your soul.

And there was something else. The fact that everyone's masks were so similar this evening was even stranger. It hid their individuality, and that anonymity was deeply disturbing.

7

It was a cold crisp evening. The threatening dark streaks in the sky had been replaced by a black velvet cloth, with a host of stars crowned by a silver moon.

'It's a perfect night for the walk,' said Zoe. 'Dad would be able to name all those constellations. Remember when we used to sit on the seat at the top of the garden in Ventnor?'

Susan took a breath. Happy memories from her marriage were somehow harder to cope with than the bad. But still, as always, she tried to protect Zoe from her hurt. 'Yes, of course. He knows so much about the stars.'

'Where is he at the moment?'

Susan felt annoyed. Her ex was the last person she wanted to think about. 'Somewhere in Spain, I think.'

'Honestly, I can't believe he's still with that awful woman.'

Fortunately, at this point they entered the gift shop and joined the group waiting for the ghost walk.

Although all were adults, there was an excited air of a children's party, where the Coke and Sprite had been replaced with small tots of local gin and whisky.

A member of staff called them together, and they were led outside, back to the courtyard.

They were met by two men in Victorian dress: cloaks, top hats and canes, carrying lamps. They were asked to stand in a circle to evoke the spirits of the castle to come and join them.

Susan joined the circle, embarrassed, sure a number of other people felt the same. Despite this, everyone conformed and repeated the words they were asked to say. As she looked around, Susan started to wonder what kind of walk she had come on.

They were then taken up the first flight of stone steps, which led to the battlements, using their torches as the tealights were of little help. The guides then led the group along what would have been the terrace to Carey's Mansion.

Susan realised she had never been along here and was fascinated when they paused at a rather beautiful, glassless, stone bay window.

'This window is named after Isabella de Fortibus, a remarkable woman who inherited the castle in the thirteenth century. She was widowed at the age of twenty-three after giving birth to six children and managed to stay single living in the castle for many years after,' the guide explained.

He and his partner then began a performance, calling up Isabella's spirit. It was entertaining and not in the least bit scary, so Susan found herself relaxing.

She was brought back to the present by the voices behind her on the steps leading to the platform. She glanced back and through the darkness she could make out the masks, knew it was someone in their group. She was soon able to make out LeAnne's leather jacket, and Maxine's white wool coat. They were speaking in urgent whispers. Susan couldn't make out their conversation until the leader of the group stopped his story for a dramatic pause.

'I can't. Not now,' said LeAnne, her voice red hot. 'Maxine, I will not let you destroy me.'

Although she'd lowered her voice, LeAnne's words rang out crisp and clear through the cold night air. Most of the group were facing away as they were focused on the drama. But Susan caught her eye; they held each other's gaze for a few seconds. What she saw shocked Susan, for she observed anger but also vulnerability, a desperation in LeAnne's eyes she'd never seen before.

The leader returned to his performance, until bringing it to a conclusion and suggesting they move on.

Susan's mind was now very much in the present. What had Maxine and LeAnne been talking about? It didn't seem to fit with Wesley's case. This sounded more personal to LeAnne. Of course, Maxine had said she had other matters to resolve with her. Susan wondered what they were.

She carefully descended the next flight of steps to an area close to the keep. There were nearly eighty steep steps which led up there and Susan was relieved to discover they were not going to climb them.

Instead, they were taken down behind some buildings and told to take care by the moat to their left, where apparently the ghost of a young man in a brown jerkin was frequently seen.

Maybe it was having the black silhouette of the keep looming down on them, or the closeness of the buildings behind, but Susan felt less comfortable here. The atmosphere in the group had changed as well. There was less giggling. One couple were now clasping hands with an air of trepidation.

It was not only the feel of the place that unnerved Susan, but she was suddenly aware of the very real physical dangers of this castle. During the day she worried about the battlements but in the night, she was made aware of many secret dark places, treacherous smaller flights of steps, the dangers of falling down this smaller moat which she hardly noticed in the day.

It seemed to Susan that the castle was slowly taking control and demanding to be taken seriously. As they walked along the path, she started to notice other features she'd missed in the day: the long, tall chimney stacks, the towers. Also, the trees took on a new significance: enormous, leafless branches stretched over paths like bony fingers and threatened rather than reassured her.

The guide conjured up the picture of the Grey Lady of the castle, in her long dark cloak and ghostly hounds, and this time Susan found herself carried along with the story, imagining the woman standing there in front of her.

One of the last places they visited was the Privy Garden. Part was lit up by the chapel lights, but most was in darkness. They crunched along narrow gravel paths, the leaves of tall bushes brushing against her face. It was like some mini maze and at one point she managed to lose the group and felt a wave of panic. The walls of the curtain walls looked down on her, as she reached the centre, by the fountain and the small statue of the war horse and rider.

'Mum, we're over here,' Zoe called.

Susan was glad to rejoin the group.

A bell tolled, and they were taken to the last stage of the walk. Leaving the garden, they went up a shorter flight of stairs. To the left was the old armoury Maxine had told her about, but they continued up the steps and entered the gatehouse itself, where it was cosier inside.

They listened to the guide summon Charles I who, in this scene, was looking for his daughter. Unlike her father, she had died in the castle, her body buried close by in St Thomas's church.

At the end of the walk, they returned to the gift shop where people talked and joked loudly, all quite pleased with themselves for completing the tour. A member of staff checked they were all there, and everyone apart from two members of staff and Zoe's group left.

'Fancy coming to the apartment for a drink?' Maxine asked Susan.

'No, thanks. I've someone dog sitting. I should make my way home but thank you. It was really interesting.'

Susan undid her mask and was grateful to return it to LeAnne.

'See you later, Mum,' said Zoe.

Susan watched them all leave the gift shop to return to the apartment. She could see the members of staff were ready to go and so she followed them out of the shop, and down to the metal gates.

As they clanged the enormous gates together, locked the padlock, it felt more as if Zoe and her friends were being imprisoned than left in a holiday home.

The idea seemed even less fun now. The castle had taken on a new persona. It wasn't a tourist attraction any more. The castle, which had seen centuries of people come and go, stood unconquerable now.

For the first time, Susan was scared of it and wanted to run back, make Zoe come home with her.

Susan shook herself; the ghost walk was making her fanciful. But, in her heart, she knew it wasn't simply that. The conversation with Maxine, the rows in the apartment, those words between Maxine and LeAnne – it was disturbing. They weren't a group of kids: they were adults with very grown-up issues.

There had been threats, sadness, fear. Nothing about this get-together was going to be easy.

Standing at the car, she looked back at the castle. The only visible light was over the gatehouse, the rest a silhouette of a giant sleeping on his side, which of course was an illusion: the giant was very much awake.

Susan was pleased to drive up her close and park to the side of her house, seeing lights on. There was no denying it was comforting to know someone was there, waiting for her to return.

8

Susan was pleased to be greeted by Robert opening the front door. He gave her a hug of welcome. 'So, how did it go?'

Rocco and Libs had run to meet her and she fussed them as Robert closed the door. 'The actual ghost walk was much better than I expected, really interesting. The guides did well.'

The kettle had boiled, and Robert made Susan the decaffeinated coffee he knew she liked.

She sat down on the sofa to be immediately joined by Rocco and Libs.

'It was a good evening, but there's a difficult atmosphere among the group.'

'Who exactly are these friends of Zoe's?'

'There are six of them, counting Zoe. The four sleeping at the castle are Maxine, the barrister, and her husband Gino, who live in Portsmouth, and Nick and Annika, a couple who live on the island. LeAnne, an islander, is coming back here with Zoe to sleep. You may know of her. She owns a restaurant over in Ventnor – her family are the Alnwicks.'

Susan was pretty sure that from his years working in the island police force, Robert would have heard of them.

'Let me think. Yes, there were four brothers, all got into trouble. One is in prison. I remember the case. Aggravated burglary, I think it was, nasty: there was a knife involved. LeAnne's father has been to court a few times, he's known for selling on stolen goods but has always managed to avoid prison. His saving grace has always been his wife, LeAnne's mother, she desperately tried to keep her children on the straight and narrow.'

'You remember them well.'

'I was based in Ventnor. We all knew the Alnwicks. I was pleased to see LeAnne making a success of things. I've eaten at her restaurant. It's very good.'

'Oh. I hadn't realised you'd been there.'

'I took a friend a few weeks ago. We had a really good meal, not steak of course, but the fish was so fresh and loads of chips.'

They exchanged a look. They both knew what was happening here. Susan had been very firm in insisting Robert date other women. It helped her feel more comfortable with her lack of commitment and, anyway, she knew he had the right to look for a stability she might never feel able to give. It didn't stop her feeling jealous, although she did her best to hide it.

'So, what about this couple who live on the island?' Robert asked.

'That's Nick and Annika. Nick's a teacher and Annika works for the health service. Nick was charged with drunk driving earlier in the year. It was outside LeAnne's restaurant after a party there. I don't suppose you heard about it?'

Robert shook his head. 'None of my mates have mentioned it. I miss stuff now I'm retired.'

'Nick was given a fine and banned from driving but is back

teaching. There's a lot of tension between him and LeAnne, though, which is awkward.'

'Did she worry about it being connected somehow with her restaurant?'

'I hadn't thought of that but, no, her concern is her brother, Wesley. He was arrested the same night for possession of cocaine. Now Wesley claims Nick set him up, and LeAnne believes him. Nick, of course, denies it.'

'So, what is this young woman Nick is with like?'

'That's Annika. Nick lives in her flat over in Cowes. She's quite quiet, very devoted to Nick. You have probably heard of her father, David Lee? Big noise over in Ventnor.'

'I know him. He's on the council, got a CBE for charity work. A bit of a know-it-all but to be fair he has done a lot for the town. I always imagined he'd go into national politics. He'd fancy himself as the island MP. Wasn't his daughter big in singing? I'm sure I remember her picture being in the *County Press* all the time. She was always winning competitions and the like.'

'That's Annika, their only daughter. She's very musical. She's stayed on the island, devoted to Nick. The only tension I picked up from her this evening was when Nick seemed to be getting too effusive over one of the other women, Maxine.'

'A love triangle? Didn't you say Maxine was there with her husband?'

'She is. Maxine is a barrister. She represented Nick in court, and he seems to have been treating her like some kind of guardian angel since then. I had quite a long chat with her when we arrived. She's pretty stressed about the week. Her marriage to Gino sounds a bit rocky and she's aware of the tension between Nick and LeAnne. I think there's something else going on between her and LeAnne as well—'

'Goodness. They have a few issues there. How is Zoe finding it?'

'I haven't had much time to talk to her. The person she's closest to is Maxine, so hopefully they can support each other a bit this week.'

'I hope so. It would be a shame not to enjoy their stay.'

'I agree. So, how have things been here?'

Robert stroked Dougie's head. 'Very quiet, a few more young trick-or-treaters and that was it. Oh, I had a text from Vicky—' He pulled out his phone and Susan sat next to him.

He showed her a photo of a hole in the ceiling of an old house.

'Oh, no. When did that happen?'

'This week. They've had a lot of rain.'

Robert's daughter, Vicky, with her husband and young children had moved to a rundown farmhouse in France earlier that year.

'They knew there were going to be problems. The roof is in a terrible state, but they were hoping it would hold for a few months while they sorted out other things. The whole house is a massive undertaking. I hadn't realised quite how much until I visited. They will have to do a lot of the work themselves as well. Savings only take them so far.'

Susan remembered Robert showing her photos of his daughter and family over the summer. With an enormous garden for the children, trees and a river, it had looked idyllic and she could quite understand why they had moved out of their tiny town house in England.

'They're young. Hopefully they will work things out. It looks such a lovely place to bring up children.'

'I hope they make a go of it as well,' said Robert, who then checked his watch. 'I should be making a move. No staying over tonight, I guess, as all the spare bedrooms are taken.'

'No, um—' The words came out too fast, too harshly, but he'd caught her off guard. He hadn't even hinted at sharing a room for weeks and, added to that, the idea of him coming down in the morning to Zoe filled her with panic.

'You needn't sound quite so horrified,' he said, frowning, but there was a twinkle in his eye.

'Sorry, but well, you know—'

His face relaxed into its usual warm smile. 'Of course. Right. Let's get these dogs organised.'

Robert gathered his things together and put both his dogs on leads. He leant forward and kissed Susan warmly on the cheek.

'I do hope you're not going to be sitting up for your daughter as if she was fourteen again.'

Susan smiled gratefully. 'No. I think she would be very insulted if I did and, anyway, I'm shattered.'

'Don't go listening for creaks and ghosts then.'

'Certainly not.'

'I hope all goes well this week. I'll be in touch.'

'Thanks. See you soon.'

Susan watched Robert drive away and went back into the house alone.

* * *

Back at the accommodation in the castle, the group had removed their masks. Nick poured himself a large glass of wine. Maxine joined him, drinking one glass quickly and pouring another. Zoe was surprised. Maxine didn't normally drink like this.

Gino didn't sit but walked around restlessly. Finally, he threw back his glass of wine and declared, 'Right, I am going out to make the most of this castle.'

'Shall I come with you?' said Maxine, but her offer seemed half-hearted as she remained engrossed in whatever she was reading on her tablet.

'No, I would rather go on my own if that's OK with you. I'm going to climb the steps to the keep.'

His comment seemed to grab Maxine's attention. 'You don't want to go up there. Those steps will be treacherous at night.'

The good-natured smile slipped and was replaced with a scowl. 'I'm not a child. I want to go up there and I'm perfectly safe to do so. I was reading about the castle online and, even at night, I should get a sense of looking down over the island.' Avoiding further discussion, he grabbed his coat, checked his pockets and left.

LeAnne was also hunched over her laptop, frowning in concentration. Nick walked past, glanced down. 'You're not working, are you?'

'Some of us have no option,' she replied, her voice cold, angry.

Zoe heard a thump as Maxine threw her tablet on to the table. 'I've had enough of that.' She glanced at her watch. 'Half eleven. I might as well go out now, make the most of having the place to ourselves. I fancy the battlements.'

'The battlements?' queried Zoe. 'You just tried to warn Gino off climbing up to the keep.'

Maxine dismissed the comment with a flap of her hand. 'The steps to the keep are really bad, narrow and very steep. Only a fool would go up there at night. But it's much easier climb up to the battlements. I want to go and look down on the Privy Garden in the moonlight. Yes, I'm off now.'

'You've been drinking—'

'I'll be fine.' Maxine grabbed the coat she had flung over a spare chair, threw it on and left.

Zoe watched her leave but was uneasy. Maybe it was the drink, but Maxine didn't sound like her usual, controlled, sensible self. There was a recklessness, a defiance in the way Maxine spoke that worried her.

She couldn't relax, so after a few minutes she said, 'I'll just go and check on Maxine.' Looking over at LeAnne, she said, 'If I get caught up chatting, I'll meet you this side of the metal gates by the shop at twelve.'

LeAnne looked up from her laptop and repeated, 'Meet at the gate at twelve? Good, I'd like to get off. Oh, but we haven't got a key to get out.'

Zoe looked over at the spare key hanging up. 'I expect Maxine would rather that stay here. I expect she'll let us out. I'll phone a taxi later.'

'Great, see you there,' said LeAnne and she returned to her laptop.

'Actually,' said Nick, getting up from the sofa, 'I'd like to see what the castle looks like at this time, with no one else around. I quite fancy sitting in that Privy Garden, and looking at the stars. Fancy coming?' he asked Annika.

'I'll stay in the warm if you don't mind.'

He kissed her cheek. 'Fine, see you later.'

Zoe and Nick put their coats on and headed out, leaving the stable yard and then crunching across the courtyard.

They were close to the garden entrance when Nick theatrically threw out his arm. 'It's incredible.'

Zoe had noticed he'd been stumbling, and remembered he'd been drinking a lot at the flat. 'Do you think you should go back? It's very cold to sit around.'

'Miss all this? No way,' he shouted, his words slightly slurred. 'We have the castle to ourselves. Maybe I'll have a chat with some of those ghosts.' He giggled, moving very close to her. 'We are all alone, aren't we? Totally cut off from the outside world. It's amazing, isn't it?'

Zoe felt uncomfortable but said, 'I suppose it is. It's like we are on our own island.'

He gave her a strange smile. 'We're stranded, all alone. Anything could happen in here but no one out there would know.' He looked up at the battlements, the crenellations silhouetted against the night sky. 'Walls can see but they can't speak. Anything they witness tonight will remain a secret forever.'

9

Zoe gasped, suddenly frightened of not just the words, but of Nick himself. She'd never heard him like this before. She turned and looked at him, horrified. But he laughed. 'Sorry, only joking.' With a large grin on his face, he left and disappeared into the Privy Garden.

Zoe rolled her eyes. Nick was obviously pretty drunk. Hopefully the fresh air would help settle him down. Taking a deep breath, she headed for the steps up to the battlements.

Holding onto the metal rail, she climbed the three flights and then paused to catch her breath at the top. Looking around, she realised it was very different up on the battlements tonight. In fact, once at the top, Zoe felt a wave of panic that nearly sent her straight back down. Although it was quite exhilarating to be up here so close to the stars, there was no doubting that darkness ruled up here. She was totally at its mercy and felt very vulnerable.

Zoe reached out and clung to the stone wall, somehow feeling safer keeping close to the wall above the interior of the castle.

She shone her torch and followed the beam as she edged her way around, calling Maxine's name.

'I'm over here,' Maxine shouted back through the darkness.

'Shine your torch, so I can see where you are.'

'I can't. It's not working. Hang on, I'll use the one on my phone, but it's pathetic in comparison.'

Zoe spotted a tiny light ahead, and slowly made her way to her friend.

'My God, it's scary up here. How can you cope with just your phone?'

'Your eyes adjust. I was up here before I even took my torch out and couldn't be bothered to go back when it didn't work. I've got my phone for emergencies, but I'll switch it off. I don't want to wear the battery down.' She slipped her phone in her pocket, took out her torch, and tried the switch again. 'Nope. It's definitely not working. That's odd, though. It feels very light. Hang on. Can you shine your torch over here?'

Zoe moved closer, and shone the light over where Maxine was fiddling with the battery compartment. 'This is so fiddly,' she grumbled, until she finally opened the casing and looked inside. 'How strange. There are no batteries in it. I put batteries in all the torches. Even if I picked up another, it should be working.' She shrugged and put it back in her pocket.

Zoe pressed her smart watch. 'You know, I've only done eleven thousand steps today. I know I've reached my ten thousand, but I thought it would be more.'

Maxine laughed. 'All my friends are obsessed with their steps. You should stick to an old-fashioned watch like the one Gino gave to me on our wedding day.' She held it in the beam of Zoe's torch. 'See. One hundred per cent accurate and just does the job it's meant to: tells me the time.'

She laughed and then fished out a small bottle of gin from her pocket, took a swig, and offered it to Zoe.

'No, thanks, particularly not up here. What's up with you? I haven't seen you drink like this for a long time.'

'Calms the nerves, I guess.'

'And why do they need calming?'

Maxine shrugged. 'You've got to admit things are pretty tense in the group.'

'I hadn't realised how angry LeAnne still is about Wesley—'

'No, nor had I,' said Maxine.

'Still, you know LeAnne. She just has to get things out in the open. It will get better now.'

'Oh, I don't think so. I'm trying to resolve another issue with LeAnne and have discovered she's more complicated than we think. I guess we always saw her as some hot-tempered working-class girl with a heart of gold. Now I know she can be impetuous, but she's also very bright. She plans. Out of us all she has the strongest instinct for survival.'

'You make her sound quite Machiavellian.'

'I'm simply saying we can easily underestimate her. Maybe that's always true of people you've known since childhood. We summed them up when we were fifteen and we've not allowed them to grow and change. We keep them innocent, when in reality they are as capable of violence as anyone else.'

Maxine leant against the castle wall with a confidence Zoe certainly didn't feel. She was able to hold a conversation as if she was sitting in a coffee shop rather than standing high up on the battlements of an ancient castle on an icy October night.

'This evening, just before coming out here, I tracked down some of that stuff Wesley posted online about Nick. It's highly offensive and could certainly give Nick a motive to set up Wesley.'

'I still can't believe Nick would do that.'

'I didn't think so, but you forget people change over the years. I realised that when I started working with Nick on his case. It's one of the reasons I regret ever taking it on.'

Zoe listened with interest, remembering her earlier encounter with Nick. He'd seemed so different to the Nick she knew, and she'd felt deeply uncomfortable. 'Would you want them to reopen the case against Wesley?'

Maxine shook her head. 'There's not enough evidence for that. But I can't ignore the fact that my opinion of Nick has changed lately. His job carries a lot of responsibility. I've decided I can't stand by and do nothing. I know the head of governors at Nick's school very well. I'm going to talk to him, but don't say anything to Nick, will you? I want to do this discreetly.'

'You need to be sure before you say anything. Nick might lose his job.'

'That's for the head and the governors to decide.' Maxine looked away. 'As I say, I've been getting increasingly worried about him, particularly after my visit to Annika's flat last week.'

'You were invited over to Annika's?'

'It wasn't a social visit. No, I made an appointment to inspect the place. I pretended to do a smoke alarm check.'

'Pretended? Were you checking up on Nick?'

'Not initially. I went because of Gino. You heard Nick say Gino was using Annika's safe. He'd already told me. It set a few alarm bells ringing. I needed to see what exactly Gino was keeping in there.'

Zoe felt her legs starting to tire but didn't dare lean completely against either of the low walls to her sides. Instead, she rested her leg against the cold stone, before asking, 'Why didn't you just ask Gino?'

Maxine played with her hair, looked down at the cold stones. 'I wouldn't get a straight answer now, it's hopeless.'

'You'd told me he was angry about you not letting him expand, buy more properties to do up—'

'I guess that was the start of things going wrong between us. He wanted me to release all my savings, and I wasn't prepared to do it. He'd have bankrupted us. Since then he's got so moody, staying over here without explaining why—'

'Didn't you say he'd taken on a building job at the island prison?'

'Yes, it's been a long job, but he could have commuted. We're only over in Portsmouth. You know, I looked at his laptop and saw he'd been going back and forth to Italy as well, without telling me.'

Zoe frowned. She'd had no idea how bad things had been. No wonder Maxine had grown so suspicious.

Maxine sighed. 'If we could have talked it would have been better, but he changed; he was moody, difficult, and then I found these wads of cash in his drawer.' She paused. Zoe saw tears bright in her eyes. 'Remember when we studied *The Great Gatsby* at school, that quote, "The loneliest moment in someone's life is when they are watching it fall apart." That's how it's felt.'

Zoe's face creased with compassion. 'I'm so sorry, Maxine, I'd no idea how miserable you were.' She paused, then asked, 'Why did the cash worry you so much? Was it stolen or was Gino working cash-in-hand?'

Maxine shook her head. 'I was sure it was neither of those things. No, combined with the change in his behaviour, I was pretty sure what was going on. Think about it, Zoe. There's not many reasons people need cash like that now. Then Nick told me about the safe. I was pretty sure what I'd find, but I had to see for myself.'

'What were you looking for?'

'Confirmation that Gino had returned to his old ways. If he'd broken the solemn promise he made on our wedding day; he'd crossed a line which spelt the end of our marriage.'

'And is that what you found?' asked Zoe.

Maxine's face creased in pain, she raised a shaking hand and pressed it hard over her mouth, stifling a heart-rending sob. She looked away and went to look over the Privy Garden. The chapel lights were now switched off. Most of it was in darkness. Zoe could just make out the sound of the fountain, and the flanks of the statue of Warrior shining in the moonlight.

Finally Maxine spoke. Looking down into the garden, she whispered, 'No more fairytales, no more happy endings.'

Zoe went and stood next to Maxine, slipped her arm around her shoulder, and stood quietly besides her.

Maxine let out a sigh that came from a place of unhappiness deeper than any castle well. 'That was only last Wednesday, and yet it feels a lifetime ago.'

She blinked and turned to Zoe. She spoke more firmly now. 'That visit to Annika's flat grew increasingly bizarre, you know. I kept searching in the safe, looked through the albums and my mind dashed off in a completely different direction. Maybe I was glad to escape the pain of thinking about Gino, maybe it was the case I was working on influencing me.'

'What do you mean?'

'It started with the albums, and then I kept rummaging about in there. I got this feeling something wasn't right and so started looking around the flat. Then I saw the music, the stuff in Nick's bedside cabinet—'

'You said you were worried about Nick before you went.'

'I was, and this made me even more concerned. I was worried about Annika as well.' The words came tumbling out. Zoe pictured Maxine frantically rushing around Annika's flat. 'I knew I had to speak to her straight away.'

'Sorry, you've lost me. What exactly were you worried about?'

Maxine flung her hand out in a distracted manner. 'It's complicated, but I was very concerned, so I sent Annika a text. She was at one of the care homes, so I went straight to see her, which was a nuisance actually. I hadn't brought the car over. I was doing it all by taxi.'

'So why the urgency?'

'I had to find out how much she understood of what was going on, and I could only do that by talking privately before we came away.'

'And did you sort things out?'

Maxine shook her head. 'Not really. It was all very frustrating. Annika is very good at making you feel she is answering your questions but at the same time gives nothing away. I'd hate to cross-examine her in court. We have to speak again.'

Maxine paused. Her eyes were wide. She was breathing fast, adrenaline fuelled.

Suddenly their attention was grasped by a white shape flying above them, its feathery silent wings caught in the light from Zoe's torch. Without a sound it disappeared into the darkness.

'How long was that there?' asked Maxine, her voice barely above a whisper. 'It's been watching us. We were being hunted by a ghost.'

'Sorry?'

'That was a barn owl, called the ghost owl, silently hunting. I wonder why it came to me tonight?' She shivered, and took a swig of gin.

Zoe stepped forward. 'This is crazy,' she said firmly. 'Stop drinking up here.'

Maxine grinned. 'Sorry, miss.' She screwed the cap on the bottle and put it away in her pocket.

Zoe's heart went out to Maxine. She looked so desperately unhappy. What was this line Gino had crossed? Why exactly had she needed to rush over and see Annika? Maxine was usually so coherent and logical. Maybe the gin was getting her confused?

As if reading her mind, Maxine said, 'It's not the drink talking. I've just been realising how little I really know anyone here.' Maxine looked out over the village, most houses now in darkness, only a few with lights on. Her voice seemed to carry as she spoke. 'We should never have come.'

Zoe had never seen Maxine so low, and was sorry she wasn't looking forward to the week away. However, it was understandable, hearing the tension and stress Maxine was having to handle.

She noticed Maxine was unzipping her small cross-body bag and taking out a small object.

'I found this just before the ghost walk. I usually only keep my phone in here. It definitely wasn't there before.'

Zoe shone her torch on to it.

Maxine was holding out a small model of a Grim Reaper, the scythe painted scarlet.

Zoe laughed, 'You're not seriously worried about that are you? Someone is playing a joke on you.'

However, there was no flicker of a smile from Maxine as she replied, 'Oh, no. This is serious. The story is that the Grim Reaper comes out at midnight on Halloween. He is gathering souls for the underworld. This person is warning me that the Grim Reaper is coming for me.'

'That's nonsense.'

'I wish it was. No, someone is warning me and it has to be a person in our group. No one else could have put it in my bag.'

'You're making too much of it.'

'I'm not,' said Maxine, her voice higher, tense, full of fear.

Zoe grabbed the figure from Maxine's hand. 'This is ridiculous. Get rid of the damn thing.' Zoe walked back a few steps and then looked down into the darkness of the old armoury, flung her arm back, ready to propel the model into it.

However, Maxine grabbed her arm. 'No, stop. I need to keep it.'

Maxine grabbed the model from Zoe's hand, thrust it purposefully into her bag and zipped it up.

She stepped back, took a breath and seemed to compose herself. Looking directly at Zoe, a slight smile now playing on her trembling lips, Maxine said, 'I know I'm sounding rather desperate this evening, but you are not to worry about me. We both know there is a chink of light, and it has given me hope.' But then the warmth that had crept into her eyes was quickly replaced with alarm, as she glanced around and lowered her voice. 'You've not told anyone about my secret have you?'

'Of course not. No one but you and me know. You know you can trust me.'

Maxine moved her fingertips along the top of the stone wall. 'How many secrets these stones must have heard. This whole castle is made from stone: strong, impenetrable, but cold and intractable. It must be a harsh judge.'

She looked over the castle. 'This place is so oppressive tonight. Halloween, a night of darkness. You can feel it, can't you? Menace and danger—'

'No ghosts are going to hurt you.'

'But people can, and there are people here who would definitely find their lives a lot easier if I wasn't around – and that is a nice way of saying: their lives would be easier if I was dead.'

Zoe gasped. 'Don't say that—'

'It's true. The Grim Reaper was given to me as a sign. Someone brought it with them: they have a plan. There is premeditation here.'

Zoe's mind was racing now. Why on earth was Maxine thinking these things?

'Stop this, Maxine,' she said, her voice sharper than she intended. 'This isn't like you. You're so clear sighted and rational. You know that what you're saying is crazy.'

Maxine shook her head. 'It's because I think logically that I see what's going on. Of course it sounds mad, but I've seen things and know things about people in this group you don't. In particular, I now know there is one person in our group who has been playing a part for years. Every day without fail they put on a mask, appear good, kind, respectable. But recently I saw that mask slip. It was only for a second, it was a shock. I saw cruelty, coldness. It scared me. In fact, even now I'm hoping I was wrong, but my head tells me I know what I saw.'

Zoe stepped forward. She put her hand on Maxine's arm. 'I think you must be mistaken. We are all your friends. No one is going to hurt you. We love you.'

Maxine smiled warmly. 'Thank you. I know it's true of you. I trust you, Zoe, and there are very few people in the world I can say that of.'

'I'm glad, I will always be here for you.' Zoe placed a gentle hand on Maxine's arm. 'Come down from here. Let's go and have a cup of coffee, get away from all these terrible thoughts.'

'I can't. I'm meeting someone here at twelve.'

'Meeting someone? Why? Who?'

'I know it seems odd to meet up here, but I need to speak to this person on their own. Some things are better discussed in private.'

'But it's so cold. Come down. Text them and have a talk at the apartment.'

'No. No, we need to be here.'

'I'm worried about you.'

'Don't be. I'm prepared now, and I will handle this. I always do. I'll survive.'

'I'm glad.' Zoe wiped a tear from Maxine's face. 'You're so strong. You know that. Listen to me. You will come out fighting. I'm sure of it.' She took a deep breath. 'Now, LeAnne and I are planning to leave soon. I'm meeting her at twelve.'

'Let me give you my key. The spare is hanging in the apartment. We won't need that until tomorrow. I was going to suggest we all go to Compton for a walk.'

'That sounds great. Mum could take me and LeAnne straight there.'

'Good. I'll check with the others and text you.'

Maxine rummaged in her pocket and handed Zoe a large key.

'Thanks. Right, I'll see you in the morning,' said Zoe.

She turned on her torch and made her way carefully back along the battlements.

Realising that descending these steps was even more treacherous than going up, she carefully started to make her way down the first short flight. To her surprise, however, she nearly collided with Gino standing at the base of the steps.

'Gino?'

He looked up. He blinked as if surprised, breathing fast.

'I'm glad to see you,' said Zoe, 'Maxine's still up there. I'm worried about her. Can you see if you can get her to come down?'

He shook his head, his eyes flashing around. 'No, no.'

Zoe was shocked at how distracted he seemed. 'Are you OK?' she asked. 'Maybe you'd better come down as well.'

She reached out and touched his arm but he roughly pushed her hand away.

'I'm going back to the keep. Just leave me alone.'

With this, he turned and stumbled back along the walkway.

Zoe made her way carefully down the two remaining flights of steps. Across the courtyard she saw Nick coming out of the Privy Garden and walked over to him.

'I'm leaving now,' she said.

The drunken smiles and giggles were nowhere to be seen now. Nick appeared sober and deadly serious.

'Good idea, escape from this place.'

Zoe touched his icy cold hand. 'You need to go back to the apartment too. You're freezing.'

'Annika phoned. She's coming to meet me.'

'Well, take care then.'

He shrugged, glanced back at the battlements. 'Take care?' He gave a hollow laugh. 'See you tomorrow.'

Zoe was tempted to accompany him to meet Annika. Like Maxine and Gino, Nick was in a strange mood this evening. She noticed he was lingering as if waiting for her to make the first move.

'Right then,' she said. 'I'm off.' She turned away and walked towards the wooden gates. There were no sounds of footsteps, and as she twisted the iron door handle, she glanced back and saw that Nick was still watching her. She gave him a wave and left. The wooden gate was always unlocked. It was the metal gates further down she needed the key for.

There was no sign of LeAnne, so Zoe stood close to the gift shop. It was only just midnight. LeAnne would arrive soon and so she stood shuffling her feet to keep warm.

It wasn't a pleasant place to wait, with the wind whistling around her.

When she looked up at the castle, she was surprised when she realised how close she was to the area of the battlements she'd been standing with Maxine. She was too low down and it was too dark for Zoe to make out anyone on the battlements, but she was guessing Maxine would still be up there.

Zoe stared for a while at the stars and tried to identify any of the constellations, but her feet were getting icy cold now. She started to walk back and forth to warm herself up.

As she did, she occasionally glanced up at the battlements. And then she saw something that caught her notice. As she saw a flicker of torchlight, she heard a voice whisper Maxine's name on the wind. So, Maxine was still up there and Zoe guessed whoever had arranged to meet up with her had arrived. She screwed up her eyes, but she could only make out the vaguest of shadows. A whistling, 'whooshing' sound came down. It was an odd noise, not the wind, not wildlife, but not a voice either. And then the light disappeared, silence. There was no sign of life up there. Hopefully that meant the meeting had been cut short and they were returning to the apartment. After that disturbing conversation Zoe would much rather Maxine was back at the apartment. Tomorrow she would have a good talk with Maxine.

The cold was creeping through her coat now, and Zoe rang LeAnne to urge her to hurry up. Annoyingly, there was no reply. She carried on walking back and forth, trying to keep warm as time ticked away. She thought about going over to the apartment, but what if LeAnne was out walking in the castle and they missed each other? No, best to wait here.

Finally, she saw the wooden gates open and could make out LeAnne coming towards her.

'Where have you been? We were meant to meet at midnight. I've been trying to phone you.'

'Have you rung for the taxi?' asked LeAnne, ignoring Zoe's question.

'Of course not, and it's just as well I didn't. You're really late.'

'Well, we'll have to wait ages now.'

Zoe bit her lip to stop herself giving an angry retort and rang the number Nick had given her. Fortunately, they said they would be along in five minutes.

They went to the metal gates. Zoe unlocked the padlock. The gates clanked open and once they were through, she made sure she locked them securely behind them.

They crossed the space in front of the castle and as they were waiting for the taxi, they saw torchlight at the metal gate and heard someone unlocking it.

'That's Gino,' said Zoe. 'He must have gone back and got the spare key. Where's he off to?'

LeAnne shrugged. Zoe wasn't sure what was up with her, but she seemed in a very bad mood.

They watched as Gino walked off down the hill. Zoe was relieved to see their taxi arrive.

To her surprise, the taxi driver jumped out of the car and opened the back door.

A young couple clambered out of the back of the car, both were wrapped up in dark coats and woollen hats, their eyes bright and excited. They looked at Zoe and LeAnne. 'Have you been ghost hunting around here?' the woman asked, her words slurred.

'We went on the ghost walk earlier,' said Zoe.

'We've done that a few times. You have to do the Ventnor one next year, you know there used to be a hospital where the gardens are? Honest to God, we heard this weird moaning sound and I definitely saw the shadow of this young girl. It was amazing.'

The young man, who had been paying the taxi driver and seemed slightly more sober, spoke. 'We're going to walk home from here to Bowcombe – reckon we'll see a few more around here.'

The young man waved back to the taxi driver. 'Thanks for the lift, mate, good of you to come all the way to Ventnor.'

They staggered away, and the driver grinned at them. 'I'd guarantee they will see all sorts, the state they're in. Right, ladies, I'm Liam. Good to meet you.'

Zoe smiled at their driver, a good-looking young man with blond hair and a warm smile, in his late twenties she'd guess.

'You said you wanted to go to Bishopstone?' Liam continued. 'In you get.'

Zoe and LeAnne got into the car. As they did up their seatbelts, he said, 'I've friends staying in the castle tonight,' looking up at it.

'We've just left them. It's an incredible place to stay,' replied Zoe.

'Yes. Annika and Nick were excited about it.'

'Nick recommended you to us.'

'That was good of him. Lovely couple, him and Annika. I often give them a lift. They've been very supportive of me setting up the business. Cowes is very different to Ventnor, but I like it.'

'Oh, you're from Ventnor?' said LeAnne. 'Hang on. Are you the son from the big house – the family where Annika was a nanny?'

'That's me,' said Liam, laughing. 'Small island. How did you know?'

'Just piecing things together. I'd heard about your family, knew Annika had been with them, and I'd heard you'd started a taxi firm over here.'

Liam threw back his head and laughed. 'You're a typical islander, honestly. Everyone knows your business over here. Guess you know all the terrible stories about me,' he said. 'Still, I'm well settled now, business going well. Right. Let's get you home.'

Zoe settled into the back seat. She remembered Maxine's warnings, but she was inclined to agree with Nick that he was doing well at making a fresh start.

As they made their way down the hill, looking out of the window Zoe saw a parked van. On the side was lettering which she couldn't read, but she could make out a logo depicting a castle and a lion. The light inside the van was on, and she could see the back of one man's head, the face of the other.

'That's Gino,' she said to LeAnne. They were already driving past. 'What's he doing there?'

LeAnne scowled. 'That wasn't Gino.'

'I saw his face. It was definitely him.'

'No, you're wrong.'

Zoe wasn't in a mood to argue, but she was sure she was right.

She glanced back up the hill at the castle. It dominated the skyline. The gates were locked. Zoe remembered Nick's description of it as an island and that was how it looked from out here. Those inside were alone, cut off. The walls alone would see what happened in there tonight.

10

WEDNESDAY, 1 NOVEMBER – ALL SAINTS' DAY

The next morning, Susan went for an early-morning walk with the dogs. There was a heavy fog up on Brighstone Down, so she decided to take them into the woods.

The fog was low, covering the trees like a shroud. It muffled the sound of the dogs as they rummaged among the fallen leaves. It was damp and cold, yet Susan enjoyed the drama of it all. She always felt that autumn was like nature's party before winter set in, its last chance to surprise and show off before the long sleep.

As she crunched through the woods, she heard a tiny 'chuck' sound, and stood very still. Fortunately, the dogs were a fair way down and wouldn't scare it away. She waited, then she saw a small, autumn-leaf-coloured squirrel, scurrying along the ground. Suddenly it froze; its dark, jewel-like eyes spotted her and, with lightning speed, it raced up the nearest tree, disappearing from sight.

Susan smiled: a rare moment meeting a red squirrel here, maybe a gift from the fog that had dampened the sound of her approach.

'Morning,' she heard through the mist.

Susan saw a young woman approaching her.

'Morning,' she replied to Holly and leant down to stroke her gorgeous little dog, Ralph. He was an elderly shih tzu-toy poodle cross, and usually kept on a lead as his eyesight was not so good.

'How's Ralph today?'

'He's doing well. The vet is pleased, and he still loves his walks. How are Rocco and Libs? Were they upset by trick-or-treaters last night?'

'A friend stayed in with them, but it's pretty quiet in Bishopstone on Halloween.'

'Yes, our farm is much too far for anyone to bother with. Right, better get on. Good to see you again.'

And with that she walked away. Susan smiled. She loved these casual acquaintances she made when dog walking.

Sometimes the conversations would get surprisingly personal as she experienced that strange phenomenon of people finding it easier to share quite intimate stories with a relative stranger than with those much closer to them, but usually it was an easy chat about their dogs or the weather.

What amused her was that in the same way that on the school gates she'd been 'Zoe's mum' to many, now she was 'Rocco and Libs's mum' to her fellow dog walkers.

When it was time to return home, and time to check up on Zoe and LeAnne, she called the dogs and took them back to the car.

They were very wet, and she dried them off as best she could with the towels before driving home.

No one else was up yet, so she gave the dogs their breakfast and went to feed the birds. They hadn't used the feeders much over the summer as there were plenty of seeds and insects in the fields, but nature was starting to get less bountiful, and they were hungrier now. She put in an extra handful of mealworms, hoping the crows and magpies didn't pinch the food she wanted to provide for the robins.

Most of the flowers in her garden had died off for the winter now, although her Japanese anemones still proudly held their pink heads to the sky. She also still had two pots of geraniums, their flowers almost fossilised. She guessed they would all drop at the first sign of frost.

As she put the kettle on, there was a knock at the door. To her astonishment, it was a delivery of a bouquet of flowers. Maybe it was for one of the girls but, reading the card, she realised they were indeed for her. She was just wondering what to do with them when Zoe appeared down the stairs.

'An unknown admirer?' she asked.

Susan blinked. 'Um, they're from Robert.'

'Gosh, he's such a nice chap. Dad never gave you flowers.'

'He never had time.'

Zoe screwed up her lips. 'Still making excuses for him. Don't do it on my behalf. So, how are things between you and Robert?'

'We're friends—'

'Flowers suggest a bit more than that, and I noticed an unfamiliar deodorant in the bathroom.'

Susan groaned. Zoe never missed anything. 'He's stayed occasionally, but in a spare room. Honestly, we're just friends. Robert understands that.'

'Does he? What's holding you back?' Zoe screwed her eyes up. 'Are you secretly hoping you and Dad will get back together?'

'No, love. I don't want that. To be honest, it's a relief having him off travelling. I hated him turning up unannounced.'

'So, what about Robert? He's a lovely chap, really fond of you, Mum.'

'I know, but I'm not ready for commitment. I'm very happy a lot of the time here on my own.'

'But I don't want you to get lonely. I know Jamari and I have come over a lot over the summer, but it's not so easy now. We only have weekends. The ferries get cancelled all the time with the weather.'

'I have my own life here. Don't ever come because you feel obliged to.'

'It's not that. Jamari has had the most wonderful summer. I love coming to the island as well. I'd be so sad not to be able to come over whenever I wanted. But you never know how life is going to work out, do you?'

Susan noticed how Zoe picked at her nails. 'Is there something you need to tell me?'

'Um, no. I'm just saying Robert is a good man. He takes care of you.'

'Maybe I don't need someone taking care of me—'

'You're not getting any younger.'

'Not this again. I'm perfectly fit and only in my sixties. As Alice said to me, my life is full of possibilities.'

'But living here on your own, I worry about you. I would like to think you had someone here with you.'

'Well, stop. I'll be fine. Look, I'll sort out Robert. Now, I need to do something with these flowers.'

Susan found a large vase, plonked the bunch of flowers in and filled it with water.

'Now, breakfast. I've got cereals and the like in.'

She noticed Zoe picking red paint off her finger. 'It came off a miniature Maxine showed me,' Zoe explained.

LeAnne appeared, coming down the stairs, and the dogs rushed from Zoe to her.

'Are you OK with dogs?' Susan asked.

'Never had them, but I can cope.' She leant down, patted them lightly.

They sorted out breakfast and sat down at the small table in the kitchen.

Susan had been trying to have more than a biscuit for breakfast and had had some granola already. She also had a box of oats as she kept meaning to make porridge or overnight oats she'd heard about. She'd read so many recipes for them and could recite why they were good for you, but hadn't quite got round to making them.

'Did you enjoy the ghost walk?' Susan asked LeAnne.

LeAnne shrugged. 'It was OK. I'm not sure it's possible to feel the presence of the spirits with a group of people like that. Most obviously didn't believe. You can't expect the spirits to appear when it's like that.'

'But I learned a lot about the history of the castle,' said Zoe.

'That wasn't meant to be the point of last night,' said LeAnne bluntly. 'You can read that in a book. Last night was meant to be about experiencing the past in a supernatural way, letting the spirits commune with you.'

Zoe put down her spoon, looked over at LeAnne. 'Are you joking?'

'No. I'm serious about this stuff now.'

Zoe cringed in apology. 'Sorry, I didn't realise. I was surprised Maxine was so nervous about it. She grabbed my arm at one point.'

'Maxine is full of surprises,' said LeAnne.

Susan caught the sharpness in LeAnne's voice and remembered the row she'd had with Maxine. Susan could still hear the desperation and anger in LeAnne's voice as she accused Maxine of trying to destroy her life.

'Things got pretty heated between you and Maxine in the apartment before the walk,' said Zoe.

'I hated the way she treated going to court as some kind of game.'

'She's bound to see it differently to us: it's her job. Surely your real problem is with Nick, not Maxine.'

'Obviously, he's the one in the wrong over the charges brought against Wesley. I was disappointed Maxine never saw Wesley's side of things, although I think she's changing her mind now. Did you see her face when I told her about the stuff online?'

'She obviously had no idea about it,' said Zoe.

'Yes, and I reckon she saw it gave Nick reason to hate Wesley, it makes Nick setting him up and driving at him all the more believable. That would upset Nick. Maxine's opinion of him really matters. God, he worships Maxine, doesn't he? Annika noticed. Did you see her face when he was going on about how wonderful Maxine was? Good job Annika didn't have a knife in her hand. I wouldn't have fancied Maxine's chances.'

Zoe laughed. 'As if! She wasn't that upset.'

'She was! You don't realise how obsessed Annika is with Nick. She has been since school. She's riddled with jealousy and fiercely protective of him.'

Zoe gave an exaggerated sigh, shook her head. 'You're massively overdoing this. Annika is not like that. Honestly. I feel I've gone back to the dark ages. It was bad enough when Gino told Annika to "control her man".'

LeAnne grinned. 'Gino was joking. I've got to know him since the party in February. He's been over to the restaurant a few times. He really supports me running my own business.'

Zoe pursed her lips in frustration. 'I should think so. However, it doesn't excuse what he said and you shouldn't be describing Annika as some desperate woman whose only aim in life is to get Nick. Annika is a bright, intelligent, gifted woman. She has done a degree in music, pursued careers.'

Susan was pleased to hear Zoe standing up for Annika in this way. Even so, LeAnne was not to be deterred.

'You've got it all wrong,' said LeAnne firmly. 'Annika has just been filling in time. I bet it annoys her father that she's not off singing her way around the world, but Nick will always come first. Her father was always so ambitious for her. I'm not sure what he thought when she became a nanny. Although she was working for a posh family. He'd have liked that.'

Susan realised they'd finished their cereal. 'Toast and coffee?' she asked.

There was a nod for both, and she went to slice the bread. She also dug out her cafetiere to make 'posh' coffee for them.

As she did this, Zoe called over, 'We met the elder son of the family Annika was nanny to last night. He was our taxi driver. He seemed a nice chap, very chatty, charming I'd say.'

'He did seem a decent bloke,' agreed LeAnne.

'What did he mean about you hearing terrible things about him? Maxine said she didn't like him,' said Zoe.

'She must have picked up about his court case, and the prison sentence.'

'He went to prison?' said Zoe, her eyes wide.

'He got in with a bad lot, got sentenced for supplying drugs. Unlike my Wesley, it was clear Liam was guilty. Still, he seems to be trying to make good now. His dad set up the taxi firm for him. It's good he's still looking out for Liam even though he had a new wife and the toddler Annika looked after.'

'You know an awful lot about them all,' said Zoe.

'People gossip over our way, and the fact Liam went to prison meant he was in the paper.'

As Susan poured boiling water into the cafetiere, and put the bread in the toaster, she said, 'Annika was telling me she was painting now. I was so pleased, she seems to really enjoy it.'

'She always loved it at school. That's great.' Zoe turned to LeAnne. 'See, she's not just been sitting around waiting for her man as you would say.'

LeAnne laughed. 'I'm glad you haven't changed, Zoe, but you can't assume all women are as enlightened as you.'

Zoe scowled, and Susan felt it was time to change the subject.

Susan brought over the toast and spreads, and went to pour the coffee. As she did, she asked, 'What have you all got planned for today? Once the fog lifts, I think it should be a decent day.'

'Maxine is going to let me know. She was talking about us all meeting at Compton Beach. If we do, Mum, could you take me and LeAnne down there?'

'Of course. I'll take the dogs for another walk while I'm there.'

At that moment, Zoe received a text. Susan saw a look of confusion, then consternation, spread across her daughter's face.

11

Susan put down her coffee, very concerned about the anxious look on Zoe's face, whatever was the matter?

'What's up?' asked LeAnne.

'Nick says Maxine has disappeared. No one has seen her since last night. Gino says he crashed out, woke up this morning to find she wasn't in bed, or anywhere else in the flat.'

LeAnne shrugged. 'She probably went off for an early-morning walk. Honestly, people do fuss.'

'They've tried her phone, but no answer. They're searching the grounds now. They can't find her.'

'It'll be nothing.'

'Maxine was in a strange mood last night, she said some things that really worried me. I think we should go there, see what's going on. Is that OK, Mum?'

Susan didn't know what Maxine had been saying to Zoe but she was concerned. 'Of course. I'll take you now. The dogs can stay here in the warm. They've had a good walk this morning.'

Despite LeAnne's protests, they set off for the castle.

Susan put on her fog lights, and drove carefully along the

country roads, through Shorwell and into the village of Castleford. Usually, in daylight, she would see the castle clearly up on the hill as she approached, but today it was hidden by fog. She drove up Cedar Hill and turned right at the roundabout to the castle. The red traffic light shone weakly through the fog, but eventually changed to green, and allowed her around the sharp bend to the castle entrance.

There were a few cars there this morning, a few dog walkers walking the public path and heading for the fields below, but the castle stood separate, alone. The fog emphasised its isolation, the padlocked iron gates warning them to keep away: this was a foreign land where they were not welcome.

Zoe phoned Nick to say they had arrived and that she had a key to let them in.

Zoe, Susan and LeAnne went inside, locked the gate behind them and heard muffled voices calling Maxine's name.

Nick came over to them. 'We can't find her anywhere. The castle isn't open to the public yet, so no one else is here.'

'Could Maxine have left the castle, gone off for a walk?' asked LeAnne.

'But we've got her key. She gave it to me last night,' said Zoe.

'I've got the spare key here. It was hanging in the apartment,' said Nick.

'So, she wouldn't have been able to get out.'

'It's very odd.'

'I know. We're at a loss. Gino and Annika are out on the bowling green. Gino's already walked the battlements.'

'But why would she be up there all night?' asked Zoe.

'We don't know,' said Nick, an edge of hysteria in his voice. 'Maybe she's lying unconscious somewhere. We have no idea.'

'How can we help?'

He took a breath and calmed himself down.

'This place is like a rabbit warren. There are always more places to look. LeAnne, can you do the battlements again? Zoe, you could go over to the right of the courtyard behind the wall at the back? There's the toilet block and the steep steps down to the gunpowder store. What if she slipped or something? We just have to keep looking.'

Susan was impressed with how well he was organising them all. It was very different from the Nick she'd seen before the ghost walk. She could actually imagine him teaching, taking control of a class or an orchestra.

'Has anyone searched the keep?' Susan asked him. 'Maxine mentioned she liked it up there.'

'I'm not sure if Gino covered that.'

'Mum, you mustn't do those steps in this fog.'

'Of course I can,' said Susan sharply.

Nick nodded. 'Just be careful. Good luck, everyone.'

Susan began to walk across the courtyard, her steps wrapped up in the cotton wool of the fog.

When she reached the steps leading to the keep, she called Maxine's name, hoping she would hear a call back, but she was greeted with silence. She had no option but to climb up. These steps were even more uneven and slippery than those to the battlements. Maybe Zoe was right, she shouldn't have come up here. Still, she'd committed to this now.

Susan held on tightly to the cold damp rail. She was soon breathing heavily, which she tried to blame on the fog making the air thicker. There was a natural rest point halfway up, where a rail had been constructed across one half of the steps, in an attempt to break anyone's fall. Once she'd caught her breath she carried on her climb.

Eventually she reached the top of the steps. Breathlessly, she called Maxine's name but, again, there was no reply.

The keep always felt to Susan like the heart of the castle and it was indeed the ultimate place of safety. There were small rooms tucked into the walls, including one that had housed the original well. She glanced around and saw the light catch what appeared to be shards of glass and when she looked closer, she found that it was parts of a broken mirror.

Leaving the room, she realised she was going to have to climb the internal steps that led to the keep's battlements. She hated going up there even in the daytime, despite the views being spectacular, so that you could see right over to Osborne House and the Solent. The low walls and the height frightened her.

She made herself do the entire wall walk. At one point she clung on to the outer wall, tried to look down. She called Maxine's name, but there was nothing. Her heart sank: Maxine wasn't here.

Then the thought came to her that maybe someone had already found Maxine. Perhaps the group were all in the apartment drinking coffee and had forgotten to phone her.

Cheered by the thought, she began the challenging descent of the keep's steps, harder than the ascent as they were so steep that she felt she was constantly being thrown forward.

It was a relief to be back safely on the ground. Taking out her phone, she called Zoe but, no, Maxine had not been found.

Zoe suggested Susan go to the bowling green to help Annika, so she walked through the small gate in the wall, and out on to the green. In the distance, she could make out Annika.

'Any luck?' Susan asked when she'd walked over to her, although the question was clearly pointless.

'None. I was scared to go too close to where the cannons are. There are steep drops around there. Gino is down that side.'

'I'll go to the other.'

'Be careful then.'

Susan made her way over and laid her hand on the cold black metal of the cannon. She called Maxine's name.

There was no reply. She felt her jaw tighten, a churning in her stomach. Where on earth could Maxine be? What had happened to her?

As if in answer, her phone rang. It was Zoe, her voice trembling with emotion, 'Oh God, mum, come here, quick—'

'Where are you?'

'The gatehouse steps.' With this, Zoe burst into tears.

Susan threw her phone into her pocket and raced across the green shouting to Annika. 'Zoe has found something. Tell Gino.'

She could make out Zoe and Nick at the foot of the short flight of steps that led to the armoury and the rooms above the gatehouse.

Zoe grabbed her arm, and led her up the steps.

Susan was going to make her way into the room ahead, but Zoe guided her into the stone ruin of the old armoury. There on the ground lay Maxine, her body unnaturally splayed. She was lying on her stomach, her face to one side. On her forehead was a gash of dried blood and on the collar of her beautiful white coat more splashes of dark red. Her cross-body bag, the strap still looped around her body, lay beside her, undamaged and zipped up.

Susan clasped her hand over her mouth. She felt sick as she stared down at Maxine's broken body. This couldn't be happening. Maxine couldn't be dead. And yet she was lying there, no sound from her parted lips. Those eyes which had been so full of passion and purpose, now blank, unseeing.

'I checked for a pulse, but it was pointless. Do you think she fell?' whispered Zoe.

Susan blinked, and looked up to the battlements. The

distance down to here was not as great as in some parts, but there was a metal support which Maxine might have knocked into, and this was one of the few places where the fall would be directly onto concrete.

'Maybe—' said Susan, her voice trembling.

'I was talking to her up there,' said Zoe. 'There's no barrier at that part, although the wall must be about thigh-height. If only she'd been just a little further along where it looks over the Privy Garden, she'd have fallen onto grass. She might have stood a chance.'

Zoe began to sob. Susan knelt close to Maxine's body, not touching anything but looking at her wrist. The beautiful Gucci watch was smashed, but she could read the old-fashioned analogue face: ten minutes past twelve.

Susan stood up and looked around. You could still see the remains of an original stone fireplace suggesting cosier times, but today it was a soulless place, cold and bleak. It was a terrible place for Maxine to die.

As if to emphasise the sense of neglect, a small pile of rubbish had accumulated in one corner. It consisted of a few torn-up tissues, discarded Coke cans, an aerosol tin, remains of tatty leaflets, and a mouldy, half-eaten sandwich. It was a desolate setting for Maxine's body.

'Where is she?' a voice screamed behind them.

Gino and LeAnne came in. Susan held out her arm, a barrier.

'I'm so sorry,' she said quietly.

'No!' he screamed and pushed past her. He fell on the ground next to Maxine's body, but just sat staring at her in horror, not moving, not touching her.

Nick came up. 'I've called for an ambulance. They're on the way. I'll go and let them in.'

Zoe handed over her key and then stayed waiting with Susan.

They stood, frozen, trying to take in the horror of what they were looking at. It wasn't long until they heard the emergency vehicles.

'We'd better get out of their way,' said Nick and all but Gino made their way back down the steps.

Susan noticed a police car arriving. A sudden death: of course they would come. Nonetheless, seeing the police subtly changed the nature of what was expected of them. It wouldn't be enough to cope with the shock and grief. There would be questions to answer.

A police officer walked over to the paramedics who were up with Maxine, and then returned to them shortly after.

'Maxine's husband told me you're all staying here. I suggest you return to your accommodation. We'll come as soon as we have something to tell you.'

'Gino needs someone with him,' said LeAnne before she ran up the steps. The rest made their way slowly over the courtyard.

The apartment felt cold and neglected. Susan switched on the lights, and they sat on the edge of the sofa and chairs.

'I'll make us a hot drink,' she said, desperate to do something. She put the kettle on. Zoe helped her.

Soon they were joined by Gino and LeAnne.

'The police will be over in a minute,' said LeAnne. She was helping Gino to a seat. He was shaking his head. His eyes were unblinking, his lips moving, but no sounds came out of his mouth.

Susan handed them drinks. Gino didn't touch his, but LeAnne hugged hers close.

Soon there was a knock on the apartment door and Susan let in an older woman in her day clothes but wearing an English

Heritage fleece. She looked as shocked as they felt, although desperately trying to remain professional.

'I wanted to come and pass on my deepest condolences. We're all so terribly sorry for the tragedy that occurred last night. I'm sure you're all in shock, but please, if there is anything we can do, don't hesitate to call us over in the reception. Of course, we won't open the castle to the public now.' She glanced around the group. 'Um, I have a message for Annika?'

Annika looked up and the woman explained. 'Your father rang reception. Somehow, he knows what's happened here. He's naturally concerned. He rang reception as he was worried about phone signal. I said you'd call him when you felt able.'

'Oh, thank you,' said Annika. 'I'll phone him back later.'

Zoe said, 'We're just waiting for the police to come over to speak to us.'

'Of course. As I say, if there is anything we can do, please get in touch.'

She left the apartment, leaving them sitting there, stunned.

'It's impossible to take in, isn't it?' said Nick. 'Accidents are like that: they come out of the blue. There's no preparing for them. We shouldn't have let her go up there. She'd been drinking, and in the dark it was dangerous.'

'I tried to persuade her to come down,' said Zoe.

'How did she seem to you?'

'Stressed. As I said, I wanted her to come down, but she said she was meeting someone.'

Gino burst into angry sobs. 'I should have gone to her.'

LeAnne put her arm around his shoulders. 'Shush, shush,' she said quietly, comforting him, calming him. 'I hate that I had that row with her. Thank God we sorted everything out on the walk. I had such a lovely chat. We were closer than ever.'

Susan thought about those words she'd overheard. That hadn't sounded like a 'lovely' chat to her.

At that moment, there was another knock at the door. Two police officers entered.

'Good morning, Susan,' said one of them, looking directly at her.

12

'Have you met before, Mum?' asked Zoe glancing between Susan and the police officer.

'A few times,' replied Susan. 'This is DC Kent.'

'Actually, DS Kent now,' said the officer.

'Oh, congratulations.'

'Thank you.'

Susan was stunned. Coping with Maxine's sudden death was hard enough, but to be confronted with DC... no, DS Kent was totally disconcerting. Here, Susan was again at the scene of a sudden death, the third time she'd come face to face with the same officer. She stumbled out an explanation. 'I've not been staying here, but I've been running Zoe, my daughter, back and forth. I helped in the search for Maxine this morning.'

DS Kent didn't comment, but gave a brief nod, before turning her attention to the rest of the group. 'We are so sorry. This must be very traumatic for you all.'

'How did she fall?' asked Gino, desperation in his voice. 'What happened?'

'We have a way to go to be able to answer questions like that,' said DS Kent gently.

'But you know she fell off the battlements—'

'It appears that way.'

'How long had she been lying there? Did she spend hours in agony?' asked Gino. 'I was so tired when I came back. Even though she wasn't here, I crashed out. I should have gone to look for her. I might have saved her.'

'Don't let your mind go there. We will be able to tell you more very soon. I would like to just check a few general details. Gino tells me there were four of you sleeping here: himself, Maxine, Nick and Annika. And you, Zoe, with LeAnne are sleeping at your mother's house in Bishopstone?'

'That's correct,' said Zoe.

'Good. So you all arrived yesterday afternoon. How many keys did you have for getting in and out the castle and who was in possession of them?'

'There were two,' replied Nick. 'Maxine had one. The spare key was hanging up on a hook by the door.'

'And all of you went on the organised ghost walk in the evening? What time did that end?'

'It was about nine,' said Susan.

'The staff tell me they had all finished work and vacated the castle by half past nine. The main metal gates were locked.'

'Yes, I left the castle with them at that time,' said Susan.

'So, it left the six of you. The staff had locked the gate. When was it next opened?'

'I should think that was at twenty past twelve when I left with LeAnne,' said Zoe.

'No one else left between nine thirty and twelve twenty?' DS Kent checked.

They all shook their heads.

'Right, so the only people in the castle were the members of this group. Maybe we could go through the events of last night. You all went on the ghost walk?'

'That's right and then we all came back to the apartment,' said Nick. 'We sat around for a bit and then, um, then it must have been you, Gino, who went out for a walk first?'

'I went up the keep,' agreed Gino.

'It was about ten minutes before Maxine went out. That was half eleven: I noticed the time,' said Zoe.

'So, Gino went to the keep at about eleven twenty and then Maxine went out at eleven thirty, alone?'

'Yes. She told us she was going to the battlements above the Privy Garden,' continued Zoe. 'I was a bit worried about her, so after a few minutes I followed her. Nick walked out with me. He went to the Privy Garden while I went up to see Maxine.'

DS Kent glanced at LeAnne and Annika. 'You two remained in the apartment?'

They nodded and Zoe continued. 'I went up the battlements and talked to Maxine for a while. Shortly before twelve, Maxine gave me her key to the gates as I was meant to be meeting LeAnne to leave at midnight. As I was coming down the first flight of steps from the battlements I met Gino. We talked briefly. He went back to the keep. Down the bottom I saw Nick over at the entrance to the Privy Garden. He told me he was meeting Annika, which I was pleased about. He was in a strange mood.'

'I wouldn't say that,' said Nick. 'Anyway, Annika had rung me and so I walked over to the bowling green to meet her.'

'And you Zoe?'

'I left through the wooden gates, inside the castle, waited by the shop for LeAnne, who met me at about twenty past twelve.'

'Were the metal gates locked when you left?'

'Yes, I had to unlock them to leave and locked them behind us when we went to get a taxi.'

'So, were you the only ones to leave the castle last night?'

There was no reply. Zoe looked over at Gino, who looked the other way.

'Gino, you went out,' said Zoe. 'LeAnne and I saw you while we were waiting for the taxi. We saw you coming out of the castle and walk down to see someone in a van.'

Gino sat up. 'Sorry, I'd forgotten. I left the keep, came to the apartment and picked up the spare key at about twenty past twelve to go for a walk outside, but I never went to any van.'

DS Kent gave him a hard look but didn't say anything more on the matter. 'Thank you all. Now, I'd like to have a short chat with you all individually. I'm so sorry. I know how trying this is, and you are all in shock. But the sooner we get a clear picture of last night, the quicker we'll have answers for you all. Now, maybe we could start with you, Gino. We will be using the café, which is close by.'

Gino walked out with them, head bent, like a prisoner. Another police officer quietly entered the room and stood to one side.

Susan glanced over at Zoe. She was staring at the floor, rocking slightly, very pale, picking at the quicks of her nails.

'Poor Gino,' said LeAnne. 'This is the most terrible shock for him.'

'It is for us all,' said Nick. His voice was quiet, as if it hurt to speak. 'How could this have happened?'

They all fell silent.

Eventually Gino returned; he was taken quietly into a separate room by the police officer.

'Honestly,' said LeAnne. 'None of us have to go in if we don't want to.'

Nick frowned. 'Why wouldn't we? They obviously have to ask how Maxine was in herself and figure out when she fell.'

'Well, I don't see why Gino has to be in that room on his own,' said LeAnne.

'They don't want us to influence each other's stories,' said Nick.

He was called in next, followed by Annika and then Zoe.

Susan felt nervous as she saw Zoe going. It was ridiculous, of course. Her daughter was an adult, probably more articulate than her. She'd be fine.

Finally, it was Susan's turn.

She followed DS Kent into the café. She had not been in this building before. When Zoe was little, a building close to the entrance but outside the main castle had been used for a café. The new café was in one of the original castle buildings. It was rather dark and cold. Susan's eyes took a few moments to adjust.

She sat on a wooden chair opposite DS Kent. The table and chairs were clearly meant for café use. She glanced over at the empty counter, imagining the cakes and sausage rolls piled up.

'So, Susan, here you are again.'

Susan blinked, shocked she'd let her mind wander to something so trivial. 'Um, yes. Sorry I keep turning up. As I said, I'm not part of this group. My daughter Zoe and her friend LeAnne are staying with me.'

'I see. Well, I guess it might be helpful to have your insights into the group. Apart from Gino, Maxine's husband, they are all school friends. Did you know any of them back then?'

'Yes, I knew them all. They would come to my house over in Ventnor after school, but I've seen very little of most of them since.'

'OK, now you said Zoe and LeAnne are not sleeping here, but at your house?'

'That's right. I came up to join them all for the ghost walk here, then left them. Zoe and LeAnne were going to get a taxi back to my house.'

'What time did they arrive home?'

'I can't tell you that. I don't wait up for my daughter any more.' Susan gave a half smile.

'Of course not, but they both returned?'

'Yes. We had breakfast together.'

'And how did they seem?'

Susan looked around, saw the menus, the knives and forks laid ready for the next visitors. It all seemed so mundane, gave the interview a dream-like quality.

'How were Zoe and LeAnne at breakfast this morning?' repeated DS Kent.

'Fine. They'd had a good evening, I think. They were all planning to go to the beach together.'

'Zoe said she had a text this morning saying Maxine was missing. What time was that?'

'I'm not sure. About eight?'

'And how did they both respond?'

'Zoe was a bit worried.'

'And what did she think had happened?'

'I don't know, but she'd found Maxine a bit stressed last night. Maybe she thought she had wandered off somewhere. I don't know. LeAnne took it less seriously, but Zoe was the one who wanted to come and find out what was going on, so I brought them up to the castle.'

'And what were your movements then?'

Susan went through the events leading to the finding of Maxine's body.

'That must have been very upsetting. How did people react?'

'Zoe was in shock, Gino, just frantic. As you can imagine they were all pretty much traumatised.'

'Maybe you could tell me what you know about Maxine.'

'I've not seen her for a few years. I know she was a very successful barrister. I liked her when she was younger. A very bright, talented girl, always fighting some cause. She had a good heart.'

'What was your daughter's relationship with Maxine?'

The confrontational way in which the question was asked made Susan sit up. 'They were good friends, always had been. They were both living in Portsmouth, so still met up for a drink.' Susan hesitated. 'It would be much better to discuss this with Zoe. She's an adult, married with a child. She leads her own life.'

'Of course. Now, can you tell me anything about the other members of the group?'

'I'm not really up to date. Nick is a teacher. Annika now works for the blood service, and LeAnne, of course, runs her own restaurant. I hadn't met Gino before. I know nothing about him apart from him being married to Maxine.'

'Do you think he and Zoe get on well?'

It seemed a strange question. 'They hardly know each other.'

'I see. Now, is there anything else you think might be useful for our investigation?'

'I did notice that Maxine's watch had broken when she fell. The time was about ten past twelve?'

DS Kent raised an eyebrow. 'We of course noticed that. It would be very useful if that gave us a time of death. But I'm sure you realise the many pitfalls of relying on that—'

'Of course. I just thought I'd mention it.'

DS Kent closed her notebook. As she did, she added, 'As

with any sudden death, we will be investigating this carefully. I realise you have become involved in other sudden deaths that have happened around you and, of course, your daughter is involved, but I am strongly urging you to keep out of this, Susan.'

'I had no intention of doing anything else.'

'That's good. I will give you a card I've given the others, one with my direct line on. If there is anything at all, please phone me. Thank you. That will be all for now.'

Realising she'd been dismissed, Susan tucked the card in her pocket and left the café.

It was a relief to be outside, although the fog still hung heavily.

The group were back together in the main room in the apartment. The police had taken some of Maxine's belongings, including her laptop, but everything else looked very much as it had before.

'If it's OK, I'm off home now,' Susan said to the group. 'I was thinking you might need a break so if you want to come to my house for lunch, you're very welcome. Zoe, can you give people directions?'

'Actually, Mum, I think I'd like to come back with you now. LeAnne, are you all right to show everyone the way?'

'Of course. See you about one? If anything else crops up, or they want us to stay, I'll text you.'

'See you later.'

Susan and Zoe walked out of the courtyard together.

'I wish this fog would lift,' said Susan.

There was yellow tape barring off the long flight of steps to the battlements and also the short flight that led to the old armoury.

'It looks like something off the telly,' said Zoe. 'Last night we were all full of the fact we had the castle to ourselves and now it's been taken away. It's horrible, like the castle has become a crime scene. I feel almost guilty, like we've spoiled it somehow.'

'The castle has seen a lot of death and killing over its time. Just think, people have been coming in here for hundreds of years. This will be one more chapter in its history.'

A police officer was standing at the gate. Susan and Zoe explained who they were and where they were going.

It felt wonderfully quiet in the car, and Susan sat back and breathed more easily.

However, Zoe sat clasping her hands, holding herself tightly, her face pale and strained. Of course, it had been horrendous, discovering her friend had died in such a tragic way, but Susan knew her daughter too well, there was something else on her mind.

13

As she began to drive them back to the house, Susan asked Zoe how her interview with DS Kent had been.

'I've no idea. I think I made a mess of it. It was weird.'

'They're just gathering information at the moment. That's all. What are you so worried about?'

'I don't know, Mum,' said Zoe sharply. 'I don't want to talk about it.'

Susan knew it was better to leave her for now, give her space. They drove back in silence.

Rocco and Libs greeted them, and Susan watched Zoe sit on the floor cuddling them both.

'I'd better pop to the shops if everyone is coming back here. Are you OK if I leave you?'

'Of course, thanks.'

Susan left the house. On her way she phoned Robert, always her first call in an emergency. He answered quickly and Susan told him as briefly as she could what had happened.

He listened well, as he always did. 'How are you all?'

'Zoe is at home. She's kind of numb, I think. It was awful,

Robert.' Susan felt tears welling up in her eyes, her hand started to shake. 'I'm sorry—' She began to sob.

'Hey, it's OK,' Robert said gently. 'I'm out with the dogs at the moment. We're over in Freshwater as I had to drop something off. Would you like me to pop, or are you both in need of peace and quiet?'

Susan checked her watch, sniffed, but felt calmer. 'It's only half ten. Gosh, it feels so much later. It would be lovely to see you. I think Zoe may find it helpful to talk to you.'

'OK, I'll be along in about twenty minutes. See you soon.'

Susan smiled, felt the tight frown across her forehead relax a little. It would be good to see Robert.

Drying her eyes, she entered the shop. News that something had happened had miraculously reached Bishopstone and Tracy was eager for more information.

'I heard they had an ambulance and police car go to the castle. My cousin lives in the village there. So, what's happened?'

'I'm afraid there's been a fatality. One of Zoe's friends has died.'

'Oh, no, but that's just terrible.'

It took a moment for the enormity of the news to sink in but, of course, Tracy wanted the details, and for once Susan was ahead of the news.

'So, what happened? I told you it wasn't safe for them up there.'

'No one knows exactly what occurred, but the body of Zoe's friend Maxine was found this morning.'

'How awful. Where did she live?'

'Maxine was a barrister working on the mainland. She was so bright, a lovely young girl—' Susan felt her voice break again, but took a breath and added, 'As I say, the police haven't given any more details yet.'

Their eyes met. Tracy gave her a gentle smile. 'I'm so sorry, Susan. It must have been awful.'

Susan appreciated her kindness but could see she was itching for more detail.

'I wonder where the poor girl was found. It might give an idea of what had happened,' said Tracy.

'She was found in the old armoury – it's off a flight of steps that lead to the gatehouse. It's in ruins now, looks over the Privy Garden.'

Tracy nodded. 'I know where you mean – you can look down on it from the battlements?'

'That's right. There's no roof.'

'So, Maxine could have fallen from the battlements?'

'It's a possibility. We know she'd been up there.'

'I always knew someone would fall off them, always wondered why it's not happened before. I never let my kids go up there. What a tragedy.'

'It is. I've invited the group of friends all for lunch, so I'd better get some food in.'

Susan simply topped up the food she'd bought the day before.

Tracy was busy chatting to another customer and Susan was able to pay a young girl who helped out and return home quickly.

She mentioned Robert's impending visit to Zoe.

'I hope you don't mind. If you need to go to your room and be quiet, I quite understand.'

'No, I'd like to speak to him. Could we all go out for a walk, Mum? My head is thumping.'

'Of course, I'll text Robert to meet us up the downs. At least the fog seems to be finally lifting.'

They wrapped up the dogs and drove to Jubilee car park. It

was so much clearer than first thing. Robert arrived, gave Susan a much-needed hug and they began the walk up the path.

'I'm so sorry to hear about your friend, Zoe,' said Robert.

Zoe glanced around. 'Coming up here, it feels like a dream. It's hard to believe that only a few hours ago, I was staring down at my lovely friend on that cold, bare floor—' Her voice started to shake.

'It's a terrible shock,' said Robert.

'The police interviewed us all. It was awful. It made me feel like I'd done something wrong.'

Robert took a ball out of his pocket and threw it for the dogs. Only Libs looked up and went chasing after it.

'They have to ask questions in a case of sudden death. Do you know any of the names of the officers who came?'

'It was DC, or should I say DS Kent, would you believe?' said Susan, grinning.

'Oh, she's been promoted to Detective Sergeant now? Impressive. Was she pleased to see you?'

'Not overjoyed and, of course, my daughter is involved as well.'

Ignoring the digression, Zoe said, 'The point is the police aren't just asking us about Maxine, but about what we were doing when she died, how we got on with her—'

'They have to get a full picture of Maxine and what happened that evening.'

'But it makes you feel so guilty. Questioning everything you say. It's like when I said I got a taxi home she asked me the time and the name of the taxi firm. Also, this DS Kent said a few times that it appeared I was the last person to speak to Maxine. I told her I wasn't, but she didn't seem to believe me.'

Susan felt uneasy. Robert paused, looked at Zoe carefully. 'Why are they so sure you were the last person up there, then?'

Zoe shrugged. 'Well, no one else in the group is owning up to being there, but I know someone was up there. Maxine told me she was meeting someone at midnight and then while I was waiting for LeAnne I saw a light, heard voices up there.'

'The police will discover who it was. Try not to worry.'

Susan looked over the downs. In the distance she could see the grey wintry sea. Rooks called from the trees in the forest, and below she could see seagulls flocked on a brown ploughed field.

Zoe seemed oblivious to it all and walked head down. 'I do worry, though. I keep thinking I should have done more, persuaded Maxine to come down. She wasn't in the right state of mind to be up there.'

'Had she been drinking or taken anything?'

'She was drinking but I wouldn't say she was drunk. No, she was just so unhappy. Her marriage was falling apart, and she seemed to feel, well, unloved. She was almost paranoid, talking about someone wishing she was dead.'

Susan took a sharp intake of breath. Had Maxine really said that?

'Have you told the police about this?' asked Robert, a sharpness in his voice.

'I told them everything.'

'That's good. That's all you can do. And Zoe, try not to go over it all too much. We all think about the things we wish we'd said or done when someone dies, particularly when it's unexpected.'

They walked on, the wind blowing through the gorse bushes, but Zoe was still looking down, still preoccupied. Robert picked this up and, with the voice of an experienced police officer, asked, 'Is there something else worrying you, Zoe?'

Zoe took a breath. 'Someone has told them they saw me involved in a violent struggle up there with Maxine. It's rubbish. Why would anyone say that?'

Susan glanced at her daughter. Was she trying to play down something here? She was concerned to see the lines of unease start to reappear on Robert's face.

'Have you any idea who said that? Is there any basis for it?' asked Robert. To Susan the warmth in his voice seemed to have gone, and he sounded more official, more serious.

'I've no idea who said this and, no, of course there is no basis to it.' Susan could hear a change in Zoe's voice, a defiance was setting in. 'We were close, very good friends. What are you saying?'

'I'm simply asking if you had a row of any sort,' said Robert patiently.

'Are you accusing me of lying?' demanded Zoe.

Susan groaned. Zoe could be so defensive: heaven help if she'd been like this with the police.

Robert stopped, looked at Zoe and said calmly, 'You have to try and see this from the police point of view. They don't know any of you. They don't know who they can trust. Who do you think told them this?'

'I've no idea,' said Zoe. She picked up a stick, broke it in half and threw it to the ground.

'The police are just trying to find out what happened. They aren't out to trap anyone. I promise you.'

'But someone is feeding them lies about me.'

'The police will get to the bottom of it. By the way, do the police have any idea when the accident happened?'

'It had to be after twelve. That's when I left Maxine.'

Susan interrupted. 'I saw Maxine's watch. It was broken at ten past twelve. It could be when she fell.' Before Robert could add the warning, she said, 'I know. The watch might have been wrong or set to a different time. I'm just saying what I saw.'

'And that's fine. Just because it's not foolproof doesn't mean it's irrelevant. It's possible the watch was accurate and really did break when she fell. If it corroborates other more scientific measures used to estimate her time of death, it may be valuable.'

Robert picked up the ball which Libs had finally returned, threw it again and turned to Zoe. 'Try not to worry. The police will be testing everything they are told.'

To Susan's relief, Zoe seemed to find some reassurance in his words and smiled. 'Thank you.'

They walked on. Robert and Susan chatted about his morning over at Freshwater, until they reached the summit of the downs. The views up here looked over the Tennyson trail and out to sea.

Zoe walked ahead.

'Thank you,' Susan said to Robert. 'This is all very stressful for her.'

'I'm not surprised. She hasn't had as many dealings with the police as her mum,' he said with a gentle smile.

'I'm a bit worried, though, about the police focusing on Zoe being the last person to speak to Maxine and the struggle—'

'The police are bound to pick up on things like that, but they're only just starting to get a picture. You know Zoe. She'll be OK.'

As they talked, Susan watched a kestrel hovering above a spiny bush, waiting to pounce on its prey. Usually the sight fascinated her; today it felt more sinister.

'Shall we get back?' she said. 'I've got them all coming for lunch.'

'Ah, you said. It's good of you to look after them all. You have had a nasty shock. Take it easy later.'

Susan smiled. It was nice to feel looked after. 'I will.'

'I'm always at the end of the phone. Remember that.'

'Thank you.'

Back at the car park, Robert turned to Susan. 'I could keep an ear open if it's any help?'

'Thanks, it would be.'

'Right. Contact me if you need me. See you soon.'

Robert returned to his car, with Gem Gem and Dougie jumping into the boot.

With a wave, he was gone.

Zoe's group arrived pretty much on time at one o'clock. Susan gave them all hot drinks and they sat huddled together.

Gino looked up, eyes red, tapping his chin with his fingertips.

'First of all,' he said, 'I spoke to Maxine's father this morning. He's naturally devastated and is speaking directly to the police. He's on holiday in Mexico and is now travelling home. Now, I wonder if I could ask you all a favour?'

'Anything,' said LeAnne, leaning forward.

'I should imagine that you would all like to get away from this nightmare—' He paused and wiped his eyes. 'I know I want to find it's a horrendous dream, but it's not. This is real. My beautiful amore, Maxine, has gone.' He started to shake and then sob. LeAnne put her arm around his shoulder.

'It's OK, Gino. No one can believe this has happened.'

He sniffed. 'Look, I would be so grateful if you could stay around for a few days. We have the apartment until Sunday and I'm not ready to move out yet. I need to stay and try to come to terms with what has happened, but I'd hate to be there on my own. I think the police would also appreciate us all being close at hand. The police have informed somebody called the coroner and it's up to her or him when anything like a funeral can be arranged. I feel in limbo. I would still like to support the concert on Saturday evening. It meant so much to Maxine. Of course, some of you may find that too difficult.'

LeAnne laid her hand on his knee. 'You know we will do anything. We will be here for you. I shall stay around here and will be at the concert.'

'I feel the same. We should stay,' said Annika. 'Dad was desperate to come and get me earlier but, even then, I felt we should stay together. I want to be here for you, Gino.'

Gino looked over at her. 'Thank you. I will understand if you don't feel able to sing at the concert on Saturday.'

'I would like to do it in honour of Maxine. Nick, will you still be OK to accompany me?'

'Of course. I'll be honest. I'd have liked to go back to Cowes, but I'll stay if that's what you all want.'

Susan mentioned the food on the table, and slowly people started to help themselves.

The conversation naturally returned to Maxine and again how shocked they all were.

Zoe carefully put down her mug and cleared her throat in a way that gathered people's attention.

'There is something I'd like to talk to you all about. I had a hard time when I was interviewed by the police. Someone said I'd had a violent argument with Maxine last night up on the battlements. Why on earth would anyone say that?'

There was a moment's pause and then Gino coughed. 'Actually, I told the police that.'

Zoe stared at him. 'Why the hell did you say that?'

'That is what I witnessed. I heard voices when I came to speak to Maxine. As I looked along the battlements, I saw you both close to the wall, physically struggling. It looked to me as if you were trying to push Maxine over the wall.'

Zoe gasped. 'Of course I wasn't.'

'I heard her say, "No, stop. It's not what I want." She was grabbing your arm.'

'Oh, that. I was trying to chuck away some miniature she'd found in her bag. It was freaking her out and I wanted to get rid of it. However, she insisted on keeping it.'

'A miniature?'

'Maxine had found a small model of the Grim Reaper zipped in her bag. It frightened her. I told her it was a joke, but she was upset by it. When you saw me, I was trying to throw it away, but she was stopping me. She wanted to hold on to it.'

'It was a joke,' said LeAnne.

'Did *you* put it in Maxine's bag?' asked Zoe.

'No. Of course I didn't.'

'Well, someone did, and Maxine didn't see it as a prank. She saw it as a threat. So, who put it there?'

14

Susan glanced around the group sitting quietly in her room. Zoe was on the edge of her seat, waiting for an answer but no one spoke.

Her eyes narrowed in frustration. 'One of you put that model of the Grim Reaper in Maxine's bag. Who was it?'

Susan could see a look in Zoe's eyes, the teacher in her coming out. This was the kind of penetrating look she gave when the class were not responding.

'I'm not blaming anyone, but I would like to know why you put it there—'

Gino looked at her sceptically. 'I'm finding the story of this model thing hard to believe. Maxine never said anything about finding one, and I never saw it in your hand.'

'I'm not inventing this,' said Zoe crossly. 'Why would I?'

Gino shrugged. 'To explain the fight you were having?'

Zoe threw her hands up. 'That's ridiculous. Of course it was there. In fact, I asked the police to look into it. Maxine was upset by it.'

'It looked a lot more than a row about some toy.'

'If you were that worried, why didn't you come and help her?' demanded Zoe.

He scowled, and leant forward.

'Because I saw the way things changed. You moved back and then Maxine started talking about some secret she was keeping, something only the two of you knew about. Maxine was very anxious you didn't tell anyone – I certainly had no idea what it was.'

Zoe looked away as she responded. 'We were close friends. We shared and supported each other—'

Zoe might be trying to sound nonchalant but Susan heard the tremor in her voice, noticed her picking her nails.

'You have no right to keep this from me,' said Gino, his voice hard and cold. 'You were the last person to speak to Maxine, you need to share everything.'

Zoe shook her head. 'But I wasn't the last person up there with Maxine. I saw torchlight up there after I left. I heard voices.'

'That could have been Maxine.'

'Maxine's torch wasn't working and why would she be talking to herself? Who was up there?' She looked around the group. No one met her eye.

'It had to be one of you. DS Kent said no one else was in the castle. You should own up.'

Still there was no reply.

'We only have your word that Maxine arranged to meet someone, or that there were lights and voices later,' said Gino.

'For God's sake. I'm not making any of this up. Why would I?'

'I have no idea, but Maxine said nothing to me about meeting someone,' he countered.

'Apparently it was a private meeting. But hang on. Before she left the apartment, didn't Maxine say, "I might as well go out now"? That must have meant she was going earlier than planned. You heard that: Annika, Nick and LeAnne?'

They shrugged. 'None of us are going to remember that,' said Nick, 'but neither Annika nor I went to see Maxine. We were together on the bowling green, weren't we, Annika?'

Annika blinked, then nodded.

'And I was in the apartment until I came to meet you, Zoe, at twenty past twelve,' said LeAnne.

'Are you sure about that?' asked Annika.

LeAnne blinked, looking surprised. 'Sorry?'

'I noticed you said that to DS Kent. But when I left around twelve, you were putting your coat on.'

LeAnne blushed. 'Um, I changed my mind after you left. I stayed in and didn't leave until I went to meet Zoe.'

'But why did you stay instead of coming to meet me at twelve like we arranged?' asked Zoe.

LeAnne tutted. 'I got the wrong time. I was sure we'd said twenty past. Honestly, why am I getting the third degree from you all?'

'Look,' said Nick, 'we don't need to keep going over and over last night. We just need to wait for the police to come back and tell us how this terrible accident happened.'

He stood up. 'If it's OK, Susan, I'll go into your garden. I need some fresh air.'

'Of course. I'll open the patio door but close it behind you. The fog's lifted, but it's quite cold.'

Some of the others went to fetch more food. They hadn't had breakfast and were hungrier than they realised.

Susan was checking the table when she overheard Annika speaking to Zoe in a low voice. 'I'm sorry, Zoe. This isn't fair. Please don't think anyone is blaming you for anything.'

'I should hope not,' said Zoe, no hint of a smile. 'It's horrible enough without people making up rubbish like this. I have to admit I was concerned about Maxine. She was stressed out. Did she say anything to you when you met last week?'

Annika frowned. 'I haven't seen Maxine since the party in February.'

'But she said she came to see you at work last Wednesday.'

'God, no. Why would she do that?' Looking totally bemused Annika walked away.

Zoe looked over at Susan. 'How odd. Maxine definitely said she'd spoken to Annika last week. She can't have forgotten so soon, can she?'

Susan shrugged. 'Sorry, love. I've no idea.'

Annika meanwhile was taking one of Susan's old stamp albums from the shelf. Her eyes shone with excitement as she brought it over to Susan. 'Is this the stamp album you used to show me?' she asked.

'It is.'

'Can I look through it? Do you mind?'

'Gosh, no,' said Susan as she and Annika settled themselves down on dining chairs. Annika opened the album carefully.

For a moment they were back in the kitchen of the old Victorian house in Ventnor where Susan previously lived. Annika sat next to her chatting about stamps, although now her knowledge far exceeded Susan's.

'You've kept up your interest?' asked Susan. 'I remember that you – and Maxine for that matter – were both interested. It was unusual, not something most kids your age were into.'

'I know. I guess it's one of the reasons we bonded as a band. We allowed each other to be a bit nerdy. I'm glad you sparked the interest. It gives me a lot of joy and you don't have to be rich to collect them, do you?'

'No, it's something anyone can do.'

'Nick doesn't get it, but I find stamps quite magical. These tiny squares of paper tell so many stories. I've been experimenting in my own painting, creating tiny pictures the size of stamps, inspired by these. Look, they have so much detail: head of a monarch, flowers and butterflies. Tiny works of art.'

'I agree, endlessly fascinating. Do you have much of a collection?'

'Not that many, I tend to stick to UK stamps, and I like attractive ones like animals, seasonal ones like those brought out at Christmas. I'm not into the monarch heads ones although they are often the ones that go on to be worth a lot of money. Patrick, the father of the child I was nanny to, was into antiques of all sorts. He taught me a few things about stamps and their value. I even went to some auctions with him. I knew of course that rarity was important and there are the ones with errors, but hadn't thought about the condition and that, even for someone like me whose collection is pretty basic, it matters. You see, who knows what these stamps will be worth one day, and so I should be looking after them now.'

'I just attach mine with those hinges and put them in an album.'

'But there is more you should do. Patrick said to handle them like good wine. Humidity is your enemy. Keep them in the dark, and don't handle them. I keep some of mine in the safe at the flat. It's perfect conditions.'

Susan laughed. 'I suppose if you have very expensive stamps, you'd do all that, but people like me don't need to.'

'Mine aren't worth much at all yet, but you never know when they may become collectable. One day, you or your kids might be able to sell them.'

'Patrick clearly installed some good habits into you.'

'He did. He's an amazing man. He'd started out as a cabbie in London and was left a painting by an aunt. He had it valued, and it turned out to be worth a lot more than anyone realised. It set him up money-wise and got him into antiques.'

Annika went back to looking through the album. 'Ah, you have some of the Christmas ones I have. Awesome. I have these castles as well from 1988. Did you know they're worth about fifty pounds? They can only increase.'

'I never knew that.'

Annika continued to look through, totally engrossed, commenting occasionally. Finally, she closed the album. 'No million-dollar. Me neither. Usual collection, but still precious. Take care of them. One day there will be no more stamps and that will be really sad.'

Annika glanced out of the window, down the garden at Nick. He was pacing up and down, eating sweets from a tin, and for a moment Annika's gaze remained fixed on him, her face screwed up in consternation.

'Maxine's death is so tragic and very difficult for you all to handle,' said Susan gently. 'I can understand why your dad wanted you home. How did he hear about the accident so quickly?'

Annika rolled her eyes. 'Dad never misses anything, and you know what it's like on the island. A friend of his came dog walking by the castle early, saw an ambulance, talked to one of the paramedics, who told him there'd been an accident in the castle. He told Dad who then rang in – I bet most of the island knew by then.'

'You're probably right.'

Annika looked down the garden at Nick. 'This has hit him hard. He was so grateful to Maxine. She stood by him when a lot of people turned their backs.'

'She was a good friend to him.'

'She was. I was so grateful. Obviously, nothing like this had ever happened to Nick before. Neither of us had a clue what was going to happen. Maxine was our rock.'

Susan was watching Annika carefully but could see none of that jealousy LeAnne had been talking about.

She could see Nick coming up the garden and he was soon back in the house. He came over to Susan and Annika.

'Ah, stamps, again!' he said as he approached.

He pointed down at the album. His hand was shaking and Annika gently held it. 'I'm afraid so. You're so cold. You stayed out too long,' she said tenderly. Nick smiled at her. 'It's warm in here though.'

Susan went upstairs to the bathroom. She noticed Zoe's bedroom door ajar. She was sitting on her bed, cuddling a teddy.

'Are you OK, love?'

'Of course not,' she snapped. 'What the hell is Gino playing at? Why is he saying this stuff about me and Maxine? He's making me out to be a liar, and I'm not. Why isn't anyone owning up to being up there with her? They should come forward, tell the police what happened.' Zoe's face was red, hot angry tears threatening to spill down her cheeks.

Susan hated seeing her this upset and sat down next to her.

'They're in shock just like you. It was only this morning. No one has had time to process it yet.'

'But I don't understand why they're all acting like this. The sooner the police get answers, the sooner they can tell us how the accident happened.'

'People get scared, they're not thinking straight.'

'Well, I wish they would. I'm trying to, and I was closer to

Maxine than most of them.' She started to sob. 'I can't believe she's gone, Mum.'

Susan put her arms around her daughter and just held her while she cried.

Zoe wiped her face and sat back. 'I wish I could speak to Dad.'

Susan bit her lip. Zoe had always turned to her father in a crisis, particularly in her teenage years. She found his pragmatism, his sense of perspective, comforting.

'You can ring him. He's not on another planet. He'd want to help you.'

Zoe shook her head. 'I don't know how to speak to him at the moment. I know I stood by him at first, but I can't stand that woman he's with now. And I find myself angrier now about how he treated you. I can't ever imagine treating Fay like that. If he was so unhappy he should have talked to you, gone for counselling. He shouldn't have just told you one evening that he was off and just disappeared like that.'

Part of Susan was tempted to simply agree and rant against her husband, but she didn't feel that would be of any help to Zoe. 'Look, what he did wasn't fair or kind. But Zoe, that was between me and your dad and slowly we are moving on from it. I'm building my own life now. He loves you so much. He'd be back in a flash if he felt you needed him.'

Zoe voice softened as she said, 'He sends postcards, you know, to Jamari, with such sweet little messages, and he signs them just from him.'

Susan had known nothing about the cards. Hearing about them hurt. It emphasised their separate lives, being grandparents had always been something she'd imagined doing together. It also reminded her that despite the terrible way he'd ended their marriage, there had been many times when Steve had been caring and kind. However, the thought was not comforting, it just seemed to emphasise what they had lost.

'I know he loves me, Mum,' continued Zoe, 'it's just a difficult time. I don't feel like phoning him, not today.'

'Well, if you change your mind, you know he will always be there to listen.'

Zoe kissed the teddy. 'It smells like Jamari, she let me bring this one away with me... it's her third favourite teddy, I must have some FaceTime with her. I miss her so much.'

'And she and Fay miss you, I'm sure.' Susan stood up. 'Have a rest, love. I'll go and see how everyone is getting on. I'm due to go and see Alice at the care home soon, but everyone is welcome to stay.'

'I think they're going for a walk but, Mum, do you think I could come and see Alice with you? Would she mind?'

'I'm sure she'd love to see you.'

'I found her to be a very sensible person when I spoke to her after Jamari's celebration. I think it would help.'

'Then of course come.'

Zoe blinked, bit her lip. 'Will it upset her if I talk about Maxine? I mean, Alice is very old now—'

Susan grinned. 'I'm sure she will know a surprising amount already. Tracy will have been on the phone to her. To be honest, she'll be itching to talk about it and rather thrilled to have a first-hand account.'

Susan went downstairs to the main room and found the rest of the group putting on coats ready to leave.

'Thank you so much,' said Nick. 'Is Zoe coming?'

'She's staying here for a while. There's someone we need to see.'

15

Susan and Zoe arrived at the care home to find Alice sitting in her chair, her tablet in her hand, the home cat, Princess, on her lap.

Alice looked up and her grey eyes sparkled at the sight of Zoe.

'How lovely to see you again. How are you?'

Zoe and Susan sat down and Zoe leant forward. 'A lot has been happening, but it's lovely to see you, Alice. How are you?'

'I'm doing very well, thank you. How is that beautiful daughter of yours?'

After everything that had happened it felt strange to start chatting about Jamari and family matters, but Susan could feel Zoe relax. She took out her phone and started to show Alice photos, which she clearly enjoyed. After a while though the conversation naturally returned to events at the castle.

'I was so sorry to hear about what happened to your friend,' said Alice.

'You know about the accident?'

'Oh, yes.' Alice glanced over at Susan. 'Tracy rang after you'd been in the shop.'

Susan smiled to herself, her earlier theory had been confirmed. She wondered how many more people Tracy had shared the news with, how the speculation had grown.

'That's right, it was Maxine. I'd been up on the battlements talking to Maxine not long before it happened.'

'Tracy said she fell into the old armoury?'

'That's where she was found. The police haven't confirmed how the accident happened as yet.'

'What a tragic start to your holiday. What friends were you over here with?'

'There were five of us from school days and Maxine's husband Gino.'

'I have a photo of everyone,' said Susan taking out her phone. She found the selfie she'd taken the night before. She pointed out Maxine, told Alice a little about her background, then briefly explained who the others were.

Alice's face creased with sadness as she looked at Maxine. 'What a waste. A bright young girl, fighting for others. It's tragic her life was cut short. And very hard for you to lose a friend in this way, Zoe.'

'It's a nightmare. I've known her since school and we'd started meeting up again.' Zoe was blinking fast, and patted her lip with trembling fingers.

Alice continued looking at the screen. 'There are only five in the picture?'

Susan glanced over. 'Ah, Gino arrived later, I have one of him, but he's in his mask.'

Susan scrolled through and found it.

'I see. Well, even in his mask I can see he's a very good-looking young man. They'd have made a handsome couple.'

Zoe grimaced. 'I can't say I'm that keen on Gino, he's been spreading all kinds of nonsense about me.'

Zoe explained about him overhearing her and Maxine on the battlements, and him telling the police she'd had a row up there.

'I feel he's got it in for me, maybe he's jealous because he knew me and Maxine were close.'

'Did she tell you things she kept from him?' asked Alice.

'We were friends, she trusted me.'

Zoe blushed and shot a look at Susan and then continued, 'Their marriage was very unhappy.'

'I got the impression Maxine felt her marriage was over,' said Susan.

'I'm sure you're right,' said Zoe, who turned to Alice. 'Maxine was talking to me about it last night. She was so upset. She talked about them falling out about money a while back. After that Gino became very moody and difficult. He started staying over here without explanation, even visiting Italy without telling her.'

'Did Maxine suspect her husband was having an affair with all these absences from home?'

Zoe blinked. 'Maxine never suggested that.'

'I wonder why,' said Alice. 'It would be the first thing most people would think of if their partner was evasive and missing from home.'

'Maxine was far more preoccupied with some promise Gino was meant to have broken: a line crossed, she called it.'

'And what was that?'

'I don't know exactly. She said she first suspected him when she found wads of cash in his drawer and then she heard he was keeping something in Annika's safe.'

'Annika lives with Nick over in Cowes?'

Zoe smiled. 'Well remembered, yes. It's Annika's flat, or at least she's the tenant. Gino had renovated it. Maxine and Gino are her landlords.'

'I see, but isn't it strange that Gino is going into the flat and using the safe?'

'It is. Nick doesn't like him just turning up without warning.'

'So, Maxine came over, you say last week, to look in the safe, but we don't know what it was she found.'

'No, but it had to be significant. It confirmed her worst fears that Gino's broken a solemn promise to her.' Zoe scowled. 'It's very odd. Maxine told me she went to speak to Annika after going to the flat, but Annika denies it.'

Alice scrolled back to the previous photo, and enlarged some of the faces. Suddenly she looked up, an excited smile on her face. 'I thought she looked familiar,' she said, pointing to Annika. 'She comes here to take blood samples. We have nice chats. She shows me photos of her latest paintings.'

Susan, temporarily distracted, asked Alice why she was having blood tests. Alice quickly explained that her doctor was very thorough and insisted on a blood test every month, but all the tests were fine. She then returned to the photo.

'Yes, I thought Maxine looked familiar as well. I remember now. She came to see Annika here last week. I saw them in the garden.'

Zoe leant forward, excited. 'Do you remember what day?'

'It was last Wednesday. I know because I usually do my chair yoga that day but missed it as I knew I was having a blood test. Annika was on her way over to me when she was called away. I looked out at the garden and saw her talking to Maxine. They looked very serious. I wondered if it was bad news.'

'That was the day Maxine said she came to the flat and

sought out Annika. So Annika is wrong. They did meet. Why is she denying it?'

'After they talked, I remember asking Annika if everything was all right. She said her landlady was telling her she'd checked the smoke alarms and they were all working. I thought it was very odd to interrupt work to tell her something that could be put in a text.'

Susan remembered Annika's description of Alice as a sweet old lady pretending to do her crossword. How she'd underestimated her!

Alice stroked Princess thoughtfully. 'Did Maxine tell you why she came?'

'Not really. It was after she'd been to Annika's flat to look in the safe. Maxine told me she'd found other things that concerned her, nothing to do with Gino, and needed to urgently discuss them with Annika.'

Susan listened intently. She knew nothing of this.

'Didn't Maxine give you any hints at all about what concerned her?'

Zoe screwed up her face in concentration, and then her face cleared. 'Maxine said she'd seen some albums in the safe. After that, she scouted around, and noticed some sheet music and something in Nick's bedside table.' Zoe shrugged. 'I don't know much more than that.'

'I see. She gave no other indication what had sparked this concern?'

'Oh, she mentioned that she could have been influenced by a case she'd been working on, but I've no idea what it was.'

'That could be important. It would be interesting to know what that was.'

Susan glanced at Alice. After three investigations she knew

that voice: it wasn't idle curiosity. No, Alice clearly believed this mattered. But why?

Alice looked up, her eyes bright. 'I shall talk to Donna, a nurse who works here. She and Annika are good friends. If Annika told anyone what Maxine came about it would be her.'

Alice picked up the phone and looked again at the photo. 'So, tell me again, who are these two?'

Zoe looked over her shoulder. 'That's LeAnne and Nick.'

'I see. Tell me more about LeAnne.'

'She lives in Ventnor, runs a fish restaurant. Big family. Some have got into trouble. Uncle in prison.'

'What's her surname?'

'Alnwick.'

'Mm. Rings a bell, sounds as if some of her family might have been in the paper.'

'Probably, but as far as I know LeAnne is trying to build an honest business.'

'That's good to hear. So, she's here on the island. Is she married?'

Zoe smiled. 'No, and no children. Her life is her restaurant. I really admire her. She can be abrupt, but she means well.'

'I noticed she'd been very supportive of Gino today,' said Susan.

'Yes, I hadn't realised he'd been to her restaurant again since the party in February.'

Alice's eyes twinkled. 'Interesting. Maybe she's the reason Gino has been staying over here?'

'Oh, Alice, I can't imagine they're having an affair or anything like that,' said Zoe.

'It's possible,' said Alice gently. 'And if it's crossed my mind, surely it must have occurred to Maxine.'

'She never said anything. I suppose LeAnne does seem

closer to Gino than I realised. But I doubt Maxine suspected anything. LeAnne talked about them having a nice chat on the ghost walk.'

Susan sat forward. 'But that's not true. LeAnne's lying about that.'

'How's that?' asked Zoe.

'I heard LeAnne say to Maxine something like, "Maxine, I will not let you destroy me."'

'Now why did LeAnne think Maxine was going to destroy her?' asked Alice.

'Would it be by not letting Gino have a divorce?' asked Susan.

'I don't think so,' said Zoe. 'Maxine had written off her marriage. It sounded as if she was the one who would be initiating a divorce. Could it be anything to do with Nick and Wesley's court cases?' She glanced at Alice. 'Sorry, I should fill you in on that. We've not really talked about Nick.'

Fortunately, at this point the tea trolley was brought round and they were able to have much-needed refreshments. 'Right,' said Alice after sipping her tea, 'tell me about this court case.'

'It was the night of LeAnne's party held at her restaurant last February,' explained Zoe and she detailed the main events of the evening.

Alice listened intently. 'Goodness, what a tangled mess.'

Zoe agreed. She went on to describe Maxine's growing concerns about Nick and the possibility of her reporting him.

'My daughter Jo is back supply teaching after retiring. I wonder if she knows about Nick?' Alice paused, took a breath and sat back in her chair.

'There was clearly a lot of tension in the group.'

'There was, and Maxine was very aware of it all. She was in a very dark mood last night,' said Zoe.

'You told Robert she felt threatened by someone in the group,' said Susan.

'She thought someone wanted to harm her?' asked Alice.

'Well, yes, I suppose she did.' Zoe explained about the model of the Grim Reaper. 'I told her it was a joke, but she took it seriously, said it was a warning. Actually, Maxine said that she thought life would be easier for someone if she was dead.'

Alice gave a sharp intake of breath; her keen grey eyes narrowed. 'She said that. Did she give any indication who this might be?'

Zoe shook her head. 'No, but she said that someone in our group has been playing a part for years, that they put on a mask, appear good, kind, respectable. But she'd seen that mask slip. She saw cruelty, coldness. Maxine said it was only for a second and then they quickly replaced the mask.'

Susan gripped the side of her chair. It was a sinister portrait, who on earth could Maxine have been thinking of?

Alice glanced at Susan and then back at Zoe. 'The words seem rather extreme, melodramatic you could say. However, the fact that within hours of saying those words Maxine was dead, well, it means we must take them seriously.'

Zoe blinked. 'Hang on, are you saying you actually believe that this person in the group had something to do with Maxine's death?' She shook her head. 'No, it's not possible, Maxine's death was an accident – she fell.'

16

Alice nodded. 'I'm afraid, after listening to everything you've told me, we have to consider the possibility that Maxine's death was not accidental, that someone else was involved. You said yourself there was a lot of tension in the group.'

'But who in our group would have hurt her,' said Zoe. 'I never seriously believed Maxine was right about someone wanting her dead.'

Zoe sat back. She was very pale now. 'My God, Alice. I came here thinking you'd give me tea and sympathy and I'd go away feeling better.'

'I'm sorry, but it's better to be prepared, my dear.' Alice put her head to one side. 'So, let's try and break this down. We know a killer needs opportunity, means and motive.' Susan smiled as she watched Alice apparently totally unaware of the incongruity of sitting in a comfy nursing home armchair calmly discussing murder.

'So, opportunity?' Alice asked in a very matter-of-fact voice.

Zoe explained how she had been accused of being the last

person to speak to Maxine, but that she was sure someone had been up there after her.

Alice nodded. 'It sounds pretty obvious to me that someone was there.'

Susan let out a long breath, felt herself relax: at last, someone who believed Zoe wasn't the last one up there.

'Who could that have been then?' asked Alice.

Zoe went through each person. LeAnne and Gino were alone. They had no one to confirm their alibis. Nick and Annika said they were together. 'But of course they could be lying, covering for each other,' said Alice.

Zoe grinned. 'You seem to find it very easy to imagine people lying.'

'Oh, people lie all the time. Most of the time it's not important. Our job is finding the ones that matter... Now, means.'

Susan shrugged. 'I guess it's not difficult for any of them to push Maxine over the wall. Everyone was fit and able and Maxine had been drinking.'

'She wasn't drunk, though,' interrupted Zoe.

'No, but maybe less stable,' replied Susan.

'As you say Susan, any of your group, given opportunity, could have done it.' Alice took a breath and continued, 'and so we come to motive.'

Zoe tapped her chin thoughtfully. 'I suppose Gino has the motive of being able to get his hands on Maxine's money. He may have realised she was going to end their marriage, been scared she would leave it all to someone else. You say LeAnne may have been having an affair with him: well, she could have killed Maxine to keep him or it could be to do with her brother's case somehow.'

'And then there's Nick and Annika.'

'LeAnne described Annika as being capable of stabbing

Maxine. She was so jealous of Nick's clear admiration of her,' said Susan.

'LeAnne was exaggerating,' said Zoe.

'But Annika did lie about Maxine's visit,' added Susan.

'Yes. We need to know more about that,' said Alice.

'And then Nick,' continued Zoe. 'On the face of it he seemed to adore Maxine. Although we know Maxine was going to report him to the governors, he had no idea. She asked me not to tell anyone what she intended to do.'

'I wonder what Maxine found in his bedside cabinet?' asked Alice, adding seriously, 'There's a lot to do.'

Zoe grimaced. 'I don't know, Alice, all this talk of motive. Somehow whatever the provocation I can't imagine any of my friends committing premeditated murder. You know, actually sitting down and coldly deciding to kill someone.'

Alice nodded, her face serious. 'Susan and I have discussed this before. After all, planned murder is mercifully rare. Fortunately, most people do not resort to it. But I have decided that there has to be something different about someone who kills, an X factor if you like. That means that for them, given the right circumstances, it is perfectly acceptable to plan to take the life of another human being.'

Zoe shivered. 'Their life would be easier if someone else ceased to exist. It's horrible, Alice.' Zoe suddenly sat up, took a breath and forced a smile. 'Still, we don't need to get too heavy about all this: we're probably wrong.'

Susan caught Alice's eye. Neither smiled, they knew the signs that all was not well here. They were keenly aware of the difficult road ahead. Added to this, for the first time someone very close to Susan was involved.

Alice, as ever, seemed to read her mind. 'This is hard, isn't it?'

Susan nodded. Her lips trembled. She couldn't speak.

'This is much closer to home,' said Alice.

Zoe was oblivious to their concerns though and, still smiling, said, 'But just in case, I could ask around, check people out a bit. Is that a good idea, Alice?'

'You could,' said Alice thoughtfully, 'but you have to be careful. This isn't a game, Zoe. We could be dealing with someone who has taken someone's life, a killer.'

'Don't you think the wisest course of action would be to step back, say nothing, leave this to the police?' asked Susan.

Zoe shook her head. 'No way. If there's any possibility someone hurt my friend, I'm going to find out who. Maxine would have done the same for me.' She patted her mother's hand. 'You can't expect me to do nothing: I am my mother's daughter.'

Susan realised that if she argued any more, she would only make Zoe more determined to act. So, she moved the conversation on. 'I'll speak to Robert again, see if he has any inside news about how the case is going from the police point of view.'

Zoe smiled. 'Good, a plan of action. Now, I'll take the cups back over to the trolley before we go.'

When Zoe was out of earshot, Alice turned to Susan. She spoke quietly but firmly. 'I'm always here if you need me. You know that.'

Alice had never said anything like this before.

'Like I said, it's close to home,' said Alice.

'I hope we're wrong. I so hope it's not—'

'You hope it's not murder? So, do I. We both know that as wicked and ugly the act itself is, the repercussions can be devastating. Zoe has no idea—'

'No. I hope she doesn't have to find out.'

They held each other's gaze again. Neither spoke.

Zoe returned. 'Right, Mum. We'd better get going. It's been really helpful to talk, Alice.'

Alice sat back and calmly stroked Princess, clearly feeling enough had been said for now.

In the car, Zoe discovered everyone was back at the castle, and so Susan dropped her there and returned home.

* * *

Later that evening, Zoe sat with the others in the apartment. It was never going to be an easy time. They put on the television, but no one could settle.

'Look, it's impossible to act as if nothing has happened,' said Zoe. 'How about we go over to the Privy Garden? It's somewhere Maxine loved. We could sit there quietly and just have a moment to remember her.'

'That's a lovely idea,' said Nick. 'It's been so hectic. No one has had time to take anything in.'

Everyone agreed they would like to go.

They put their coats on and got ready to leave.

'As Maxine would have said, don't forget your torches,' said Zoe.

Saying this reminded her of Maxine's torch and the missing batteries. As the others put on their coats, she went and checked the box Maxine had brought the torches in. It was empty. She frowned: surely there should be a spare?

Zoe noticed that although they had put their coats on, no one was actually walking to the door, as if they were afraid to go out.

'We need to do this,' she said firmly. 'Let's go.'

As they walked, the crunching of the gravel beneath their feet seemed to bounce off the stone walls. There were no fairy lights dotted around this evening, no crowd of excited visitors. They were alone.

In the garden they found a bench to sit on. It was very peaceful. The trickle of the water in the fountain was soothing. No one spoke: they all needed silence.

* * *

Back at home, Susan was up in her bedroom, finding a jumper for her last walk that evening with the dogs. As she left the room, she glanced over at where LeAnne was staying. The door had been left open. On the bed, Susan saw a line of stuffed toys, and beanies on her pillow. She remembered the soft toys on the beds at the apartment.

Susan went out for a short walk around the village. She always enjoyed these late-night walks. Tonight she walked down to the church and looked up at the tower. It didn't look like a murder scene, but then she guessed neither would the castle in a few weeks. And yet Susan was a firm believer that places somehow held onto their past, the memories would be locked there in the stonework, never completely erased.

She walked quickly back down the road to the park, and then returned home.

Susan was about to go upstairs when she heard LeAnne and Zoe return.

'Hi,' she said. 'Shall I put the kettle on?'

Susan made drinks, the dogs getting out of their beds in the hope of treats and fuss.

'It must have been a difficult evening,' said Susan.

'It was. We had a takeaway. No one could cook. It was miserable. We did go over and sit together in the Privy Garden though.'

'That was a good thing to do. Tell me about it.'

'Well, I thought it would be good to go and remember Maxine. It had been such a hectic day. It was pretty emotional. Oh, before we left I did notice that there was no spare torch. There should have been, shouldn't there?'

Susan nodded. 'Yes. Maxine brought eight. There were six of you. She gave one to me. That meant there was one left. That's odd.'

'Nick was pretty out of it,' said LeAnne. 'I'm sure he's on something.'

Zoe shook her head. 'Of course he isn't.'

'I'm probably a lot more familiar with people taking drugs, and I'm telling you: he's taking something like ketamine, or even cocaine.'

Zoe pursed her lips. 'My life has not been completely sheltered, you know. If Nick has a problem with anything, I reckon it's alcohol.' She screwed up her eyes. 'Maybe you want him to be on drugs so that you can prove he has access to them and could have planted cocaine on Wesley.'

LeAnne went very red. 'That's rubbish.'

'Is it?' said Zoe. 'You need to be careful. I know how it feels to be falsely accused. I wish to God Gino would keep his nasty insinuations to himself. It's awful.'

'He's only saying what he saw. He saw an argument and then he heard all that about a secret. You can't blame him for feeling put out that you and Maxine had been keeping secrets from him. I think he has a right to know what they were.'

Zoe slammed down her mug. 'I made a promise. I don't intend to get bullied into revealing that. For God's sake. Just leave it alone, LeAnne. I'm going upstairs to phone my wife.'

She stormed off. LeAnne shrugged. 'I can't say anything

right tonight, can I? Better go to bed as well. Hell of a day. G'night, Susan.'

Susan sat on the sofa. The dogs jumped up to join her. Feeling the warmth of their bodies and stroking their soft velvet ears gave her a sense of comfort she badly needed that evening.

What if Alice was right? What if one of these friends of Zoe's was a killer? She thought about LeAnne, her name possibly associated with violence: she would be sleeping there tonight!

Susan shuddered and reminded herself they were only on the very edge of suspecting something sinister. It was literally only a matter of hours since Maxine's body had been found.

Her thoughts turned to Maxine, the full enormity of what had happened starting to sink in. Maxine was dead. She had fallen from the battlements in that beautiful old castle, the place of so many wonderful fairytales but also of imprisonment and death.

Susan thought about Maxine's father: how would he ever be able to cope with the loss of his talented, beautiful daughter?

And putting aside any questions about how the accident had occurred, Zoe was having to cope with the shock of losing her friend. Everything about the death was foreign to her: the involvement of police, questions to be answered. It would be helpful if Gino would stop throwing around accusations. It was so hurtful. They said anger was part of grieving, but his reaction did seem extreme. Or was it? Maybe when we lose someone we love, we all look for someone to blame?

Susan sighed. It was getting late: time for bed. She settled down the dogs and went upstairs. As she changed, she could hear Zoe in the next room talking on the phone to Fay. Although the old cottage walls were thick, this was a wall that had been added to divide a larger room, and it was not made of the solid materials that had been used to build the rest of the house. She could make out the odd word but tried not to listen.

By the time she got into bed, though, Zoe's voice was much louder. The hard laugh rang very loud and the words that followed were very clear.

'Don't worry. It will be OK. Accidents happen. I'll be fine.'

It was all so loud and over-cheery, and the words didn't ring true. Why was Zoe minimising everything that had happened today? Surely if there was anyone, she could talk to it would be Fay?

Soon afterwards, she heard a loud, confident goodbye, and the call ended.

Susan switched her light off, tried to sleep, but in the darkness her thoughts seemed to run wild.

Her mind summoned up horrific pictures of Maxine lying on the stone floor, the blood around her head, Gino's screams of grief. And in the middle of it, Zoe, at times lost and afraid, at others prickly and evasive.

Susan turned over in bed. She tried to distract herself and managed finally to drop off. However, she fell into a dark, nightmarish world of ghouls, black-cloaked, faceless spirits, and at one point she was standing in the garden at the castle watching Zoe fall, screaming, from the battlements.

Susan woke sweating and shaking. She turned on her light. She had to break this cycle. She got out of bed, crept out of her room and along the landing, but then she heard terrible heartrending muffled cries from Zoe's room.

Susan knew that Zoe was crying into her pillow like she'd done when she was a little girl. Susan could feel tears falling down her own cheeks. Nothing destroys a mother like the tears of her child, whatever their age. Zoe was obviously going to be distressed at the events of the day, the shock of losing her friend, of finding her body. But was there more? Why hadn't Zoe been able to talk to Fay?

She desperately wanted to go into Zoe's room and hug her, tell her everything would be better, but Zoe wasn't a little girl. She was a grown woman. Susan went to the bathroom and returned to bed.

She felt the heaviness of anxiety, layer upon layer with nowhere to go. For a moment she even directed the anger at her ex, Steve, off sailing around the Mediterranean, abandoning Zoe. He'd always been able to calm Zoe in a way Susan could not. The two of them had an invisible thread of understanding, but what was the use of that now?

No, he was far away and the responsibility of supporting Zoe came down to her, and her alone.

17

The light early the next morning was extraordinary: light peach horizon, white, blue-grey sky. The underbelly of the seagulls screeching above reflected that gentle creamy light, the black silhouettes of the rooks flew gracefully across the sky.

Susan walked up the central path, high up on the downs. The views here were amazing: the Solent, Tennyson Down, the cliffs. They lifted her heart. Despite the lack of sleep, the sight of a new day gave her hope.

Yesterday had been a black day. How could it have been anything else when it began with the discovery of the dead body of someone who had been such a close friend of her daughter's?

The dogs ran ahead, as always. They were full of optimism. Did dogs wake each day thinking that this could be the best day ever?

She reached the top of the downs and looked towards Tennyson Down. There was a sparkle on the sea from the weak sun. The freshly laundered chalky white cliffs shone.

Susan returned to the car and made, for her, a big decision: it would be pancakes for breakfast. They had always been Zoe's favourite as a little girl. Maybe they would be a tiny consolation in the bleakness.

On her way back, she stopped off at the shop for eggs and lemons.

Tracy was fortunately tied up with a customer complaining their newspaper had been late the day before, and Susan was able to dash in and out.

Zoe came down, pale. Clearly, she had not slept well.

'I thought I'd make pancakes for breakfast this morning,' said Susan.

'Good grief, Mum, you're cooking. Is something up?'

Susan smiled. 'I thought you needed a treat.'

'Thank you.'

Susan set about making the batter. She didn't need a recipe. It was surprising how it came back to her. She heard LeAnne on the stairs, and she too seemed very subdued; no mention of the row the night before.

The first pancake Susan put aside on a plate for herself, as it was a bit of a disaster. The rest, though, worked well.

'These are good, Mum; you always could cook.'

'Thanks,' she replied but her sarcastic tone was wasted on Zoe.

'There's no reason you should be living on ready meals just because you are cooking for one,' said Zoe.

'I haven't been having such easy meals because I'm bereft. I've been giving myself a holiday. After forty years of cooking and baking most days of the year, I thought I deserved a break.'

'Fair enough,' said Zoe, a hint of a smile on her face.

'I cook when I feel like it now.'

Zoe's smile grew. 'And you wonder where I get my fighting spirit from. Jamari is the same, you know. I see her little fists tighten when I suggest she try broccoli again and I know the battle has begun.'

'I haven't asked you much about your little girl,' said LeAnne. 'You must have photos on your phone.'

Zoe went to find her phone and started scrolling though photos of Jamari, some of which were new to Susan as well.

Breakfast passed quietly. They chatted about Jamari, and LeAnne talked about her dream of having children.

'I definitely want them. Mum would love grandchildren.'

'You will know when you meet the right person,' said Susan as she watched LeAnne carefully.

'Sometimes the right person is tied up somewhere else. They may not be in a position to ride off into the sunset. Still, nothing worth having is easy. I've learned you have to fight your own corner. It's survival of the fittest.'

Susan listened intently. LeAnne could be indicating an affair with Gino and, if she was, that talk of fighting her corner had to be significant.

'Tell me more about your restaurant. I guess it's mainly fish?' enquired Zoe.

Susan was surprised. She had expected Zoe to ask more questions and was surprised when she changed the subject.

'Sustainable fish, yes,' said LeAnne. 'I'd like a chain of restaurants. It could be done. The menu comprises a few regular dishes but the emphasis will be on meals based on that day's catch. We've shown it can work if you get the backing. It's the way we should go forward with fish cookery: get people away from their obsession with cod and chips.'

'I can see it happening in the restaurants. Whether it catches on in fish and chip shops is another matter.'

'People will have no option soon. I've been getting some great ideas from Gino. The Italians are so brilliant with fish. He's given me his mother's recipes for pasta with shellfish, sardines and cuttlefish.'

Susan grabbed her chance at the reintroduction of Gino's name. 'He was talking about the joy of eating long meals outside. Do you think he'll return to Italy now?'

LeAnne picked up a slice of lemon, carefully squeezed it over her pancake. 'I don't know what his plans are.'

Finally, Zoe seemed to pick up where Susan was going. 'You get on very well with Gino. You were very good at looking after him yesterday. You're closer than I realised.'

LeAnne shrugged. 'We got chatting at my party in February. He was friendly, met the family. Over the summer he enjoyed coming to the restaurant and eating out on the patio on the sunny days. He was so relaxed. As much as he loved Maxine, he found her quite controlling. She didn't let him have any autonomy with his money. She was always checking his accounts.'

'It sounded to me like she had to. He'd have got them in debt otherwise.'

'That's her side of it. Maybe she didn't want him to be more successful than her.'

'That's ridiculous. She simply didn't want to end up in debt. I can understand that.'

'You have no idea just how controlling she was. You know, she'd go through his pockets and wallet, asked him about the cash. That's not on. He said she was always interfering, sneakily checking his phone and laptop and always complained if he came in smelling of smoke—'

'But you know why she had a thing about people smoking,' interrupted Zoe.

LeAnne shook her head.

'It's how she lost her mum while we were at school. She was devastated.'

'I knew her mum died but she didn't say much.'

'She kept a lot to herself.'

'Funny, I never gave it much thought,' said LeAnne, 'which is awful really. At that age you are so taken up with your own world. I look back and think how close we all were, but I missed all that. Anyway, it doesn't really excuse her being so controlling of Gino. He works so hard and is determined to make money independent of family. I admire that, but I don't think Maxine understood at all.'

Susan saw the passion burning in LeAnne's eyes. There was little doubt in her mind now that there were strong feelings, at least on LeAnne's side.

At that point, Zoe took the conversation in a different direction. 'Maxine admired the way you built your business—'

'Initially, yes, but a restaurant like mine needs support long term. She didn't get that. She always had money.'

'But she had it hard in other ways. She had to cope with the loss of her mother when she was so young and while she was trying to sit exams. It was tough.'

'I realise that, but she doesn't understand what it's like to struggle financially.'

'Plenty of her client base were from disadvantaged backgrounds.'

LeAnne thumped her spoon in the bowl. 'That's not the same as living it. Obviously, Annika's parents were obsessed with her singing. But you all had parents who understood about you wanting to do music and who had the money to pay for instruments and lessons. You all learned a few instruments while I had to choose only one. My parents paid for my drum kit in instalments. Mrs Strong, our music teacher, was so kind. She gave me a load of music free, and some really decent drumsticks that her son had used.'

'I'm sorry,' said Zoe quietly. 'I didn't realise what you went through either. I was lucky: you're right. I took it for granted.'

LeAnne picked up her spoon and went back to eating her breakfast. 'Thanks. I appreciate you saying that. Mrs Strong was a one-off, wasn't she? Really backed us as a band, letting us use the music room to practise, giving us slots in concerts even when we were right at the beginning. The band kept me out of a lot of trouble.'

Zoe looked up. 'Oh. Do you think Mrs Strong knows what has happened to Maxine?'

'I would think so, but we should get in touch, make sure.'

'I could speak to her if you like,' said Susan. 'I was teaching at a different high school. But we got on well at Zoe's parents' evenings. I liked her a lot.'

'That would be great, Mum. Thanks.'

They began to clear away the breakfast dishes, but as they did, they became aware of the rumble of a large van coming up the close.

Susan looked out the window and saw removals signage on the side of the vehicle. 'That must be my new neighbour arriving.'

Zoe joined her. 'How exciting. You should go and say hi, Mum.'

'Do you think so? I don't want them to think I'm some nosy neighbour who will always be interfering.'

'They won't. It's friendly, Mum. Go and say hello. They might be glad of a cuppa.'

Reluctantly, Susan put her shoes on and opened the front door.

It was easy to pick out the new neighbour from the removal

men. He was standing slightly apart, with a concerned look on his face, an air of someone who felt he should be helping but was not too sure what to do.

Someone called from inside the house. 'Dad, you forgot to get milk.'

As he turned, he caught sight of Susan, and he gave a nervous half smile.

She walked over to greet him. 'Hi, I'm Susan. I'm guessing you're my new neighbour?'

'I am.' His face relaxed into a warm smile that reached his brown eyes. He was quite short, with scruffy black hair and glasses. She guessed about fifty. He was wrapped in a thick waterproof and brown cords.

'My name is Harri. It's very nice to meet you.' He spoke with great sincerity, lending the words a gravitas not usually associated with a casual hello.

'How is it all going?' she asked.

He blinked through clear-rimmed glasses. 'Chaotic. We've had so many problems completing on our old house. It's been a nightmare. I've been commuting from Cardiff to Southampton.'

'Oh, no. That's a long way.'

'One train but, yes, a long way.' He looked around. 'It's good to finally be able to make a fresh start.'

Susan noticed hurt in his voice and wondered what had happened to cause it.

Suddenly she heard barking, a familiar sound that always brought a smile to her face.

18

Susan soon saw that the sound she heard coming from her new neighbour's house was indeed the one she thought.

For at that moment a beautiful orange roan dog came racing out of the house next door. Taking one look at Susan, he bounded over to say hello.

She was fussing him when a young woman in her early twenties with short black hair streaked with blue, came out of the house, ran over and attached a lead to his collar.

'Oh, God. Sorry. Luca, come here,' she called to the dog, who ignored her. 'He loves everyone.'

'That's fine. I have two of my own. Lovely to meet you, Luca.'

'This is my daughter Jasmine,' said Harri smiling warmly. 'I'm relieved you like dogs. I'm afraid Luca is very lively.'

'Wait till you see mine,' said Susan with a smile.

'Luca's two now,' said Jasmine, 'but still very much a puppy.'

Susan grinned. 'I'm Susan. It's good to meet you. I was going to ask if you'd all like a drink?'

'Thank you, that would be great. We all drink coffee. Dad

and I take milk. The two removal men take milk, two sugars each.'

'Right, I shall get on with that,' said Susan and returned to the house.

'Did I hear a dog barking? What are they like?' asked Zoe.

'You did hear a dog.' Susan looked down at Libs and Rocco, tails wagging and definitely picking up on the excitement. 'You have a new friend,' Susan said to them. 'He's called Luca and he's a cocker spaniel.'

'That's brilliant,' said Zoe, 'and what about the human?'

'Two, actually. A man, I guess in his fifties, called Harri and his daughter, Jasmine.'

'How exciting. I'm so pleased there will be people next door.'

'I've promised them drinks so I'd better get on.' Susan went back out with a tray of coffee, with sugar and spoons at the side and a packet of biscuits.

Harri came over and took the tray. 'That is so kind. Many thanks.'

Jasmine struggled to take a cup of coffee, as she was holding Luca's lead.

'Can I help?' asked Susan.

Jasmine smiled, gratefully handing Luca's lead to Susan. 'Oh, do you mind? I just need to keep him on the lead until we can shut the front door.'

'Of course not.'

At that point Zoe came out with Libs and Rocco. The dogs tugged at their leads and were soon sniffing and greeting each other in a friendly way.

'This is my daughter Zoe and my dogs, Rocco and Libs,' said Susan.

'Excellent,' said Jasmine. 'They're going to get on just fine. They'll be able to bark to each other over the fence. Don't worry, though. Luca will be coming to work with me most days, so he shouldn't be too much of a bother.'

'I don't mind at all.'

'Jasmine will be starting work in the vet's practice in the village,' explained Harri.

'How exciting,' said Susan. 'My dogs are signed up there. It's great to have a surgery here.'

'I'm not a vet,' said Jasmine. 'I'll be working as a veterinary nurse. I had a post back in Cardiff, but then Dad got the job over this way and, well, I decided it was time to move in with him.' She paused, glanced at her father. 'It's complicated but, anyway, I saw they were opening the practice here. I was lucky they kept the job open for me after all the delays.'

One of the removal men, holding a large box, shouted over, 'Is this up or down?'

'That looks like more books,' said Jasmine. 'I'd better go and help.'

'Would you like me to take Luca in?' offered Susan. 'I've a few minutes before I need to go out.'

'That's brilliant. Thank you. Just bring him back when you need to.' She turned to her father. 'Dad, we need to get those drinks to the men before they go cold.'

Harri looked down at the tray as if surprised it was still in his hands. 'Oh, yes. I'm so sorry,' he said, and walked over to the van.

Jasmine rolled her eyes but laughed affectionately. 'God knows how I'm going to learn to live with him.'

'We'll leave you to it,' said Susan, and Luca happily trotted into the house with her.

She took him through to the back garden and let him off the lead with Libs and Rocco. The dogs ran madly around.

Feeling the cold, Susan went back in, grabbed her old parka and returned to watch the dogs.

Above, she heard the familiar high pitched 'kee-yaa' call of a buzzard and, looking up, saw two frantic crows trying to chase it off.

The bird feeders were practically empty, and a robin was protesting noisily from the fence.

'OK, I'll get some more mealworms and seed, but you lot are costing me a fortune,' she said and went into the house to find a packet.

Zoe and LeAnne were in the kitchen, clearing the table and stacking the dishwasher.

'Thanks,' she said.

'They're all getting on well,' said Zoe, gesturing to where the dogs were playing in the garden.

'Yes, it's a good chance for them to get to know each other.'

Susan filled the feeders and, without waiting for her to retreat into the house, the robin and two bluetits began busily pecking at the food. Some seed fell to the ground, no doubt to be cleared up soon by the pigeons or even one of the odd stray pheasants which made their way into her garden.

It wasn't long before Susan saw Jasmine looking over the fence. 'You've made yourself at home, Luca,' she called over.

'He's lovely. I'm sure he'll enjoy going to work with you. He's very sociable.'

'Yes, I took him to my interview. It was a bit of a deal breaker, whether I could take him in or not. Even though we are very close to the surgery, I wouldn't want to leave him all day. Dad's no help with the hours he works.' Susan was curious as to what Harri did but, before she could ask, Jasmine said, 'I'll come round and get Luca, I've got lots to do upstairs. I can keep him up with me.'

There was soon a knock at the front door. Luca ran to Jasmine and they left.

'Well, they seem friendly enough,' said Zoe. 'Was there a partner or wife there?'

'I think it was just Harri and his daughter. Tracy talked about a single man. Maybe he's divorced or something.'

'What does he do?'

'No idea. I've no doubt Tracy will wheedle that out of him very soon. Right, now, I think I've time to ring the music teacher before we go. Can you give me the phone number?'

Susan went to her bedroom to make the call. The teacher had heard about Maxine and was naturally very upset. She was glad to get a few more details from Susan. She also asked her to pass on the message that she quite understood if anyone didn't want to take part on Saturday night. Susan assured her that as far as she knew, everyone would be there.

They were just putting their coats on to go down to the beach when Zoe received a text from Nick. She raised one hand to her mouth, Susan thought she was going to be sick.

'What's up?' she asked.

'We've got to go back to the castle. The police are coming to talk to us all.'

'OK. Maybe they're just checking up on everyone.' Susan tried to sound casual but was concerned.

'No. They've found something.'

Susan felt her stomach clench with anxiety. 'I see. So, what time are they coming?'

'In about half an hour.'

'I'll drive you both over there now. The dogs can stay here. They've had a good walk this morning.'

Despite the stress, the drive was much pleasanter than it had been the day before. On the horizon the sky was tinted with soft salmon and pale lemon from the early sunrise. Above, the light blue accentuated the white clouds streaking across its surface.

Susan was starting to calm down and even managed to half convince herself of the routine nature of this visit by the police.

LeAnne, who was sitting in the passenger seat beside her, broke the spell.

'Bloody police, why can't they just leave well alone? It's obviously an accident. They're just layering on the stress.'

'They have to be sure—' said Zoe, from the back of the car.

'They never tried very hard with my Wesley, did they?'

Susan wondered why LeAnne couldn't see that it was only natural that the police would commit more resources to a case of sudden unexplained death, but was sure if she pointed this out it would only enrage LeAnne further. And so she let LeAnne continue uninterrupted.

'The police saw his surname and assumed Wesley was guilty. It never even crossed their minds that Nick could have set him up. Well, it's up to me then. I will get to the truth.'

Zoe sighed. 'I'm sorry, LeAnne, but I don't see what more you can do. You only have Wesley's word against Nick's, and he's adamant he never planted any drugs, never drove at Wesley. That's it.'

'But I can force Nick's hand, make it so he has no option but to confess.'

'How on earth will you do that?'

'Ah, I have plans for this evening.'

Susan inwardly groaned; what was LeAnne planning? Surely the group had enough to cope with.

Zoe echoed her thoughts. 'Not more drama. We've all had enough.'

'I'm sorry. I'm not letting this go. Anyway, you might even find it fun.'

'What have you planned?'

'You'll have to wait and see.' Susan glanced at LeAnne, saw her give a cold smile. 'This is going to upset Annika: her hero brought down. Just when she thought she was sitting pretty.'

'What do you mean?' asked Zoe.

'She's not exactly been mourning the loss of Maxine, has she? Haven't you noticed? I heard her laughing yesterday when we went for a walk. She was chatting away to Nick looking very cosy.'

'I think she's just trying to look after Nick,' said Zoe.

'That's her problem. Her life is totally centred around him now. It's an obsession. I wasn't joking when I said that I saw murder in her eyes when he was all over Maxine.'

'You're exaggerating.'

'Am I? Annika will feel a lot more secure with Maxine off the radar. In fact, I could just see her giving Maxine a gentle push.'

Susan could hear in her voice that LeAnne was serious. It was the second time she'd brought this up: did she really believe Annika was that jealous of Maxine? Susan wasn't convinced. Annika had appeared upset that evening, but she wouldn't have described her as looking murderous.

LeAnne twisted round to look at Zoe. 'Look, if Gino can throw accusations around about you, aren't you glad I'm looking elsewhere?'

'Of course,' said Zoe, 'but don't you think it's odd the way Gino is throwing accusations around about me? I reckon he may be trying to distract the police from himself.'

It dawned on Susan that LeAnne could be making accusations against Annika for the same reason, to distract the police from Gino. LeAnne must realise that, of them all, Gino had the strongest motive for killing Maxine. Maybe she was trying to protect him.

She could see LeAnne's hands firmly clasped together, see that she was breathing fast. 'Are you saying you think Gino killed Maxine?' Her voice held threat as well as anger.

Zoe continued undaunted. 'Maxine told me she was ending her marriage. She didn't trust Gino with money. Maybe she'd written a will leaving her money elsewhere – that's a motive, surely.'

Susan heard LeAnne give a sharp, quick intake of breath. Her voice shook as she spoke. 'Maxine would never have ended her marriage.'

'Oh, she would have. I'm sure of it.'

LeAnne unclasped her hands. She was now frantically tapping her fingernails on her lap. She was staring out of the front window now, and talking more to herself than to them. 'But no – no – that's not possible,' she stammered. 'And Gino knew?'

They'd arrived at the castle. Susan parked, but LeAnne sat very still, as if frozen on her seat.

19

'We're at the castle,' Susan said to LeAnne, who had still not undone her seatbelt.

'What?' LeAnne turned to Susan and blinked, as if coming to from a dream. 'Of course, sorry.'

They walked to the gate. Zoe, who still had the key Maxine had given her, unlocked the padlock. Susan wasn't sure if she was included in the invitation from the police but her concern for Zoe meant she was going to hang about until they asked her to leave.

The others were sitting around in the dining room of the accommodation. Nick and Gino looked dishevelled and tired. Annika was making drinks.

The police arrived almost immediately. It was DS Kent with another officer.

'Thank you so much for being here,' she began. 'I wanted to let you know where we have got to. Obviously, it's still very early days. However, there are a few things you should know.'

She paused. Everyone was on edge.

'We have some postmortem results which we requested were done urgently.'

'Why the urgency?' asked Gino. 'Is something wrong?'

'A case of sudden, unexplained death is always going to take priority,' said DS Kent, choosing her words carefully. 'Firstly, we believe Maxine died as a result of injuries sustained falling from the battlements. There were superficial wounds, scratches on the front of her legs from the wall over which she fell. The fatal wound was actually caused as she fell.'

'As she fell?' queried Nick.

'Yes, there's a metal support across the ruin. We now know the gash on her forehead was caused by a fatal blow against that as she fell. Of course, falling onto concrete may well have proved fatal as well, but the cause of death was the blow to the head.'

'So, she was dead before she landed?' asked Gino.

'She was certainly extremely badly injured.'

'Does this mean you are sure her death was an accident?' asked Zoe.

'No. We can't be sure of anything at this point. Maxine had been drinking. Toxicology supports that. I wonder if you could tell me, did Maxine have a history of abusing alcohol?'

'No,' said Zoe. 'One of the reasons I was concerned was that she didn't normally drink like that.'

'You're not quite right there, Zoe,' interrupted Gino. 'Maxine had been drinking a lot more at home. I had spoken to her about it.'

'Were you concerned she might have a problem?' asked DS Kent.

'Maxine had a very stressful job. She had problems sleeping. Yes, I was concerned about her. This recklessness of going up to the battlements while drinking: the rest of you see this as totally out of character. But that is because you were out of touch with who the real Maxine was. She was living close to the edge.'

DS Kent was sitting, head to one side. When she spoke, her voice was serious.

'You have not shared this with us before.'

Gino shrugged, looked down. 'She was private, and I don't want to muddy her name. Maxine was an exceptional person.'

'We have gathered that,' said DS Kent gently, 'but it is important to have a complete picture of Maxine. She had an extremely stressful job. Anyone would need to find ways of coping with that. If she chose alcohol that may not have been the best choice, but it was understandable. Thank you for sharing that.'

She turned to Zoe. 'When describing the conversation you had with Maxine, you gave us a picture of someone struggling to cope. She sounded hypervigilant, paranoid.'

'That's not what I was trying to say,' said Zoe, sounding frustrated. 'I don't agree with Gino. I don't think Maxine was unable to cope with the pressure of her job. She truly believed someone had come away this week planning to hurt her, and I agree.'

'It is possible to take what Maxine said literally. However, if we look at the person speaking, there is another picture. Someone who believed it was too hard to carry on—'

'If you're suggesting she died by suicide, you're completely wrong,' said Zoe.

'We have to explore every possibility.' DS Kent took a breath, as if drawing a line under that part of the conversation.

'Now, let's return to the investigation so far. We have a much clearer idea of a time of death for Maxine.' She glanced over at Susan. 'There was of course the evidence of the watch.'

'What was that?' asked Gino.

'Maxine's watch appeared to have been smashed at the time of her fall and read ten past twelve.'

'I've seen that on TV. It gives you a precise time of death,' said Nick.

'It can do,' said DS Kent. 'But of course, the watch may be inaccurate. The hands can be moved. It was an old-fashioned analogue watch.'

'It was a Gucci watch, a wedding present from me,' said Gino.

'Ah, was it? Yes. Well, the pathologist has a far more scientific measure for estimating time of death.'

'Like rigor mortis?' asked Nick.

'Exactly, but there is also body temperature, liver mortis, stomach contents, corneal cloudiness, and many more indicators to use.'

'So, do you know what time she died?' asked LeAnne impatiently.

'We feel the time of the watch could well be pretty accurate. The closest we can get to a time is between quarter to twelve and twenty past twelve. The watch has been examined. Before the glass was smashed by the fall, it would appear to have been in good working order.'

'It was the correct time when I was with her,' interrupted Zoe.

'I know she always kept it to time,' said Gino.

'All I can say is that ten past twelve is a viable time of death. Now, as I said, we will need to look at a few things more carefully, and that includes what you were all doing at the time Maxine died.'

Suddenly an idea came to Susan. 'Hang on,' she blurted out.

DS Kent raised an eyebrow. 'Sorry, Susan?'

'It's just we've been assuming this group were the only ones in the castle and, yes, I saw all the people who came to the ghost talk checked off, and the final staff left at the same time as me, the gate was securely locked. But I've just realised the staff have keys, maybe one of them came back.'

DS Kent nodded. 'You're quite right, Susan, and we did think of that. Apart from the two sets of keys given to the people staying in the apartment, there are only three more sets and we tracked them down. To start with, we are as sure as we can be that none of the key holders knew Maxine or had any kind of motive to kill her. We did check up on their movements during the time we estimate she died. It was of course very late. One person was watching TV in bed with their partner, one playing a video game online, and the third was actually on a phone call to a relative abroad. They all keep the keys securely.'

After such a long speech, DS Kent paused to take a breath but then gave Susan a dry smile, adding, 'We are absolutely certain their keys were not used by them or any other person to gain entry to the castle that night.'

Susan felt her face burning but, for all that, she was glad she'd asked.

DS Kent turned back to the group, 'So, as I say, it would be very helpful if you could remind me exactly where you all were around the time we now know Maxine died.'

The words slipped out easily, but Susan knew only too well that the implications were huge. 'If we are suspects,' said LeAnne, appearing to be the first to recover, 'we should have solicitors here.'

'This is not a formal interview. No one is being arrested. I am simply asking you to help us with our inquiries. Any information you can give as to where you were or what you saw during that half hour would be extremely useful.'

Before anyone could respond, DS Kent turned to Zoe. 'Now you at least admit to being up on the battlements with Maxine, so let's start with you.'

Susan saw her daughter take in a deep breath, her face red.

'You told us you were up there from eleven thirty-five until eleven fifty-five according to your smart watch.'

'That's right.'

'You left her just before twelve, and you say she was waiting to meet someone else.' DS Kent glanced around. 'Has anyone remembered this arrangement yet?'

There was no reply.

'So, Zoe, you left Maxine and you met Gino on the way down.'

'That's right, and I met Nick coming out of the Privy Garden. He said he'd heard from Annika and was going to meet her. I then left through the wooden gates and waited for LeAnne by the gift shop until twenty past twelve.'

'Your smart watch is certainly coming into its own,' said DS Kent, one eyebrow raised. 'I don't think I've ever had a witness be so precise about timings before. Well, unless they have been preparing an alibi.'

Susan wasn't sure if the officer was implying that she didn't believe Zoe or that she was genuinely impressed at the accuracy of the times being given.

DS Kent continued. 'While you were waiting, you saw a light on the battlements and heard a voice, but you can't identify when this was.'

'I don't know exactly what time that was,' said Zoe, giving DS Kent a straight look. 'I was starting to get cold and a bit fed up waiting for LeAnne. I guess it was about ten minutes after I left Maxine.'

'Right, and then LeAnne joined you at twelve twenty and you took a taxi at twelve twenty-five to your mother's house. That has been verified. Right, now Gino. You left the apartment, and went to the keep. You met Zoe just before twelve, and say you witnessed an argument before that. When did you leave the keep and how long had you been close to where Maxine and Zoe were?'

Gino shrugged, sending a cynical smile in Zoe's direction. 'We don't all have smart watches. I've no idea, to be honest. I left the keep to go and speak to Maxine, just to have a chat. We'd not seen much of each other since I'd arrived. I saw the struggle and heard the row and was totally thrown. That's why, after I met Zoe, I went back to the keep.'

'But at some time, you decided to leave the castle. What time was that and why?'

'I know the time because I saw the clock in the apartment. It was about twenty past twelve. There was no one in the flat when I went in. I picked up the spare key. I walked over to the gate and unlocked it. I simply wanted to get out and walk about. That was all. I came out, locked the gate, saw Zoe and LeAnne waiting, and went for a walk.'

'You went down the hill to a van?'

'No way.'

'You did,' said Zoe. 'I saw you, from the taxi. We drove down the road and I saw Gino in a van parked further down. He was talking to someone. I couldn't see their face, but I clearly saw it was him.'

LeAnne shook her head and interrupted. 'No, I disagreed with you at the time. I definitely said that the person wasn't Gino.'

'It would have been very dark,' said DS Kent. 'Can you describe the van?'

'There was writing on the side, like some kind of business lettering.' Zoe screwed up her eyes. 'Orange writing... I think there was an A and a drawing of a castle and a lion. Sorry, that's it.'

'OK. Well, we can ask around. Gino, are you sure you didn't meet somebody?'

'Absolutely positive,' said Gino. 'I went down the hill and then right at the little traffic light to the path that runs parallel to the outside of the castle. I walked for a while, returned at about one, unlocked the gate, locked it behind me and returned to the apartment.'

'OK. One thing I have been wondering about, Gino. You say you saw a struggle between your wife and Zoe. Whatever you felt was between them, why not go to your wife's aid?'

He blinked, fiddled with his wedding ring. 'I told you. I saw them separate.'

'But surely you were concerned things had become very heated?'

'They had calmed down quickly and then they moved on to talking about some secret of Maxine's that only they knew about. I couldn't interrupt.'

DS Kent sat up. 'What do you mean by a secret?'

Gino scowled. 'I've no idea. They didn't say what it was. Maxine was anxious that Zoe should keep it to herself, whatever it was. I've asked Zoe about it since, but she still won't tell me what it was. Maybe she'll tell you.'

DS Kent looked directly at Zoe, clearly waiting for an answer. Susan held her breath. Zoe had to reveal the secret now: she had no option.

But then Susan saw Zoe shake her head. 'I'm sorry. Maxine told me that in confidence. I have no intention of ever breaking that.'

'We need to know everything, Zoe,' said DS Kent, her voice tense.

'I can't. I'm sorry. I can't break my promise.'

DS Kent coughed. 'We will need to talk about this another

time. Now, LeAnne, you say you were in the apartment the whole time until you went to meet Zoe at twelve twenty?'

LeAnne shifted in her seat, glanced over at Annika. 'I was, yes. I left here just before twenty past twelve and went straight to meet Zoe.'

DS Kent sighed and consulted her notebook. 'Nick, you went out with Zoe and then went alone to the Privy Garden?'

'Yes. I sat there for quite some time on my own. It was a lovely night, and very peaceful in there. Annika rang me, saying she would like to come out and have a walk, so I got up and left. That's when I met Zoe. We exchanged a few words and then, um, I went over to the bowling green and waited for Annika.'

'It's no distance to walk between the garden and the bowling green, so you two met a few minutes after twelve?'

'I think so,' said Nick.

'Um, it was a little later,' said Annika, quietly.

'Where were you then?' asked DS Kent.

'I left the apartment at midnight after speaking to Nick. Then I had a call from Dad. He's not been well. I stood by the apartment chatting and then went to the entrance to the stable courtyard – I thought it was odd Nick wasn't there, but I waited.' She gave Nick an apologetic smile. 'I waited a few minutes, then I remembered we'd said we'd meet at the bowling green, and so I came and waited for you there.'

'What time was this then?'

'I've no idea. About ten past twelve, maybe? Maybe a little after.'

'You say you waited for Nick. So, he wasn't there when you arrived.'

Annika blinked quickly, glanced at Nick and then back at the officer. 'Sorry. I meant to say I went to the bowling green and Nick was there waiting for me.'

DS Kent tutted.

'The point is we were on the bowling green together most of the time,' said Nick. There was a slight defiance in his voice and from the raised eyebrow and questioning look on DS Kent's face, it hadn't gone unnoticed.

'How long were you on the bowling green?'

Nick shrugged, but Annika replied, 'I know that. After a while we decided to go back in. I stopped to answer a text, which was half past twelve. I was only a minute or two, then I joined Nick in the apartment.'

'And was anyone else in the apartment?'

Nick frowned thoughtfully. 'No, the place was in darkness when I arrived. I put the kettle on.'

'It was just me and Nick,' concurred Annika. 'We took our drinks to bed.'

DS Kent did not look entirely satisfied. She sighed. 'Thank you for your answers. I have one bit of admin. Part of our investigation process can involve checking people's financial positions. We of course are very careful how your private information is handled, but it is a useful box for us to tick.' She leant down and pulled some forms out of her bag. 'I'd be grateful if you could all sign one of these, giving us the necessary permission.'

'You want access to our bank accounts?' said LeAnne.

'As I said, unless it has a direct bearing on the case, it is just a matter of course.'

DS Kent handed around the forms. Susan understood LeAnne's reservations, it did seem quite intrusive, but as is the way, once one person signed their form no one else felt they could refuse.

DS Kent collected the forms, thanked them and said, 'Now, do any of you have any questions for me?'

'Yes. I have one,' said Zoe. The others looked at her. 'Have you found that miniature of the Grim Reaper in Maxine's bag? It really scared her. I think it's important.'

DS Kent shook her head. 'I did check because you asked but there was no miniature in her bag or in any of her pockets.'

Zoe glanced over at Gino, who returned a knowing look.

'Well, it should have been there. I saw Maxine zip it back into her bag,' said Zoe.

'I'm sorry, there was nothing. By the way, you mentioned that Maxine said her torch didn't work because it didn't have batteries. I followed it up, but there were batteries in the torch. It worked perfectly well. She must have been mistaken.'

'No. I watched Maxine take the cover off the battery compartment. We both saw it was empty.'

'Um, it was very dark. Maxine had been drinking.'

'I'm sure the torch was empty. There is something iffy about the torches. I looked in the box over there on the table, and there are none left. There should be a spare. It means one torch is missing.'

DS Kent glanced over at the box, but didn't comment. Instead, she looked around for more questions, but no one appeared to have any. She stood up. 'I understand you're all going to continue your stay here until Sunday? Of course, Zoe and LeAnne will be at Susan's?'

They nodded.

'Good, well, we will probably need to speak to you all again soon, so I'll just make sure I have all your mobile numbers.' She checked her phone for a moment. 'I'll see you all again soon. Oh, and Nick, could I have a quick word?'

Susan saw a look of alarm in Nick's eyes, but he replied, 'Of course,' and followed the officer outside.

'Good God, it's like a police state,' exclaimed LeAnne, who

Susan noticed was always a lot more vocal when the police were not around. 'We ought to have solicitors if they're going to be questioning us like this.'

'I don't see the point,' said Gino. 'It's not like they're accusing anyone.'

'But it's not far off, is it? What are they asking Nick about, do you think?'

Everyone shrugged.

'I'll put the kettle on,' said Zoe.

She was pouring fresh drinks when Nick returned. He was quite flushed but didn't seem unduly worried.

'What was that about then?' asked LeAnne.

20

Nick replied to LeAnne's question with an enigmatic smile. 'You'll have to wait to find out what the police wanted to talk to me about,' he said and turned to Gino. 'Why did you say that about Maxine drinking? She was nowhere near having a problem.'

Gino pulled at the gold necklace around his neck, seemed to sneer at them all. 'You all think you knew Maxine so well: all this bullshit about being friends since school. None of you had really kept in touch – well, apart from Zoe. I am the only one here who knew the real Maxine. You remember some brilliant, saint-like person, but I remember who she really was. Yes, she was clever, passionate about her work. But she also needed to control every aspect of her life. She was scared life would run away from her, and so she desperately tried to control everything around her, including the people who loved her. Occasionally the realisation that this was impossible came crashing in, and then she would drink. I'm sorry, but that's the truth of it.'

'You're right,' said LeAnne, 'I hadn't seen the drinking, but I've seen that side of Maxine recently.'

'I loved her,' said Gino, 'but we have to be honest.'

'You really believe that she could have died by suicide?' asked Nick.

Gino looked towards Zoe. 'No, I don't. I'm simply saying she had more issues than the rest of you realise.'

'I admit she was stressed, but she was in control, talking about the way forward in her life,' said Zoe. 'The police will see that. I think their job will be to decide whether Maxine died on her own up on the battlements, accidentally fell, or if someone was up there with her and was involved somehow in her death, maybe even caused it by pushing her – and the police officers clearly think we are all suspects.'

Annika sat with clenched fists placed on her lap, Nick was breathing fast, Gino crossed his arms and glowered. They looked tense, afraid. Only LeAnne, her head held high, her eyes squinting, looked defiant.

'If anyone pushed Maxine, killed her on purpose, it had to be a stranger,' said LeAnne.

'But it couldn't have been. DS Kent showed that. At the time Maxine died, the gate was locked. No one could get in. We were the only ones here,' said Nick.

'None of us would have wanted to kill Maxine. It's ridiculous,' said Annika.

'You'd have thought so, wouldn't you?' said Zoe. 'But there is no getting away from the fact, it has to be possible.'

'But why would any of us do such a terrible thing?' asked Annika. 'It's beyond belief. This has to be a mistake.'

Zoe cleared her throat, played with her wedding ring. 'The night before she died, Maxine was scared. She told me that one of us was not who they appeared to be, she talked about violence and that one of us would find life a lot easier if she was no longer around.'

She had taken the pin out of the grenade.

'Are you serious?' asked LeAnne.

'I am. That's what Maxine said.'

'Did Maxine say who?' LeAnne's voice was quiet, lacking its usual assurance.

Zoe shook her head. 'No, but she had issues with everyone here.' She glanced at Gino. 'Maxine told me there were problems in your marriage.'

Gino shrugged. 'Every relationship has its ups and downs.'

'It was a lot more than that, wasn't it?'

A look of fury swept across Gino's face. 'Maxine and I loved each other. We were working everything out.'

Susan looked at Gino thoughtfully: did he really believe that or was he bluffing?

Zoe raised her eyebrows, in an expression of scepticism, and continued, 'Nick, you must have realised Maxine was becoming increasingly concerned about you—'

'I could see she was thrown by what LeAnne said about the online abuse, but I was going to talk to her about that. She'd have soon realised I had no reason to set up Wesley.'

'It was too late for that,' said LeAnne. 'I'm sure Maxine had realised you'd stitched up Wesley. Your guardian angel was on the turn.'

Susan saw Nick scowl but noticed he didn't try to defend himself.

'You could be right about Nick,' Zoe continued, looking at LeAnne, 'but of course Maxine had issues with you as well. In fact, she warned me not to underestimate you. Now, why would she do that?'

'Maybe she'd come to respect me for setting up a successful business,' said LeAnne stiffly.

'I'm sure she appreciated what you had done. But there was

something going on between the two of you. Mum heard you arguing on the ghost walk—'

Susan realised she had suddenly become the focus of attention. 'You sounded desperate, LeAnne, talked about Maxine being about to ruin your life.'

Susan waited for an explosive reaction from LeAnne but instead LeAnne gave her an ice-cold look. 'I'm not sure why you were trying to eavesdrop, but you misheard. We were talking about Wesley and by backing Nick, I did feel she'd played a part in ruining my brother's life. However, if you'd kept listening, you'd have heard Maxine apologise. She said if she'd known everything she'd never have stood by him and was very sorry. At the end of the walk we'd reconciled our differences and I'm really grateful for that.'

Susan was aware of LeAnne's eyes on her the whole time she was speaking, challenging Susan to contradict her. In that look she saw a different LeAnne, maybe the one Maxine had been warning Zoe about. And so, although she disagreed with LeAnne, she didn't respond. She noticed that Zoe didn't challenge her either.

Instead, Zoe turned to Annika. 'And then there's you.'

'Maxine and I were good friends. There were no issues as you call them between us,' said Annika. She sat very upright, a small red patch on either cheek.

'Although you deny it, I know Maxine came to your flat last week,' said Zoe. 'Something worried her enough to make her decide to see you at work. Alice at the care home told me that she saw the two of you talking in the garden.'

Annika looked thoughtful. 'Last week? Oh, God, yes. Sorry, I forgot. She was concerned about one of the smoke alarms; told me she'd changed the battery. That's all.'

Zoe screwed her lips in disbelief. 'Now why would Maxine

disturb you at work just to tell you something she could have put in a text?'

Annika blinked innocently. 'I thought it was odd. After all, it's a bit awkward to be interrupted at work. She apologised.' She sat back and crossed her arms. She clearly had no intention of saying any more. Susan found Annika's response fascinating. Most people would have rushed in, tripped over words trying to defend themselves. It took a great deal of nerve just to say nothing. She felt she'd seen a more calculating, more confident Annika today, a woman to be reckoned with.

Before Zoe could continue, Gino interrupted. 'You're hitting out at us because you feel threatened. You lied about the miniature and the batteries in the torch: the police have proved that. You were the last person up there. You say Maxine was fine when you left her, but we only have your word for it. Now you're trying to make us look as if we had reasons to want her dead.'

Susan watched Zoe scratch nervously at the side of her finger, and took a sharp intake of breath as she recalled something she'd seen the morning after Maxine died. She felt a wave of relief, not that she had doubted her daughter, but it was good to have some solid proof of one key fact she'd been maintaining since Maxine's death.

Zoe continued her fight. 'I'm not lying. I saw the miniature and there were definitely no batteries in the torch. Most importantly, I know I saw someone was up there with Maxine after me.' She looked around. 'That person should own up. You may be innocent, but the police need to know what happened. I've pointed out that everyone has potential motives; the police will discover that. Is that why you are all letting Gino attack me? I've noticed none of you are trying to defend me now.'

The silence that followed was painful, the air thick with confusion. It was as if no one could breathe, let alone speak. Zoe shook her head, stood up and headed for the door. Susan quickly followed.

Without speaking, they walked out of the main castle grounds through the gate in the thick walls and on to the expanse of the bowling green, which was surrounded by high grassy banks. Although outside the castle proper, there were further fortifications which prevented public access from outside.

It was such a contrast this morning after the fog of the day before. Today the sun shone, not with an August warmth, but enough to take the chill off the day and give a lightness to the sky.

Zoe dashed ahead, clearly fuelled with adrenaline, while Susan rushed along beside her trying to keep up.

'I thought I knew these people. I thought they were my friends,' cried Zoe, 'but no one is being honest, and no one is sticking up for me. Don't say they are all still in shock: there's something else going on.'

'You're right. I felt it as well. Shock has been replaced by something more powerful,' said Susan, 'and that is fear. DS Kent made it clear that the police are investigating Maxine's death carefully and are not ruling out one of them being involved in her death. No wonder everyone is on edge.'

'I guess so. It's bad enough to think of your friend being murdered, let alone be suspected of being the killer. Even if someone is innocent, that's a nightmare. When we were talking with Alice I didn't really think it was possible, not really.'

Susan didn't respond. She felt her stomach twist in dread of what lay ahead of them. Unlike Zoe, she had been prepared for this outcome, but part of her had been desperately hoping that the police would magically prove that Maxine had definitely died accidentally. Well, that wasn't going to happen.

Susan paused, her attention was caught by the sound of the clear wistful singing of a robin in a tree close by. The beauty of the song seemed to draw Zoe in as well and for a moment they stood, silently, enjoying a moment's respite from the ugly conversation about death and murder.

After a few minutes, Zoe laid her hand gently on Susan's arm. 'I have to ask you something, Mum. It's really important.'

Susan turned to her daughter.

Zoe spoke quietly, but with passion. 'I need to know you believe me. That matters more to me than anything. I promise you I'm not making anything up. I'm not lying.'

Susan patted her hand, looked deep into her daughter's eyes. 'I know you are innocent, and I don't just say that because I'm your mother. When you were all talking to DS Kent I remembered something that proves to me you definitely saw and handled that miniature.'

Zoe frowned. 'And what was that?'

'Yesterday at breakfast I saw you were scratching red paint off your finger. You told me it had come off the miniature.'

Tears sprang into Zoe's eyes. 'You're right.' She let out a deep sigh of relief. 'I'm glad I'm not going mad.'

She could see Zoe was more at ease, but Susan's mind was racing, trying to piece together the implications of what they were saying. 'I need you to think carefully, Zoe. This is important. After Maxine stopped you throwing away the model, what did she do with it?'

Zoe screwed up her eyes, and after a moment's thought answered. 'I know. She put it back into that little cross-body bag she had and zipped it up.'

Susan nodded. 'Right – so she didn't put it in her pocket with the torch?'

'No. She definitely put it in her bag.'

Susan clasped her hands together. 'Right, so we know it was in the bag. I saw the bag was still zipped up when we found Maxine the next morning. So, if that model was not in the bag when the police looked, then either Maxine or someone else had removed it.'

'That's true,' said Zoe eagerly.

'Could Maxine have thrown it away?' asked Susan.

Zoe shook her head. 'No, she said she needed to keep it. Maybe she was going to confront the person she thought had put it in her bag?'

'That seems likely,' said Susan. She spoke earnestly. 'If Maxine didn't discard the model, then someone else was involved. Maybe Maxine showed it to them and they took it away, or they removed it from her bag.' She looked at Zoe excitedly. 'This must confirm what you have maintained all along, someone spoke to Maxine after you.'

Zoe gasped. 'Of course. Yes, you're right. I wish whoever it was would own up—'

'But they're not going to if they were somehow involved in Maxine's fall,' said Susan quietly.

They both paused, trying to wrestle with the enormity of what Susan had said.

'So Alice could be right? Someone here might have killed Maxine?' whispered Zoe.

'I'm afraid so.'

'Maxine was right then to be frightened by that miniature: it had been a warning. My God, Mum, did one of my friends came on this holiday with the specific aim of ending Maxine's life?'

They recommenced their walk but at a slower, more considered pace, both deep in thought. Soon they'd reached the far side of the green and climbed up a short steep path that led to one of the black cannons. From up here they could look down on the public path outside. They saw a woman chatting on her phone, her dog running crazily up and down the moat.

'About this torch,' said Susan in a more pragmatic voice. 'I agree with you something is off here. There shouldn't be batteries in the one the police found on Maxine, and one is missing from the box.'

'I agree, but I can't explain what's happened. We'll have to forget about it, I think.'

'Oh, no,' said Susan, clenching her hands. 'That's the last thing we do. It's the unexplained, the missing pieces, that are the most important. They can be the difference between solving a case and failing.'

Zoe grinned. 'A case – is that what this is now?'

Susan nodded but her face was grave. 'I'm afraid that is exactly what this is now.'

She turned to Zoe, choosing her words carefully. She didn't want Zoe marching off in temper. 'There is something else we need to talk about. This secret between you and Maxine. It could be really important. You need to share it. If nothing else, not telling the police looks suspicious.'

Zoe kicked the concrete plinth the cannon was mounted on.

'I can't tell anyone, not even you, Mum. I made a promise, but it has nothing to do with Maxine's death. I'm sure of it.'

Susan tutted in frustration. Zoe had no way of knowing that. But still, she knew her daughter: the more she pushed, the more stubborn she would become, and so for the time being she would have to put this aside.

They walked along the ridge leading to another of the cannons. Susan waited.

'So, what do we do next?' asked Zoe.

'We keep digging, I guess. The means of killing Maxine hasn't changed. We have to assume the killer pushed her. We have a new one on opportunity. Did you notice how Annika changed her story about meeting Nick? Now she says they were apart during the crucial time.'

'The call to her dad and then the mix-up about where they were to meet makes sense but did you notice her stumble over meeting Nick? First, she said she waited for him, and then that he was waiting for her. If Nick wasn't there when she got to the bowling green, what on earth was he doing? It's such a short distance from the garden.'

'Did you see where Nick went after you spoke to him?'

Zoe shook her head. 'No, he waited for me to leave.'

'That's interesting in itself. Of course, Annika was alone as well.'

'You're right,' said Zoe. 'So no one has an alibi for the time Maxine died?'

'No. As Alice would say, we need to look at motive.'

'We went over that with Alice. I can't see we are any further forward.'

'No, but we will be more vigilant now. By the way, did you notice how shocked LeAnne appeared when you said Maxine had talked about ending her marriage?'

'I did,' said Zoe. 'I'm sure she didn't know. Maybe she'd felt the only way to get Gino was to kill Maxine?'

'It has to be possible. Of course, Gino, on hearing Maxine was going to divorce him may have killed Maxine to be free to go away with LeAnne,' said Susan.

'A divorce would be a lot easier,' said Zoe.

'Yes, but he would have been a lot less well off. I wonder if she'd made a will leaving him everything?'

'If she did, he must be a good candidate for the person whose life would be easier if she died,' said Susan.

'We've a lot to find out, haven't we?' said Zoe.

'We have. But remember what Alice said: be careful. It's looking even more likely now that one of your friends here is a killer. Up till now, they thought the police had accepted Maxine's death as an accident. They're on the defensive now. They're more dangerous.'

Zoe pulled her coat tight around her. 'You make it sound really scary.'

'It is,' said Susan. 'But you know, you can leave this. If the police allow it, you can go home.'

'You know I can't do that. Maxine told me I was the only one she could trust. I told her I would always be there for her. I have to keep that promise even though she's died. If this had happened to me, I know she'd keep digging until she found out the truth.'

Susan nodded. 'I understand. Well, we must do this together then and keep you as safe as possible.'

At that moment, they saw LeAnne heading towards them.

Zoe frowned. 'Has she come to tell me to leave?'

But then she saw the nervous smile on LeAnne's face and felt a wave of relief as LeAnne said, 'Look, no one wants to fall out over this. We thought we might all go out. Fancy the beach? Please come.'

Zoe smiled. 'Thank you. Yes, it would be good to go down there.'

It was agreed that they would all go to Compton, although Susan would go back and collect the dogs first.

Gino drove Nick and Annika in Maxine's car. LeAnne and Zoe went with Susan.

The furniture van was no longer parked next door. Susan could see her new neighbours through the windows moving things around, and decided it was best now to leave them to it.

After collecting the dogs, they drove to Compton, stopping off at the shop to pick up fresh doughnuts.

They parked at Hanover Point car park, and Susan battled with a gust of wind as she opened the driver's door. But it wasn't the wind that occupied her thoughts.

Susan had been far more aware that one of this group might have killed Maxine. But for all that, part of her had been clinging on to a thread of hope that the police would quickly and conclusively tell them Maxine's death was accidental.

Susan knew that she had to let go of this thread now. One of the people she was about to meet on this beach was a killer. Someone had sat down and methodically made a plan to take the life of either their friend or wife. And her own daughter was caught up in this nightmare, suspected by the police and putting her own life in danger as she searched for the truth.

As Alice had said, this case was very close to home.

21

The view over Compton Bay this sunny, crisp autumn morning was everything Susan could have wished for. The sea glistened. The tide was out. As they reached the top of the steps, blissful miles of sand stretched before them.

Libs and Rocco barked excitedly, noses up in the air, tails wagging furiously. Susan let them off to bound down the steps rather than being pulled down herself, and they raced onto the beach.

Susan handed over the bag of doughnuts to Zoe, before deciding to walk away from the group, heading off after the dogs.

However, Gino made a beeline for Susan and, munching on a doughnut, walked beside her.

'These are delicious,' he said, wiping the sugar off his lips. 'In Italy we have bamboloni. My favourites are full of custard, but I love this jam, it's very good... So, tell me, have you always lived on the island?' he asked.

Susan was caught off guard by how friendly he was being, after the set-tos with Zoe.

'Yes. I grew up around here but then for forty years I lived over in Ventnor with my husband. It's very different over there: a classic Victorian seaside town with lots of hills. Zoe grew up there, went to the same school as the rest of the group.'

Gino, having finished his doughnut, pulled his coat more closely around him. 'It's very different here to the beach at Ostia where my parents would take us. There are many places to eat, a lido, a lot to do. It's so wild here, untamed.'

Susan nodded. 'It is, and that's why I love it. You must miss Italy, particularly Rome—'

'Of course, but there are so many tourists now. You can't move in the summer.'

'Are your parents still there?'

'Oh, yes, but they have a large house on the outskirts. Mum teaches in the university. She's English actually.'

'I thought your English was very good.'

'Thank you. My mother always spoke English to me growing up. She loves Rome, but she loved talking to Maxine about England. They got on well. She is so upset – of course – about all that has happened.'

Susan realised she had never thought about his family. She had forgotten the ripples on the pond created by a death.

Gino's face relaxed into a warm smile. 'I remember taking Maxine to meet them, that first summer when we met. They were very impressed, of course, that she was so clever, and she loved sitting on the veranda of our house, looking over the olive trees, drinking wine.' He looked out at the cold grey sea but he smiled, transported back to a happier, warmer time. 'I knew the moment I met her that Maxine was special. She was on holiday in Rome. I was working in one of the hotels. I came down to buy a coffee. She was ordering her lunch, getting confused.' He blushed. 'Now, of course, in Rome, I often dated women who were on holiday. I would take them out, show them the city. When I started chatting to Maxine, I saw straight away she was different. I took her to a very intimate restaurant, one I very seldom took people to, and, well, that was it. I managed to get time off work and spent all my time with Maxine. I have many connections in the city. I could get the early-morning tickets to Vatican City, access to areas of the Colosseum few people see. I used up so many good favours, all to impress her.'

'And you succeeded.'

She saw the warmth of an Italian sunshine spread over his face. 'I did. Her father came over and we married at the end of that summer. I then returned to England with her.'

Hearing Gino speak was a revelation, as if Susan was seeing a totally different side to him. It made her realise that what is hidden isn't always dark and disturbing. Sometimes disappointment or grief hide gentleness and light.

'It's a very romantic story.'

'Yes. It started like a fairytale but, real life, it is not so easy. England is not Rome. It can be cold, dark, and oh, so wet.' Susan remembered Maxine's heartbreaking words up on the battlements when she had first arrived: no more fairytales, no more happy endings.

'You miss Italy?' she asked gently.

'I do, but for Maxine I happily gave it up and I would do it again. I loved her very much.' Gino spoke with such passion and sincerity it was hard not to believe him.

'I'm sure.'

'It's so awful losing her suddenly. It's why I'm finding it so hard Zoe keeping this secret from me. It's not like I can talk to Maxine about it, but it feels like this is something I should know about.' He paused and added, 'You're Zoe's mother. I can see you're very close.' He leaned in too close.

Susan backed off. Was this why he'd come to talk to her?

'I'm sorry. I have no idea what it was. I don't know anything.'

He raised his eyebrows, clearly not believing her. However, even if she wanted to, she had nothing to share. Instead, she moved the conversation on.

'LeAnne was telling us about you visiting her restaurant,' said Susan.

He blinked, wrongfooted by the sudden change.

'Oh, um, sometimes, yes.'

'She's built such a good business there. And she's such good company.'

'I'm sure she is. I wouldn't really know.'

Gino had effectively shut that topic down. Susan had no way of judging his feelings for LeAnne from what he said. Instead, she changed tack. 'So, will you return to Italy now?'

'I'm not sure. I promised Dad I would come to England and make my own money. Inheritance would not be making my own way, would it? He believes we should prove ourselves. Basically, he said if I can make a certain amount, he will then back me in buying land over there. It seems fair to me, but more difficult than I imagined. It's not easy raising money for these projects.'

'But you're very good at your job. Annika speaks very highly about what you've done with her flat.'

'Thank you.'

Susan's mind was racing. What was an easy way to bring up the safe? She shook her head; nothing came to her. It was no good, she was just going to have to jump straight in. 'I hear you put a safe in for Annika. That's a good idea, with them being out all day, the flat must be vulnerable to break-ins.'

He knitted his brows together. 'Um, yes, I thought so.'

He looked around, clearly about to change the subject. Feeling she had nothing to lose, Susan said, 'I hear you used it as well, um,' she said desperately, adding, 'Maxine was curious about that, I think – wasn't it why she visited the flat last week?'

Susan waited, half expecting him to simply refuse to answer and walk away.

However, Gino scowled and went very red indeed. He bent down, grabbed a pile of pebbles and threw them to the ground. 'I loved Maxine so much, but she never stopped prying and digging into my business.'

Susan found it interesting that there was no denial about the safe. There seemed no harm in keeping going.

'Maxine said the visit had upset her for a few reasons,' she continued. 'In fact, she went straight from there to talk to Annika at work.'

Gino frowned at her now. 'You seem very interested in all this.'

Susan grasped at an explanation. 'I visited an elderly friend, Alice. Annika was working in her nursing home the day Maxine visited her. She told me the conversation looked very serious and Annika was upset. I naturally wondered what had gone on.'

Surprisingly Gino seemed to accept the explanation. 'To be honest, I had no idea Maxine went to speak to Annika.'

He looked out to sea, took a breath, then looked at Susan searchingly. 'I can see where your daughter gets her curiosity from.' The laugh he gave was as cold as the wet pebbles on the beach. 'Right, I shall go and speak to Annika.'

Susan felt quite relieved when he had gone. The conversation hadn't taught her much, but she did feel she had got to know Gino a little better.

She was prepared to turn around and walk back on her own as the group seemed to have changed direction, but she saw Nick was approaching her.

'I asked Gino earlier to play a round of golf with me over at

Freshwater,' he said. 'I wonder if Annika could go back with you?'

'Of course, no problem.'

He continued to walk quietly by her side and so she asked, 'How are you coping, Nick?'

'It's been a terrible shock for us all.'

'You were very fond of Maxine,' said Susan.

His reply was interesting.

'Of course, to have someone of her standing come to court with me meant the world to me.' He smiled sadly. 'I always envisaged asking her to be godmother to our first child. Annika agreed. She'd have been perfect for the role.'

'Annika understood how highly you regarded Maxine then.'

'Oh, yes. The problem when you've known someone in their teens is that you forget they grow up. I always knew Maxine was clever, but she was an amazing barrister. I was so proud to know her.'

'I suppose everyone thought she'd marry someone in a similar field of work—'

Nick shook his head. 'You're right, and it would have been much better if she had. Maxine and Gino had so little in common. I'm not saying anyone would find Maxine easy to live with. I used to say to Annika how exhausting she would be, and very demanding. But if she'd been with someone from her own walk of life, they'd have understood the pressures she was under. You know: another lawyer, or a doctor, for example.'

'So Gino struggled? It sounds as if you understood Maxine very well, would even have made a better partner for her.' Susan added a smile to try and lighten what she was saying but she still held her breath, wondering how Nick would react.

Nick threw his head back and laughed. 'Good God, no.'

Then he gave a warm smile. 'I've found my life partner. Annika is a real treasure. She always supports me. She's my rock.'

His sounded very sincere. 'That's lovely,' said Susan. 'I hope she realises how much she means to you.'

'She's very modest but, yes, I'm sure she knows it. She would never have asked me to move in with her if she hadn't been sure of my feelings for her.'

Susan looked over at Rocco and Libs. Feeling they were getting too far away from her, she called them back. Fortunately, they came straight back. She gave them a fuss and a treat, and they continued their walk but closer by.

'I remember Annika's father being pretty strict.'

'That's an understatement. I've always been scared of him, but he was fine when we first got together. Then I got arrested. I thought he'd have put an end to us then.'

'Annika is an adult. She'd have stood by you, surely?'

'It's difficult to say. She's very influenced by her father. He was also helping her with the rent. He bought her a car. At the very least, she may have pressed pause on our relationship. I was worried we'd be over before we'd even really got started.'

As Susan listened, she realised she was seeing Nick and Annika's relationship in a new light.

'The fact you're still together means, I guess, that he must have accepted the situation.'

'He was pretty reasonable, all things considered. The main thing is that it was nothing to do with drugs. Neither he nor Annika would have coped with that. Still, I was able to go back to work, prove myself as you say. He told me straight before the hearing that if I was sent to prison that would be it.'

'But there was no question of that?'

'I didn't think so, but I suppose you never know. Anyway, after the verdict he said to me, "Nick, I'm relieved, and now we can move on. But remember this: I only allow everyone one mistake."' Nick laughed, nervously. 'He made it clear that this was my one and only chance, so it will keep me on the straight and narrow. I think the fact I would like a career in music plays in my favour. I think he hopes I'll encourage Annika to do the same.'

'And do you? Push her?'

Nick shook his head. 'No, I wouldn't do that to her. I think she's probably had enough of it all, to be honest. There's a lot more she wants to do with her life. Have you seen her painting? It's wonderful.'

'It's lovely you are so supportive of each other.'

'Oh, yes. Moving in with Annika gave me a real fresh start. I was worried about getting to work. My school is over the other side of the island, but I get the floating bridge over to East Cowes and a lift from a colleague.'

'We're so dependent on cars, aren't we? Mind you, Annika was telling me she hates driving—'

'She does. I suggested she go for hypnosis or something, but she says it's good to manage as much as we can without the car. The bus route is easy and she uses Liam a couple of times a week – says it's good to support him, and he gives her very good rates, so it seems fair.'

'LeAnne was talking about Liam at breakfast. She said he was the son in the family where Annika was a nanny?'

'That's right,' said Nick. 'Liam was a bit of a black sheep, but he's on the straight and narrow now. Good for him, he's making a good job of it.'

Susan looked out to sea and noticed that the wreck was visible today. It was an old tugboat which hadn't been worth saving. Further along the beach, she knew, were the fossils of dinosaur footprints, a great deal older, of course. But she liked to think this was a place that valued and held on to its past.

Turning to Nick, she said, 'I was pleased to hear Annika is doing gigs with you.'

'Yes, just for fun.'

'Of course, but it's good she's still using her music. You both have choir as well. Oh, and she mentioned you both volunteer in the prison—'

'We do. It's good to give something back, isn't it? The inmates appreciate it.'

'I'm sure.'

'It's not easy, though. I find it so oppressive in there. No one should ever call it an easy option. It's dehumanising. You arrive and are searched, questioned. Someone is always locking doors behind you. It's so demeaning. Gino doesn't seem to mind. He told me he likes working in there. He's asked for more work. I don't know how he can do it.'

'But they have to have tight security. LeAnne was telling me about the drug problems.'

'Of course. Her uncle is in there, isn't he? Gino told me about this drug spice. I'd never heard about it. Apparently, prisoners pay good money for it and it's hard for the authorities to detect. Fortunately, we've not encountered kids at school using it.'

'Good. It sounds a horrible drug, very dangerous.'

'Yes. It's good to think when we go into the prison that it contributes something positive to the prisoners' lives. Music can be very healing: relieving of stress, lifting depression.' Nick smiled at Susan. 'You should consider volunteering. You'd enjoy it. Annika has a singing group. I teach keyboards. We would both love some help.'

'Thank you. Maybe I'll think about it.'

He breathed in the cold air, looked up at the seagulls circling above them. 'Even on days like this it's stunning down here, isn't it? I'd find it very hard to leave.'

Susan was surprised to hear him say this. She hadn't realised that he or Annika had thought of leaving.

Nick continued. 'I want to seriously move forward with my composition. I should move to somewhere like London or even LA. I never thought Annika would want to but she's all for it.'

'Really?'

'She hasn't said anything to her parents because she knows that, although her father would help, he'd make it conditional on her doing something with her singing. My parents are all for it but can't help us. So, we have to do it alone, and that's no bad thing. We'll manage, I'm sure.'

'So, you see yourself leaving teaching?'

'Yes. I have to leave it soon. It's so stressful. I used to love teaching but—' He leant down, picked up a pebble and threw it with surprising force into the sea. 'It's brutal. The stress locks you in a room where there is no colour, no sweet melody, no light, no warmth. You're completely alone, and there's no way out.' He paused.

Susan was shocked by the depth of pain and despair in his voice. 'Is there someone at your school who you can talk to?'

'I daren't talk to anyone.'

'But people are more enlightened now about mental health problems—'

'Yes, but since my conviction I have a point to prove – to the kids, the staff, to parents. It's a small island; everyone knows what went on. There are plenty of people who don't trust me, who don't think I should be back in teaching. It makes the job so much harder. I'm scared to put a foot wrong.'

Listening to LeAnne, Susan had been persuaded that Nick had practically got off scot-free from the incident. But, of course, that wasn't true. He gained a criminal conviction, lost a huge amount of respect. Of course, he was responsible for those terrible choices, but there was no doubt he was living with the consequences now.

Nick sneezed violently, and clamped his hand on his nose. 'Oh, no.' He rummaged with his spare hand in his pocket as blood dripped down to his chin.

'These wretched allergies. Mind you, I haven't had one of these for ages.'

The single tissue he was holding to his nose was totally inadequate for the job. Susan, as always, had a packet of tissues in her bag and handed him a couple, which helped him staunch the flow.

They had reached the steps which led back up to the car park. Susan called the dogs to put their leads on.

Gino and Annika came over.

'Oh, no. What's happened?' Annika asked Nick.

'It's nothing.'

'Not another one. Are you OK?'

'Of course.' He looked at the tissues, which seemed to have stemmed the flow of blood. 'I'm fine to go and play golf with Gino. Susan is OK to give you a lift.'

'Thanks so much, Susan.'

They left the beach. LeAnne, Annika and Zoe prepared themselves to return to the castle in Susan's car, the dogs in the rear.

'Everything OK?' Zoe asked Annika.

Susan glanced in her mirror to where the two sat in the back seat. Annika was bent over her phone, texting.

'Fine, just booking a taxi from the castle. I need to go to my flat. I would drive but I don't feel up to it today.'

'It sounds like you find driving really difficult,' said Zoe.

'I do. I hate it. I have nightmares about accidents, see hazards everywhere. I know it sounds stupid. I brought the car to the castle in case we were planning days out, but now, with everything that's happened, I can't really face it.'

Susan was listening to the conversation and suddenly realised this might present an opportunity to see inside Annika's flat.

'How about I drive us to Cowes?' she suggested. 'I just need to drop the dogs off, and then I can drive you over. I've not been to Cowes for a while.'

'Oh, no, please. I'll get a taxi.'

'No, I insist,' said Susan firmly.

22

Susan parked along the parade that looked out over the harbour in Cowes and walked back towards the town with Zoe, Annika and LeAnne.

They stopped at a baker's, picked up some sandwiches which they ate outside looking over the water, then LeAnne went to do some shopping while Annika took Susan and Zoe to the flat.

Part of Susan would love to have joined LeAnne. Cowes had a vibrant and lively high street with lots of independent shops including a great bookshop, grocers, a florist, a butcher, and clothes shops.

However, today Susan had more important things to do. She was trying to remember the items that had concerned Maxine – there was the safe, of course. Susan would like to see inside it, but she had no idea how she'd persuade Annika to open it. There had also been something about music, Nick's bedside drawer: at least that shouldn't be difficult to find.

Susan caught Zoe's eye. She grinned excitedly. Obviously the same thoughts were going through her mind.

They followed Annika to a small front door next to a fancy gift shop.

'My flat is above the shop,' Annika explained, unlocking the door.

Inside, they climbed tidy stone steps up to Annika's flat and she let them into a light, bright room. The decoration was immaculate, although the room was crammed with stuff. Every surface had piles of paper, bags, coats, spilling off it.

The most organised spot was a large table, one half occupied with small miniatures and paints, the other with paper and acrylics, pencils and a range of artistic equipment. 'This is where we relax,' said Annika, smiling. 'Nick loves painting these.'

'For such tiny models there is a lot of equipment,' said Susan, taking in the array of paints, cans, brushes and display cases.

'I know,' said Annika, laughing. 'He's such a perfectionist about the whole thing.'

Zoe moved to pick up one of the miniatures.

'Don't touch them,' Annika intervened. 'Nick hates me handling them. They may look dry, but he has so many different layers of work to each one. I always say they would withstand a nuclear war if they had to: layer upon layer of special paint, primers, air sprayed to dry and keep any dust off them, and then varnished. Finally, they go in these special acrylic cases – it's a serious hobby.'

'He does them very well.'

'Yes. He doesn't play games, just loves painting and collecting them.'

'Has he ever had a miniature of the Grim Reaper?' Zoe asked. She smiled over at Annika as if to lighten the question, but she held her gaze, clearly expecting an answer.

Annika frowned. 'Definitely not.'

'I'm guessing this is your side of the table,' said Susan, pointing at the paper and paints.

'It is.' Annika picked up a small, beautifully detailed painting of an orange and brown chequered butterfly and showed it to Susan.

'That's beautiful – a Glanville fritillary?'

'Exactly right,' said Annika with a smile. 'I went out walking and took lots of photos of them before starting this. We're so lucky to have them here on the island.'

Zoe had wandered over to another table on which rested an electric keyboard with a laptop, wires, and a headset.

'That's where Nick does his composing,' explained Annika. Piled around the keyboard was manuscript paper with bars of music scrawled over them. Susan saw that some of the notation had been written with a heavy hand, the blackened crotchets filled in over and over again with black ballpoint, sometimes making a hole in the paper. There were also complex, tangled doodles in the margins, written in the same heavy hand. She could feel the stress, the frustration of the writer. She glanced at Zoe who, looking down at the music, raised an eyebrow.

Annika spotted the look between them.

'Nick is very intense when he's composing. I say he's like my Beethoven: a troubled genius.'

Annika picked up some other papers, her hands shaking, and covered up the doodles.

'When Maxine came to see you,' Susan asked gently, 'did she talk to you about Nick? He's been under so much pressure with the court case and teaching—'

Annika swallowed hard. 'OK. Maxine did ask me about how Nick was coping. She asked me how much he is drinking. I said he was much better and please not to mention it in front of everyone when we were away.' Annika shook her head. 'It was why I was so angry with her for mentioning it that evening. Fortunately, no one picked him up on it. I assured her everything was in hand. Nick doesn't know anything about Maxine's visit. Please don't mention this to the others. I'm looking after Nick. Everything will be fine.'

Susan heard the tightness in Annika's voice, saw a twitch in her cheek. Those words, 'everything will be fine,' rang hollow.

Susan nodded. 'Of course.' She looked over at the keyboard. 'Nick was excited to share your plans for moving. It's really giving him something to look forward to.'

Annika's eyebrows shot up. 'He told you? Well, it's true. I just haven't said anything to my parents yet.'

'It would be a massive step to leave the island.'

Annika's face relaxed. There was warmth and excitement in her voice.

'Of course, but it would be great for Nick.'

Susan glanced around, trying to think of a way of getting Annika to show them the safe. Then she remembered Annika's visit to her house.

'While we're here,' she said, desperately trying to sound casual, 'could you show me your stamps? I'd love to see them.'

Annika bit her lip. 'They're locked away—'

'But we're in no rush.'

Annika sighed. Zoe and Susan followed her over to an innocuous-looking cupboard. Susan's heart raced as Annika opened the door to expose the safe.

'Fay and I have been thinking of having a safe fitted,' said Zoe. 'We could keep things like our passports in it.'

Annika seemed to relax. 'That's a good idea. Nick wouldn't put his in. He refuses to use the safe for some reason. But I could. I find it useful.' She looked towards Susan. 'Particularly for my stamps.'

She leant down and started putting in the code. 'Gino insisted the number was really easy to remember – 1950, the year thirteen was made a lucky number in Italy for some reason. I can't say it's helped me remember it though!'

Annika opened the safe. It was larger than Susan expected. In one side of the safe there were some small metal boxes and a small album, in the other were a pile of long boxes of Italian cigarettes.

'Every time Gino goes to Italy he buys these cigarettes. He treats them like the crown jewels. We're not to touch them.' Annika glanced at the boxes, leaned her head to one side. 'He says he has to keep them here because Maxine doesn't approve of him smoking but, to be honest, I've always thought it a bit odd. Surely he could find somewhere more convenient to stash them? He started when he was coming over here for work at the prison and just carried on.'

'Nick was talking about Gino working in there.'

'Yes, I think he's trying to get more work there.' She took a breath. 'Anyway, on to more important things: stamps.'

Annika took out the first metal box and started to open it. Suddenly Susan's heart leapt: of course, Maxine had mentioned albums. What had she seen here?

'The safe is the perfect place to keep them, dry and dark. These are some featuring flowers. Aren't they pretty?'

Susan turned the pages carefully. 'You have them in slip covers. You don't use hinges?'

'No. It's better this way. I never handle them. I always use tongs.' Her face shone like a child's when opening an advent calendar.

'They will keep a lot better than mine.'

Annika opened another tin. 'I think you have these bird ones. They're so cool.'

Susan smiled but wasn't quite so impressed by them. They looked rather dull.

Annika excitedly picked out another. 'You'll like these. These are my Christmas stamps. You've got this one as well,' said Annika.

Susan studied it more closely. 'I have, but you can tell you look after yours better. The angel looks so much brighter.'

Annika smiled. 'It makes all the difference.'

Susan carried on looking through the stamps. Zoe leant forward and picked up a larger album that lay beside the metal boxes. She opened it and exclaimed, 'Oh, this isn't stamps. It's photographs.'

Annika reached out to take the album from her, but Zoe started turning the pages. Her attention seemed to get caught by one photo in particular. 'Isn't that Liam? The taxi driver? This is you and him and, I assume, his family?'

Annika blushed. 'Yes. This is us all last Christmas. It was such a happy day.'

She opened the final metal box and, to Susan's surprise, using tongs, carefully removed a stamp and placed it in a spare bag.

'This is for you,' she said.

Looking at it, Susan saw the image of a black cocker spaniel.

'That's lovely, but don't break up a set for me.'

'It's OK. It's actually a one-off. The others, you can see, are all terriers, but I know how much you love spaniels.'

'Thank you so much. I will treasure it.'

Annika blushed and smiled. 'I know.' She replaced the boxes carefully and relocked the safe.

Annika looked up at Zoe. 'Would you choose a couple of

bottles of wine from the rack? Nick buys them all. I'm pretty hopeless.'

Zoe picked out three bottles while Susan looked out of the window. There was a wonderful view out to sea. 'This is a lovely location. It's a great flat.'

'I know. When I was looking round, I saw some really rundown places.'

Susan noticed a box with file dividers, with 'choir music' written on the outside. She pulled out some sheet music for 'Frosty the Snowman' and 'Silent Night', some yellowed sheets of Rossini warm-up exercises and, rather incongruously, the music for 'My Way'.

Annika laughed. 'Those are the songs the men at the prison have requested. I suggested some Christmas songs and those are the ones they asked for. I was surprised they went for such sentimental ones.'

Susan held up the Frank Sinatra and Annika laughed again. 'I know. Can you believe it? I'm not sure if that was chosen as a joke, but I took them at their word. You can imagine what it was like to try and adapt it for them with such a wide vocal range, complex phrasing. Still, they love it.' She paused. 'You should come along sometime. It can be fun, and it's very worthwhile.'

'Nick mentioned. I shall think about it.'

Next to this box was another with random books for beginners' keyboard lessons and assorted sheet music. Annika laughed. 'That's Nick's stuff – he may be a teacher but he's less organised than me. Right, to find my inhaler: that's why I came.'

'You have asthma?' Zoe asked.

'I do. But nothing like as bad as Nick. Poor thing with all his sneezing and nosebleeds.'

'Does he have them often?'

Annika blinked in confusion. 'Um – oh, no. Not at all.'

A Halloween Murder

Annika headed towards the bedroom. Susan was pleased. Maybe this could be a chance to look in Nick's bedside cabinet. Zoe gave her a tiny nod, clearly thinking the same and they followed Annika into the bedroom.

It was a large airy room but, like the rest of the flat, very cluttered.

Annika went to one side of the bed and rummaged in a bedside cabinet.

'Here it is.' She took out an inhaler and put it into her pocket. Susan wandered around what was clearly Nick's side of the bed and noticed his bedside drawer hung open. She started to walk towards it, but Annika threw herself across the bed and slammed the drawer shut.

'Sorry about the mess. Right, come on. We need to get back.'

They left the flat. Annika headed off to find LeAnne while Susan and Zoe walked back and stood by the car. Looking over the Solent, Susan was struck by what a busy stretch of water it was, with a number of recreational boats alongside the Red Funnel ferry just making its way to Southampton.

She turned to Zoe. 'So, what do you think we learned from the flat?' she asked.

'Quite a lot, actually. Well done for thinking of a reason to look in the safe.'

Susan frowned. 'Yes, but do those cigarettes give us any answers? Would finding them be enough for Maxine to want a divorce?'

'It could be. She hated smoking with a vengeance. If he'd promised to give up when they got married and then she saw them, well, it could have been the line she said he must never cross.'

Susan leaned back against the car. 'I suppose so. I can't help feeling there is more to it than that, but maybe I'm wrong. What did you think about those doodles on the music?'

Zoe's eyes widened. 'They were very disturbing. We know why Maxine said the music alarmed her. Did you see anything in Nick's bedside cabinet before Annika shut it?'

'No. Which is a shame as I reckon there was something interesting in there. Why else would Annika dive over to shut it?'

'I was thinking that.'

Susan pulled on her gloves. It was getting chilly but she was reluctant to get back in the car yet. It was good to feel the clean, fresh air on her face.

Zoe stepped closer to Susan, lowered her voice. 'There was something else, Mum. Remember Maxine said about the albums in the safe? I think I know what it was.'

'Yes, I loved looking at the stamps, but couldn't really see what was so special.'

'That's because it wasn't stamp albums she was talking about, but a photograph album.'

Susan heard the excitement in Zoe's voice, and wondered what she'd missed.

'Remember I saw photos of Liam, the taxi driver, and the family where Annika was a nanny?'

'Oh, yes. What about them?'

'In a few he had his arm around Annika. Mum, don't you see they were in a relationship? I could see it in her face in the photos: she was glowing.'

Susan blinked. 'But why would Nick be so enthusiastic about them using Liam's taxi if he knew Annika used to be in a relationship with Liam?'

'I'm sure she's kept it a secret from Nick. She certainly would have kept it from her father. It's interesting she keeps those photos in the safe, somewhere Nick never looks.'

Susan frowned. 'I can see all that, but why would Maxine be worried about Annika having had a fling with Liam?'

Zoe leant forward, her eyes bright. 'Because she realised that Annika is still seeing Liam.'

Susan blinked. 'Why on earth would she think that?'

'Remember Maxine's reaction when Nick suggested I use Liam's taxi? Maxine was dead against it. Nick looked surprised. It didn't really make sense. Maxine had heard all about Liam from Nick and used him last week when she went to Annika's flat.'

'And then found the album, saw the photos—' said Susan.

'Exactly. So she'd met this charming chap who she knew Annika knew before and whose taxi she is still using a lot. I mean, even I can see that's excessive and expensive, isn't it? It's a simple bus route from Cowes to the hospital if she really didn't want to drive. Maxine saw the photos I did, realised the relationship, knew Nick was unaware of this. The photos, which were hidden in a safe Nick never used, told Maxine a different story.'

'Nick would be devastated if he realised,' said Susan.

'That's right, and so Maxine went over to Bishopstone to speak directly to Annika.'

Susan sighed. 'Does this mean Annika is just using Nick?'

'I don't reckon it's as simple as that. I think Annika can see a future with Nick, but, Liam is perhaps more exciting. Maybe she tells herself it's still a fling, a bit of excitement before she settles down.'

Susan nodded. 'You could be right, yes.'

'Annika thinks everything is going along nicely, and then Maxine confronts her with the truth – maybe even threatens to tell Nick. Don't you see, Mum? This gives Annika a prime motive for wanting to kill Maxine.'

They both leant back on the car and caught their breath. It was a lot to take in.

'I feel sorry for Nick if this is true,' said Susan. 'I realised on the beach how much Annika means to him. He called her his rock. Maxine was right to be worried about how he would react.'

The wind coming in off the sea had become stronger and Susan was about to suggest they sit in the car when she spotted LeAnne and Annika walking towards them.

Susan said quietly to Zoe, 'By the way, what do you think LeAnne has planned for this evening? She said about catching Nick out.'

Zoe groaned. 'I'd forgotten about that. Heaven knows, but we really could do with a quiet time. We are all exhausted.'

'Hiya,' called LeAnne. 'I had a good mooch around. It may be a bit posh over here, but they've some lovely shops.'

Susan dropped them all back to the castle and drove herself home. She wondered how their evening would go and what LeAnne had planned for them.

23

One of the things Robert and Susan really enjoyed doing lately was going out for meals together. They took it in turns to choose a different pub or restaurant on the island. There were so many now to choose from.

Tonight, Susan was meeting Robert at a country pub which specialised in pies. It was a place that was very happy for them to take their dogs and, as they had four between them, it was quite a pack.

As she arrived at the car park, Susan spotted Robert's car. Inside, Susan saw he'd found them a cosy table close to the fire. She sat down opposite him and the dogs quickly settled down under the table.

They began by looking through the menu. Susan chose the vegetarian hotpot; Robert, steak and kidney pie. He went to order their food at the bar while Susan sat back and relaxed, enjoying the warmth from the fire.

Robert returned, with a pint for himself and lemonade and lime for Susan. He took a long sip of beer and then said, 'I hear the police went back to the castle.'

'Now how did you know that?'

'I haven't been idle since our walk. I rang around and found an officer I used to work with who knows about the case. She was very helpful actually. Amazing what people tell you after a drink.'

'Gosh, how indiscreet, but also how useful,' said Susan. 'It would be great to know what the police are thinking about it all.'

'I think they're leaning towards accident, but there were obvious tensions among the group. They're looking very carefully at the husband.'

Susan eagerly sat forward. 'Why Gino?'

'They picked up all wasn't well in the marriage and then found out about Maxine's will.'

'I was wondering if she'd made one.'

'She made it when they got married. It's clear that she was the careful one, and she'd kept substantial savings in her own name. He couldn't get to them without her say-so. The will makes it clear that they will go straight to him.'

Susan gasped. 'He gets everything of hers. That has to be a motive.'

'It could be. Of course, we don't know if he knew about it.'

Susan frowned. 'Hang on. Yes, on the beach he was talking about proving himself to his dad, making his own money and he said, "Inheritance might not count." I think he knew. I'm sure of it.'

'You seem very excited about this. The man might have loved his wife, you know.'

Susan remembered listening to Gino on the beach. 'Of course, yes. I have wondered about that. However, he knew Maxine was planning to divorce him. She told Zoe in the conversation he overheard. And something else: I now know he was having an affair.'

Susan explained what she knew about LeAnne and Gino.

'Goodness, that does give them both a very real motive, doesn't it?' Robert grinned. 'You've been sleuthing again, haven't you?'

'I have to. Something is definitely amiss here. I am now convinced Maxine was killed.'

Robert took a long swig of his beer. 'And why is that?'

Susan told him about her conversations on the beach and the visit to Annika's flat.

'You're getting motives together, certainly, and it sounds as if someone was definitely up there after Zoe. You're right the torch and miniature need explaining. But there's no real evidence.'

'No, but we can keep looking. So, have you heard anything else?'

Robert drew his finger around the rim of his glass. 'A few things about money.'

'Oh, DS Kent got them all to sign forms so they could look into their finances.'

'Yes, well, it was quite interesting. Annika is very well organised with her money. Pretty frugal. She does have a kind of basic membership to the local sailing club via her dad, which allows her and Nick access to the bar and restaurant. Her father pays the rent on the flat. She pays all the bills. She has a small amount of savings. It looks like she manages to save about a hundred pounds a month, savings amount to about five thousand. Nick is managing to save some money, not a huge amount, a few thousand pounds. Oh, now this is interesting—'

Susan was aware of Libs sliding her head onto her lap. She stroked her ears and soon Libs returned to lying on the floor.

Meanwhile Robert continued, 'One thing they noted was

that on 15 September two thousand pounds was paid into Nick's account by someone. The following week, Nick withdrew most of it and then a month later he withdrew five hundred pounds, a large amount for him.'

'Who gave him two thousand pounds?'

'The man concerned is a member of the sailing club, a bit of a dodgy character: Frank Sheen. He makes money in antiques and the like. Why he was giving Nick that amount of money hasn't been answered yet, but the police were intending to ask Nick about it when they revisited.'

'Ah, DS Kent did ask to speak to Nick. I wonder how he explained it?'

'I'd love to know. And, by the way, I asked around about that incident involving Nick and Wesley which resulted in them both being in court.'

Susan sat up eagerly. 'What did you hear?'

'Obviously Nick was guilty of drink driving, but he had a very good reputation as a teacher up until then. Wesley, on the other hand, had previous on accusing authority figures of being "out to get him". He'd even accused a neighbour who complained about him swearing and being abusive of driving their car at him at night.'

'The same allegation he made about Nick?'

'Also, Nick's crash was literally feet away from where he was parked. He started the engine and swerved left, straight into the wall. The only way Wesley could have been driven at is if he was directly in front of the car. When the police arrived, very shortly after the crash, Wesley was screaming at Nick from the opposite side of the street.'

Susan took a deep breath. 'So it looks like Wesley is making this whole thing up?'

'Certainly about the crash, yes. Now, LeAnne appears to be

doing well at the restaurant, has some pretty hefty loans but she's building a good business there. They checked on Zoe, of course.' He smiled. 'You'll be pleased to know she's fine financially.'

'Good, so what else are the police considering?'

'Well, of course, there's a problem with alibis. LeAnne and Gino both claim to have been alone, so no alibi. Nick and Annika say they were together.'

'Ah, Annika clarified that. She went to the stable courtyard around midnight to meet Nick who was meant to come straight from the garden, but it sounds like he took his time getting to her – well, that's her story. He says he went straight to the bowling green and waited for Annika. The trouble is, he sounds pretty out of it, so his word isn't that reliable.'

'That's a mess then. Of course, Zoe was on her own.'

Susan opened her mouth to protest but Robert held up his hand. 'They have to consider her. She's the last one to admit to being up there with Maxine, and then there's Gino saying he witnessed a struggle.'

'But she explained that, and we have proof now someone went up after her.'

Robert grimaced. 'The problem with the miniature and the torch is that they are both dependent on Zoe's account – the fact you saw the red paint on her hand isn't going to be persuasive.'

'That's not fair—'

'But Zoe is also refusing to explain some secret she was told?'

Susan could feel the anger bubbling up inside her. 'I told Zoe to explain. She insists it's nothing to do with Maxine's death. Zoe is not a liar. It wasn't a violent struggle, and someone did go up after her. Robert, she's my daughter. I expect you to be more supportive of her.'

Robert seemed to turn uncharacteristically pink, a twitch of annoyance on his lips. 'I'm not much help to you if I don't stay at least a bit objective. You wanted the police point of view and that is what I'm giving you. I know it's personal, but the best way to help Zoe is to be in possession of all the facts.' Robert squeezed her hand. 'I do understand, though. Try not to worry.'

She pulled her hand away. 'That's impossible, and you know it. This is very close to home for me.'

Fortunately, their meals came at this point. Susan's hotpot smelt wonderful, and she tucked into the crispy slices of potatoes, chunks of tasty carrots and parsnips, and swede. It was delicious.

'Now, would you mind if I share a dilemma with you while we eat?' asked Robert.

A change of subject seemed a good idea. 'Of course you can. What's happened?'

'It's my daughter in France. Remember I mentioned the problems they're having out there with the state of the house, the leaking roof and the like. I had a long chat with her last night. I'm concerned about the stress all this is putting on their family life and their marriage. They've not allowed enough money to buy in the help they need to sort that place out.'

'Maybe they should sell up, come home.'

'But this is their dream. I hated hearing her so upset on the call. I feel so far away from her. I've made a decision. I'm going to go out to help them.'

Susan's stomach turned over in alarm. 'You're moving to France?'

'Not permanently, but I'll go out for a couple of months.'

'That's a big decision. What about Dougie and Gem?'

'They can come as well; they'll have a good time. There is so much land there for them to run around and explore.' He paused. 'Do you think it sounds a good idea?'

'If your daughter needs you, of course you must go – but, um, me and the dogs would miss you, of course.'

He leant forward, rested his hand on hers. 'And that's my dilemma. I hate the thought of being away from you for that long.' He grinned. 'And I do mean you, and not the dogs.'

Susan looked down at her food.

'The thing is,' continued Robert, 'I was going to ask – do you fancy coming with me?'

Susan gripped her glass, totally thrown by the suggestion. 'You want me to come to France?'

'For a few months. You can bring Rocco and Libs—'

'Leave my home?'

'It's not the end of the world. Only France. You could come back and forth, but yes. We'd basically be over there helping out. I'm sure you'd get on well with my daughter. You'd be great with the kids.'

'When are you thinking of going?' Susan asked, playing for time, as she was finding the whole idea very hard to take in.

'Soon... in a few weeks' time. I'll be out there for Christmas, but it could be good fun, Susan, and we could really set them up.'

'But what about my family? I didn't see Jamari last Christmas. We were at the manor, and that wasn't exactly a typical Christmas.'

'You could come back for Christmas if you wanted to.' Robert sounded irritated.

'Yes, but that time of year to be travelling can be awful. I'm only just settling in. I can't imagine leaving the house empty all that time—'

'I was hoping that you'd find this an exciting change. You've seen a lot of Zoe and Jamari over the summer, but they won't be coming over as much now.'

'But I can pop over and see them for a Saturday if I want to.'

'Yes, and you're lucky. I've not seen my daughter for a few months. It's different when they move away.'

'You were just telling me it's not the other side of the world.'

'It's not but, also, it's not a matter of seeing her for a day or an evening. I miss her. We were always close. Calls just aren't the same.' He played with the wedding ring he still hadn't removed since his wife's death six years ago.

Susan sighed. 'How can I leave Zoe? Things are difficult with Fay's dad being unwell. And Jamari is growing up so fast. How can I just leave them?'

They sat silently eating. Susan found the chatting and laughing from the other diners only emphasised the awkward silence between them.

Finally, Robert spoke. 'I know it's asking a lot, but tell me you'll think about it.'

'I just can't imagine it. Listen, maybe your daughter should call it a day out there, come home. We all make mistakes.'

'It's her dream and I need to support her as long as it takes. My son and his family on the mainland are talking about coming out to France for Christmas. It will be the first time we've all had Christmas together since Carol died.'

The name of Robert's wife came as a shock. He seldom talked about her. Susan knew she shouldn't mind, but it seemed to push her away from him.

Robert's eyes sparkled as he added, 'Anyway, I think it could be exciting, getting to know a new country. I've started to learn a bit of French online.'

Susan put down her knife and fork. She'd lost her appetite. Robert had made plans with his family, been learning French?

He'd been preparing for this visit and she'd had no idea. It took her back to that horrendous night her husband had revealed not only that he was leaving her to go off sailing, but that he'd been secretly organising it for months.

Robert was doing exactly the same thing. He invited her along, but these were his plans and he was clearly going to do what he wanted with or without her, it showed little or no commitment to her. Just as she was starting to trust him, he was happy to abandon her.

'Look, Robert, you have obviously got this all planned out; you might as well just get on with it. To be honest, it seems to me you have nothing to lose, while I would be making all the sacrifice.'

There was a coldness in his eyes Susan had never seen before.

'Fine. You've a week or two to change your mind before I book tickets.'

They finished their meals in awkward silence. Susan was finding it hard to swallow, she was so full of emotion. She just wanted to leave.

Neither suggested dessert.

Susan drove home, tears falling down her cheeks. All the pain and heartache she thought she'd left behind came flooding back. She thought she'd moved on but now she felt she was right back where she started.

Meanwhile, back at the castle, tensions were mounting.

24

Everyone in the group was silently waiting for midnight. LeAnne had told them that whatever it was she'd planned would be happening then. Too exhausted to push her, they sat around idly watching TV or on their laptops and phones. However, although on the surface they appeared relaxed, Zoe could see people checking watches and phones, counting down time.

At quarter to twelve, LeAnne turned the TV off, and spoke to them all.

'OK. Now, I know everyone is still reeling over Maxine. But there is another matter that has to be resolved.'

Gino groaned. 'And what would that be LeAnne?'

'I want to prove that Nick set up my brother the night he was arrested.'

'You won't be able to prove it because it's not true,' said Nick. 'One day someone may be able to make you understand that Wesley is lying, but I will certainly not be that person.'

'You're right. We need a neutral person to adjudicate here.'

'It was done in court—'

'But they didn't have all the facts. They weren't impartial.'

LeAnne had everyone's attention now. They looked up. She looked at her watch. 'Ten to twelve. Time to prepare.'

'What are you talking about? Have you got a lie detector?' asked Nick. He sounded nervous now.

'Yes, a spiritual lie detector. I believe spirits see everything. They know what you did. Are you prepared to be judged by them?'

'What are you talking about?'

'We're going to ask the spirits if you planted those drugs on Wesley and then tried to kill him.'

Zoe was aware of the darkness outside. She longed to pull the curtains, make it cosy in here. Most of all she wanted LeAnne to stop, but she felt totally helpless. LeAnne was like some force of nature, and they were all at her mercy.

LeAnne went over to the table at the side of the living room. It was meant to be a dining table, but they preferred to eat sitting on the comfy chairs.

Instead it had slowly been accumulating debris, and LeAnne began to remove all the clutter: a hairbrush, keys, masks that had been removed after the walk, make-up and nail varnish LeAnne had brought over as well as the empty box for the torches.

She picked up the dining chairs and arranged them around the table, and went into the hallway where she had left a bag that first night when they arrived. From it, she took a wooden board which she opened and placed on the table.

Zoe went to see what LeAnne was doing and gasped in astonishment. She saw a board covered with the letters of the alphabet, the numbers zero to nine and the words 'yes', 'no' and 'goodbye'.

'Wow! It's a Ouija board. I haven't seen one of them since school,' said Zoe in horror.

LeAnne looked directly at her. 'We didn't know what we were doing back then but, used properly, I've found the board never lies.'

Zoe grimaced. 'Seriously, LeAnne, I may not believe in any of this but to suggest we try to contact the dead is insensitive after we've all been through. Put it away.'

LeAnne stood very upright, her hands on her hips, her eyes scanning the faces of the group. 'No. It's because of what we've been through that we have to do this. We are so close to the other side. I can feel spirits in this room. We have to talk to them.' She turned to Nick. 'Are you prepared to let them speak or are you too scared of what they might say?'

'Will this settle it once and for all?' asked Nick.

'It will. Whatever the board decides, I will go with.'

'You can fix it so easily. Push that wooden thing—' interrupted Annika. 'This is stupid.'

'I promise on my life and Wesley's life there will be no cheating on my part,' said LeAnne. 'My mum needs this. She believes the board. She needs proof that Wesley is innocent. We both do.'

Zoe could hear how desperate LeAnne was: maybe they needed to do this for her.

It was as if Nick picked up on this as well. He stood up, 'OK, look, if you need to do this, then let's get on with it. If any verdict is given, which I very much doubt, then you might finally have to start to come to terms with what Wesley did and maybe then you, your mum and Wesley can move on.'

Zoe checked her watch: three minutes to twelve. Nick took his seat at the table, and was joined by Annika, then Gino and finally Zoe sat with them. At any other time she would have been joking, but everyone seemed so serious. She thought, at least for LeAnne's sake, she should remain silent.

They sat very still. 'Everyone must turn off their phones,' LeAnne instructed, and they complied.

The room was eerily quiet, the only sound was the tapping of the bony branches of the trees on the window.

LeAnne took a metal plate and small bundle of sage out of her bag. To Zoe's surprise, she lit the herbs, waving them over the plate and chanting, 'I cleanse this space of all negativities.'

She placed the herbs on the plate. Soon only ash remained, but the woody, musky, peppery smell of sage lingered.

After this, LeAnne took candles out of her bag and lit them, placing them around the edge of the board. 'I shall use white candles for our protection.'

She also lit an incense stick, which released the strong, sweet, lemony smell of frankincense.

Nick sneezed. 'Do we have to have all these strong smells?'

'We have to do this properly, Nick. It's important. We're opening portals to another world. We must be protected.'

Zoe was inclined to agree with Nick that the smells were cloying and overpowering.

LeAnne turned off the lights. The only illumination was from the candles flickering on the table.

Zoe usually found candles comforting, romantic, but tonight the flickering flames seemed to dance menacingly on the faces of the people sitting around the table. Like the masks, the flickering light hid more than it exposed. Was that how it really was with people: more was hidden than we ever saw?

'Right, I'd like us all to hold hands,' said LeAnne.

No one responded. They all sat self-consciously with their hands in their laps.

'Come on, hold hands,' instructed LeAnne again.

Zoe reluctantly held hands with LeAnne on her right, Gino on her left. Then others followed suit. It felt uncomfortable, too intimate.

'We call upon our guardians to protect us.' LeAnne's voice changed. She spoke in soft chant-like voice. 'We call upon the spirit world and welcome any kind spirits to talk with us.'

There was a moment's silence. Then, in the same voice, LeAnne said, 'And now we stop holding hands, each lay one finger lightly on the planchette.' They did as they were told as LeAnne continued, 'Spirits, are you there?'

Zoe glanced around the group. Certainly everyone looked engrossed now, but she felt like an outsider, an observer.

Nothing happened, as Zoe expected. She wondered how long they were going to have to sit there.

No one moved. They all seemed content to wait.

Slowly the planchette began to move, to spell out a word.

LeAnne was prepared with a pen and paper.

The first letter was M, followed by A, then X.

'Maxine, are you here?' asked LeAnne.

'Stop!' screamed Annika.

Zoe felt Gino's body tighten, but he didn't speak.

'Welcome, Maxine,' said LeAnne. 'We are sorry for what happened to you. You know we love you and we miss you. We want to ask the spirits if Nick has been lying to us.'

The planchette moved to G then each of the letters U I L T Y.

Zoe heard Annika gasp. She looked at Nick, who was staring, horrified, at the board.

'Maxine, are you telling us you now know Nick was guilty of planting the drugs?' asked LeAnne. Zoe could hear she was desperately trying to keep her voice calm, but the excitement was bubbling through.

NO.

'What are you trying to tell us then?' asked LeAnne, confusion in her voice.

The planchette moved, slowly spelling out: I W A S K I L L E D.

There was a collective gasp. Everyone quickly withdrew their hands as if the planchette had burnt their fingers.

LeAnne's eyes were wide in terror.

'We have to continue,' she said, her voice shaking.

The group members reluctantly placed fingers back on the planchette.

'Who is the killer?'

Slowly it began to spell out: G I N O.

There was a crack as a huge branch hit the window. The candles flickered and were extinguished. They were in darkness.

Gino pushed back his chair violently, but LeAnne shouted, 'Don't move.'

They all froze, while LeAnne quickly thanked the spirits and spoke words to the effect that they would close the portal.

Without waiting to be released, Gino marched to the lights, and switched them on.

'Who did that? This is a sick joke,' he screamed, his face red with fury.

Zoe scanned the group, once again able to see everybody properly.

LeAnne was breathing so fast that she was on the verge of hyperventilating.

Annika was very still, pale, with small red patches on her cheeks. Her middle finger and thumbs on both hands tapped together and her eyes flickered around the group as if, like Zoe, she was judging their reactions.

Nick had flopped back in his chair. His arms hung loosely by his side, but the fast blinking of his eyes conveyed a mixture of relief and confusion. 'What the hell?' he exclaimed. 'Who did that? Gino has a right to know who moved that damn thing.'

No one spoke. No one looked him in the eye.

Gino came back and thumped his fist on the table. 'I demand to know who did that.'

Zoe shrunk back. The anger in his voice had the full force of a hard slap. This was a side of Gino she'd never seen.

'LeAnne, what just happened?' he demanded.

She was very pale. 'I don't know. Honest to God, I have no idea.'

Annika turned to Zoe and spoke calmly, with no fear in her voice. 'Was this you? Are you getting your own back on Gino?'

'Of course not,' she replied.

'I did not kill my wife,' said Gino, red with anger. 'How dare anyone insinuate this.' He stood up, leaned over the table, and shouted in Zoe's face, 'You did this. I know it.'

Zoe could feel the heat in his breath. She tried to hide her fear. 'Of course I didn't.'

'If you threaten me again you will regret it,' he snarled. Nick sat forward, spoke quietly. 'I think we need to calm down. Whoever did this needs to own up and apologise to Gino.' He spoke like a teacher handling a difficult group of children. 'But we all need to cool off first.' He looked at LeAnne. 'Maybe that wasn't such a good idea. We're all very stressed. I shouldn't have agreed to go along with it.'

'I agree. This was a stupid idea,' said Annika. 'Everyone is upset, and you got no answers about Nick.'

'No. Interesting. The spirits didn't seem to want to talk about him,' said LeAnne. 'I wonder why not.'

'Well, I'm not going through that again,' said Nick. 'Now, I need a drink. Wine, anyone?'

'I'm going out,' shouted Gino. Grabbing his coat, he stormed out of the apartment.

LeAnne started to put the board away carefully. Avoiding their gaze, she said, 'I'm sorry, everyone. I didn't expect that. But the spirits have the right to take us where they will.'

Once everything was cleared away, she looked at them, a fixed smile on her face. 'Now, on a lighter note, I would like to invite you all to come over to Ventnor tomorrow to my restaurant for lunch. I was thinking we could meet earlier, walk around by the school, relive a few memories, then eat at my place. How about we meet at the school gates at, say, ten?'

Those present agreed. Zoe just wanted to leave now, and told LeAnne she was about to call a taxi. LeAnne decided to leave with Zoe.

As they walked across the dark courtyard, Zoe breathed in the cool air and felt calmer. She could make out Gino from the light of his torch, he seemed to be heading to the keep.

'What do you make of what happened?' she asked.

'I've always trusted the board,' said LeAnne, quietly.

'Do you honestly believe Maxine visited us?'

'Of course I do.'

Zoe unlocked the metal gates locking them behind her. She was glad to get away tonight.

She phoned Liam. He was able to come for them, but he was in Cowes: he would be about fifteen minutes.

They decided to wait for him. As they stood, Zoe remembered the last time they'd stood here in the dark ringing Liam, unaware that Maxine was dead. Liam had come quickly that night.

For a moment, her heart raced. Why had Liam come so quickly? Was he a suspect she'd missed? Annika could have let him into the castle. Did he kill Maxine to protect his relationship with Annika?

But Zoe remembered the couple falling out of the taxi. Liam had definitely driven them from Ventnor. He had a cast-iron alibi for the time Maxine died.

Eventually they saw the taxi coming up the hill. Liam flashed his lights at them, came to a halt and jumped out of the taxi with his usual enthusiasm.

'Back to your mum in Bishopstone?' he asked, smiling, opening the back door.

'Yes, please,' said Zoe. She found herself grinning back: he certainly had a lot of charm.

As they fastened their seatbelts, Liam said, 'I was very sorry to hear about the death of your friend. What a tragedy. I know Annika and Nick were very fond of her. They must be shocked.'

'It's been very difficult,' said Zoe. 'It's hard to believe it was only a few days ago. I think you gave Maxine a lift last week, didn't you? Over from Ryde to Cowes and then out to the nursing home?'

Their eyes met as he glanced in his mirror before driving off.

'That's right. It ended up a long drive. I was only thinking about her the other day. A very nice lady: very generous, quiet though.'

'Did she seem upset to you?'

'Not particularly, just preoccupied. You learn to pick up signals from your customers, the ones who want to chat and the ones who don't. Still, as I say, she seemed a nice woman. I'm sorry about what happened to her.'

It wasn't long until they were back in Bishopstone. Zoe paid Liam. Zoe thought that LeAnne had been unusually quiet throughout the journey. As she unlocked the front door, she asked, 'Are you OK?'

A Halloween Murder

LeAnne shrugged, but Zoe could see she was close to tears.

* * *

Despite the late hour, Susan had decided to stay up reading. The evening with Robert had been strained. She hadn't been able just go to bed when she returned. Instead, she had made herself a decaf coffee and sat with the dogs, reading.

She'd got lost in her novel, an Agatha Christie she'd borrowed from the village library. She'd been brought up reading the classics, or non-fiction, and had only recently been branching out. The book she was reading was actually called *Hallowe'en Party*, a rather dark mystery surrounding the death of a thirteen-year-old girl.

She was so involved in the plot that she'd missed the sound of the taxi drawing up. She was startled by the front door opening.

'Oh, hi,' she said to Zoe and LeAnne. As the words, 'Good evening?' slipped out Susan could tell from the look on LeAnne's face that it had been anything but.

'I'm off to bed,' said LeAnne quietly, and she made her way up the stairs.

Zoe came and sat with Susan. The dogs switched allegiance, moving from Susan to rest their heads on Zoe's lap.

'What's happened?' asked Susan. 'LeAnne looks very upset.'

Zoe lowered her voice. 'You're not going to believe this, Mum. LeAnne produced a Ouija board.'

'Oh, no. Really?'

'I know. She did the whole thing: candles and incense.'

Susan frowned. She'd never felt easy with seances and the like. Too often people came away frightened or disturbed, and this group of friends were particularly vulnerable and stressed.

'How did it go?' Susan asked.

'As I expected, nothing happened for ages. There were no answers about Nick or Wesley, which was supposed to be the point of doing it.'

'Is that why LeAnne is so upset?'

Zoe cringed. 'Not exactly. You see, the name Maxine was spelt out: she visited us. She told us she had been killed and she named the killer.'

Susan gasped. 'Oh, Zoe. What a shock! Who did she say killed her?'

'The name spelt out was Gino.'

Susan sat back, but looked closely at her daughter. She could see her eyes were bright with excitement as she bit her lip. At that moment, Susan knew exactly what had happened.

25

Zoe grinned at her mother. 'Yes, it was me. I moved the planchette on the Ouija board. We were sitting there. Clearly, nothing was going to happen, so I thought, why not liven things up?'

'For goodness' sake, Zoe,' said Susan crossly.

Zoe rolled her eyes. 'It's no big deal, Mum. It all fell a bit flat. Nobody broke down and confessed to killing Maxine.'

'But you accused Gino.'

'It won't hurt him to experience what I've been through.' The smile had gone, and Zoe crossed her arms in defiance.

'Zoe, you shouldn't have done that. You've really upset LeAnne. It doesn't matter you thinking the séance is nonsense. It matters to her. And also, you were playing with fire accusing Gino like that. I know it's been awful for you, but you knew you were innocent. What if Gino is guilty? We said earlier how the shock has been replaced by fear, and fear makes people, innocent or guilty, unpredictable.'

Zoe bit her lip. 'No one will take it that seriously. They'll forget it soon enough.'

There was a creak on the stairs. The dogs pricked up their ears.

'Was that LeAnne?' Zoe whispered.

'I don't know.'

Zoe cringed. 'Maybe it was a mistake. I hadn't thought about it upsetting her.' She shrugged. 'I'll own up to her tomorrow and apologise. I'm not worried about Gino, though. He can cope. I hope I do get some kind of reaction. We've only got a few days left here. I don't want Maxine's killer to leave feeling like they've got away with it.'

'Just be careful, Zoe.'

'LeAnne has invited us all to her restaurant for lunch tomorrow. We're going to go round Ventnor beforehand. That will give us all a break. Um, can you take us over? You could go and see Robert. He could join us for the meal—'

'I'm not sure he'll want to see me at the moment.'

Zoe's forehead wrinkled in concern. 'Oh, no. What's happened?'

'It was a bit difficult this evening. Although he did answer one of the questions we keep asking.'

'What was that?'

Susan looked around and checked LeAnne wasn't still on the stairs.

'He discovered that Maxine's will left everything to Gino.'

'Oh!' exclaimed Zoe. 'He finally gets his hands on her savings.'

'He does and, what's more, he gave away that he knew about the contents of the will before Maxine died.'

'The police should be out arresting him now,' said Zoe.

Susan smiled. 'They need more before they can do that. Oh, and there were one or two other interesting bits of info from Robert.'

Susan told Zoe about Nick and the two thousand pounds.

'That's weird. What's that all about? Why is this chap Frank putting that amount of money into Nick's account?'

'No idea. Oh, and by the way, the police were totally convinced that Nick was completely innocent of Wesley's allegation that he deliberately drove at him.' Susan explained the details of the crash.

'LeAnne must know this. Why is she continuing with her campaign against Nick?'

'Wesley's her brother. Maybe it's simply misplaced loyalty. Of course, this doesn't prove that Nick didn't plant the cocaine—'

'True,' said Zoe. 'Robert did well. He's a useful contact, as well as a good friend. What was the problem between you then?'

Susan started to tell Zoe about Robert's plans to go and help his daughter in France and his invitation to Susan.

'It's very good of him. What a nightmare for her.'

'She chose to go there—'

'Yes, but it's easy to underestimate how much work and money something will be. It sounds such a beautiful place to bring up the family. But you know all that, Mum. It's not like you to be so judgy.'

Susan knew Zoe was right. 'It's complicated. I think what most upset me was how Robert started out saying how much he wanted me to go and then I realised he'd already been making all the plans.'

'But he's bound to have been having conversations with his family about it.'

'I know, but I suppose it made me feel like I didn't matter, that he was just going off.'

Zoe put her head to one side. 'Like Dad?'

Susan nodded.

'Robert's not Dad. You know that. He's asking you to go with him. Would it be so awful to go out there for a month or so?'

'But I'm just building my home here, and I need to be close for you and Jamari. You need the support.'

'Well, maybe now is the right time to tell you. I said earlier that I was prepared to do anything for Fay. I promised I'd tell you exactly what I meant by that.'

Susan waited.

'The thing is, Mum, we may have to move to be closer to her parents.'

'You're moving to Scotland?'

'We might. Part of the reason for Fay's visit this week is to try and gauge whether we should move up there.'

'Move to Scotland?' repeated Susan.

'Um, yes. I'm so sorry, Mum, but we have to think about it. I hate the idea, I'll be honest. We have you and the island, but also our friends. Jamari has her playgroup here. It would be difficult, but we can't carry on like this—' Her eyes filled with tears. 'I'm sorry.' She wiped the tears away as Susan furiously tried to take in the implications of what she'd just been told.

'So, when would you go?'

'Soon. We would have to live with her parents to start with, get an estate agent to sell the house for us. Her dad isn't going to get any better and her mum is starting to crack under the pressure.'

'Have they got help going in?'

'They have some but, of course, they have no other family up there. It's her father's family who are Scottish, and he's the only one left. Her mother is from down here. Her sister and brother are here. Her mother gets lonely.'

'Would they think of moving down?'

'I suggested that,' said Zoe, with a weak smile. 'The problem is her that father loves being in Scotland. I think Fay's mother is scared that if she moves him away it will be like taking a snail out of its shell. He'd give up.'

Susan nodded. She could see the sense in what Zoe was saying. She could feel her lip quivering, but was desperately trying not to cry. That wouldn't help Zoe, and she had to go with her family.

'You must do what is right for you and Fay, love. Scotland isn't on the other side of the world, is it? I can fly from Southampton to Edinburgh.'

'You're so kind, Mum, but we both know nothing would be the same.'

'I know, but we could make it work.' Susan looked at the clock. 'It's nearly two, love. We should both get some sleep. It's been quite a day. But thank you for talking to me.'

Zoe kissed her mother on the cheek. 'And thank you for listening. I feel so much better for telling you everything. Sleep well, Mum.'

Susan watched Zoe go upstairs. It had helped her, unburdening herself, being reassured by her mother.

When Zoe was out of sight, Susan sat back on the sofa. What a night it had been. The dogs were relaxed, but she realised if she didn't go up to bed, she would fall asleep there and that wouldn't do her any good. And so, she locked up, settled the dogs and went to bed.

In bed, she switched off the lights and took comfort in the dark. She felt tears burn her eyes. The idea of Zoe and Jamari being so far away hurt in a way she'd never imagined it would. All those lovely impromptu Saturdays on the beach that they'd had this year wouldn't happen if they moved away. They might come down for a week, but it wouldn't be the same. As things currently stood, not only could Zoe come here, but Susan could also pop over to help out, babysit for a night, take Jamari to toddler time, just spending time together. That would all end.

Susan tried to reason with herself. Fay's dad had been so unwell. It was hard on Fay always being so far from him. And there would be positives for Zoe and the family moving up there. House prices in the area outside Edinburgh where Fay's parents lived were lower than down here. They could get a bigger house, a nicer garden. Zoe's and Fay's jobs were both transferable. They could have a good life up there.

Compared to friends whose children had moved to Australia, this was nothing. But, said a voice, scratching away at her, it was still a lot further than it was now: everything would change.

Susan wiped away the tears. She'd adapted to the momentous change of her husband leaving her, started to build a life without him. She could do it again.

Of course, they might ask her to move to Scotland. Would she want that?

Susan stepped out of bed and moved towards the window. She looked over the village, where lights sparkled comfortingly from the houses nearby, to the distance, through the blackness, the sea. The move here had been huge: a new village, a new part of the island after forty years in Ventnor. However, it was still her island. Could she ever bear to leave it?

Susan climbed back into bed. Her thoughts turned to Robert. He had been coping with his daughter moving away, living in another country, but hadn't really said much about it until this week. Susan realised she hadn't been very supportive, had not appreciated how much he'd been quietly handling on his own. She hadn't reacted at all well to him talking about going to France. This needed sorting.

***

The next morning, Susan felt exhausted, her eyes sore from lack of sleep. Zoe and LeAnne seemed in better spirits, looking forward to the visit to Ventnor. It was a cold, crisp November morning, but the weather was good. There was sunshine.

Susan nervously sent a text to Robert saying she was going over to Ventnor, half expecting him to make an excuse not to meet up. However, she should have known better. He replied immediately saying that he would love to see her and would have the kettle on ready.

Susan drove Zoe and LeAnne along the military road, catching glimpses of the sea until they turned inland after Blackgang towards Whitwell, St Lawrence and finally Ventnor.

Susan dropped Zoe and LeAnne at their old school and drove around to see Robert, having arranged to meet the group at LeAnne's restaurant later.

The dogs, as always, were excited to see Robert's dogs and they all ran out into the garden.

The atmosphere was naturally rather strained, but Susan waited until Robert had made them coffee to talk. As well as the drinks, Robert produced two plates, each bearing enormous croissants.

'Wow, where did they come from?'

'I went down to the baker's this morning. I thought you'd enjoy it.'

'Thanks, it's perfect.' Susan bit into the buttery pastry, flakes falling down her jumper, but she didn't care. She tried to smile, but maybe it was lack of sleep, maybe it was the emotion of the night before: she felt tears on her cheek.

She wiped them away. 'Sorry, bad night's sleep.'

'It's more than that. What's happened? I'm sorry. I came on too strong last night.'

'No. No, you didn't. I was being very selfish. Of course you want to go and help your daughter. I was wrong to criticise her for the move and wrong to make this a choice between her and me.'

Robert bit into his croissant and smiled warmly. 'Goodness, this is a different side of you.'

'Well, I was wrong. Something Zoe said made me realise I hadn't appreciated what you've been going through.'

'And what was it that she said?' He sat forward, patiently listening in that way he always did. 'So, what's happened?'

Slowly Susan described the conversation with Zoe, occasionally gulping back a tear. 'I'm so sorry, it's stupid.'

'No, it's not. You and Zoe are close. It's lovely. Jamari is your only grandchild.'

Susan sniffed, feeling much better for spilling out the words. 'There's all that talk about letting your children fly, and I understand it. I really do. I agree with it but, well, change is always hard.'

'Of course it is. It sounds as if Zoe is dreading the idea as well.'

'I think she is, but she's right.' Susan sipped her coffee. 'I'll cope. I know I will. It's just the shock.'

'Exactly. And about me and France—'

Susan cringed. 'I don't know.'

Robert held his hand up. 'It's OK. Look, I want to go over and help out but, after we talked, I realised I'd not seriously considered making a permanent move over there.' He paused. 'I'm not running out on you, not going to abandon you.'

Their eyes met, and Susan realised he'd known exactly what she'd been thinking.

Robert continued, 'The island is my home. All my memories are here and, of course, so are you.' He laid his hand on hers. 'I didn't set out with the intention of making this some kind of test of our relationship, but it turned into one. I think I should go this time on my own, see how things lie. I haven't seen the house yet. Also, I might find living under one roof, albeit a leaky one, for weeks on end may prove too much for me or my daughter. So, I will suggest I go to stay with her until the new year, and then return home. I think going out for short periods of time might be the way to do it.'

Susan smiled. 'That sounds good. I'll miss you. You do know that, don't you? But we'll chat online, and I can even come over here, keep an eye on the house for you.'

'That's perfect. Thank you. Tell you what, let's go down on the beach: give the dogs a good run.'

The brisk walk along Ventnor beach was just what Susan needed. It took her back to the days she lived there and would take her dog, Rocco, down to the beach most winter mornings. It was how she'd met Robert and become involved in investigating her first murder. Little Libs, her black cocker spaniel, had also come into her life as a result. It was lovely how close Libs and Rocco had become.

She couldn't stay with Robert long as she was due at LeAnne's restaurant at twelve, so once Robert had safely put all the dogs in his car, she made her way up there.

26

Susan started the climb up the hill, one of Ventnor's steepest, and was glad to turn off into the side street she knew LeAnne's restaurant to be on. She met Annika, looking in a shop window.

'On your own?'

'Nick's gone off to his model shop so I'm having a wander.' Annika glanced at her watch. 'I'd better go and dig him out. He'll lose all sense of time. It's quite fascinating in there. Do you want to come?'

'Yes, all these shops have arrived in Ventnor since I moved. It's great.'

The model and games shop had the same cluttered air as one selling haberdashery or antiques. Rows of models, every type of primer and paint, brushes, aerosols, stands and many different styles of boxes to display the models in... the list went on. So much stock that you wondered how the owner ever kept track of it.

Nick was engrossed in inspecting a selection of miniatures. He seemed startled when Annika called his name.

'Are you buying more?'

'I will definitely buy this.' He smiled. 'I only came in for a new tin of primer, but this caught my eye.'

Susan glanced around the shop. A young man with long hair was arranging a display. She approached him.

'Excuse me. This may sound odd, but do you have a miniature of the Grim Reaper?'

The assistant looked completely unfazed. He answered her seriously. 'We usually do, but with Halloween—'

Susan glanced around, impressed that he knew immediately they were out of stock.

'I can order them in for you,' he offered.

'No. It's OK. Thank you.'

'Asking about Grim Reapers?' Nick's voice made Susan jump.

'Just interested.'

'You believe Zoe's story that Maxine had been given a miniature?'

'I do. In fact, I remembered seeing red paint on Zoe's finger the next day. She told me it had come off the model.'

'Well, that must have been a cheap model. Done properly with primer, the paint would never peel off. I'd like to see it.'

'It seems to have disappeared, so you're not likely to.'

Annika came over to them. 'Right, come on. Pay for those, Nick. We need to get going.'

The restaurant was three doors down. It was decorated in a smart grey paint with white writing. It simply said 'Sustain'. Susan smiled. It was a good name.

Inside, she walked through the smart, modern eating area. A few tables were occupied by people drinking and perusing menus.

LeAnne had prepared a table for the group at the far end of

the restaurant. This was close to a large window which looked out onto an outdoor area.

Susan was fascinated. There appeared to be a number of small greenhouse-type structures, but the insides looked cosy, with rugs and heaters.

'They've been a huge success,' said LeAnne, coming over to her. 'People love sitting out there in the evenings, looking up at the stars. I take them down in the summer, but it gives us extra dining space when the weather's less warm.'

'It looks wonderful in here, LeAnne. You should be so proud of what you've created.'

'I am. Thank you. It's everything to me.'

Watching LeAnne here, it was clear that this was where her heart was. She stood more confidently, looked very much in control.

Susan sat next to Zoe, opposite Annika and Nick. LeAnne joined them, sitting opposite Gino.

As LeAnne had told them, the menu was a few regular dishes and a large part was a simple list of 'today's catch'.

A young woman came and took their order. She showed good understanding of the food being prepared, and Susan could see she was receiving encouraging smiles from LeAnne.

Susan, of course, was vegetarian, but she was also provided for. She ordered a vegetable tagine made with local vegetables, including fresh Isle of Wight tomatoes.

The food was beautifully presented. It was good to be together away from the pressures at the castle, and Susan noticed people chatting in a more relaxed way than they had for days. They started asking about everyday matters: work, family, as well as remembering their times back in Ventnor. They were the kind of conversations that would have been natural on the holiday if the tragedy had never happened.

As the meal came to a close, LeAnne took most of the group out to see the pods on the patio, while Susan remained sitting with Zoe.

She glanced around the restaurant. This was where the party was last February. The effects of the events of that evening were clearly still being felt by members of Zoe's group, particularly LeAnne and Nick. But did it have anything to do with Maxine's death?

'Sitting here, can you tell me what you recall about Nick and the party?' she asked Zoe. 'I don't think it's directly related to Maxine's death but it's like an undercurrent in the group: you can feel the effects of it all the time. I need to understand it better.'

Zoe concentrated. 'OK, let me think.' She looked out through the patio windows into the garden. 'Earlier in the evening I remember being out in the garden. I was phoning Fay to see if Jamari had settled down at bedtime. Nick was smoking and Wesley was with his mates. I did see Nick go over to speak to them, briefly. I came back in. Nick returned a while later. He'd been drinking and was a bit loud.'

'What happened next?'

'Puddings were brought out for a sort of buffet. Wesley and his friends came in and were gathered around the table. Nick, as I say, was noisy. He glanced over at Wesley and said that he'd called the police, told them someone there was using weed.'

'Could anyone apart from those on your table have heard him?'

'I think so. As I said, he was pretty loud. Anyway, he started to leave. I went with Maxine and Gino to get dessert – they were really good, individual strawberry pavlovas, lemon possets, chocolate mousse: so much to choose from. When I went back to our table I told Annika to get one, but she stayed sitting down. I think she might have been worried about Nick. He was meant to be going to stay with a friend in Ventnor. It's why she let him leave. Nobody thought he'd be getting in a car.'

'Where was LeAnne?'

'Oh, wandering around. I was just tucking into my dessert when it all kicked off. Wesley came over, asking where Nick was. We told him he'd left. Wesley swore and ran out of the restaurant, screaming that Nick had set him up. The police arrived. We dashed out, and saw that Nick had crashed his car.'

'And Wesley was screaming at him from the opposite side of the road?'

Zoe paused. 'That's right. I remember Annika pushing past him, hysterical. She crossed the road, but Nick was already getting out of his car. LeAnne was trying to calm Wesley down, but he was just screaming. One police officer went to check on Nick. The other went over to Wesley. LeAnne tried to drag Wesley away, but he then started swearing and hitting out at the police officer and was taken to the police car. LeAnne had to stay with us. It wasn't long until an ambulance and more police arrived. We were asked to go back into the restaurant. Annika, though, stayed with Nick. LeAnne was furious, wanted to be allowed to go with Wesley, but they wouldn't allow it. Annika also rejoined us.'

'What was Wesley wearing that night?'

Zoe gave a confused look, but Susan simply waited.

'OK then, let me think. Yes, it was baggy cargo trousers and an enormous jacket. He and his friends looked lost in their clothes, but I guess that is the fashion. Why does it matter?'

'Just that it would have been pretty easy to slip something into one of those pockets... for Nick or for anyone else.'

Zoe grinned. 'Gosh, Mum, that was clever. You sound like a

real pro. Yes, Nick could have slipped something into a pocket when he went over to Wesley in the garden.'

'But also, you, Maxine, Gino and LeAnne could have had contact with him when he came in for pudding.'

'Yes, I suppose that's possible. Why suggest LeAnne though? She wouldn't have any reason to go planting drugs on her brother. You can see how upset she is.'

'But she may have been doing it as a precaution. Either she had drugs herself or she knew a member of staff did. If the police had found them, it could have ruined her business.'

'But she would never have planted them on her brother,' said Zoe.

'No? She may have thought he would get off with a caution, not expected it to be taken so seriously. Her business means everything to her.' Susan reached out to one of the small bowls of handmade chocolates that had been placed on the table at the end of the meal. She'd been trying to avoid them, but they were irresistible. She bit into a soft praline, and for a moment forgot talk of the investigation while she savoured the rich, creamy filling.

Susan dragged herself back to their conversation. 'You're probably right though about LeAnne. The obvious person had to be Nick, but why would he have cocaine on him?' She paused, as an idea had come to her.

'I've just remembered Nick's nosebleed. That can be a sign of snorting cocaine, can't it?'

'It can be,' said Zoe, 'but lots of people get them who aren't using drugs.'

'Maxine picked it up, though. Remember, she said, "Annika, we need to talk about Nick's allergies."'

'Oh, God, Mum, yes. Did Maxine think he was using

cocaine? Is that what she saw in the bedside table? No wonder she was going to the governors about it.'

'Yes, but of course, Nick didn't know she was planning that. However, Maxine did hint that she was going to tell Annika... I'd forgotten that. On the beach yesterday, Nick told me the one thing Annika would not tolerate was him taking drugs. Nick would have known that was the end—'

'I've put all Nick's moods down to alcohol, but he was very odd the night Maxine died, and LeAnne said she thought he was on something. Maybe she was right... my God, Mum, you've found a motive for Nick. He killed her to stop her talking to Annika.'

Susan poured them both fresh glasses of water from one of the bottles on the table.

Zoe leaned back. 'We've covered a lot and definitely learned more about Nick and Annika, but it still doesn't give us any solid proof or clues as to who killed Maxine.' Zoe looked at the group laughing in one of the pods outside: suddenly the task of solving this murder seemed impossible. 'There are so few physical clues in this case. We can't go looking for a dagger or a gun.'

'There's the miniature,' said Susan. 'We have to think where the killer may have got hold of such a model and what they have done with it. We know it's possible Gino, Annika or Nick may have found one in the flat but today I found out that LeAnne could also have got hold of one very easily.'

Susan told Zoe about the model shop. Zoe laughed at the idea of her mother asking about Grim Reaper models. 'Honestly, Mum: the lengths you will go to.'

'Seriously, though,' said Susan, 'we ought to follow up this miniature business. The killer either took it from Maxine when they were shown it or they removed it from her bag after she fell. What did they do with it? Oh, and one small thing. Nick said that the paint should never have come off the model if it had been painted properly. I'm not sure if that's relevant, but we could remember it.'

'I wonder why the killer didn't just leave the model. It's a bit daft to carry around something that links them to Maxine,' said Zoe.

Susan nodded. 'I agree. I wonder if they took it as insurance. If they sense the police are getting suspicious, they may plant it on someone else to divert them.'

Zoe cringed. 'I don't like the way you seem to be able to get inside this killer's head.'

'But that is the key to solving this. We need to search the apartment, look for that miniature—' She hesitated. 'Of course, the killer may have simply chucked it somewhere. Let's hope they held on to it.'

The others were coming back in now. Susan thought it must be time for everyone to leave. However, Nick cleared his throat and asked for everyone to listen.

'I would like to ask someone the most important question I can ask. I want you all, my close friends, to be my witnesses.'

27

The group gathered around in the restaurant, and watched as Nick slipped his hand in his pocket, took out a small box, and stood in front of Annika. He knelt on one knee, opened the box and said, 'I have loved you from the day I met you. It's taken me all this time to realise just how much and so today I'm asking you to do me the great honour of becoming my wife. Will you marry me?'

Annika's bright eyes filled with tears. Her expression was one of delight rather than surprise.

'Of course I will. This is the best thing ever.'

Nick stood up, kissed Annika, and put the ring on her finger, a beautiful diamond. Slowly, the group began to join in a round of applause, smiles slowly replacing confused expressions. Sensing they may find the timing of his proposal odd, Nick explained, 'I know this may feel a strange time to propose to Annika, but it was slightly out of my hands. Sorry about the timing of this but, well, this has been planned for a few weeks. I intended to propose this week and have the celebration this evening. A few of our family and friends have been alerted and I have booked the small function room for us all at the sailing club in Cowes tonight. After such a terrible week we have something to celebrate.'

'Of course,' said Gino. 'We will all come and, LeAnne, it would be good to open a bottle now?'

LeAnne blinked and disappeared into the kitchen, returning with a bottle of champagne, which she handed to Gino. He deftly opened it and poured it into glasses. Everyone toasted the couple, and final arrangements for the evening were made.

Susan stood slightly apart. She was sure the timing of the proposal had been a surprise to Annika. She looked happy enough but, given her relationship with Liam, she must have mixed feelings. Or maybe this would help her make the decision between the two men. Susan glanced over at Nick. She couldn't help feeling sorry for him and angry with Annika. He was glowing, ecstatic, completely unaware that Annika had been cheating on him.

It was agreed that Annika, Nick, and LeAnne would return to the castle with Gino in Maxine's car. Zoe said she would go with Susan to pick up the dogs from Robert.

As they left the restaurant, Zoe whispered to Susan, 'I wonder how Annika is feeling about all that?'

Before Susan could answer, Zoe caught her mother's arm: in fact she wrapped it around so tightly that Susan flinched.

'That's it, Mum. That's the van I saw Gino getting into the night Maxine died. I recognise the writing on the side.'

'No, it can't be,' said LeAnne sharply, from behind them. 'That's my dad's work van. He wouldn't have been around the castle that night. You're wrong. It was very dark. Zoe, you've made a mistake.'

'I'm certain that van was there, and Gino was talking to someone in it.'

'What would my dad be doing over there meeting Gino, who he hardly knows? No, you're wrong.'

LeAnne marched ahead of them, catching up to Gino.

'I'm right, Mum. I'm fed up with her saying that I imagine things. So why was Gino having a clandestine meeting with LeAnne's father?'

'Was her father at LeAnne's party last February?'

'Oh, yes. All the family were there. I remember early in the evening LeAnne took Gino round the restaurant to show him the work that had been done and then she introduced him to her family. At the time I wondered what Gino would make of them, but he stayed chatting to them for quite some time.'

'Do you think Gino was working cash-in-hand for him?'

'Maxine didn't think so. LeAnne's father is known for selling on goods. Maybe Gino was bringing over the cigarettes to sell?'

'There weren't that many though,' said Susan. 'It would be a very small operation.'

Zoe tutted, frustrated. 'You're right, but what else could it be?' She let out a long sigh. 'I wish I could go and search the apartment now, but everyone will be there.'

'I suppose we could go back to where Maxine fell, see if we missed anything. You never know, that miniature may have been thrown away.' Susan checked the time. 'Two o'clock. We should have enough light if we get on with it. We'll pick up Rocco and Libs from Robert, drop them home, and go to the castle. What do you think?'

'I think it's a brilliant idea,' said Zoe.

And so, an hour later, Susan and Zoe were back at the castle.

They started climbing the steps up to the battlements.

Susan was aware Zoe had gone very quiet when they reached the first landing point. 'Are you OK?' she asked.

Zoe frowned. 'It just brings it all back to me. This is where I met Gino after I spoke to Maxine. He was so odd that night.' Zoe looked around. 'I still don't understand why he didn't go and talk to Maxine if he was that upset by what he'd overheard. Why go back to the keep?'

Susan looked along the wooden platform. 'Gino seems a bit obsessed with the place, and it's quite a hike up there. I went up there that morning, when we were searching for Maxine.' She paused. 'Hang on: I saw something... what was it? I need to go back up there and check.'

'But let's go along the part where I met Maxine for now.'

They climbed the final flight of steps. When Susan reached the top, as always, she had this feeling of being on top of the world, with views over the island. It came to her that the last time she had been up here, it had also been with Maxine.

Turning to their left, they followed the battlements over the gatehouse until they arrived at the area which overlooked the armoury.

'This is actually where I had the conversation with Maxine,' said Zoe, 'and look, the wooden barrier that protects you doesn't come this far. I can see why I wanted us to move further along.'

Susan looked over the low stone wall, down into the ruined armoury. 'Yes, I don't think you could just stumble and fall here but if, say, you leaned over far enough, you might fall.'

'Particularly if somebody helped you over. I need to cast my mind back, see if there's anything I've forgotten.'

Susan waited as Zoe collected her thoughts.

'The first thing was the torch. We've not got any further with that, have we?'

'You're sure, are you, that the batteries were missing? Like DS Kent said, it was dark up here.'

'Yes, there were no batteries in the torch, but the torch

Maxine used earlier on the ghost walk worked. So maybe the killer for some reason had swapped the torches – but why?'

'Maxine was more vulnerable up here in the dark. She had her phone but that wouldn't have been as bright and she wouldn't have wanted to use up the battery.'

'The killer was lucky. Maxine said she couldn't be bothered to go back and get one that worked—'

'I guess it wasn't vital, but helpful for the killer,' said Susan.

Zoe bit her lip. 'But swapping the torches wasn't as easy as it sounds. I remember Maxine threw her coat down on a chair in the living room.' She paused. 'Of course: they took the batteries out of the spare and switched that with the one in Maxine's pocket. That would be much easier.'

'So they had Maxine's working one when they came up here, and swapped them back, which is why the police found one that worked.'

Susan nodded. 'Yes, they must have thought it would be suspicious for Maxine to have a torch which wasn't working, but how did they swap them back?' She held onto the cold stone wall, her forehead creased in concentration as she tried to imagine the sequence of events.

Eventually she said, 'I think the killer must have switched the torches after Maxine fell.'

Zoe shuddered. 'They must have been desperate to go down to her body and mess around with her pocket.'

Susan agreed. 'It's not a pleasant insight into the killer's head, is it? But then it's a very dark place to be, being prepared to kill.' She paused, then added, 'The killer must still have the spare as well as their own torch.'

They were distracted by a rustling in the garden. Zoe glanced down. 'It's only a blackbird,' she said, then looked around. 'It's so quiet up here. Every sound seems significant.'

She turned, looked out over the houses and fields, then down at the roof of the gift shop.

'That's where I stood waiting for LeAnne,' she said, pointing towards the castle side of the shop. 'I was right. I had a good view back up here. I saw the light, heard the voice. Oh, and that sound, the whooshing. I'd forgotten about that. I wonder what it was?'

'A bird maybe?'

Zoe shook her head. 'I don't think so. No.'

'Hopefully it will come back to you,' said Susan. 'Let's search around just in case the model, or the torch for that matter, were discarded around here.'

They searched that area of the battlements but found nothing. They then went back down to the armoury. As they entered, Zoe shivered. 'It's all horribly real, isn't it? I can still see her sprawled out here. Poor Maxine.'

'It was tragic, love.'

Susan looked around. She poked around the small heap of rubbish, but there was no sign of the model. They were leaving when Susan turned around and looked back.

'What's the matter, Mum?'

Susan went back into the old armoury, over to the rubbish. 'Why is that pile worrying me?' She walked over to it, then she saw it.

'Zoe, I know what made that sound you heard.' Her voice shook. She spoke quietly, in awe of what she'd discovered.

She pointed down at the aerosol can. 'That's a can of condensed air. People use it for cleaning laptops, or for model making—' She stared at Zoe.

'Nick had one of these on his desk. I saw it.'

'Yes, and there were loads in that shop.'

'So, Nick and Annika had access to it, or Gino... and LeAnne in the shop.'

'But how exactly did they use it?'

Susan grabbed Zoe's hand and led her back up to the battlements.

'Right,' she said. 'Imagine you are Maxine. I'm the killer. You're waiting for me. But you can't see well. It's very dark. We know Maxine was on edge, listening out for noises. The killer takes the can from their pocket, without Maxine seeing, leans over and presses the button, emitting that sound you heard down by the shop. "What's that?" the killer asks. Maxine looks down and then the killer acts. They drop the can, as they need two hands to push Maxine to her death.'

Zoe nodded. 'Yes, it could have been like that, but we thought they went to Maxine's body, removed the miniature and the torch. Why not pick up the can?'

'They forgot,' said Susan with a smile. 'It was a mistake, not just an act of over-caution. They simply forgot it.'

'Do you think there are fingerprints on it?'

Susan shook her head. 'I doubt it. No, the killer would have been wearing gloves, but it supports our theory. It confirms what you heard.'

'Should we tell someone?'

'Yes. Maybe you should speak to DS Kent,' said Susan, grinning. 'She sounds more receptive to you than to me.'

Zoe took out her phone and placed the call, but this time she got DS Kent's answerphone, so she left a message.

'Right,' said Susan. 'We need to finish our search.'

They went down to the Privy Garden and looked amongst the plants. It was easier this time of year with so many losing their leaves, and flowers so scarce, but they found nothing.

They took a break and sat on the wooden bench.

'This is where we all came the evening after Maxine died.'

Susan looked carefully at Zoe. 'Of course. Hang on, you mentioned something. What was it? Go through that evening again—'

Zoe talked through the events, then looked around. 'We should get on. There's the bank on the other side of the curtain wall, outside the castle, not as easy to search but we must look,' said Zoe. There was an urgency, a frantic edge to her voice.

'It will be difficult, muddy and slippery.'

'But, Mum, we have to look. Come on. I'm inspired by our success with the can.'

She walked away, and Susan rushed after her.

They exited the castle, clambered down the empty moat, up the other side and along the base of the castle walls, but they found nothing.

They went back into the castle, both muddy and tired after the fruitless search. Dusk was creeping in. Black clouds were joining together and covering the dark blue backdrop.

'Let's go to the apartment and wash our hands,' suggested Zoe. 'Do we tell the others about the aerosol can?'

'No. We don't want anyone removing it. Leave it for the police.'

As they approached the apartment, they saw Annika outside talking on her phone. She looked very serious. As they approached, she smiled, waved to them and ended the call.

'Mum is already talking hats! They're so pleased for me. And I'm so excited about the party this evening. It came as a complete surprise.'

They walked back into the apartment together, to find the others drinking coffee. Nick looked up at Annika, his eyes bright. 'Ah, my future wife,' he said, and gave her a hug.

'You two look a state,' said LeAnne, looking over at Susan and Zoe. 'What on earth have you been doing?'

28

Susan glanced down and saw just how muddy she'd got on the search in the castle grounds.

'Searching for that miniature of the Grim Reaper,' said Zoe in response to LeAnne's question, a note of defiance in her voice.

'And did you find it?' asked Gino.

'Well, no—'

'Of course not,' said Gino smugly, 'because there was no model and no missing torch. Why put on this façade, Zoe? Why not simply admit you made all this up?'

Nick sat forward and spoke gently but firmly. 'Zoe, you must realise we all need you need to back off now. We've all been very tolerant of the accusations you've been throwing around but it's very upsetting and offensive. It's up to the police to investigate, not you. I still believe Maxine's death was an accident.'

'I'm sorry, but I can't accept that,' replied Zoe. 'You may doubt my word, but I know someone was up there with her after I was. The fact that they won't admit to it is very suspicious and I know Maxine was scared.'

Nick shook his head. 'If that was the case, the police are the people to investigate, not you.'

Zoe pursed her lips, her hands clenched. 'I'm sorry, but I don't trust them to get to the bottom of this. They seem to be ignoring what I've told them about someone being up there after me, not looking for the miniature, not investigating the torch. I don't want to think like this, but we have to find out the truth. Maxine would have done it for any of us. Most of us are innocent. We don't deserve to have suspicion hanging over us.'

Nick sat back, face creased with anxiety. Annika reached over and rested her hand on his.

Gino leapt across to Zoe. 'You aren't pinning this on me. I had nothing to do with Maxine's death. You fixed that board last night.'

Susan's heart raced: so they'd come back to this. She heard the anger in Gino's voice. It frightened her.

However, Zoe seemed calmer now than she had been with Nick, and simply replied, 'I'm afraid I did. Yes, that was me.'

Susan waited. Gino's temper scared her. She wasn't sure how Zoe could appear so cool.

There was a silent gasp. Gino's face was red with rage. 'I knew it!'

'Come on. You've been happy to throw around accusations about me.'

'But I had foundations for them.'

'And I have for you. No one can corroborate your alibi for the time Maxine died. You say you were in the keep, but no one was with you. You had motive; you wanted to grow your business. Maxine was stopping you. I was right about you meeting someone secretly the night she died. I saw the van today at LeAnne's restaurant. Were you frightened Maxine had discovered some dodgy dealing?'

Gino threw his head back and laughed. 'This is nonsense, and if anyone killed Maxine, it was you – you're blaming us to distract us.'

Zoe shook her head. 'No, it wasn't me. Someone here had definitely arranged to meet her after I left, and they kept that appointment.'

Nick spoke up again. 'Look, Zoe, I repeat. Please give this up. Let the police do their job. We have to move on with our lives.'

'Maxine's death was a few days ago, Nick. How can you say that? We can't move on until we know what has happened.'

'And that's the police's job to find out,' Nick shot back. 'Now, why don't we all get ready to go out and celebrate? This is such a special day for Annika and me.' He threw Annika a loving smile, then turned to LeAnne. 'I know we've had our differences, but I hope you can be happy for us and will join us.'

LeAnne looked directly at Annika. 'I wish you every happiness and, yes, I will come out.'

Zoe nodded. 'Look, Nick. I don't want to ruin your celebration. I will leave off this evening, but I can't promise anything after that.'

Nick smiled. 'Thank you.' He glanced at Susan. 'You are, of course, invited to the party this evening. I do hope you will come.'

Susan smiled in acknowledgement. 'That's very kind, but I need a quiet night. It's been quite a week, and my dogs need me to spend some time with them. Have a wonderful evening though.'

Nick nodded in an understanding way, looked at his watch and said, 'Right. Time to get ourselves ready.'

Susan, LeAnne and Zoe returned to Susan's house to get ready for the evening. The dogs were excited to see them, and for their tea.

All three women were still feeling pretty full of lunch, so they had a few biscuits with cheese. Susan lit the log burner, and they sat close by.

Zoe engaged LeAnne. 'I should apologise for fixing the Ouija board.'

'It wasn't a wise thing to do. You shouldn't mess with the spirits, you know.'

'Look, I don't believe in it, but I realise you might feel it was disrespectful. I was surprised you didn't say anything when I confessed this afternoon.'

'I already knew. I heard you talking to Susan after we came back. I was more frightened for you than upset.'

'You don't need to worry about me.'

'You say that, but it doesn't stop the spirits being offended. They will have retribution.'

Zoe smiled. 'It's a good job I don't believe, or you'd be scaring me now.'

'I'm sorry, but you need to be careful, Zoe.'

Susan shot a glance at LeAnne. Was she threatening Zoe?

'I can't be hurt by something that doesn't exist,' said Zoe, but Susan heard a note of unease in her voice. 'Now, we'd better get ready for this party.'

LeAnne and Zoe went upstairs while Susan busied herself in the kitchen, Zoe returning far more quickly than LeAnne.

'I've got nothing glitzy, just the black cords and red jumper I brought for the concert. This will have to do. We're about the same size, I guess,' she said to her mother.

'I've nothing you could borrow, love. You're much slimmer than me. You look fine, really lovely.' The smile slipped from Susan's face. 'Now, listen. You need to be very careful tonight.'

'You think the spirits are out to get me?'

'No, but someone far more real might be. I certainly don't

want you putting yourself in harm's way. Stay with the group. No walking down dark alleyways on your own.'

Zoe laughed. 'Of course not. Now, don't worry. I'll be fine.'

LeAnne came down in a short black bodycon dress with heels Susan would never have been able to stand in, let alone walk.

'Gosh, you came prepared,' said Zoe.

'This was for the concert. That's your posh outfit then?'

Zoe grinned. 'It's the smartest I'm prepared to go, and I'll be warmer in the Great Hall tomorrow than you.'

Susan drove Zoe and LeAnne to Cowes where they were all meeting.

She dropped them at the top of the high street but couldn't ignore a growing feeling of unease, deep in the pit of her stomach. She understood why Nick wanted them all to have a good evening, but there was no hiding from the tension among them and her Zoe was right at the centre of it. Susan admired her daughter's passion for the truth, her courage in speaking out. She knew that she'd passed that on, but she knew only too well how much danger Zoe could be putting herself in.

She drove straight home, and decided to take the dogs out. Once outside again, she was struck with how cold the air felt. Winter seemed closer than it had a few days before. Tomorrow morning, she must remember gloves and her woolly hat. A warm coat was not going to be enough.

Next door was in darkness. Susan wondered where the new neighbours were sleeping that night. It would be good to have the house lived in properly soon.

She enjoyed her night walks with the dogs through the village. There were always a few more dog walkers out at this time and they greeted each other when they crossed paths. She noticed a small Christmas tree in the window of the hairdressers. Lots of people grumbled about creeping Christmas. Susan actually quite liked the effect of the lights. If it cheered up somebody's November evening, she really didn't see the harm.

The village shop was still open. Tracy worked such long hours, and she would be up early in the morning to do the papers. Maintaining a small shop as a viable business was not easy. Susan was pleased that Tracy at least enjoyed her work, even though she must be hiding exhaustion at times.

She walked down past the church, the school, then took the short lane into the park. It was too dark to let the dogs off lead, but Susan walked briskly around and returned home feeling refreshed.

She didn't feel relaxed enough to go to bed. Just like when Zoe had been a teenager, she needed to see her safely in tonight.

And so Susan put on an old series of *Sewing Bee* on TV and settled down with the dogs snoozing either side of her.

* * *

Friday night in Cowes was not the hectic, crowd-filled evening of a city centre. The pubs were comfortably full, but there were no bouncers on the doors, as couples and small groups stood outside restaurants reading the menus. It seemed pretty tame.

As Zoe walked down the dark passageway that led to the entrance of the sailing club, she remembered her mum's warning, but, of course, she was with LeAnne, who was walking surprisingly gracefully in her heels down the cobbled slope.

Inside was warm and welcoming. Sailing was a side of island life Zoe was unfamiliar with. Her father had not become interested in it until she was in her teens and, as with her mother, it wasn't something that had ever appealed to Zoe.

They went up two flights of stairs to a small function room. Annika's and Nick's parents and some friends were already there. Some were dancing to the music that was playing. It felt very odd to be out in the 'real world' after such an intense few days.

Annika and Nick had clearly been back to the flat. Nick wore a smart navy suit, but the real transformation was Annika. She looked younger and more fashionable than Zoe had ever seen her. Her hair was half up in a messy updo, her dress clingy, showing off her figure.

Zoe noticed Gino was chatting amicably to them, and he had the dashing appearance she remembered from the first time they'd met at LeAnne's party. His black hair was immaculately styled, his beard trimmed, and the perfectly fitted black suit and gold jewellery gave him an exotic edge over his more conservative male counterparts. There was no doubt he stood out. Zoe observed a blush spread over LeAnne's face as she noticed him.

'I have to say Annika has stepped things up a notch,' LeAnne said to Zoe. 'I've never seen her look so on trend. It's not just the clothes: she's holding herself differently.'

Zoe had to agree. Annika looked very happy and confident this evening. Maybe she'd realised that her future was with Nick. Hopefully, she would now end things with Liam.

Zoe was sure that LeAnne had no suspicions about this. No way could she imagine LeAnne keeping it to herself. No: LeAnne's thoughts were still close to her brother. 'It doesn't seem fair though that Nick's life goes from strength to strength when I know he ruined Wesley's.'

'But you can't be sure of that, and I'm not sure you'd ever be able to prove it.'

'I choose to believe my brother. It's all the proof I need.'

A waitress came over with a small tray of champagne and orange juice, another with canapés.

Annika's parents were working their way around the room and came over.

'We're Philippa and David. You're Annika's friends?'

'Maybe you don't remember us? I'm Zoe and this is LeAnne. We were in the band at school with Annika and Nick. It's lovely to see them as a couple.'

'Of course,' said Annika's father. 'You've changed. We can't have seen you since you were teenagers. We were terribly sorry to hear about Maxine's accident. What a tragedy. I have close friends in the police, although I have to say I was one step ahead of a lot of them. I knew about the accident before most. I hear Maxine had been drinking up on the battlements, a very foolish thing to do.' He looked stern. Any warmth in his eyes had gone, and the thinly veiled criticism upset Zoe.

'Accidents can happen to anyone,' she said firmly.

'Of course,' said Annika's mother. Zoe guessed she was used to smoothing out her husband's tactlessness. 'Her poor father. Annika is our world, I can't imagine what we would do in such circumstances.'

David picked up on the change of tone. 'Of course, it doesn't bear thinking about. I always admired Maxine. She used her talent and was building her career successfully. It's awful to think of someone who had so much left to give dying so young.'

'It's nice to be able to celebrate something this evening,' said Zoe as a conciliatory gesture.

'Indeed,' said Philippa quickly, 'and we were so thrilled when Nick talked to us last week. David has been unwell, and we know how worried Annika has been. It was wonderful to have some good news. So, what is it you do now, Zoe?'

'I'm a teacher like Nick, but with primary-aged children. I

live with my wife and little girl over in Portsmouth. My mother is still on the island, though. She lived in Ventnor for years. Susan Flynn. My father was a GP.'

'Oh, yes. We knew of him. He's, um, moved away now?'

Philippa clearly knew about her father going off and it was irritating to think of her mother's heartache being a juicy piece of gossip in the town.

'He has. Mum is living in Bishopstone now.'

'It's a lovely village. So much wilder over there on the west though, isn't it?'

Zoe smiled. Philippa spoke of a place only a few miles from her own as if it were a foreign land.

'It's different to living in a seaside town, I admit. Mind you, she doesn't miss the hills.'

Philippa laughed. 'I can understand that. I can't run up and down them like I used to.'

'LeAnne, you're still in Ventnor, aren't you? I understand you have a restaurant,' said David. 'We keep meaning to come down to it. Lovely to see a local person setting up a business in Ventnor. Your mother must be so pleased to have someone in the family adding so much to our community.'

Zoe groaned inwardly. That last sentence was loaded. They all knew that.

'My mother is proud of all her family,' said LeAnne pointedly.

'We all had a fabulous lunch there today,' said Zoe. 'The meal had the perfect ending, when Nick proposed to Annika.'

'We knew, of course,' said Philippa. 'But Nick said not to come. He wanted it to be a surprise for Annika and she'd have been suspicious if we'd made an appearance.'

David was glancing around restlessly. Zoe guessed he was a

man who liked to do most of the talking. 'We ought to move on. Lovely to see you both.'

They were barely out of earshot when LeAnne said, 'I'd forgotten what a prick he was. Good luck, Nick, with him as a father-in-law. I almost feel sorry for him.'

Zoe finished her glass of champagne, then decided to go to the toilets. As she was leaving, she noticed Nick with his back to her, talking in the hallway to an older man.

There was nobody behind her, so Zoe paused in the doorway to observe what was happening. She watched as Nick handed over an envelope. The man accepted it with a rather unpleasant grin, and slipped it into his pocket.

As he did this, a woman approached him. 'Frank, good to see you.'

The woman glanced at Nick. 'Oh, so sorry. I didn't want to interrupt.'

'Not at all,' replied Nick. 'I need to get back to our party. Annika's father is about to make a speech.'

Before he walked away, he turned quickly and seemed to catch sight of Zoe. However, he didn't acknowledge her, even with the faintest of smiles, but instead walked quickly back to the function room.

Zoe's heart was racing: she knew that name. Her mother had told her someone called Frank had put two thousand pounds into Nick's account. She also said Nick had been taking out large amounts of cash. What was going on?

29

When Zoe returned to the engagement party, she saw that Annika's father was about to make a speech and people were gathering to listen. Glasses were being charged with more champagne. The speech was mercifully short and Annika's father soon invited everyone to partake of the magnificent buffet that had been prepared in the kitchens at the club.

Zoe, aware of how much she'd been drinking, helped herself to food. She was relieved to see that for once most of the dishes had been labelled, and there was a decent spread for vegetarians. She selected bite-sized vegetable roulades, hummus, falafel, and carrot and caraway crackers. The food was delicious, and after she'd finished her plate she went enthusiastically to help herself from the array of puddings: mini eclairs, pastries, and French fruit tarts.

She congratulated Nick and Annika, who were both glowing. She also chatted to a few of their relatives and finally met up with LeAnne again.

'You're not eating much,' she commented, looking at the half-eaten pitta bread on LeAnne's plate.

'I'm not hungry. Too much tension around, I guess.'

After a few minutes and a glass of white wine, Zoe decided that maybe it was time for her to leave. LeAnne, though, wanted to stay, so Zoe went outside to find a taxi alone.

As the fresh sea air hit her face, she felt the effects of the champagne. Maybe she should clear her head before heading on home?

The atmosphere in the town had changed now. Approaching eleven o'clock, it was a bit more edgy. People out for meals had gone home: it was just the drinkers left.

She walked down the alleyway that led onto the seafront.

The parade had streetlights and she could see groups of people in the pubs, chatting and laughing. She walked along, taking in the fresh air, started to feel better and decided to turn back.

As she walked back along the parade, she looked out to sea, saw the silhouettes of the larger boats. It was noisy as the waves crashed on to the shingle, as if trying to reclaim it.

The alley that led to the sailing club and then the high street was across the road. Before going over, Zoe noticed a slipway and, feeling drawn to the sea, she carefully made her way down the damp path, until she reached the edge of the water.

Finding the sea far more mysterious and compelling at night, she stared out into the darkness. Zoe was so absorbed that she missed the sound of footsteps behind her. Her first indication that she was not alone was when—

She felt the violent push between her shoulder blades, hard and purposeful. Zoe fell crashing to her knees but managed to grab onto a metal ring in the wall to stop herself being propelled any further forward and into the sea.

She pulled herself up, and swung round but her attacker

had gone. All she could hear was footsteps running up the alleyway and then stop.

Staggering back up the slipway, nausea gripped her. She noticed someone walking further along the parade, but the person glanced over and crossed the road, avoiding her, probably assuming she was drunk.

She longed for Fay to put her arm around her, comfort her, take care of her, but she was abandoned and alone, frightened.

Her knees were stinging. Looking down, she saw the front of her trousers were sodden. She wanted to get back to Susan's and she began to hobble across the road. There was no one around now. The quickest route to picking up a taxi in the high street was up the alleyway. She looked up. She could see it was deserted and began making her way up.

Zoe became aware that her hands were filthy, and her coat was streaked with muddy water. Would a taxi driver even allow her into his cab?

Of course, she could ring her mother, but then she realised she was at the sailing club entrance. The toilets were just by reception: she could nip inside, tidy herself up and then get a taxi.

However, as she walked in, a member of staff entered the reception area and caught sight of her.

'Are you OK? What's happened?'

'Nothing, I fell.' She looked up the stairs. 'I came to the party, then went for a walk.'

The woman came over. Her name tag indicated she was Penny. 'Why don't you come and let me help you? That's blood seeping through your trousers.'

Maybe it was the gentle way Penny spoke, or maybe the enormity of what had happened was starting to sink in, but Zoe found herself sobbing.

Penny put her arm around her and guided her into a small office behind reception.

'Where did you fall?'

Zoe was shaking now. 'I was pushed,' she said, and started to sob again.

'Let me fetch someone from the party—'

Zoe panicked, as she remembered the footsteps disappearing up the alley. Of course, her attacker could have come in here. That push had been purposeful. It wasn't random. Her mother was right: she had become a threat to someone in her group.

'No, please don't,' she said.

Penny gave Zoe a glass of water which Zoe sipped. She then rolled up the legs of her trousers. As she thought, both knees were badly grazed.

'I could see to those knees,' said Penny. 'But first, I know there's a police officer on duty in the town this evening. How about I give him a ring? He should know someone is going around doing things like this.'

Zoe realised it was pointless, but Penny was already on her phone.

While they waited, Penny bathed Zoe's knees and applied plasters. It wasn't long before a uniformed officer arrived at the sailing club. Zoe gave him the few details she could. As she did, she was aware her words were slurring from the champagne, but the officer was gentle and polite. He didn't seem to be judging her. He wrote down all she told him and took her details, including Susan's address. He offered to take her to the hospital.

'I don't need it, seriously. I just want to get back to my mother's. There's a taxi rank close by, isn't there?'

Zoe thanked the receptionist for her help. The officer was

very kind and considerate, but it was clear to Zoe there was little follow-up he could do. The officer walked her up to the taxi rank. Zoe noticed Liam in one of the cars. He waved to her, then seeing the officer, got out of the car.

'What's up?' he asked.

'Um, I fell,' said Zoe. She looked up at the officer. 'Thank you so much for looking after me. I'll be fine now.'

'Take care now, and if you remember any other details don't hesitate to call us. Thank you for reporting the incident. We need to know what's going down and we'll make sure we patrol that area for the next few nights.'

As he walked away, Liam asked, 'Needing a lift?'

Zoe nodded, feeling her lips tremble. She was close to tears again.

Liam helped her into the car and she sank back into the seat.

Liam got into the driver's seat but looked at her in his mirror. 'Where are you heading?'

'Mum's please, in Bishopstone.'

Liam started to drive away.

'Nasty fall,' he said, glancing in his mirror. 'The police were involved then?'

'Actually, I was pushed over, down by the harbour. I think it was a kid or something.'

Suddenly, a terrifying thought inched its way into Zoe's mind : could Liam have been her attacker? Maybe he was protecting Annika? Panicking, she looked down at the door handle. She saw a light: the automatic lock was on. In any case, it was ridiculous to think of throwing herself out of a moving car.

She caught Liam watching her from his mirror. Their eyes met.

'I'll take the country route if that's OK. They're doing night work on Horsebridge Hill.'

He turned off and soon they were on dark, unlit country roads. Zoe knew there was an entrance to Parkhurst Forest not far from here. Her mind was racing. Where was he taking her?

30

Zoe dug into her handbag and grabbed her keys, the only thing she could think of to use as a weapon.

'So, what were you doing down the harbour on your own?' Liam continued to chat as if nothing was amiss. 'I guess you'd been to the engagement party?'

Momentarily distracted, she said, 'You know about Annika and Nick?'

'Annika sent me a text about the proposal. I'm so made up for her. What a lovely couple they make.'

He sounded genuinely happy. Zoe guessed he was putting a brave face on it, but then he added, 'Actually, I knew about the proposal before Annika. Nick had already invited me to the party but I told him it's not my kind of thing. I'd been booked for a stag do over in Yarmouth, so I stuck to it.'

Zoe wondered if he just couldn't face the celebration.

To Zoe's relief, they turned on to the main road and the route back to Bishopstone.

'You look done in,' said Liam. 'You rest now; not long till I get you home.'

At that moment he received a call and started chatting to someone trying to arrange a lift to Heathrow the following week.

Sitting back, Zoe caught her breath, closed her eyes. Liam seemed to pick up her need for quiet and let her be.

And then finally, thank God, she was home.

Liam, without speaking, opened the car door, helped her out.

* * *

Inside the house, Susan heard the slamming of a car door, guessed Zoe was returning, although it was before twelve, earlier than she had expected. She opened the door, saw the taxi driver helping Zoe and rushed over to her.

'What's happened?' Susan asked Zoe.

'She's had a bit of a shock,' Liam explained. 'I've no doubt she'll tell you all about it.'

'Thank you,' Susan said.

Zoe fumbled for money and jammed some notes into the hand of the driver. 'Keep the change. Thank you.'

'You take care now.'

With her arm around Zoe, Susan helped her into the house.

Inside, she saw the scratches on Zoe's hands, the wet knees, how red her eyes were and that her make-up was smudged by tears.

'What has been going on?'

'I was pushed, Mum.' Zoe burst into tears.

Susan's stomach turned over. She was close to tears herself now. All the primaeval emotions that stir when someone has purposely hurt your child raged around her: the need to protect, to fight back.

'Who did it?'

Between gulps of tears, Zoe described being pushed down by the edge of the harbour.

'The police know. I went back to the sailing club, really just to use the bathroom, but the receptionist kind of took over.'

'She sounds very kind. I'm glad the police know.'

'They're not going to be able to do anything. I couldn't tell them anything about the person who pushed me, and it's not even as if I was badly hurt.' Zoe gave a weak, watery smile, calmer now. She rolled up her trouser legs and showed Susan the plasters. Blood had seeped through.

'Oh, love, that looks painful. Knees take a while to heal. I'll fetch your dressing gown if you want to slip out of those things.'

Susan was not gone very long, returning with a comfy dressing gown. She took the clothes Zoe had taken off into the kitchen and left them inside the washing machine.

'Incidentally, did you notice the taxi driver? That's Liam, the man we think Annika is seeing.'

'Oh, right. He seemed very kind actually, and he's handsome.'

'I know; seems a nice bloke. He knew all about the engagement. Nick had told him. I guess he's putting a brave face on things.'

'Maybe. So, back to this push: was there definitely only one person?'

'It was.'

'Did you hear or see anything?'

Zoe tried to think back. 'No, nothing. I didn't even hear them coming up behind me. The waves were making a lot of noise crashing on the shore.'

'So, you have no idea who it was?'

They looked straight at each other.

'I'm certain it was someone from the group, Mum. The attack was purposeful, it wasn't someone messing about. I think they were warning me off.'

Susan's heart sank. This had been her greatest fear all along: that Zoe was putting herself in danger, that the killer would strike back.

Zoe gave a weak smile. 'I guess it proves we are on the right path.' She shuddered. 'That push had such force in it. It felt like real anger. That's what frightened me so much.'

Zoe placed her hands over her face, and she sobbed.

Slowly she removed one hand from her face, reached for her handbag and opened it, searching for a tissue. However, she suddenly froze, stared at Susan.

'What is it?' Susan asked.

Zoe pulled out an object, a grisly miniature figure of the Grim Reaper, the scythe painted red, blood dripping down.

'Oh my God,' she said. Her teeth started to chatter. Her whole body shook.

'Who put that in my bag? It wasn't there before I went out. I'm sure. I sorted out my bag.'

Susan went and found a sandwich bag and suggested Zoe put it inside, then placed the bag on the table.

'I should imagine the killer wore gloves, but we'll put it in here just in case. It needs to be handed to the police. Listen, love. I really think you should leave the island now. You have to think of Fay and Jamari.'

Zoe frowned thoughtfully. 'I admit I'm tempted. But, Mum, I can't go. You've always said truth matters. I want Jamari to have a mother who cares about it, will fight for it. And then there's friendship, loyalty. I owe Maxine all of those things.' She shook her head. 'No. I can't leave. I have to see this through.'

Susan nodded. 'But you are in danger.'

'I was stupid this evening. I'll be really careful tomorrow. It's the concert and I'd like to be here for that.'

Zoe stared down at the bag containing the miniature. 'The police won't suspect me because of this, will they? We said the killer took it to cast suspicion on someone else—'

Susan shook her head. 'I don't think so. The worst they can conclude is that you had it all along and are trying to use it to confirm your story.'

'It seems a bit stupid for the killer to give this to me. Like the push, it simply confirms to me I'm on the right track.'

Susan nodded. 'I agree. It does seem foolish, but the killer is getting frightened and desperate. It makes them dangerous but it can also lead them to make mistakes. They may simply be hoping you will be scared off.' She squeezed Zoe's hand.

'Whatever they all think, our time is running out, isn't it?' said Zoe. 'We have tomorrow. Everyone goes home on Sunday. One day to try and get to the truth.'

'You mustn't allow that to push you into taking any more chances. Now, you need to shower and rest.'

'OK. Oh, before I go up, I should tell you what I saw happen with Nick.'

'What was that?'

Zoe told her about seeing Nick with Frank and how she thought he was giving him money.

'Paying back a loan seems to make sense,' agreed Susan. 'Do you think he needed money to pay for drugs?'

Zoe grimaced. 'I've a nasty feeling you could be right. I also met Annika's father. I didn't have anything to do with him when I was a teenager, but I can't say I warmed to him. He was rude to LeAnne. He obviously knows the reputation of her family. He also kind of boasted about knowing about Maxine's accident before anyone else, then seemed to almost blame her, saying he'd heard she'd been drinking.'

'That was uncalled for.'

At that moment, they heard a knock at the door. Susan let in LeAnne.

'I'm so sorry to knock,' said LeAnne. 'I didn't realise until Zoe left that I had no way of getting in, but it looks like you were still up.'

Susan looked at Zoe but caught the quick warning shake of the head.

'We've been chatting,' was all Zoe said.

Fortunately, LeAnne accepted this at face value and went straight to bed.

Susan turned to Zoe. 'I think you should go up now. Have a shower and try and rest.'

'Thanks, and Mum, I was thinking: could we make a visit in the morning?'

Susan smiled. She knew exactly who Zoe meant. 'Of course. I think that would be a very good idea.'

* * *

The next morning, Susan got up early, ready to walk the dogs before the others were up. She was just putting the coats and leads on Libs and Rocco when she heard footsteps.

'Morning, Mum. I thought I'd join you for the walk if that's OK?'

'Of course. It's going to be very cold, so wrap up.'

They drove to the car park close to the local manor house where Susan had stayed the Christmas before. There was no snow today, but the ground was hard with an early frost.

They climbed the steep path which circumvented the manor

grounds and led to woodland. In the spring it would be carpeted in bluebells, but today it was covered in crisp, frozen autumnal leaves. They kept walking, the dogs rushing around, foraging in the undergrowth.

One final steep path led them up on to the downs. Here they were greeted by the ancient Longstone, a solitary house and downland.

'I haven't been here for years,' said Zoe.

'I was here a lot last Christmas.'

'Oh, yes, of course. Your last investigation.'

'It's good to come back. The Long Stone looks exactly the same. So many dramas and tragedies have happened up here and yet the stones stand solidly the same. I find that comforting.'

'I guess it's like the castle. When we leave, the walls remain, to see the next tragedy unfold.'

'Or joy: the walls see it all.'

'I always feel the island knows its own, remembers them. It's why I love bringing Jamari here. I feel this will always be her home. Remember, you gave her a fossil at her birth celebration? I keep it next to her bed.'

'That's lovely. I'm glad.'

'Wherever we go, we'll have that with us. And wherever I live, the island will still be part of me.'

'It will.'

They watched the dogs run up the hill and followed them. They reached the brow of the hill which looked down on to the village and over to the sea beyond. Looking at Zoe, though, the frown on Susan's daughter's face showed her mind was in a far less pleasant place.

'What's wrong?'

Zoe sighed. 'It's the concert this evening. I'm dreading it.'

'But Mrs Strong will appreciate you being there.'

'I know, but it's going to be incredibly hard and sad not having Maxine there.'

'You're stronger than you realise. You'll cope, love. Now, last night you mentioned a visit. I was going to check with Alice if she's free – I'm assuming I've got this right?'

'You have, and yes, I'd love to see her.'

They walked back down to the car and returned home. LeAnne was still in her room. Zoe knocked on the door and explained they were off to see their friend Alice. LeAnne replied that she would have a lie-in and catch them later.

Alice had replied to Susan that she was free early that morning and so they set off straight after breakfast.

Alice was sitting with a cup of tea on the table, her iPad in hand and Princess on her lap. She greeted them with the same warm smile and twinkling eyes that she always did. Princess gave them a glare and pointedly turned to face away from them.

'Good to see you too, Princess,' Susan said, laughing.

'Well, you have a warm welcome from me,' said Alice.

'So much has happened, Alice. I need your perspective on everything,' said Zoe.

'I find that very flattering. Tell me the news.'

'First there is our discovery.' Zoe told Alice about the aerosol can.

'That's excellent. It's always reassuring to have confirmation you are on the right track.'

'That's how we feel,' said Susan.

Zoe sat forward excitedly. 'Now, I have something really interesting to show you.'

Zoe produced the small bag containing the miniature, handed it to Alice and explained how she came to be in possession of it.

Alice frowned. 'It's a horrible thing. I can understand why it upset Maxine.'

'I feel someone is warning me as well. And then there's the push.'

'The push?'

Zoe gave her account of the attack.

'That's very serious,' said Alice. She handed the bag with the miniature back to Zoe.

'Yes, I was scared, I don't mind admitting.'

'It sounds like a warning to me. I think, as you said, this is someone telling you to back off.'

'I have been stirring things up, I guess. I was frustrated. I didn't feel I was getting anywhere.'

'Well, you are getting results now. Interesting that it's the same tactics, the model and the push. Killers often lack imagination,' said Alice.

Susan hid a smile. Alice had spent her life as the village shopkeeper in Bishopstone, seldom venturing outside the village, let alone going on trips to the mainland. And yet she had this amazing insight and understanding into human nature.

Alice continued, 'It's fortunate because it's how the killer is often caught. We are all creatures of habit. It's natural. We repeat what has worked for us. The killer knew the miniature scared Maxine. They're hoping it will do the same for you.'

'But they didn't seriously hurt me.'

'Which is interesting. You were alone in the dark. They could have done a great deal more harm.'

Susan shivered: the same thoughts had occurred to her.

Alice continued, 'but they intended this as a warning. I'm sure about that.'

'It's not going to put me off,' said Zoe defiantly.

'No. I didn't think it would,' said Alice, 'but of course—'

'I know I have to be careful,' said Zoe. 'Oh now, something else I found out yesterday. Remember I said I saw Gino in a van the night Maxine was killed?'

'I do. White with writing on the side.'

Zoe beamed. 'Exactly. Well, I've found the van.'

'Does it belong to LeAnne's family?'

Zoe stared, open-mouthed. 'Now, how did you know that?'

'I spoke to Tracy. We remembered LeAnne's surname was Alnwick. You said the van had lettering on it, and a picture of castle with a lion, which is the symbol of Alnwick castle, in Northumberland.'

'That's very good detective work.'

'It sounds cleverer than it is. I was already wondering if this was someone from LeAnne's family. To be meeting secretly at that time of night strongly suggests some illegal dealings. I knew members of LeAnne's family had been at the party in February. The really interesting thing here is what business Gino was cooking up with LeAnne's father.'

'Yes, we think it was selling on cigarettes Gino brought into the country, although I'm not sure he's bringing in enough to make a very profitable business.'

Zoe told Alice about the contents of Annika's safe.

'It doesn't sound that many, and you did say Maxine found wads of cash. I was thinking about that. I wonder why Gino needed cash. My granddaughter hardly uses cash any more.'

Zoe blinked. 'Actually, I remember that Maxine said that the fact Gino needed cash bothered her more than how he got it.'

'Ah, now that is very interesting,' said Alice, her eyes shining.

'We're sure now he's been having an affair with LeAnne. She seems very keen on him.'

'Remind me. Does LeAnne have an alibi for when Maxine died?' asked Alice.

Zoe explained that LeAnne claimed to have been in the apartment until twenty past twelve. But she added, 'Of course, Annika did say that LeAnne was putting her coat on when she'd left at twelve, so she could have gone out.'

'She could. Could you remind me of everyone's alibis?' asked Alice.

Zoe went through the group: Gino at the keep, Nick and Annika missing each other. Alice was particularly interested in Nick and Annika. 'Interesting. Annika at least seems to be able to account for her time, but where was Nick?'

'We have no idea. Oh, by the way, he proposed to Annika yesterday. We had all been invited to LeAnne's restaurant for lunch and he did it in front of us all.'

'Goodness – an odd time to do it.'

'He'd had it planned the week before we came. He'd spoken to her parents, booked the room in the sailing club for the party in the evening. Oh, but there's so much more about Annika.'

Zoe told Alice all about Liam.

Alice raised her eyebrows. 'That's very surprising. Now, I talked to Donna who works here. Annika seems to have shared her hopes and dreams with Donna. She talked about having saved up a lot of money, how she was going to leave the island, start a new life.'

Susan smiled. 'I know she'd like to leave with Nick, but it'll be quite some time. She hasn't much money saved yet. I think she must have embellished that for Donna.'

'She may well have.' Alice turned to Zoe. 'Talking of Annika, I was thinking again about her conversation with Maxine.'

'Oh, she agrees it happened now.'

'Good, it was a stupid lie. Now, I was thinking of Maxine after Annika left her. I was watching her out in the garden, scrolling through her phone. I may have this all wrong, but it seemed to me as if her face lit up. It was an expression of someone feeling the warmth of the sun on their face after a long time in the cold and dark.' Alice looked closely at Zoe. 'I will make one guess. Don't be angry if I'm wrong. Had your friend Maxine maybe met someone new?'

Zoe stared.

Alice gently patted Princess. 'I just wondered. You'd mentioned her marriage was very unhappy, that she confided in you. You blushed, looked nervously at your mother when you talked about Maxine confiding in you. It all added up.'

Zoe shook her head. 'You don't miss anything, do you, Alice?'

'Am I right?'

Zoe glanced over at Susan. 'I promised, Mum.'

'But if Maxine was having an affair, the police will find out,' said Susan.

'But she wasn't. That's the whole reason I haven't said anything.'

'Maybe you'd better explain,' said Alice.

Zoe sat back. 'OK, but I'm not promising to tell the police. Maxine wasn't having an affair. I promise you. About a month or so ago, she went into an art gallery in Portsmouth, met the owner, got chatting. He's an artist, and she bought some postcards of his paintings. He'd asked her out for a drink before we came away. She didn't go, but she was tempted. She told me she'd forgotten what it was like to feel warm and excited by someone. It's been so hard and cold with Gino for so long. She was scared but I think it gave her a glimmer of hope that maybe, one day, she could, well, be happy again.'

Zoe turned to Susan. 'You see why I can't say anything to the police. They would make a huge deal out of it. They will never believe there was nothing there and I can't bear seeing Gino using it to justify his own affair.'

'But they would only go and talk to this dealer. He would be able to confirm there was no affair, if that's actually the truth.'

'It is, Mum. I'm positive.'

'Then you have nothing to fear. You are making this a much bigger thing by keeping it to yourself now.'

Zoe sighed. 'I guess you're right. Maybe I have to trust the police with this.'

'Good. That's the right thing to do,' said Susan.

'True. Now I have learned something else of interest,' said Alice. 'You mentioned that Maxine had referred to a case she had recently been involved in and how it had influenced her. I thought it would be interesting to look it up.'

31

Susan sat up. Of course, she'd forgotten to research the case Maxine had been involved with before she came away. Trust Alice to remember. 'Tell us, did you manage to track it down?'

'It takes time, but I have plenty of that.'

'So how did you go about finding the information on Maxine's last case?'

'The first thing I did was google her name. It wasn't difficult to track down Maxine and her chambers. I took a guess and hoped that her last case had been heard at Portsmouth Crown Court. To my surprise, I was able to see all the cases that had been listed over the past few months and found her most recent one. Disappointingly, little detail was recorded. They had simply named the people involved and the charges. I jotted the names down, and thought maybe the local paper had covered the case.'

Susan smiled. 'That was inspired.'

Alice grinned. 'I have to admit I was rather pleased I thought of that. I tried googling each of the names of the people involved, and actually found quite an extended piece written about it.'

'So, what was the case about?' asked Zoe.

'It was very interesting. It was something I know little about. Two women had been charged with smuggling drugs and mobile phones into prison at visiting time. The article looked at their case and explored more generally the situation in prisons. LeAnne is right: smuggling is a huge problem.'

'Who was Maxine defending? Was she defending one of these two women?'

'That's right. Maxine's client had a child with her, and they found ketamine in what should have been the battery compartment of a toy. The sniffer dogs discovered that. Then they found spice sprayed on a child's painting, and a mobile phone in the sole of one of her trainers.'

'Good grief. She was really taking a chance, and it seems worse somehow to use a child.'

'I agree, but the mitigation was that the woman had been forced into this by friends of the partner. They'd threatened her and her family.'

'That's awful. I guess her friend was doing something similar?'

'Exactly, she had ecstasy in what appeared to be a packet of sweets.'

'Hang on,' said Susan. 'This case of Maxine's involved smuggling drugs into prison. Doesn't LeAnne go there to visit her uncle? Had Maxine become suspicious of LeAnne?'

'Maybe,' said Zoe. 'But how would Maxine get to know about that?'

'I'm not sure. But we still haven't discovered what they were arguing about on the ghost walk. If Maxine was accusing her of something like this, well, it could certainly ruin LeAnne.'

'One of the women was smuggling phones inside their trainers,' mused Zoe. 'LeAnne wears those ones with very thick soles.'

'That's true,' said Susan. 'She seems anti-drug but maybe she'd take in phones for the right price? Of course, it might be that Maxine was more interested in the places drugs had been stashed than where they were going.'

'You could be right,' said Alice. 'I was amazed once I started reading how drugs were being taken in: everything from cuddly toys to birthday cards.'

Zoe sat forward, excited. 'So, if Maxine had seen an object that she thought could be used to smuggle or hide contraband in, she might have wondered if that person was taking drugs—'

'I noticed they all had cuddly toys in the apartment, and even LeAnne has them on her bed. So far we've only thought of Nick possibly taking drugs though.' She went through the conversation she'd had with Zoe with Alice.

'It must be possible,' said Alice, 'and very likely that is what Maxine saw in Nick's drawer. It would be worth just taking a look at all those cuddly toys though – just in case. Ah, back to Nick for a minute. I asked my daughter about him and his reputation at school. She said Nick was highly regarded, had done wonders for the music there. A friend of hers works with Nick, likes him a lot. Everyone was very surprised he was arrested for drink driving but they knew the stress he'd been under.'

'Was this because of the online abuse?'

'Well, he was finding the job very stressful anyway, but the abuse from Wesley had been particularly vindictive. This friend told my daughter that although it had stressed Nick out, he'd been very forgiving of Wesley, seeing him as a very troubled lad.' Alice looked around, then lowered her voice. 'Nick's only consolation was that after Wesley had left school he had treated other members of staff in a similar manner: publishing their home addresses, making accusations, telling people to burn their houses down.'

'My God! That's terrible. Actually, Robert mentioned the police knew about Wesley's reputation for stirring up trouble. They certainly didn't believe Nick had driven his car at him.'

'Interesting.'

They sat back, caught their breath.

'So how much longer are you all here?' Alice asked Zoe.

'Just until tomorrow. There's a concert this evening for our old music teacher, and then we all leave. It makes me wonder what exactly I can hope to achieve in a few hours. We can try and look at these toys, but there isn't much else.'

'I can't help feeling that things are building to a head. You need to be extra vigilant now,' said Alice.

'But we can't back off. We have so little to go on. I've a horrible feeling this person could get away with this.'

'The police won't stop. Don't forget, their investigation will continue.'

'I know, but I'm so close to everyone. I should be able to see things the police would miss.'

'I can see that, but you must pass everything on to them. Don't forget to give them that miniature and tell them Maxine's secret.'

'I will.' Zoe smiled. 'Thanks, Alice. It's been so helpful coming here and talking to you.'

'I'm glad. Now I probably won't see you before you leave. Take care. It's been a pleasure getting to know you better. You are much more like your mother than I think either of you realise.'

Zoe grinned. 'I'll take that as a compliment.'

As she stood up, Susan looked at Alice. She caught a look of consternation, warning even, and nodded. She was only too aware of the danger she and Zoe were in.

As soon as they reached the car, Zoe took out her phone. 'I'm ringing that police officer now to tell her about Maxine's secret. If I leave it, I know I'll back out.'

'You could mention about Frank and the miniature as well.'

'Of course.'

Susan climbed into the car while Zoe made the call. It wasn't long until Zoe joined her.

'OK?' she asked.

'It was better than I expected. I actually spoke to DS Kent, and she was very understanding: no lecture or anything. She also promised that unless it had any bearing on the case, it would be kept quiet.'

'What about Frank and the miniature?'

'She said they knew about Frank.' Zoe grinned at Susan. 'They're ahead of us on that one. As for the miniature, she's going to send someone round later to pick it up. She was already planning for someone to make a visit – she'd got the message about the aerosol.'

Susan smiled. 'I have to admit DS Kent is being very efficient – you have definitely got on her right side.'

'She's been OK with me. She said she'd get the officer who is coming round to text me so I can meet them. It'll be later this morning.'

'You did well. Right, let's get back to the house.'

Susan and Zoe found LeAnne was up and dressed. Susan drove them to the castle, returning home to walk the dogs and have another look at this case Maxine had been working on.

* * *

The castle was closed to visitors today, which was very unusual on a Saturday. It seemed eerily quiet for late morning. Zoe and LeAnne wandered over to the Great Hall.

Walking though the main door, they entered a very different world. Inside was a buzz of activity. People were rehearsing in corners, tuning instruments. Some were drinking coffee from flasks, eating snacks.

Zoe hadn't been in the Great Hall for a long time, not since she'd visited as a child. It was a very quiet museum, with exhibits in cases. She remembered at one time buying jumping beans in the little shop inside there. She'd always loved the enormous model of the castle. She would like to have been able to play with it, but this was obviously forbidden.

The room itself had been shaped by Isabella de Fortibus in medieval times. One end had been her chamber, the other a private chapel. Zoe had been amazed to learn that this incredible woman had six children before she was twenty-three. At that time there had been a very high ceiling, but a false ceiling had been introduced to create an upper floor.

The room spoke clearly of its many original medieval features, including the great fireplace, and merely whispered its later uses such as being the summer lodgings of Queen Victoria's daughter.

Although most people were wearing thick woollen jumpers, Zoe noticed they'd discarded their coats. Extra heating had been set up and the room was warming up.

Zoe soon spotted Mrs Strong, the music teacher, and walked over to introduce herself.

Mrs Strong looked quite a lot older than Zoe remembered, but she reminded herself that this woman was now, like her mother, in her sixties. She was looking unusually ill at ease. Zoe remembered her as always bustling around, looking very much in control.

She tapped her on the shoulder. 'Hi, Mrs Strong. I'm Zoe.'

Mrs Strong blinked and stood up, smiling broadly. 'Of course. How lovely to see you. Please call me Diane.'

Zoe grinned. 'I'll give it a go, but old habits die hard. It's wonderful to see you again.'

Diane clasped her hand. 'I was devastated to hear about Maxine. What a tragedy. I quite understand if tonight is too much for any of you.'

'We all wanted to come. Maxine had organised this week around this evening. It would seem all wrong not to be here.'

'Maxine was such a bright girl. I always knew she'd do something special. It's such a waste. Her poor father. That's her husband over there, isn't it?'

Zoe saw Gino, the sleeves of his jumper rolled up, moving a large bench. 'Oh, yes, that's Gino.'

'He's been very good, moving things around.'

'He's like us all, doing it for Maxine, I guess. Although this concert is of course all about you. We want to celebrate your work; you meant so much to all of us.'

'You were all talented. It was lovely to have kids of your age back then so enthusiastic.'

'How does it feel to be retired?'

'I can't quite believe it but, so far, I'm enjoying it, keeping busy with grandchildren.' She looked around. 'This feels a bit strange, though: being at something and not organising it. I've had strict instructions to keep out! My husband and daughter have put this together.'

Susan saw a younger woman, about forty, in jeans, holding a clipboard and batting off questions in a competent but calm manner.

'That's my Catherine,' said Mrs Strong.

'She's just how I remember you at the school concerts. You even had a clipboard like that.'

'It was mine. I've handed it down. She's a music teacher on the mainland now. How she's managed to do this on top of a full-time job and kids I have no idea.'

'She's her mother's daughter: that's how.'

'I'm delighted that Annika still feels able to sing. She's to be accompanied by Nick, I hear.'

'That's right. She's definitely the best person to represent our group.'

'And how are you enjoying teaching, Zoe?'

'I love it. Although I have a wife and child now, so it's not easy fitting it all in.'

'I'm sure you're excellent in all your roles. You were always so organised even as a teenager. Whatever you committed to, you gave your all. You have heart, passion. You care, like your mother.'

Zoe blushed. 'Thank you. Goodness. It's not often I get deluged with such praise.'

'Well, you should be. Right, contrary to my daughter's instructions, I am going to go and help that group of youngsters trying to tune their violins. I can't cope listening to them making such a hash of it. Lovely to see you, Zoe.'

Zoe smiled as Mrs Strong bustled off. Everyone in their group seemed to be in there. Annika and Nick were quietly practising. Gino was helping move chairs, LeAnne was chatting to an old acquaintance.

It dawned on Zoe that this was a perfect time to go and search the apartment for that spare torch. But she didn't have a key: she would need to borrow one.

She went over to Nick. She knew she'd be able to get away

with a vague excuse of needing to go and use the bathroom over there.

'Of course,' he said reaching for his keys. 'Actually, can you take mine and Annika's coats over with you? They're in the way.'

She picked them up and was soon on her way to the accommodation.

32

Zoe found it strange going into the empty apartment. Maybe it would have been different if she was staying there, but she felt guilty being in here on her own.

She reminded herself that someone could return at any time: she needed to get on with this. Her focus was to check the cuddly toys and look for that spare torch but really to be alert to anything unusual.

She went straight to the large table which they'd used for the Ouija board. It was covered again with all the clutter. Zoe glanced at the box that had contained the torches. Knowing it had been empty, she almost left it untouched but couldn't resist removing the lid.

What she saw made her gasp: a torch had been returned! She moved to pick it up but remembered her mother's warnings about fingerprints, and so put on her woollen gloves. She picked up the torch, hardly daring to breath. Would it work? She pushed the switch, nothing. Trembling, she managed to remove the battery cover; the compartment was empty. This had to be the torch Maxine was holding when she met her. Examining it more carefully, Zoe found that on the side was a tiny dent. That was interesting. It was supposedly spare and if it was unused, it should have been unmarked. She guessed that dent had been made when Maxine fell. She went to the kitchen area, found a plastic bag and put the torch in it, before placing it in her bag.

Zoe glanced over the table, and another object stood out. She picked up a bottle of bright red nail varnish and remembered LeAnne suggesting they might like to wear it, to have their fingers dripping with blood. From her handbag, Zoe pulled the bag containing the miniature of the Grim Reaper. She held the nail varnish next to the scythe: they were exactly the same colour.

Her heart raced. So, the killer had used varnish, not paint. No wonder it peeled so badly. Of course, this belonged to LeAnne but it had been lying here on the table. Maxine had found the miniature in her pocket after the ghost walk. Maybe LeAnne had bought the miniature from that shop, painted the scythe and brought it away, with the plan of frightening Maxine before she killed her. LeAnne had made the joke about the Grim Reaper before they left the flat.

Zoe slipped the nail varnish in her pocket and, encouraged, continued her search of the apartment.

She moved to Nick and Annika's room, and in here she was particularly looking for any signs of cocaine use. She would look for small bags of the powder, and she had picked up from a documentary the other kind of things to look out for: small tubes, spoons, mirrors, blades and the like.

She started on the bottom bunk and quickly realised this was Annika's. A pink nightdress was carefully folded with a romantic novel featuring a woman on board a cruise ship on the cover. Next to them, propped against the pillow was a pink beanie bear with an embroidered heart. Zoe guessed this was a present from Nick.

Zoe examined it carefully, but it was clear the original factory stitching had not been disturbed.

She climbed up a small metal ladder to examine the top bunk. There was a glossy music magazine. She flicked through it, but there was nothing hidden among the pages. There was a similar bear to Annika's in blue. Zoe examined this but again there was nothing suspicious. There was also a small open tin of mints. She'd seen Nick eating them off and on: green hard-boiled sweets. Maybe they helped with indigestion or something? She glanced at the lid. It wasn't a brand she recognised.

She stepped away and searched through the drawers and holdalls but there was nothing of interest.

It was disappointing, but she had to keep up her search, so Zoe headed for Gino's room. The room was pretty untidy, and she realised that Gino had made no effort to put away any of Maxine's belongings. The way the glass and books lay on the bedside table, her nightie in a heap on the floor, made it feel as if she could walk in any moment. Maybe that was what he was hoping.

Her attention was caught by the teddy bear on the bed. She hadn't suspected Gino of taking drugs but she had to inspect it. Gino had talked about Maxine's affection for it, but it was his and it was interesting he'd brought it away with him. The teddy bear lay propped up proudly on the bed close to the pillow. It was not that old. It wore a smart waistcoat and bow tie and had the name Gino embroidered on it with a heart. Maybe it had been a gift from Maxine? Zoe couldn't really imagine why else Gino would have it with him. Zoe picked it up, examined it: all the seams appeared original. She was about to replace it when she decided to take off the waistcoat. Behind this was a zip. With trembling fingers, she began to unzip it.

Inside was a large removable pad. She remembered that one of Jamari's friends had a bear like this. The pad could be removed to enable the owner to embroider the front.

It struck Zoe that this bear would provide an ideal place to stash a few packets of something illegal, and it flashed into her mind that just maybe Gino had been involved in something other than cash-in-hand work or selling cigarettes. However, this bear was empty. Disappointed, she replaced the bear and turned to look through the drawers.

One contained a number of items of male Gucci jewellery. It seemed over the top somehow. How could Gino afford this much designer jewellery? Of course, Alice had wondered what he spent his cash on. Maybe he loved expensive jewellery and didn't want Maxine to know what he was buying. Still, wasn't it rather careless to bring it away and keep it in an unlocked drawer in a holiday home?

She wandered back and went to the bathroom. There was a row of soap bags which she checked. Nothing seemed amiss. And then she glanced down at the pedal bin, which was partially open.

She leant down and opened it. It seemed to be full of tissues. She rummaged around them and then felt hard plastic.

Zoe pulled it out and held her breath. It was a pregnancy test, and it was positive.

Her mind raced. Who was pregnant? It had to be Annika, or perhaps Maxine: the bin probably hadn't been emptied since her death.

She didn't want to spend time in here thinking through the possibilities. No, she should do that with her mother later.

She left the bathroom and returned to the main room. She

was about to leave when she decided to hang her coat up with the others. As she did, she remembered all that fuss when Gino had arrived, when Maxine had found a broken torch in his pocket. Of course, that wasn't the one used by the killer but for him to still be carrying a large broken torch was a bit odd.

She took the torch out of his coat pocket and tried switching it on and off. It still wasn't working. Zoe carried the torch back over to the sofa and sat down to examine it. The battery compartment was accessed via the base of the large boxlike body of the torch. It was clearly meant to house one large battery.

A quick check showed there was no battery; however, it was far from empty. To her surprise, Zoe tipped it up and an odd assortment of objects fell out, including an out-of-date credit card.

Suddenly she heard a key being slid into the lock of the front door. Panicking, she replaced the items in the torch, but the battery cover was hard to slide on. Her fingers trembled as she fiddled with it as she walked back over to the coat rack. She was pushing the torch into Gino's coat pocket as he pushed open the door.

'Zoe, what are you doing in here?' he asked.

She swung around, felt her cheeks burning.

'I came over to use the toilet and have a drink.'

'So why are you hanging about here in the hallway?' He leant past her, his body very close to hers and reached for his coat. 'I came to change into a lighter jumper. It's very warm over there now. I'm sure you're ready to come back. Give me a second, and we can walk back over together.'

It was a matter of seconds before he returned and they left the apartment, walking in an awkward silence to the Great Hall.

Gino, however, didn't go in. 'I've got to collect something from the van,' he said, and left her.

Zoe felt she could breathe again, but she was in no doubt Gino had seen her replacing his torch. She was desperate to ring her mother, but then received a text saying a police officer would be there in about fifteen minutes and would meet her at the gate.

Zoe walked across the courtyard and decided to make a quick call to Susan. For privacy she decided to go into the Privy Garden.

'Mum, I've been in the apartment. I have so much to tell you.'

'Did you find the torch?'

'Yes, it was back in the box. The killer must have realised they needed to get rid of it. It has to be the one swapped for Maxine's. There's even a slight dent in it – and they hadn't replaced the batteries.'

'I'm guessing the killer had the torch all this time and you talking about it to DS Kent yesterday got them worried. They're panicking. I don't suppose you spotted any spare batteries around?'

'I didn't look specifically but, no, I didn't come across any.'

'OK. Well, anything else?'

'Oh, yes. To start with, there's the nail varnish.'

Zoe explained and Susan quickly picked up the implications.

'That's important. You need to pass it on to the police when they come for the aerosol and the miniature.'

'Don't worry. It's all bagged up and so is the torch.'

'So, did you find anything else?'

'Well, first there was a positive pregnancy test.'

Zoe described finding it and then asked, 'Could it have been Maxine?'

'I think they'd have mentioned that after the postmortem. No, if it's someone in the apartment it has to be Annika. Or of course LeAnne might have done the test there, not wanting to chance the test being found in the bathroom here.'

'Of course. Remember, LeAnne talked about wanting children. She also talked about fighting for what you want in life. Maybe that is Gino.'

'You've done so well, Zoe.'

'Oh, there's more.' Zoe told her about Gino's room and the jewellery and then finally about what she'd found inside the larger torch in his coat pocket. 'I don't understand any of that but, well, you might think of something.'

'Not immediately, but I'll give it some thought. I should go up and have a look around LeAnne's room as well. We're running out of time. How are rehearsals going?'

'I've not seen much. I talked to Mrs Strong. She's really shocked, of course. I hope it doesn't spoil her evening. Did you have a look at that court case of Maxine's?'

'I'm looking it up now, not that I'm finding out any more than Alice. I did get sidetracked, mind you, reading about all the illegal goods being taken into prisons. You'd never believe what people do. Drugs in the bodies of dead birds thrown over the walls, stashed in the battery compartment of children's toys, even delivered by drones.'

'Well, I'll leave you to it. I got a text from the police. Someone will be here soon.'

'That's great. Good luck,' said Susan, and rang off.

Zoe made her way to the entrance to the castle, wondering what kind of reception she was going to get from the police. She was starting to get nervous: would they treat her as an interfering busybody, or even think her involvement was suspicious?

33

Waiting at the castle gates, Zoe was pleased that the officer arrived promptly. A tall uniformed young man with a broad smile greeted her. 'I'm Constable Phillips, and you are Zoe?'

His friendliness immediately put Zoe at her ease.

'I am. I hope you don't feel I'm wasting your time.'

'Of course not. My boss was eager to hear about what you've found. I understand there is an aerosol can and a model for me to collect.' Zoe took him straight to the armoury.

Wearing gloves and carrying an evidence bag, he efficiently collected the can but also collected other individual items from the pile and placed them in separate bags.

'Thank you. That's very helpful,' he said to Zoe.

'I've the model here,' said Zoe taking it out of her bag, 'and there's something else I thought might be helpful.' She explained about the nail varnish.

Again, he listened and placed them in another bag.

Looking up at the battlements, he said, 'I've obviously heard about the accident. It's so sad. I knew Maxine's family. I grew up in Whitwell. My dad was friends with hers. They were in the same amateur dramatics group.'

Again, Zoe saw the ripple effect of a tragedy within a community like the island. There were unspoken bonds between so many people who lived here. No one made a fuss about it, maybe because they took it for granted, but often there was an aunt, a cousin, a school or club that linked them.

'Yeah,' he continued, 'my parents were very upset to hear about it. We were proud of an island woman doing so well. Were you related to Maxine?'

'No. We went to school together and had stayed in touch.'

'That's good. You grew up in Ventnor then?'

'Yes, I was Zoe Flynn then. My mother was a teacher, Dad a doctor.'

He shook his head. 'No, don't think I remember your family.' He glanced down at the evidence bags. 'Are you worried there's more than an accident going on here then?'

'I don't know but, if something doesn't feel right, it's my responsibility to let you know.'

'You're right. It's a shame more people aren't like you.' He looked towards the Great Hall. 'Big concert this evening, then? It's for Mrs Strong, isn't it? She taught my brother to play the trumpet. My mum wasn't always so keen, right racket she called it. As soon as he started, you'd hear the cat flap go as the cat let herself out. We all felt like joining her.'

Zoe laughed. 'Music can be a blessing or a curse.'

'Dad said at least it wasn't the violin.' He smiled. 'Right, better be on my way. I'll make sure these reach the right people. Bye, then.'

Watching him leave, feeling relieved, Zoe was about to make her way over to the Great Hall, when she saw Gino returning to the castle.

He nodded in the direction of the police officer. 'What was he doing here?' He was trying to sound casual, but she could detect the underlying tension in his voice.

'I called him.'

Gino scowled. 'And why was that?'

She took a deep breath. 'The miniature you said I imagined turned up in my bag—'

She paused. His face went blank. It was impossible to read his reaction to the news.

Zoe continued, 'Mum also found an aerosol can in the armoury. I thought the police should have them.'

'They came out to collect them?'

'Yes, the officer was very polite, thanked me for my help.'

Gino sneered. 'I'm sure he's done his course in how to handle deranged members of the public.'

Something snapped inside her and Zoe turned on him. 'You have been throwing accusations about me, making me out to be at best some delusional hysteric, at worse, a murderer, and none of it is based on anything. Finding the miniature, then the can, I'm being proved right.'

'You were the last person to speak to Maxine. You're the one who had a row with her—'

'I definitely wasn't the last person. It could easily have been you up there.'

'It wasn't me. I had no reason at all to kill my wife.'

'Maxine left you everything in her will, didn't she?'

'How on earth?'

'You knew? Mum was right.'

He leaned down, his face close to hers. 'I never wanted Maxine's money. I don't need her controlling me from the grave!' And with that he stormed off.

Zoe stood, breathless. In his anger, Gino had allowed her to see the levels of frustration he'd felt, and also revealed he knew that all the money was left to him. He might say he never wanted Maxine's money, but he needed it and that added to his fury.

She walked over to the Great Hall, planning to see how rehearsals were going. However, as she entered, Annika rushed past her, phone in hand, panic frozen on her face.

'What's the matter?' Zoe asked, turning around and chasing after her.

'Nick's collapsed – no signal in there—' Her hand was shaking so much that her fingertips couldn't press the numbers. Zoe grabbed the phone off her and pressed the numbers 999.

Zoe handed the phone back to Annika when it was answered and listened as she described how Nick was lying unconscious. Yes, he was breathing but, no, he wasn't conscious. Yes, they needed somebody as soon as possible. She explained where they were and ended the call.

Zoe's mind was racing but going way beyond the usual medical emergencies. Had Nick also been attacked?

'They're on their way,' Annika said, and rushed back into the Great Hall. Zoe followed and saw a group standing around Nick, who was lying face down on the stone floor.

She couldn't see any blood. He hadn't fallen. What had happened?

LeAnne was standing close by. She was staring at Nick in horror. Was she shocked or had she taken justice into her own hands, and she was just appreciating the enormity of what she'd done?

Gino was much further back, but walking nervously around: a caged animal, desperate to escape, but unable to break away.

Annika, much calmer now, was taking charge. She expertly

put Nick into the recovery position, in a way that reflected her training, and all the time she was speaking gently to Nick, reassuring him.

The paramedics arrived quickly. It was a relief to have professionals take over.

'Has he taken any medication – any drugs?' the paramedic asked.

Zoe's mind immediately went to the possibility of cocaine. She hadn't found any in the apartment but maybe he kept it with him.

Zoe saw the look of panic in Annika's eyes. Then she saw Nick's eyelids tremble and slowly open. He spoke Annika's name.

'I'm here. Don't worry, you're going to be fine,' she assured him.

He managed to turn his head slightly and speak to the paramedic. 'Get the tin of mints.'

'The tin on your bed?' asked Annika. She didn't sound surprised at the request. He nodded.

'I'll be quick,' she said, but Nick's eyes filled with panic. He reached out, obviously reluctant to let her go.

Zoe was confused by the conversation: why did he need mints?

Annika glanced at Zoe. 'I know it seems odd, but the mints aren't quite what they appear – we need to take them to the hospital. They need to check exactly what's in them.' She glanced down at Nick, who was clinging onto her hand. 'Look, I don't want to leave him. Can you go and fetch them? The tin is on his bed – the top bunk.'

'Of course. I have Nick's keys to the apartment.'

Without wasting time explaining how she had the keys, Zoe

left the hall and ran to the apartment. Once in Nick and Annika's room she climbed up to the top bunk. There was the opened tin she'd seen earlier. From what Annika said they weren't simply mints. She looked down at the green boiled sweets. It didn't seem likely they contained cocaine, but she could be wrong.

She secured the lid, climbed back down and ran back to the Great Hall.

Nick was on a stretcher now, and the paramedics were wheeling him out.

She held the tin up in front of him. 'Is this what you mean?'

His eyelids flickered and he slowly opened his eyes. His voice was weak. It was clearly a struggle to speak. 'Yes, but more at home.'

'Are they in your bedside cabinet?' asked Annika. 'I'll get them.'

Nick's eyes filled with panic, again. 'Don't leave me,' he pleaded and squeezed her hand.

'I could go,' said Zoe. 'Mum would take me, I'm sure.'

'Um, no—'

'Don't leave me,' repeated Nick.

'I don't mind,' said Zoe. 'He needs you.'

'OK, thanks,' said Annika. 'I'll need to give you the keys to the flat.'

She grabbed her handbag and thrust the keys at Zoe.

Zoe left the Great Hall and went to phone Susan.

* * *

Susan was in the garden on the patio, having just returned from a long walk up on the downs with the dogs when Zoe rang.

The events at the castle sounded alarming, and Susan was keen to help. Fortunately, she had just finished towel drying the last washed paw and took the dogs inside.

'Right, quick lunch for you two. I'm off out.'

After feeding the dogs, she grabbed a biscuit for herself and left the house.

She remembered watching Nick in her garden the day they'd found Maxine's body. He'd been eating what she thought were sweets from a tin then, while he paced up and down. What had he been taking? Her mind raced and more questions bubbled to the surface.

She saw Zoe waiting for her outside the castle and picked her up. Zoe told her what had happened in more detail.

'I was trying to think this through,' said Susan. 'These mints have been doctored in some way. Where does Nick get them and why doesn't he know what's in them to be able to tell the paramedics?'

'My guess is he's buying them illegally online, and if so, they're not regulated. I reckon he's scared something has been added to them that is making him ill, and hoping the hospital can work out what it is. As to what he thought he was taking, I've no idea, it could be cocaine in some form. I really don't know.'

'It sounds as if Annika knew all about it then?'

'I'm sure she did. She didn't look surprised, and she knew he was keeping some in his bedside cabinet—'

'Which is why she slammed it shut when I was about to look inside.'

The journey to Cowes was being frustratingly slow. There were temporary traffic lights on Horsebridge Hill, soon after the prison, and long queues as a result.

As they drove, Susan could feel a gathering excitement. They were being given another opportunity to look inside the flat. She was sure they'd missed things last time. As Zoe had said, time was running out. This visit could be the key to them unlocking this case.

34

As soon as Susan and Zoe entered Annika's flat, they headed into the bedroom.

Zoe went straight to the bedside table and found an unopened tin of 'mints'. 'This is just like the tin at the apartment,' she said, holding up the tin.

'We should check in the bathroom for any more,' said Susan. She opened what was clearly a medicine cabinet. 'There are quite a few meds in here, lots for allergies. Nick was speaking the truth about that. I'll take some for the hospital. There are no more tins though.'

Back in the main room, Zoe went to the cupboard containing the safe. 'I know we should get to the hospital, but I'd like to look in here again.'

'I agree. We're missing something.'

'The trouble is we've no idea of the code.'

'But we do,' said Susan, joining her. 'Remember, Annika told us. Something about thirteen being a lucky number in Italy. There were some numbers before it – something to do with the year. Quickly, google Italian thirteen.'

Zoe scrolled through her phone. 'Ah, here we are. Thirteen became a lucky number in Italy in 1950, an important year for some gambling changes there.'

Susan tried 195013. To their relief, the door opened.

She looked inside. 'So, what are we missing?'

She took out one of the long boxes of cigarettes and looked inside. It was indeed full of smaller unopened packets of cigarettes. She tried the next. It was the same. And then the next. Susan was about to give up when she picked up the last box. This was much heavier.

She placed it carefully on the floor, and opened it. She took a breath as she saw the contents.

'My God, Mum,' said Zoe.

Inside were a number of Gucci watches and bracelets.

'These must be worth a lot of money. Now him selling these on with LeAnne's father makes a lot more sense than the cigarettes,' said Susan. 'They must be stolen.'

'Maxine would have been so upset to discover this. He must have been involved with stealing jewellery when she met him, and has gone back to it. No wonder he hadn't been telling her about his visits to Italy... I'll take a photo of the serial numbers, just in case.'

Susan glanced around the rest of the safe. She picked up the photograph album, flicked through. She opened some of the boxes of stamps, being careful not to touch the actual stamps, but learned nothing new.

They packed the boxes back into the safe and locked it up.

Susan quickly glanced around the flat a final time. Seeing the sheet music, she wondered what would happen now about Annika's solo this evening. 'Right, we ought to get to the hospital,' she said, and they rushed back to the car.

As they drove, Zoe looked down at her phone, examining the photos of the watches she had seen in the safe.

'These are like the one Gino gave Maxine.' She sat frowning and then her face lit up.

Susan waited, and Zoe exclaimed, 'Wait! That could be it.' Without explaining, she frantically began scrolling down on her phone.

35

Susan waited for Zoe to tell her what she was so excited about – what had she learned about the Gucci jewellery they found in Annika's safe?

'That's it,' exclaimed Zoe. 'I looked at the serial numbers and saw that they were all the same. When I googled Gucci serial numbers there is loads of information about them. Firstly, they shouldn't all be the same. Secondly, there should be twenty-one numbers, not twenty.'

'That's odd.'

'It's more than odd. What it says here is that it tells us the jewellery is fake. That jewellery is not genuine Gucci. I wondered when I saw Gino's own jewellery at the apartment why he wasn't keeping it more securely.'

'So he is bringing in fake Gucci jewellery to sell?'

'He must be. It says here there is a lot of fake Gucci jewellery around in Italy. Gino must have contacts over there. I bet he was involved with it when Maxine met him and he promised to give it up when they married. That could be the line he crossed. She found the jewellery inside the cigarette boxes and knew he was selling it again.'

'And that is where LeAnne's father comes in—'

Susan heard the excitement in Zoe's voice as she said, 'I've just remembered something. Didn't Annika say Gino started stashing the boxes in the safe around the time he started working in the prison?'

Susan gripped the steering wheel. 'Gosh, yes. I'd forgotten that. But I don't see how this would work. Would inmates want fancy jewellery? I'd have thought the call was for things like drugs and mobile phones.'

They both sat quietly, trying to work it out. An idea came to Susan. 'Maxine's case was about smuggling drugs into prison. That jewellery is very chunky. Could it be used in some way to smuggle drugs?'

Zoe tapped her knees. 'I don't know. It seems a lot of work. Why not use any old jewellery? I'm not sure about the drug side of it. Maybe LeAnne's dad just sold the fake stuff through contacts and then he and Gino split the profits.'

Their conversation was cut short by their arrival at the hospital. Zoe put her phone away. Susan parked and they went in.

Someone at reception was able to tell them where to find Nick and they took the lift to the ward.

Annika was sitting next to Nick, who was lying with his eyes closed. She looked up at them. 'He's just sleeping. He's going to be fine.'

'We've got the tin of mints and brought along any medication we could see.'

'Thanks. They've done blood tests and been able to test the sweets as well. They're pretty sure they're some kind of sedative. They're much stronger than Nick realised, and he certainly shouldn't have been taking them so freely. The doctor said it was the kind of thing that should really be prescription only.'

'Where did he get them from?'

'Nick told me they were some kind of natural remedy for stress he'd seen online. He never showed me the site and he didn't seem to have any instructions as to how many he should be taking or when. I did notice he seemed to be taking a lot today.'

'That's awful,' said Susan. 'He was self-medicating. He told me he was too scared to go and get help.'

'I know. He wouldn't even trust his doctor, said it was a small island. He was paranoid.'

'You must have been very worried,' said Zoe.

'I was. It's been awful. To be honest, Maxine did ask me about it when she came over. It wasn't just the drinking. She told me she'd seen the tin on his bedside table, and was worried he was taking something.'

'Did she suspect cocaine?'

Annika frowned in confusion. 'Cocaine?'

'I ask because Maxine mentioned that the case she'd just finished, one involving drugs, had influenced her.'

'Oh, right. Yes, she did say she'd had a case where drugs were being smuggled into prison in different ways and she'd thought the tin of sweets looked wrong,' Annika smiled, 'but I told her Nick wasn't using anything like that. I wouldn't have put up with that. Anyway, even knowing these sweets were herbal, she seemed concerned, said he should be getting professional help.'

'Did you worry she might report Nick to anyone in school?'

'She didn't say anything to me.' Annika hesitated. 'Mind you, I remember the night Maxine died, when we were walking on the bowling green, Nick suddenly came out with all this stuff about what would he do if Maxine was to report him. He hadn't talked about it before, but must have been thinking about it when he was over sitting in the Privy Garden that night.'

'He was very upset?'

'He was, but I told him it didn't matter. Whatever happens, he needs to get out of teaching. We'll get the help he needs now and move on with our lives.' Annika paused, lowered her voice. 'Now I could do with phoning Nick's parents to give them an update.' She glanced at Nick, still asleep.

'We could stay here with Nick if you want to go outside?' said Susan.

'Oh, thanks. I won't be long,' said Annika. She walked quickly out of the ward.

Susan and Zoe sat next to Nick's bed quietly. However, it wasn't long until Susan realised he'd opened his eyes.

'Hi,' she said gently, 'Annika has just popped out to make a phone call. She'll be back any minute.'

He nodded, and spoke more clearly than Susan had expected.

'She's amazing, isn't she?' he said.

'How are you feeling?'

'A lot better. I scared myself. I've been stupid. I should have got help, but I was worried about losing everything.'

'People who love you will always be there for you, and that includes Annika. You know that.'

'I know Annika loves me, but it doesn't stop me being insecure. I always want to prove to her and her father that I deserve her. It's why I went to such lengths to buy her a decent ring.'

Susan frowned. 'Sorry?'

'I proposed weeks ago but said I'd save for a decent ring. There was this chap, Frank, at the sailing club. We'd got to know him, chatted a few times. Well, he noticed I looked down. I told him about the ring and he offered to lend me the money.'

Susan saw that Annika had returned to the ward and was talking to a nurse.

Nick continued. 'It was easy. I arranged to pay him back in instalments.' He looked at Zoe. 'You saw me. I didn't want to say I'd had to borrow money for the ring.'

'Did the police ask about it?' asked Zoe.

He nodded but then, with a sigh, he closed his eyes and was soon fast asleep.

Susan saw Annika coming back to them, smiling this time.

'It's good news. They want to keep an eye for another few hours and then all being well he can go home later this evening. I think they need the bed. I said I'll be looking after him. They're just going to write it all up for the GP and ask for a referral to the community mental health services.'

'That's great,' said Susan.

'Nick's parents are on their way. They want to see him, so I'm going down to meet them.'

'Do you want us to stay with Nick while you go?'

Annika glanced at Nick, who was still fast asleep. 'No, it's OK. You get on. We can walk out together.'

In the lift, Annika said, 'I was thinking about the concert.'

'You're not to worry. Mrs Strong will understand,' said Zoe.

'I know, but, really, Nick is going to be fine. He must stop taking these pills, obviously, and I promised I'd make sure he saw his GP soon. He's not going to be up to playing this evening. But I'd really like to sing. It meant a lot to Maxine, and it was our way of thanking Mrs Strong. It seems a shame not to perform.' She looked at Susan.

'What are you singing?' Susan asked.

'"Queen of the Night" – the Mozart aria. I was wondering,

Susan, and I know this is a big ask, but would you be able to play for me?'

Susan sighed. 'Goodness, I know the piece. It's notoriously difficult.'

'But have you accompanied anyone singing it before?'

'A few years ago I accompanied an advanced pupil in a recital. It took me quite a while to learn the piece and I haven't played it since.'

'But you'd have the rest of the day to go through it—'

Susan smiled. 'Well, OK, yes. I could try. I'm not promising to be as good as Nick.'

Annika sighed with relief. 'That's OK and, anyway, I'm sure you'll be brilliant. Thank you.'

'Is your music up in the Great Hall?'

'Yes, it's on the keyboard there. Sorry, it's not a proper piano. They couldn't move one in, but it's a very good keyboard.'

'I'll need to go and get familiar with it and then take the music home to practise. We will need to go through it together though as well.'

'Of course. I'll text you, when I know how things are going here. I'll either get a taxi to your house or to the Great Hall.'

As they left the hospital, Susan looked over and saw the taxi driver who'd brought Zoe home the night before. 'Isn't that Liam?'

'That's right,' said Annika, waving to him.

'He gave me a lift home last night,' said Zoe. 'LeAnne and I have used him a few times.'

Liam came over to them. 'I hope you're OK?' he said to Zoe.

'Yes, thanks. Much better.'

Annika looked at her quizzically, but Zoe didn't explain.

'We're here visiting Nick,' explained Annika. 'He's eaten something that badly upset him.'

'Oh, no. It must have been nasty for him to need to come here.'

'It was, but he's much better already.'

Further along in the car park, Zoe saw a worried-looking couple approaching them, and recognised them from the party as Nick's parents.

'Oh, there they are,' said Annika. 'Bless, they look worried to death.' She turned to Zoe and Susan. 'Thanks so much for everything. I'll text you, Susan.'

She left them and walked over to Nick's parents.

'They'll be pleased he's going to be OK,' said Liam, looking over. 'I wonder if Nick ate something dodgy at the party last night? Shame, they should all be celebrating today. I remember Annika talking about Nick when she was with my family. She was obviously keen on him then.'

Zoe looked at him sideways. 'She's been very supportive of your business.'

'She has, but then she's got this phobia thing. I told her to go and see a hypnotist. It can work if you see the right person. It helped my girlfriend get over her fear of flying. We're off to Tenerife soon.'

'Oh, you have a partner?' blurted out Zoe.

Liam frowned but in a good-natured way. 'You sound surprised?'

'Sorry, I don't know why. Um, the hours you work must make it difficult,' Zoe stammered.

'She's a nurse. Last year when she worked in A&E I hardly saw her. At least she finishes on time now she's moved wards,' explained Liam. 'In fact, she's due out soon and, as I was around, I said I'd save her getting the bus.'

At that moment a short, pretty nurse with red curly hair came out of the hospital. 'Oh, Liam, how sweet,' she shouted.

'I'm shattered. I wasn't looking forward to the bus.' She came over put her arm through his. She looked questioningly at Susan and Zoe, but Liam simply bid them farewell and the couple walked to the taxi.

Susan's eyebrows shot up. 'Well, we got that wrong!'

'We did.'

'No affair for Maxine to tell Nick about.'

'We've made so many mistakes,' said Zoe, groaning. 'There was no affair, Nick's not taking cocaine, and all that business with Frank was easily explained.'

'True, but we have the link now between Maxine's criminal case and the flat – the tin of sweets.'

'I suppose so – I don't know, Mum, what if we've got it all wrong? What if Maxine just fell and there are perfectly innocent explanations for things like the torches and that damn model?

Susan heard the frustration in Zoe's voice. 'We're bound to get some things wrong, love, but I'm not ready to give up. Now, come on, I need to go and get some practice in.'

They realised it was lunchtime and picked up some sandwiches on the way to the castle, which they ate outside before making their way to the Great Hall.

The hall was still a hive of activity. Mrs Strong came to ask after Nick and a few other people listened in.

'He's going to be fine: a bad reaction to some medication he was taking,' said Zoe, which Susan thought was succinct and tactful. 'Now, Annika would still love to perform tonight.'

'Oh, she mustn't—'

Zoe interrupted. 'She really wants to do this, although, of course, Nick is not up to accompanying her. If it's OK with you, Mum will stand in?'

Mrs Strong beamed at Susan. 'I'll tell my daughter. She'll be delighted. We were wondering what to do. That's so kind. Thank you.'

'I'd really like to practise,' explained Susan. 'Annika said her music is on the keyboard?'

'I made sure it was put aside. Come on over. I'll explain everything.'

Zoe smiled. Mrs Strong was quietly organising as much as she could.

She noticed LeAnne and Gino were missing and decided to see if they were in the apartment, to fill them in on the news about Nick.

As she approached the front door to the apartment, she was surprised to hear raised voices – well, one raised voice at least. Although she couldn't make out the words, she knew it was Gino.

With some trepidation, she knocked on the door.

36

Gino flung open the door to the apartment and Zoe walked straight in. LeAnne was sitting on the sofa in floods of tears.

'Whatever's the matter? What's happened?' Zoe asked.

LeAnne shook her head. 'It's nothing. We were going though Maxine's things. It was so upsetting.'

'I heard Gino shouting,' said Zoe, glancing at him.

Gino glowered. 'It's a very emotional time.'

Zoe was sure the row had nothing to do with sorting out Maxine's belongings, but clearly neither Gino nor LeAnne were going to enlighten her, so moved on. 'I came to tell you about Nick.'

LeAnne wiped her face. 'Of course. How is he?'

Zoe told them how he had been when they left him.

'I told you he was on drugs,' said LeAnne.

The smugness was irritating. 'I don't think he really knew what he was taking. You could show some compassion.'

'You appear very sympathetic towards Nick,' said Gino. 'Have you ruled him out for my wife's murder? Is that what you were telling the police this morning?'

'You talked to the police?' LeAnne's eyes were wide in alarm.

'Didn't you know? Zoe contacted the police, got them to come here,' said Gino. 'Apparently, she was handing over so-called evidence.'

'You need to stop this,' said LeAnne. 'Leave everything to the police. You're just throwing around accusations, pretending you've found clues. All you're doing is upsetting people.'

Zoe turned to her. 'But I'm getting closer to the truth all the time, nearer to finding out what happened to Maxine.' She looked at Gino, adding, 'I was attacked last night. It shows someone is panicking.'

'Hang on – you were attacked? You didn't tell me,' said LeAnne.

'I didn't feel like saying anything last night. After I left the party, I went down to Cowes harbour, and someone pushed me. I fell forward but I was able to stop myself falling into the water.'

'Did you see who it was?'

'No, nothing, but I'm sure it was one of our group, someone warning me off.'

'You're being ridiculous,' said Gino. 'You're paranoid. It was kids, or you imagined it and just fell over drunk.'

'You always do that, don't you?' said Zoe, annoyed. 'Always trying to make me doubt myself, but you know I'm being proved right. You saw for yourself I was able to give that missing miniature to the police this morning.'

'Where did you find it?' asked LeAnne.

'Someone put it in my bag last night at the party.'

LeAnne's face was snow-white now, her fingertips trembled. 'And you gave it to the police?'

'I did, and I gave them a bottle of red nail varnish—' Zoe was watching LeAnne closely. Would she defend herself – say that anyone could have used the nail varnish?

To her surprise, LeAnne threw her hands up and exclaimed, 'OK, I brought the damn thing here. Maybe I did want to give Maxine a bit of a fright, but that was it. The last time I saw it was when I left it in her pocket.'

Zoe stared at LeAnne. She was admitting to bringing the miniature and giving it to Maxine.

'Why didn't you own up? You let Gino make out I was lying,' demanded Zoe.

'I was scared,' said LeAnne. 'It was a joke, well, kind of. And then the person I had given the Grim Reaper to was dead and she'd told you how it freaked her out, made her feel threatened. Why the hell would I confess to having anything to do with it?'

'Because the police needed to know what had happened?'

'You don't get it,' shouted LeAnne angrily. 'With my surname I'm always going to be right in the frame. If I hinted at any involvement they'd have jumped on me.'

Zoe shook her head. 'But hiding this information makes you look more guilty. How do I know it wasn't you who put that model in my bag? And if you did, then how did you get hold of it from Maxine?'

LeAnne crossed her arms, gave a condescending smile. 'How's this for a theory? I gave the model to Maxine, who overreacted, and showed it to you. You left, she chucked it away. It was picked up by someone and to shut you up they put it in your bag last night.'

Zoe stood very still: could LeAnne be right?

LeAnne leaned her head to one side. 'You know it's possible. You've built up all these crazy theories but, at the end of the day, they'll all be explained away and we will all realise that poor Maxine just fell. Nothing more dramatic than that.'

Zoe was more shaken than she wanted to let on but she

replied, 'I don't think so. I'm going to keep digging. However, for now, I'm going back to the Great Hall.'

Outside the apartment, Zoe took a deep breath. She was making so many mistakes. Maybe LeAnne had a point. Head down, she walked slowly back over to the Great Hall.

* * *

Susan was reaching the end of the time she needed with the keyboard. Now she needed to take the piece home and quietly practise on her piano.

Looking up, she saw Zoe and, once she'd gathered up her music, she told her she was off.

To her surprise, Zoe said she would like to go with her.

'I'm so tired, Mum. I need to go and rest.'

Worried by how disheartened Zoe looked, Susan agreed a rest would be a good idea.

They were walking out of the Great Hall when Susan noticed LeAnne walking towards them.

'Are you going back to your house?' LeAnne asked.

'Yes—'

Susan saw a nervous look pass between LeAnne and Zoe.

'I could do with a break. Could I come as well?'

'Of course,' replied Susan.

There was an uneasy silence in the car on the way back. Susan wondered what had happened.

It was wonderful to be greeted by two excited dogs and the warmth and security of home. Susan knew the dogs needed a walk, so left Zoe and LeAnne to rest.

Susan walked around the village. It seemed calm after all the drama. People seemed to be in their Saturday routines. Calling into the shop, Susan picked up some pizza for their tea. Libs and

Rocco were excited to see their friend Lottie, and they had a good sniff and bark together.

Feeling refreshed, Susan returned home to her piano practice.

She opened the piano, set up her music and began to play. It was a beautiful but extremely challenging piece. Susan hoped Annika was prepared. They would be a knowledgeable audience, and they would know exactly how this should sound. Well, Susan told herself, all she could do was get her part as good as she could. Despite years of accompanying pupils and playing at concerts, Susan always got nervous, and knew the only way to overcome the nerves was to be as prepared as she could. And so she went over and over the piece until she felt it was as good as she could make it.

Once she was as satisfied as she could be, Susan bundled up the music and placed it ready to take away. She needed to try to relax a bit now.

However, as she went to make coffee, she heard retching from the bathroom. She ran upstairs, knocked on the bathroom door, and went in. LeAnne was standing by the toilet, a ghastly colour. Zoe, disturbed by the noise, came out of her room.

Without warning, LeAnne burst into tears. Susan put her arms around her and led her into her own bedroom where there was a small armchair. LeAnne sat there while Susan and Zoe sat on the edge of the bed.

'Whatever's the matter?' she asked gently.

'Are you pregnant?' asked Zoe.

Her directness shook Susan, but LeAnne nodded, clearly too tired to argue with Zoe's blunt enquiry.

Zoe crouched next to LeAnne and spoke more kindly. 'I found a test in the bathroom at the apartment this morning. Is Gino the father?'

LeAnne wiped her face, looked closely at Zoe.

'I'm sure there was something going on between you two,' said Zoe.

LeAnne frowned. 'I'm not proud of it. We got chatting at my party. He was so handsome and charming, but it was only when he told me his marriage was on the rocks that I agreed to go on a date and, yes, I fell for him. He's been over a lot, come to the restaurant, and we've found quiet places to see each other. I'd only just started to suspect I was pregnant. I used the test the night of the ghost walk. It was the first time I knew for certain that I was.'

She paused. 'I didn't stay in the apartment when I said I did. I went to speak to Gino in the keep. I was very vulnerable, hoping for reassurance, but that's not the way it went. It's almost as if he wasn't listening. He said he would never be divorcing Maxine. I was hurt and angry, and I stormed off.'

Zoe, watching her carefully, asked, 'Did he tell you he'd just heard Maxine tell me she wanted to end their marriage?'

'No. I knew nothing about that. All I knew was that he wasn't going to stand by me, that as things stood, Maxine would come first.'

'Where did you go when you'd finished talking to Gino? Did you go straight to meet Zoe?' asked Susan, realising that if LeAnne said yes and she was speaking the truth, it possibly gave her and Gino alibis for the time when Maxine died.

However, LeAnne shook her head. 'No, I went and sat on the ground at the side of the well house, in the dark, alone. I was so upset. I covered my face and cried. It hurt. I loved him and I thought he'd felt the same.'

'And maybe you also thought that if Maxine had been out of the way, Gino would have turned to you?' suggested Susan gently.

LeAnne's face hardened. 'I didn't kill Maxine to get Gino. What would be the point of that? Gino either loved me or he didn't. I wouldn't want him because he was lonely or desperate. In that moment, I knew I was on my own. But I'm a survivor. I was quickly coming to terms with it and knew I'd be OK. I'll bring up this baby on my own.'

'The day we discovered Maxine's body, you were very sympathetic towards Gino, considering how harshly he treated you the night before,' said Zoe.

'Look, I'd had the night to think things through. Of course I was angry with the way he'd reacted: he should have been kinder, gentler. But then we'd never talked about a future, never planned a baby. I wanted to talk to him properly, but then Maxine died. It was so terrible. Even if their marriage was going wrong, what a tragic end. I felt sorry for him, but I wasn't hoping to win him back.'

'Gino said he wasn't going to let Maxine end their marriage,' said Susan. 'Do you think he was so desperate to save it because he loved her?'

LeAnne screwed her eyes up tightly. 'Rather than him simply being after her money?'

Susan waited.

'I honestly don't know. Look, I knew he was no angel. He liked money.'

Susan's mind was racing. How could they be sure LeAnne didn't go and confront Maxine? Did Gino stay in the keep or did he go back along the battlements to Maxine?

LeAnne started to stand up, clearly indicating the conversation was over.

However, Zoe hadn't finished. 'I need to ask you about this business with Gino and the van the night Maxine died. I know

now the van belonged to your father and I am more certain than ever we saw Gino talking to him that night.'

LeAnne stepped back, looked towards the bedroom door.

'Don't go,' urged Zoe. 'I think this is to do with the fake Gucci jewellery we found in the safe at Annika's flat.'

LeAnne froze.

'We looked in the safe,' said Zoe. 'Is your father selling the goods for Gino?'

LeAnne's bottom lip quivered. She swallowed hard. 'I don't know how you discovered all this but, yes, that's what's happening. I saw Dad talking to Gino at my party in February, and I could see they'd quickly sussed each other out. I was so angry with Dad. But I can't stop them, can I? Gino seems to want the cash. Dad can make money.'

'And are they using the jewellery to smuggle drugs into the prison?'

LeAnne looked up, her eyes wide, and mouth open. 'What?'

Zoe repeated herself.

LeAnne grimaced. 'That's mad. Of course not.'

Zoe and Susan glanced at each other: they'd got that wrong too.

'Look, I've had enough of this confessional,' LeAnne said. 'Don't tell the others about the pregnancy. I could do without Nick crowing over that.' And with that, she walked out of Susan's bedroom. They heard LeAnne's own door shut firmly behind her.

'We didn't ask her about the miniature and the nail varnish,' said Susan.

Zoe explained what had been said in the apartment.

'Like we said, we've made so many mistakes, Mum.' Susan saw Zoe's fingers tremble as she wiped away tears on her cheek. 'Maybe LeAnne's right: we've created all these problems, imagined Maxine was killed but, all along, what really happened is that Maxine simply fell.' She sniffed. 'I've wound up a lot of people. No wonder someone pushed me, left that model to shut me up. I'd be fed up with me if I was one of them, even if I was innocent.'

Susan put her arm around Zoe. Was she right?

'I don't know. The fact we've made mistakes doesn't mean we are wrong about everything, but I can't be sure.' Susan looked at her watch. 'I need to get up to the castle soon. I had a text from Annika. She's getting a taxi to the castle and will meet me there to practise. How about we try to put this all out of our minds, at least for an hour or so? You did the right thing handing everything over to the police. We need to take a break. Let's get the dogs out for a quick walk and some fresh air without talking about the investigation.'

They walked through the village. Susan greeted a few villagers. A young mother with her dachshund recognised Zoe and asked her how Jamari was getting on. It was good to have a taste of normal life.

Afterwards, Susan made pizza. LeAnne wasn't hungry, so she and Zoe ate alone. Susan made a determined effort not to mention the case. Afterwards they both went to change. Susan decided to wear the blue dress Alice had given her last Christmas, which she'd worn to the Twixmas party at the manor. It was unlike any other dress she'd ever owned, made from silky material: the colours of the ocean, a kind of shift dress but more fitted. She wondered what Zoe would make of it and was nervous as she went downstairs.

Susan waited for Zoe and LeAnne. It struck her that this was their last evening staying with her.

Her mind went back to the day the group all came here for lunch, still stunned from the events of the morning. She remembered Gino throwing his accusations at Zoe and later her tears. It had been a difficult lunch, the only respite had been looking through the stamps with Annika. Susan glanced over at the table. Something was nagging away – what had she missed?

She decided to recreate the scene, and found the stamp albums, took them over to the table and opened them. She and Annika had sat here, looking through them. Susan flicked through the pages, glancing down. Of course, Nick had been outside, pacing up and down in the garden. He'd had that tin in his hand – Susan paused, took a sharp intake of breath: how had she missed that? Her heart raced, she didn't know how this fitted in, but it was significant and proved to her they had been right all along. Maxine's death was no accident.

'Wow, Mum. That's gorgeous. I haven't seen that before.'

Susan was startled by Zoe coming into the room. She brushed her hand down her dress self-consciously.

'It's not really a typical me dress, is it? Do you think it will be too much for this evening?'

'Not at all. It's going to be a dressy affair.' Zoe grinned at her own black trousers and jumper. 'Seriously, Mum. You should dress up more.'

'I can't be bothered usually, love, but at least this gives me an opportunity to wear it. Unfortunately, I will have to ruin it by wearing your old parka over the top. I should get a decent winter coat sometime.'

'You won't need it in the Great Hall. It's surprisingly warm. You could leave it over at the apartment if you want.'

LeAnne came down the stairs in her towering heels and black dress. She held her head high in an almost defiant air. 'Blimey Susan. You scrubbed up well.'

'Thank you.'

A Halloween Murder

* * *

It was a clear evening, stars shining, the moon bright white.

There were only a few cars parked in the castle car park so far. They made their way to the apartment where Susan, Zoe and LeAnne hung their coats up with the others.

The Great Hall was noisy with people tuning instruments and excitedly chatting. Susan enjoyed this pre-performance buzz.

Diane Strong, the music teacher, had been instructed by her daughter not to arrive before the start of the concert. Quite rightly she told her she had spent too many years coping with this nervy hour before a concert, sorting out all the last-minute crises that inevitably crop up. This was her evening off!

Annika was wearing an empire-line black velvet dress with pearls. It was a classic dress for the soloist at a concert.

'You look wonderful,' Susan said to Annika.

'Thanks. This dress cost a fortune, but it's paid me back many times over and been to so many concerts and competitions. Now, I need to get on. Goodness, I'm quite nervous. For ages now I've only been singing popular songs around pubs. I hope my voice is still up to this.'

Annika took Susan over to the keyboard. 'If we both wear headsets for practice it will be a lot easier. One of the plusses of using a keyboard. We start with the warm-up.'

The vocal warm-up was as hard as Susan expected but it was very necessary. As Annika had said, she had not been singing at this level for quite some time. However, as she warmed up, Susan could hear her relax and that beautiful voice was set free.

They moved on to the aria, even more demanding. But Annika was more than up to the task. As she was playing, Susan glanced up. The headphones had put them into their own world, but she looked around and saw everyone was slowly looking their way. The room was mesmerised by Annika's singing.

When she finished, a spontaneous round of applause broke out, and Susan nudged Annika who had her back to the room. Annika blushed and took a quick bow, smiling.

They removed their headsets.

'You've nothing to worry about this evening,' Susan assured her. 'Let's get a copy of the programme, see when you will be performing.'

The programme informed them that they would be on just after the interval. Susan wished it had been in the first half, less time for nerves to set in, but she also knew that Annika's solo would be a highlight, something to lift the second half.

Zoe came over to her. 'Fancy a coffee before the concert begins?'

'That would be great. Annika said she'd stay in the hall, there were a few other performers she wanted to chat to.'

They walked over to the apartment. The light had gone now. Above them crows, blacker than the night's sky, noisily cawed, as they swooped around, gathering to fly to their roosts. As she watched them circle above her, Susan felt a shiver of apprehension. The harsh grating calls of the birds, that murder of crows, seemed to be warning her of danger, evil ahead.

37

As she entered the apartment, Susan glanced at Gino's coat. Noticing the torch, she remembered Zoe describing it, that credit card inside. She paused, and then suddenly saw the significance of it.

Susan was surprised to find Nick sitting in the living room.

He smiled up at her. 'They let me out. I just feel exhausted now. Thanks for all the running around you did. It was lovely to see my mum and dad but Annika and I decided it was probably best not to mention it to her father!'

'I'm glad you're feeling so much better,' said Susan.

'Is LeAnne here?' Zoe asked.

Nick gestured towards the bathroom. 'She's in there. She's awfully pale, isn't she? I noticed she hasn't been drinking all week. That's not like her. Makes you think—'

It was clear what he was implying, but neither responded.

Zoe brought Nick and Susan hot drinks and they sat down together.

'How did the rehearsal go?' he asked.

'Annika was brilliant,' said Susan.

'I knew she would be,' said Nick. 'We've been practising. I do worry she's a bit wasted on gigs in pubs but it's the way she likes it now.' He sighed. 'I'm lucky she's prepared to take on someone like me.'

Susan watched him carefully as she said, 'You don't need to be ashamed of asking for help. Everyone needs it from time to time. People care about you. I know Maxine was concerned about you.'

Nick eyes narrowed. 'Was she? Do you mean about Wesley and that online business? I realised afterwards that I should have told Maxine about it but, honestly, as awful as it was, because I knew I hadn't had any kind of vendetta against Wesley, I'd never seen the point.'

He sat back and continued, 'None of that matters any more anyway. Like we said that night on the bowling green, for Annika and me it's all about the future now. I'll keep teaching, save up and then we'll go. Annika is so excited. She can't wait until she's able to paint full time, and I do my composing.'

LeAnne returned to the living room. She looked pale but when she spoke her voice was firm and sarcastic. 'I'm glad to hear life is working out well for you,' she said to Nick. 'People like you get away with anything. You can lie as much as you like but people stick up for you.'

Nick rolled his eyes. 'You accuse me of lying?' He glanced down at LeAnne's open laptop. There was no mistaking the look of alarm on LeAnne's face.

'How dare you look at my laptop—'

'You left it open on the table,' he said. 'What was I meant to do?'

Without warning, LeAnne lunged at Nick, her hands claw-like, red nails ready to dig themselves into Nick's flesh. Susan's heart missed a beat. She held her breath.

Nick must have felt the same. He held his hands in front of his face.

'You're such a bastard. How dare you judge me and my family?' LeAnne stepped back.

Nick spoke more quietly, his voice shaking, 'I'm really sorry for what happened to Wesley, but I never set him up. I'm sorry for him, but he's very troubled. You need to wake up, face who he is, and get him help.'

LeAnne backed off. 'You almost sound sincere, but you don't convince me.' She looked towards the window, the pane painted black by the night. 'I won't be sorry to leave this place.'

She pushed past them and Susan watched her leave the apartment. She looked down at LeAnne's open laptop, started reading the page, and was so engrossed that Zoe startled her when she spoke.

'Mum, we should be getting back,' said Zoe. 'I'll just pop to the bathroom.'

'I'll go and have a lie down,' said Nick. 'See you both later.'

Susan went into the hallway, trying to decide whether to take her coat. The other coats were hanging in a row: Zoe's, Gino's, LeAnne's, Nick's and Annika's.

She stared at them, and her mind began to work.

From the pocket of her own coat, she took her gloves. Susan slipped her gloved hand into his coat pockets and then worked her way along the other coats. And then she felt what she was looking for. She glanced inside. Removing one glove, she fished out her phone from her own pocket and took a photo.

She returned to the main room and opened the torch box: there was the spare torch, just as Zoe had said. She examined it, saw the dent but also something else. She carefully returned it to the box.

'Ready then, Mum?' Zoe startled her.

Susan turned. 'Sorry?'

'It's time to go – and promise me you'll leave the old parka here.'

'Of course,' Susan said, her mind preoccupied with far more important things than her coat.

The main courtyard was busy with people arriving for the concert. It was dark so extra lighting had been erected. The doorway to the Great Hall was lit, and there was an excited air as people gathered.

However, Zoe was looking over at the keep. 'There's a torch light on the steps. I'm sure that's Gino. What's with his obsession with the keep?'

Susan could make out the silhouette. She agreed with Zoe: that was Gino.

'I'm pretty sure I know. I should have realised it that morning in the fog when I went up to search.'

Zoe looked at Susan. 'You sound different, Mum. What's going on?'

'I think I'm finally starting to piece this puzzle together. I'd been forcing pieces into the places where they didn't fit; that was all.'

'Do you want me to go up the keep, check what Gino's up to?'

'No, no. Don't do that. Whatever you do, you stay in my sight this evening.'

'Well, OK. You're being a bit mysterious, that's all.'

Susan looked around at the imposing stone walls, the crenellations and towers stretching into the sky. 'The castle seems more alive than ever this evening.'

'Are you expecting the ghosts to come out?' asked Zoe.

'Someone said, only a few days ago, that you can be haunted by the living as well as the dead. They were right, and it's the living that scare me this evening. If anything is haunting me tonight, it's the killer.'

They had arrived at the Great Hall.

Zoe held on to her mother's arm. 'You should tell me what you're thinking. I'm worried about you now, Mum.'

'We'll talk after the concert. I need time to think,' said Susan. 'But no sneaking out. I mean it. I've talked to you about danger, but we are there now, on the edge of the battlements, but with no barriers, no protection. One false step and we fall.'

Zoe leant and kissed her mother on the cheek. 'With talk like that, you can bet I'm not letting you out of my sight now.'

Susan smiled. 'Good. Let's go in.'

The atmosphere in the Great Hall was very different to earlier. The lighting was subdued, casting shadows on the stonework. Susan felt herself transported back to medieval times. As people took their seats, she noticed them lowering their voices as if entering a church or a library.

The performers all sat close to the front. Susan left Zoe and went to sit next to Annika.

Annika gave her a nervous smile. 'OK?'

'Yes, thank you,' said Susan. 'This is an amazing setting for a concert, isn't it?'

'It's magical.' Annika blinked. 'I know this sounds fanciful, but I feel as if Maxine is here watching us.'

'Maybe she is. I've just spoken to Nick. He's coming over in a minute.'

'I told him to stay over there in the warm, but he insisted.' Annika smiled.

At that moment they were aware of voices at the back of the hall and turned around. Mrs Strong had arrived with her husband, who escorted her down the central aisle. Everyone stood and applauded. Diane Strong looked very emotional, and

Susan saw her husband tuck his arm through hers and give her arm a supportive squeeze.

The Strongs sat down in reserved seats in the front row. Catherine Strong stood at the front. The concert had begun.

Susan tried to concentrate on the concert, not on the investigation. She needed to stay focused on the performance.

During the interval, while others drank mulled wine, Susan went to the keyboard and made sure the music was all arranged as they were to be the first item in the second half.

Annika came over, stood with her back to the audience, and did some breathing exercises.

She picked up the sheet of Rossini's warm-up exercises and handed it to Susan.

'Can we just do a few?'

'Of course.' Susan smiled.

As they practised, she could hear Annika's voice relax and was glad that with such a difficult performance coming they had these few moments.

People started returning to their seats, some still clutching their glasses of mulled wine. The atmosphere now was easier. They were ready for a performance like Annika's.

Catherine Strong introduced them. 'We are thrilled this evening to have Annika sing to us "Queen of the Night" by Mozart. We are very grateful to Susan Flynn for standing in at the last moment to accompany her.' She sat down.

Susan took a deep breath. The problem with accompanying, Susan felt, was that people only notice it if you go wrong. In a way, the pressure on you to be perfect is greater than that on the performer.

However, once Annika started to sing, it was as if accompaniment and singer became one. Her voice soared. It filled every nook and cranny of the ancient building. The assembled people held their breath. It was one of those very special performances that, when it ends, makes the audience pause in awe. For a brief few seconds, there is silence. And then the applause.

Annika looked quite overcome. She bowed, and gestured to Susan, who also acknowledged the applause.

As they returned to their seats, Susan snatched a look to the back of the room. She was relieved to see Zoe was still there. She was sitting next to LeAnne. Gino had also joined them, sitting a few rows behind with Nick.

'That was wonderful,' she whispered to Annika. 'Outstanding.'

Annika's bottom lip was trembling. She was too emotional to speak, but the flutter of a smile said it all.

The next performance was a child playing their flute. It was a simple piece, played well, a perfect foil to Annika's performance.

Susan now allowed her mind to drift back to the investigation.

She looked at an intricate tapestry on the wall. If only she was trying to create something as beautiful, and not the picture of an ugly, cruel deed: the murder of Maxine.

38

In her mind, Susan stepped away from the concert in the Great Hall and with her eyes half closed, she forced her mind back over the events of the past few days.

She remembered arriving here, Maxine taking her up on the battlements. Then the masks, the ghost walk, searching the keep in the fog, followed by the tragic discovery of Maxine in that bleak armoury. And then the events that followed, the visit to her house, conversations on the beach and the downs, visiting Annika's flat – Susan made herself pause. The safe had hidden secrets from them, the music had more to tell them. And then there were the blackbirds rustling in the Privy Garden. There had been all those complications over the miniature and the broken torch: so many stray pieces, all so confusing.

Susan's mind was brought back to the present by a group of excited children being escorted down the aisle. Some were carrying violins and their teacher, looking considerably more nervous than them, ushered those playing instruments to their seats and the small group of singers to the front. He stood ready to conduct and they went straight into the performance.

They performed a simple medley of Christmas songs, including 'Jingle Bells' and 'Rudolph the Red-Nosed Reindeer' and then a soloist gave a simple but moving rendition of 'Silent Night'. It took Susan back to many school concerts: excited children, fraught teachers, and proud parents.

The children grinned proudly as the audience applauded. Susan loved their innocence. They'd not spent hours worrying, no warmup exercises for the singers, not even the soloist. They had given an enthusiastic, if not perfect performance, and now were confident of a job well done.

And suddenly it was if a spotlight illuminated a piece of this puzzling case that she'd been missing. She picked it up, examined it, and then slowly she started slotting all the other pieces around it.

Finally, she was able to sit back and view the picture as a whole. But it wasn't a relief: it frightened her. Maxine had found this piece and, by revealing it to the killer, had signed her own death warrant.

The killer had made mistakes, but they had also planned so many aspects of this meticulously. They were clever, cold, calculating, adaptive. They could still defeat her, and they would show no mercy.

The sense of danger, like a cobra, started to wrap itself around her. The killer could read her mind, knew she was closer to the truth. They are no longer one step ahead. Susan found herself gasping for breath. She desperately tried to calm herself, take control, or she would never be fit for the task that lay ahead.

Catherine Strong was now making her final speech. She mentioned Maxine, made a short but moving tribute to her, then all attention was on Diane Strong. Children brought up posies, adults' bouquets, chocolates, champagne and wonderful words of thanks for her dedication and love. A buffet had been laid on in a local pub to which everyone, including staff from the castle, was invited. The clearing up could wait until the following day. More hugs and tears were shed, and finally the event drew to a close. As people started to gather their things, Catherine Strong came over and thanked them both. Annika was still glowing. Nick came down and hugged her, so proud of her.

Susan looked around for Zoe, anxious to share her thoughts but, to her horror, she saw that Zoe's seat was empty. She glanced around the hall frantically, but Zoe was nowhere to be seen.

Pushing her way through the crowd, she made her way out of the hall and into the courtyard. Lights had been placed to guide everyone to the exit. The rest of the castle was in darkness. Where was Zoe?

The crowd were pouring out behind her. Susan spotted Gino weave past her and disappear into the darkness. She called Zoe's name, but her voice was lost in the kerfuffle of people.

Susan was close to tears with anxiety. Then she thought of the keep: had Zoe gone up there?

Susan located her torch. She raced round the side of the well house, along the path and approached the steep flight of steps that led up to the keep. She screamed Zoe's name, but there was no answer. Reluctantly, Susan began to climb the steep steps, clinging onto the cold metal rail as she made her way to the heart of the castle.

She stopped halfway, caught her breath, and shouted for Zoe, but again there was no reply.

At the top, she ran into what had been the old well house. Shining her torch on the ground for a moment, she was distracted. The beam picked up a glint of broken mirror. Glad she had gloves on, she picked up the pieces, wrapped them in tissues, and placed them in her bag.

And then her phone rang. The screen showed it was Zoe. Susan answered.

'Where are you, Mum?'

'I'm at the top of the keep. Where are you? I've been looking everywhere.'

'I got a call from Fay. I went outside to answer it. What the heck are you doing up there on your own? You told me not to go there.'

'I know, but I thought you'd gone your own way.'

'Mum, come down, and be careful. We're not going to the buffet in the pub. We're going to the apartment for a final drink and get-together. Come and join us.'

Susan looked around. Suddenly the keep which had appeared so threatening felt like a place of refuge. This was the last resort when under fire, the final line of defence. The walls hugged her: she wanted to stay here.

But Susan knew she had to leave. She had to meet the enemy face to face.

Holding her torch with one hand and clinging onto the rail, she carefully made her way down the steps. In the distance, the crowds were making their way out of the castle, chatting and laughing. It was all so normal, as if they were on a different planet to her.

She made her way over to the stable courtyard, and then up the steps that led to the apartment.

Before entering the apartment, she thought about the risk she was taking and decided to make a phone call. She was unsure what reception to expect, and relieved to be taken seriously. At the end of the call, she glanced at her watch, then looked through the window.

The group was sitting round with glasses of wine and orange juice. For the first time, they looked relaxed. They were smiling. It looked as if Gino was telling them a joke.

Did she really want to go in and spoil everything? Shouldn't she give them one last good memory of the castle? But then she looked up at the high stone walls.

The castle was no longer some kind of threat. No, it was there to defend her. It knew who had killed Maxine and why. It was trusting Susan to make sure justice was done.

She knocked on the door. Zoe let her in.

'Thank God, Mum. What on earth have you been doing?'

'I know everything,' Susan said, speaking quietly but directly.

She saw the colour in Zoe's face fade. 'Are you sure, Mum?'

'I'm afraid I am. I'm sorry. I don't want to do this, but I have to.'

'OK, I'm with you, Mum. Come on.'

Susan followed Zoe into the living room. As Zoe coughed loudly for attention, Susan went to where the spare key was hanging up and slipped it into her pocket.

'Mum has something she'd like to say to everyone,' said Zoe.

Susan turned and saw Nick take a deep gulp from his glass of wine and then groaned. 'Oh, come on. Let's have one night off. We've all been through hell this week.'

'But there are questions that need answers,' said Susan. 'I'm sorry to spoil this evening but, if I don't, tomorrow a killer will leave the castle. Maybe they will never be caught.'

'I think that's for the police to decide,' said Gino. 'They would be here now if something was wrong. They're clearly letting us go.'

'I think you should let Mum speak,' said Zoe.

She sat on a chair at the end of the sofa. Susan took a dining chair. She sat apart, facing them all.

Sitting very upright, she began. 'Firstly, some of you may know that I have been involved in murder investigations before. However, this one was different. As my friend Alice said, this was much closer to home. This involved my daughter. Not only was she a suspect at one point, but she became involved with trying to track down Maxine's killer. I was scared but also proud of her. Without her this would never have been solved.'

Susan caught Zoe's eye: a look of understanding, appreciation and love passed between them.

Susan took a breath. 'And so we begin. Maxine died tragically on Halloween, the night when, traditionally, the boundary between the worlds of the living and the dead becomes blurred. All of you were on edge. I could see that when I arrived. Was this caused by the fear of ghosts, the dead returning? Or was it fear of the living? An ancient castle, whose history began in pagan times, had to be the perfect setting for Halloween. It should have been fun but, no, the castle changed from a fairytale to a place of execution. Maxine sensed that, up there on the battlements. She was frightened.'

'Now, hang on—' interrupted Gino.

The others, though, shook their heads and silenced him. Susan had cast a spell. They wanted to know what she was going to reveal.

'Maxine confessed to being a little superstitious, but she was far more frightened of the real world than the supernatural. That Grim Reaper model terrified her because it confirmed a feeling she already had, a deep feeling that someone here wished her harm.'

Gino groaned. 'We all know she'd been drinking, out of sorts: that was all.'

Susan glared at him. 'Oh, no. Maxine was perfectly coherent; Zoe was very clear about that. Maxine, who trusted Zoe completely, confided in her, actually said the words that someone here wished she was dead.' Susan paused. 'There was nothing ambivalent about that. What is more, Maxine had a good idea who it was. She told Zoe that she'd seen behind the mask, seen this person was cruel and cold. Very shortly after she spoke those words to Zoe, Maxine was dead.'

'Maxine was paranoid. You're like your daughter. You sit there throwing out accusations but you have no proof,' said Gino.

'Ah, but I do now,' said Susan.

She felt a prickle of anxiety pass around the room, a nervous shifting in their seats.

'For a murder we need means, opportunity and motive.' She felt confident, for the moment, as if giving a lecture to students.

'It is clear that if Maxine hadn't fallen accidentally, someone must have pushed her. As everyone here has the physical capability to commit that act, then that tells us everyone here had the means.' Susan paused deliberately, assessed the group. They were sitting back, wary, but even Gino remained silent.

'Opportunity is also there for you all,' continued Susan. 'Anyone, in theory, could have been up there with Maxine at the time she died. I'll say more about that while I cover the main focus here, the motive.' She looked directly at each of them in turn. Gino raised a cynical eyebrow, Annika looked down. She was squeezing Nick's hand. Nick was pale, his eyes bright with fear. LeAnne met her gaze defiantly.

'I'm afraid you all have motives, and therefore you were all suspects,' said Susan. 'The first suspect, of course, was Zoe. Gino claimed she was the last person to speak to Maxine. He says he overheard an argument, saw no miniature, but also saw closeness between them that upset him. Zoe says that the argument was about a miniature and that she definitely saw someone with Maxine up there after her. Fortunately, we had corroboration about the model: paint on her hand. Zoe also found the missing torch that had been disputed. Both are now with the police.'

Susan looked directly at Gino. 'You're like a magician. You distract with words. You've made up this whole scenario of Maxine drinking excessively. You created the picture of Zoe and Maxine having an intense relationship, one of fierce rows, desperate secrets. And it was effective. If someone was to question whether Maxine really had just fallen, you had provided feasible alternatives. Maxine was drunk, depressed: she had taken her own life by suicide. Or maybe Zoe had a fierce row and pushed her. Why did you do this, Gino? What were you trying to distract us from?'

'Hey, come on now,' interrupted Nick. 'Gino, like the rest of us, was in a state of shock. None of us knew what we were saying that first day.'

'Is that your excuse for originally saying you and Annika were together the whole time?'

He went to speak but again Susan held up her hand, feeling very much in control.

'The truth came out: you were not together during the vital times.'

'But I went straight from the garden to the bowling green. I was sure that was where we were meant to meet.'

'Or you went from the garden up the battlements to speak to Maxine—'

'Of course I didn't. Why would I?'

'This is something I nearly missed. Hearing the blackbird rustling in the bushes below reminded me how easily sound travelled over there. You'd been sitting in the Privy Garden, directly below where Maxine and Zoe were talking. You heard everything. How she was planning to report you to her friend, the head of governors at your school. She had major concerns about your fitness for your work. She was concerned about your drinking, the fact you were self-medicating, the fact you'd lied to her, denied there was any reason for you to set up Wesley.'

'Of course I didn't hear anything.'

'You did. Unwittingly, Annika confirmed it, told me how upset you were when you finally met up that evening.'

Nick looked over to Annika. 'Even if I did overhear anything, I didn't go and see Maxine. I did nothing.'

Annika looked away. Nick looked desperate now.

'Your future was at stake,' continued Susan. 'Even if you'd planned a life outside teaching, you didn't want to go this way, a man accused of self-medicating on unlicensed drugs, still drinking. That would definitely be too many wrong steps for Annika's father. You admitted he influenced Annika. Could he succeed in getting her to end your relationship? No, your life would have been far easier if Maxine had ceased to exist.'

Nick shook his head, his eyes wide, burning with tears. 'Whatever the price, I would never, ever have hurt Maxine.'

'And no matter what Nick did, I would always stay with him,' said Annika quietly.

Susan put her head to one side, and looked at Annika.

'You certainly appear obsessed with him, so defensive. How far would you go to protect him? Maybe Nick did go straight to the bowling green and found you missing? He was in such a state, wasn't he? His word would never be trusted.'

'That's a lie,' said Annika. 'I love Nick but I'm not some crazy obsessive.'

'This is getting too much,' said LeAnne. 'You can't sit there judging us all.'

A Halloween Murder

'Ah, LeAnne,' said Susan. 'Maxine warned Zoe not to underestimate you. You care passionately. You act when provoked. Today you were very close to physically attacking Nick. Maxine had seen that anger in you.'

'Look, I've told you. I had no reason to kill Maxine.' LeAnne looked around at the group. 'If you haven't worked it out yet, then I'll tell you. I'm pregnant by Gino.'

'Wait one minute,' said Gino.

'Don't bother denying it. I will use DNA if I have to. I don't want to be with you, but you will support your child financially.'

She turned to Susan. 'The point is, I didn't go and kill Maxine to free her man.'

'No. I believe you. However, you did have another motive. I heard you on the night of the ghost walk. You said, "I won't let you destroy me." How did you think Maxine would do that? Nick found the answer on your laptop and I read it after him. I knew you'd had loans to set up your business, and you said Maxine had been supportive at the start. However, you also said she didn't understand about the long term. You were telling me that Maxine was demanding the repayment of a substantial loan: money you didn't have.'

LeAnne stared. She didn't speak.

'Your business is your life. You couldn't let her ruin it, could you? The row you had with Gino earlier was about that money. You hoped that Gino, the father of your child, might be more lenient, let you off the loan or at least put off repayment. But no. This afternoon, when we discovered you in tears, he had told you he wanted the money now. There was to be no leniency from him.'

LeAnne made no response, but sat digging her red nails into her hands.

39

Susan turned on Gino. Her expression was now more severe. 'And so, we come back to you, Gino, and my original question. What were you trying to distract us all from? So busy accusing everybody else, weaving stories, casting suspicion on anyone other than you. You overplayed your hand.'

'I loved Maxine. I had no reason to kill her.'

'I believe you started your marriage in love. You were also desperate to prove yourself to your father. You worked hard, making over properties, but it was difficult, slow money, wasn't it? Added to which, your new wife was watching every penny. It was frustrating. She didn't miss anything. You became unhappy and this led you back to your old ways, and to a way of life you'd promised Maxine you'd left behind. You knew if the police looked at your life carefully enough, they would find evidence that would send you to prison for a good length of time.'

'You're talking nonsense,' said Gino.

'Oh, no. The evidence is easy to find. To start with, there are those boxes in the safe at Annika's, the fake Gucci jewellery.'

Gino crossed his arms and attempted a look of defiance, but Susan saw fear in his eyes.

Nick stared. 'That's what you kept in the safe? My God, I had no idea.'

Susan continued. 'You had contacts over in Italy. You started smuggling the jewellery over here. In LeAnne's father you found someone to help sell the goods on.'

Gino threw his head back, and laughed disparagingly.

'Oh, no, I'm right about this,' said Susan, 'but the most important question for Maxine was: why did you need cash?'

Gino squirmed in his seat. He glanced over at the door, as if planning his escape.

'Maxine had suspected for a while. She'd seen your change of mood, found the wads of cash, saw the enormous teddy bear. I mean, what grown man buys himself a teddy bear that he insists on carrying around with him? From her work as a barrister, Maxine knew it was a classic place for concealment, and one you also quickly realised was just too obvious.'

Susan glared at him. 'The line you crossed, the promise you broke, was not about the fake jewellery. It was about taking drugs, wasn't it? That's what you needed cash for.'

'No way.'

'I have proof in that old broken torch in your coat pocket,' said Susan. 'Of course, the credit card, the chewing gum, the broken mirror I found in the keep: they were all the paraphernalia you need for snorting cocaine. This explains your obsession with the keep: private, away from everyone. Unfortunately, you dropped the mirror, the small pieces of which I found and will be handing on to the police. There will be evidence of cocaine on there, I'm certain.

'Maxine knew you were back using drugs, and that was the deal breaker. Because of that, she was going to seek a divorce.

You must have been desperate when you heard her telling Zoe. No wonder you were so out of sorts. And then, later, when LeAnne came to see you, it was all you could think about: "I will never let Maxine end our marriage." No, you needed her money, didn't you? You could have gone along the battlements, and ensured she'd never, ever be able to divorce you.'

All the assurance, the sneering, left Gino. His voice shook. 'I didn't go to Maxine. I was up the keep. I couldn't have killed her. LeAnne, you came and saw me up there. I was out of it, a wreck.'

LeAnne shrugged. 'I wasn't with you long. I don't know what you did after I left you.'

Susan looked around the group. 'You all have means, opportunity and motive, but there is only one killer among you. My friend Alice would talk about an X factor, something that makes an individual think they have the right to take the life of another. You may all have motives but only one of you has this.' Susan glanced around. 'I made mistakes. I forgot about the case Maxine had been working on. I wrongly interpreted what she said about the safe and the music, but Zoe and I kept searching and today I discovered the truth of what happened. I know what happened the night Maxine died, who killed her and why.'

Susan was interrupted by a buzzing sound on her phone. She took it out of her pocket, then looked up. 'Right on time. Before I came in here, I made a phone call. I'll be back in a few minutes.'

Susan walked out of the apartment, and left the stable courtyard.

It was surprising how quickly the castle had emptied. The Great Hall was shut up, the extra lighting switched off, the place was in darkness. As if to emphasise how alone she was, in the distance she heard a clanking of the giant iron gates being shut and locked. An eerie silence followed, the last member of staff had left.

Susan remembered Annika saying how much smaller the castle felt at night. She'd been right: the walls seemed to be closing in. As she walked across the courtyard the crunching of her footsteps echoed around the grounds.

But then she realised it wasn't only her own footsteps that she could hear. Her heart started to race, she'd not expected anyone to follow her. She paused, but so did the steps behind her, and as she glanced around, she couldn't see anything except darkness. However, it was as if she could feel them watching her, a wild animal stalking their prey.

Susan pushed her hand into her pocket, felt the giant key. Thank God she'd brought it, she must get out of this place.

She began to walk quickly, there were no steps behind her now – had she imagined them?

However, as she paused to take the key out of her pocket, someone grabbed her arm and she realised her attacker had crept silently along the grass at the side of the path.

Susan tried to pull away, but her opponent was stronger... and then she felt a needle pressing into her wrist.

'Stay still. Any sudden movements and you will die,' the person instructed.

Susan froze, the only sound was the key falling to the ground.

'I know exactly what I'm doing here,' the person continued. 'I know the exact spot to cause an air embolism. Not many people do. But then it's my job to know these things. Now, we are going to walk together into the garden, no sudden movements, the needle is millimetres away from breaking your skin.'

They walked together, slowly, as if over a minefield, Susan

not daring to breath, swallow, or blink. She was led to a bench just inside the Privy Garden and they sat down.

Susan looked up at Annika, her voice shaking, 'the police are on their way, you can't get away with this.'

'They are the other side of the gates. I'm guessing you were going to let them in. By the time they realise you are not coming and have tracked down the keys it will be too late. This place is a fortress. It keeps the enemies out.'

'Someone will come from the apartment,' Susan said desperately.

'Oh, no. No one suspects me, do they? They all think I've come to check up on you while I phone my dad.'

Susan felt a spark of anger at Annika's smugness. 'Lying about ringing your father again?'

Annika scowled; her eyes creased up in suspicion, 'What do you mean?'

'You lied about speaking to your father the night Maxine died. You were supposedly on your way to meet Nick.'

'I did speak to him.'

'No, at the party your father told Zoe that he had phoned the castle reception the day Maxine's body was found as he had thought there would be no signal in the castle. Well, if he'd have spoken to you the night before, he'd have known there was good signal, wouldn't he?'

Annika laughed a cruel, cold laugh. 'Very clever, but a single stupid phone call is not going to convince the police I had anything to do with Maxine's death.'

'But there are plenty of things that will. I'm in no doubt you are the person who arranged to meet Maxine at midnight, who spoke to her, used that aerosol to distract her—' Susan paused as she saw a flash of panic in Annika's eyes. Susan nodded. 'Yes,

I worked that out. After the distraction, it was simple to push her over, wasn't it?'

'You've no proof.'

With her free hand, Susan put down her torch, reached for her phone, and showed Annika the photo she had taken earlier.

Annika shone her torch on it. For a moment, the torch light revealed the panic on Annika's face.

'It's not very good, but I didn't want to remove vital evidence from your pocket or the box.'

'A torch and some old batteries? So what?' said Annika.

'That torch was the spare you swapped Maxine's torch for. The batteries are those removed from the spare. When I looked, I found tiny pink fibres on them. You should have worn a coat that didn't shed. When the police know what they're looking for, who knows where they will find the fibres – in Maxine's pocket from the spare torch, the can, the miniature you pushed into your pocket? At the very least, they'll show you were up there.'

Susan again felt the needle pressing on the skin of her wrist, but she could sense Annika was waiting, wanting to hear what she had to say.

'It would have been better not to remove things from Maxine's body after she fell. You could have left her with the broken torch and the miniature.'

'When do you think I went to the armoury? If I'd been to see Maxine, I'd have had so little time—'

'You had those moments between leaving the bowling green with Nick and pretending to answer a text. You ran to the armoury, switched the torches, took the miniature—'

Annika kept her gaze, but Susan saw a pulse of fear deep in her eyes. 'My guess is you regret taking the miniature now.'

Annika scowled. 'I don't have any regrets.'

'It was risky. I'm wondering now if there are any flakes of the red nail varnish in your pocket. It's possible. That's a lot of explaining to do.'

The tiny flicker of fear in Annika's eyes was quickly quenched. 'You've nothing, no motive, nothing.' She gave a cold half smile 'Or will you try to argue that I was so obsessed with Nick I had to stop him running off with Maxine, or even had to protect him from her?' She shook her head. 'No, neither will ever hold up.'

'You're right. Love was never your motive. I admit it was hard to find. I was slower than Maxine. It took those young children singing in the concert for me to finally piece things together.'

'Some children singing?'

'Yes. Their performance opened my eyes to the dark secret you've been hiding from the world. Maxine found it but then made a fatal error. She came to speak to you and, in doing so, sealed her fate.'

40

Annika sat slightly back from Susan. She relaxed the grip on Susan's wrist. Susan felt the pressure from the needle lift. She glanced around, should she try to make a run for it? However, Annika grabbed her hand again before speaking, 'I have a deadly secret? I'd love to hear what you think that might be.'

A biting wind rustled the bushes; the hard wooden slats of the bench dug into Susan's back. So much of the Privy Garden was in darkness, and yet she could see Annika's eyes shining, her lips thin and cruel.

'Maxine discovered it a lot more quickly than me. She gave Zoe three clues she'd spotted in your flat. The albums, the music and the bedside drawer. The last is nothing to do with the secret. But the first two are vital.

'Last week, Maxine opened your safe, found out what she needed about Gino, and then she opened one of the albums. It had photographs of you and Liam. She knew all about Liam from Nick. She used his taxi that day, and then she saw a photo of him with his arm around you. The closeness of your relationship concerned her.'

'It was just a fling, and it was before I was with Nick.'

'Even so, Maxine knew that you were still seeing a great deal of him, a man with a criminal record. Now, she'd told Zoe that it was the albums which concerned her – I nearly missed that, it wasn't just one, not just the photograph album. No, she'd looked inside those metal boxes, hadn't she and found different kinds of albums.'

'She saw my stamps. So what?' said Annika.

'Maxine knew about stamps. We talked about that. She saw something I missed. She realised that the reason the birds were dull and the angel seemed large was because the stamps you owned contained errors. Those mistakes, the lack of a colour with the birds, the missing monetary value on the angel stamp, made them extremely valuable.'

Annika gave a resigned shrug. 'For a moment, I'll let you have that, but even if Maxine had spotted that, it's not a crime for me to own them. They're not stolen. I paid good money for them.'

'Yes, and that's the interesting part: the money.' Maxine was concerned, 'How could you afford stamps costing thousands of pounds?'

'I love stamps. You know that.'

'But how could you afford such expensive ones?'

Susan was aware that Annika was leaning towards her now. The grip on her wrist tightened.

'I can imagine Maxine closing the safe, looking around,' continued Susan. 'Now you were unlucky at this point. If Maxine hadn't just finished a particular case, she could easily have missed the vital clue on the music. I missed it. I was distracted by the doodles on Nick's manuscript.'

Annika grinned. 'I noticed that. I enjoyed talking about my poor troubled genius.'

'Yes, I fell for it, but Maxine saw more clearly than me. She looked through the music you take into the prison.'

'That's just sheets of easy songs we sing together.'

'Yes, very appropriate. Like the children sang in the concert. However, there weren't just sheets of simple songs in that box. There were also copies of Rossini's complex warm-up exercises. Now why would a group of men just learning a few songs need those? The answer of course is they wouldn't. Also, unlike the copies of warm-up exercises you used, these were on yellowed paper – I didn't even think of that until this evening. However, Maxine had noticed everything – the incongruity of those exercises and the yellowed paper. Her case taught her about the many ways drugs were being smuggled into prison, one of the most difficult to detect being the drug spice, which can be sprayed onto paper. Maxine had a horrible feeling then she knew exactly what you were involved with. No wonder she came rushing over to the nursing home to speak to you.'

Susan took a breath, saw Annika's eyes widen in alarm.

'I did wonder, you know, why Maxine didn't go straight to the police,' said Susan. 'She'd seen evidence of your relationship with Liam, found the rare stamps, found the spice laced music.'

Annika gave a cold smile. 'I wondered that as well. And then I realised what she was thinking—' Annika's eyes were blazing now, her lip curled. 'She assumed I'd been duped, coerced into something I didn't understand. She told me she would go with me to the police, argue my side of the story. Have you any idea how angry that made me?'

Susan could see it in her face, in the clasp of her hands.

Annika continued. 'For a moment, I was tempted to tell her to go to hell—' Susan could imagine it. She guessed that was the moment the mask slipped.

'But no, I realised then she was a serious threat to me,' said

Annika, 'I went along with her. We agreed to talk this week. That's what the meeting on the battlements was meant to be, to plan our way forward. But I wasn't going to take any chances. I knew before we came away that she had to die.'

The cold, matter-of-fact way Annika spoke shocked Susan.

'You really thought you had the right to end Maxine's life?'

'Of course. You have no idea how hard my life has been. I deserve this break, and Maxine was not going to ruin it for me. Life with my father had been hell. You have no idea what it was like growing up knowing nothing you did was enough. There was always another exam, another competition, and they got harder and harder. But at least when I was younger, I always achieved distinction. I usually won the competitions. But at university, there were many talented singers. I started to come second or even third in competitions. I failed auditions, but my father still thought that if I worked hard enough, one day I'd be a prima donna, a goddess in one of the best opera houses in the world. He never gives up, never stops nagging and pushing me.'

'His voice haunts you,' said Susan quietly.

'It never goes away. He will never understand that there is a limit, that however hard I try, I can't ever be what he wants me to be.'

Susan heard the heartbreak in Annika's voice, saw pain etched on every part of her face, and for a moment she felt sorry for that hurt, broken child.

But then Susan saw the vulnerability melt away. It was replaced with white-hot anger, and resentment.

'Don't you dare feel sorry for me,' Annika snarled. 'I don't need your pity. I'm in control of my life now. I've known for some time I had to find a way to get away from my father. I needed money that was nothing to do with him, no strings attached. But I didn't want to go off and live on a pittance in some dingy flat. Then I met Liam. He told me about his life, the drugs, his experiences in prison. He was desperate not to be dependent on his father as well, but I was the one to put it all together, find a way we could both make really good money. I volunteered in the prison, Liam used his contacts to organise the rest. It was easy. I gave him the sheets of vocal exercises. He arranged for them to be sprayed with spice, then returned them to me, on one of our many taxi rides, for me to smuggle into the prison.'

'You don't really have a fear of driving, do you?'

'Of course not. It's not that flattering that Nick accepted it so easily but, well, it was useful. And Liam had a contact in the prison who came to my singing group. It was so easy.'

Susan noticed that word 'easy' again, heard the excitement in Annika's voice: she'd enjoyed this.

'And you had no problems with security?'

'Spice is hard to detect. And they never looked twice at me.'

'And how did the inmates pay you?'

'Obviously they don't have cash. They paid Liam via accounts, family, friends and the like on the outside. Then he paid me.'

'And rather than put the money into accounts, you bought stamps.'

'Exactly. If my father or anyone else was to look at my accounts, they would find nothing suspicious. Frank at the sailing club does the negotiations. Nothing is traced back to me, and it won't be when I sell them.'

'You weren't lying when you told Donna at the care home how much you were saving.'

'Oh, no. It was the truth.' Annika sighed. 'It's been amusing watching you and Zoe running around. I threw you the odd bone to play with – heavy hints about Gino and the prison. Of course,

I knew what was really in those cigarette boxes. I cast a bit of shade on LeAnne as well, mentioned she'd put her coat on to hint she'd left the apartment. As I climbed the steps behind the apartment to the battlements, I looked back and saw her leave. I was keeping that up my sleeve, but she broke it in any case.'

'You were willing to pin the blame on anyone.'

Annika shrugged. 'It's the way the world works. And look, Nick will benefit. Left to himself he'd never get away; never live the life he wants. With me he gets a new life.'

'But does he? I've realised that he is your ultimate plan B if the police start suspecting you. You have set him up nicely, building a picture of how unstable he is. First the misleading hints about cocaine use, drawing attention to the bedside cabinet. You'd also sown the seeds of doubt about his movements the night Maxine died, made sure there was a time when he had no alibi. But, of course, you encouraged him to keep silent about the most damming piece of evidence—'

Annika rolled her eyes. 'You were so slow. I had to spell it out to you in the hospital in the end. Yes, Nick, from where he was sat in the Privy Garden, overheard Maxine the night she died. When I spoke to him on the phone he was in a right state. He even talked of going up to speak to Maxine.'

'Which is the last thing you needed.'

'Exactly. I talked him out of it in the same way I persuaded him, afterwards, to keep secret the fact he knew Maxine planned to go to the governors. I knew how suspicious his silence would look.'

'He, at least, appreciated Maxine: someone clever, passionate for justice, who had a lifetime of helping people in front of her.'

Annika flapped one hand in dismissal. 'All this fuss about

how clever and noble Maxine was. She just had the breaks. She was lucky.'

'No. She had a heart and compassion, which you will never understand. Killing her was truly wicked, Annika. It was a terrible deed, and I am glad you will be punished for it.'

'I don't think so.' Annika pressed the needle harder.

Susan caught her eye, saw a cold determination and froze. For the first time she noticed the medical latex gloves Annika was wearing, it made it all seem so clinical. Was this it? Was she about to die?

'Everyone will know you killed me,' stammered Susan in desperation.

'Oh no,' said Annika slowly and then as if explaining to a child, with her spare hand she pulled something out of her pocket. 'I'm very good at this. I've rung Liam, told him to get himself to the other side of the castle, on the North side, along from that wooden gate. Now, this is Nick's penknife.'

Susan could see the cold gleam in Annika's eyes, she was excited, proud of herself. Annika continued, 'So, after I inject you, I shall slit your wrist, covering the injection site and also implicating Nick. I'll then use your phone to send a desperate message to Nick, pleading with him to meet you here. After that I'll rush to the bowling green, via the battlements, to that gap in the castle wall by one of the canons. I can speak to Liam on the path outside the castle from there.'

Susan knew exactly where Annika meant, it was where Libs had been barking at that rabbit only a few nights before.

Annika gave a sickening grin. 'I made sure the group knew the time I left the apartment, and Liam will swear I was with him from that time onwards. All being well Nick will be blamed for your death. Impressive isn't it! Quick thinking on my part.'

The smile slipped away, to be replaced by a cold sneer. 'Right, enough talking.'

Susan could feel the needle digging into her skin, she tried to pull away, but Annika held her in a vice like grip.

And then suddenly, like a bullet, a loud shout shot through the darkness.

'Stop, police.'

An officer appeared, charged over and grabbed Annika, the needle fell to the floor. Another officer pulled Susan off the seat.

'Thank God,' she exclaimed.

'I'm so sorry,' stammered the police officer. 'We were waiting for you, wondering if we needed to send out for a key, when we spotted this chap smoking. He was a member of staff. He gave us his key and we thought we'd better come in – thank God we did. And thank heavens sound travels, we heard you talking – hey, are you ok?'

Susan felt herself begin to shake uncontrollably, she started to sway, felt her head start to spin.

As she started to fall to the floor Susan heard a familiar voice, 'Mum, my God mum.' She felt her daughter take hold of her, lead her back to the seat.

Slowly the dizziness settled, Zoe took off her coat and wrapped her mother up.

'What the hell mum? I came out – you were taking such a long time.'

Annika was stood close by being held by an officer. She shouted over to them, 'My plan to kill Maxine was brilliant, even my father will be impressed. You were just lucky.' With that she was led out of the garden.

'My God, it's like listening to a stranger,' said Zoe. 'That had to be the Annika Maxine saw. But mum, you took such a risk—'

'It didn't go quite to plan. Remember, always do as I say, not as I do,' Susan said with a weak smile.

Zoe put her arm around her. 'You are amazing, Mum.'

Then Susan saw something up on the battlements where Maxine had been pushed.

It was a white barn owl. Susan watched as it spread its magnificent wings and took off upward into the night sky. Slowly the white shape became smaller and smaller until it finally disappeared.

'Maxine told me how the owls take away your soul when you die. I think Maxine is at peace now,' said Susan.

Zoe nodded, too moved to speak and let the tears slowly roll down her cheeks.

41

There was a long night of questions ahead of them all, but eventually Zoe and Susan returned home.

LeAnne arrived at the house the next morning.

'I thought I'd better come and collect my stuff,' she said. 'What a night.' She looked at Zoe and Susan. 'You two did well. You were right: we needed this resolved. I confess I never suspected Annika. I was so wrong about her.'

'She fooled us all,' said Zoe.

'What will you do now?' Susan asked LeAnne.

'Get back to my restaurant, plan for the future.' She tapped her stomach. 'I've new responsibilities coming up. I can't see the dad being much support – he's been arrested for possession.' LeAnne paused and looked at Susan. 'It wasn't until you were speaking last night that I realised I'd missed something pretty obvious with Wesley.'

'That Gino had planted the cocaine on him?' said Susan.

'Mum, how did you get that?' asked Zoe.

'Once I realised Gino was using cocaine, I also realised he

was the most likely to have had it on him at LeAnne's party. I guess he heard Nick say he'd called the police, panicked, and so planted the drugs on Wesley when he went to get dessert.'

LeAnne shook her head. 'What a bastard. I don't want him anywhere near me now. Me and this little one are better off without him. I guess I'll need to apologise to Nick sometime, although that's the least of his worries at the moment.'

'Better for him to know the truth about Annika now.'

'I guess so. Right, I'll go and fetch my things.'

LeAnne returned quickly. 'I've ordered a taxi to take me to Ventnor – not Liam. He's still at the police station. I don't think he'll be out of there any time soon. Shame, he seemed a nice chap.'

When LeAnne had left, Zoe and Susan sat down for coffee.

'Now, Mum, I need to tell you why I went out to take a call from Fay after the concert. For once it's good news. Fay's parents have decided to move down here.'

Susan tried to hide her excitement. 'That's wonderful. Well, it is for me, but what about her father?'

'It's fine. In fact, he brought it up. He can see how hard it's been on Fay's mother. They're going to move somewhere by the sea, maybe Worthing. They'd like to get a flat down on the seafront. He'd love that.'

Susan felt as if a huge, invisible weight had been lifted. 'That's lovely.'

'I know. Fay and Jamari are flying back today. It'll be fantastic to see them later.'

'It will. It's been hard, but we got to the truth. Your daughter will be very proud of you when she hears about this one day.'

'She will, as proud as I am of you.'

* * *

A week later, Susan went alone to see Alice. Princess, the cat on Alice's lap, turned her back to her and occasionally twitched her tail in annoyance. But they both ignored her while Susan filled Alice in on every detail of their investigations.

'You did well,' said Alice.

'And you gave us essential pointers as always. Thank you.'

'I'm very glad Annika won't be coming in here taking my blood any more,' said Alice, her grey eyes twinkling. 'So, any other news?'

Susan told her about Robert and his daughter. 'Now I know things are settled with Zoe, maybe I'll go over with him to France for a week.'

'Yes, that sounds a good thing to do.'

'Oh, and with all this happening, I haven't filled you in on my new neighbours,' said Susan.

'Tracy has told me they moved in,' said Alice, 'but she's quite frustrated at how little she knows about them. She knows the daughter will be working in the vets.'

'That's right. And they have a gorgeous cocker spaniel, called Luca.'

Alice smiled. 'This all sounds very interesting. And what about the man himself, I think Tracy said his name was Harri?'

'Yes, that's right. But so far, I've no idea what he does, or why he felt the need to move here.'

'Ah,' said Alice, her eyes twinkling, 'a new mystery – we all love them.'

* * *

MORE FROM MARY GRAND

Another book from Mary Grand, *A Christmas Murder*, is available to order now here:
www.mybook.to/ChristmasBackAd

AUTHOR NOTE

Although Bishopstone is a fictitious place, it was inspired by the beautiful village of Brighstone. The people in the book are entirely fictitious.

Carisbrooke Castle is now owned by the English Heritage. Research on the history and structure of the castle is as accurate as possible. All the staff and people in the story are completely fictitious.

ACKNOWLEDGEMENTS

I started visiting Carisbrooke Castle many years ago with my children. It's an incredible place, if you are ever on the island, you must visit. As soon as I heard it had an apartment for people to stay in, I knew I had to set a story there. I've visited the castle a lot while writing this book, climbed the battlements and the keep steps and even went on the fabulous ghost walk for the first time! I have to thank everyone who works for English Heritage. In particular thank you so much to the staff at Carisbrooke Castle. I learned so much from everyone in the reception, the office and the Well House. Your enthusiasm, knowledge and love for your work is amazing. Thank you.

A book of course, is not the work of an individual but a team. Firstly, I would like to say a huge thank you to Emily Yau. It's our first time working together, and it's been wonderful. Thank you so much for all your insights, support and encouragement.

Thank you also to everyone in team Boldwood including Claire, Ben, Megan, Marcela, and Rachel, for your dedication and hard work, for endless patience and professionalism.

In addition, thank you to everyone else who has worked on this book, on the line-edits and proof editing, and Daniel for your patience and amazing skill in producing such a wonderful cover design. Also thank you once again to the wonderful Karen Cass for the narration of the audio book. Thank you everyone who has helped bring this novel to life.

I want to also thank Sarah Ritherdon, Publishing Director at Boldwood. Thank you for all the support and encouragement you have given me on the books leading up to this, and for everything I have learned from you.

As always, I want to say a huge thank you to my gorgeous family. My husband, Andrew, always my first reader and invaluable critic, and children, Thomas, and Emily, for their unending support, humour, and encouragement.

Thank you to you, my lovely readers. I hope I have kept even those who read with notebook and pen (you know who you are!), guessing to the end. I really have the best readers; I appreciate and am so grateful to you all.

I have to say a massive thank you to the bloggers who work tirelessly in supporting writers like myself and to Rachel Gilbey for organising the amazing blog tours.

There are quite a few dogs in this story, and I'd like to thank all the owners for allowing me to use the names and descriptions of their very special dogs. Thank you, Diane Lister, for allowing me to mention Libby (Libs), Pat Pearson for Rocco, Pauline Trimmings for Gemma (Gem Gem), Fiona McGregor for Dougie and Wendy Coates for Lottie, a first appearance for Roger and Maureen's Luca and Holly's Ralph.

Last but not least, thank you to my cat Princess, who no doubt thinks she is the main character in this story!

ABOUT THE AUTHOR

Mary Grand writes gripping cosy mystery novels, including the number one bestseller A Christmas Murder. She grew up in Wales, was for many years a teacher of deaf children and now lives on the Isle of Wight.

Sign up to Mary Grand's mailing list here for news, competitions and updates on future books.

Visit Mary's website: www.marygrand.net

Follow Mary on social media:

- x.com/authormaryg
- instagram.com/marygrandwriter
- facebook.com/authormarygrand
- bookbub.com/profile/mary-grand

ALSO BY MARY GRAND

The House Party

The Island

Good Neighbours

The Isle of Wight Killings Series

A Seaside Murder

A Parish Murder

A Christmas Murder

A Halloween Murder

Poison & Pens

POISON & PENS IS THE HOME OF
COZY MYSTERIES SO POUR YOURSELF
A CUP OF TEA & GET SLEUTHING!

DISCOVER PAGE-TURNING NOVELS FROM
YOUR FAVOURITE AUTHORS &
MEET NEW FRIENDS

JOIN OUR
FACEBOOK GROUP

BIT.LYPOISONANDPENSFB

SIGN UP TO OUR
NEWSLETTER

BIT.LY/POISONANDPENSNEWS

Boldwood

Boldwood Books is an award-winning fiction publishing company seeking out the best stories from around the world.

Find out more at www.boldwoodbooks.com

Join our reader community for brilliant books, competitions and offers!

Follow us
@BoldwoodBooks
@TheBoldBookClub

Sign up to our weekly deals newsletter

https://bit.ly/BoldwoodBNewsletter

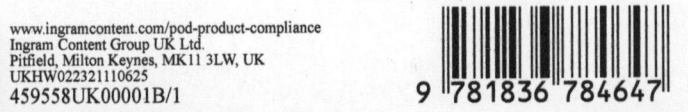

www.ingramcontent.com/pod-product-compliance
Ingram Content Group UK Ltd.
Pitfield, Milton Keynes, MK11 3LW, UK
UKHW022321110625
459558UK00001B/1

9 781836 784647